EVERLASTING

EMPIRE

EVERLASTING EMPIRE

YI IN-HWA

Translated by
Yu Young-nan

Introduction by
Don Baker

EastBridge

White Plains, New York
Norwalk, Connecticut

EastBridge

Signature Books

EastBridge is a nonprofit publishing corporation chartered in the State of Connecticut, tax exempt under section 501(c)(3) of the United States tax code.

EastBridge has received a generous multi-year grant from the Henry Luce Foundation.

This book is partially supported by a grant from the Korea Literature Translation Institute.

Library of Congress Cataloging-in-Publication Data

Yi, In-hwa, 1966-
  [Yaeongwaeonhan cheguk. English]
  Everlasting Empire / Yi In-hwa ; translated by Yu Young-nan ; with an Introduction by Don Baker.
        p. cm. -- (Signature books)
  ISBN 1-891936-02-6 (pbk.)   ISBN 1-891936-15-8 (hardcover)
  1. Korea—History—1864-1910 – Fiction. I. Yu, Young-nan. II. Title.
  III. Signature books (White Plains, N.Y.)
    PL992.9.I4767 Y6513 2002

                                                    2002016774

Printed in the United States of America

Contents

Introduction

History from the Pen of a Novelist

I am a professional historian. As such, I am expected to be able to evaluate the authenticity of historical documents. For example, I am supposed to be able to determine whether a document before me is as old as it purports to be. If I determine that it is a genuine historical document, I am supposed to then be able to evaluate it for reliability. For example, I am supposed to determine, if a document is described as a first-person account of an historical event, whether or not that claim can be trusted.

Though it is embarrassing to admit it, I was almost fooled by Yi In-hwa's *Everlasting Empire*. Yi's opening account of finding a manuscript on the back shelves of the Toyo Bunko Library in Tokyo sounded plausible enough. Moreover, his description of the factional infighting that raged around the throne of King Chongjo rang true. I have studied the deadly rivalry between the so-called Intransigent faction led by Shim Hwan-ji and the so-called Flexible faction which Chae Chegong led until his death, so many of the people and actions Yi talks about were familiar. I was a little puzzled about some of the details of his story. For example, I wondered why the sudden deaths of palace personnel were not mentioned in the entries in the official government chronicle for the nineteeth day of the first month of King Chongjo's twenty-fourth year. However, it was not until the final pages of this novel, when Yi admitted that *Everlasting Empire* was a work of fiction from start to finish, that I realized how skillfully Yi has woven his story.

He has achieved a goal that eludes most authors of historical fiction: He has created a tale so plausible that it almost can pass for the work of a historian rather than a novelist. Even though the events that form the core of his novel did not actually take place, they could have. This is what makes his novel more than just a riveting work of fiction. It is also a book that opens a window into the turbulent world of Choson dynasty politics, in which political disagreements often had deadly consequences.

The Choson dynasty lasted more than five centuries, making it one of the more stable dynasties anywhere on the face of the globe over the last two millennia. Nevertheless, the solid rock on which it rested was occasionally shaken by earthquakes of fatal intensity. During the first century of the dynasty, in 1455, a prince seized the throne from his young nephew, King Tanjong (reign 1452–1455), forcing the unfortunate Tanjong to end his own life with a drink of poison. A few decades later, another king, known posthumously as Prince Yonsangun (1494–1506), was told that some of the officials in his court had been responsible for his mother's untimely demise under the previous kings. In sorrow and anger he turned on his own bureaucracy. The death toll among court officials finally reached so high that no official felt safe from the king's wrath, so they removed him from the throne and replaced him with a less choleric member of the royal family.

This dethroning of a Choson dynasty king by his own officials early in the sixteenth century, and the dethroning of another, Prince Kwanghaegun (1608–1623), in the seventeenth century, severely weakened the throne. Their successors learned that they could not simply order their officials to follow royal directives. Instead, government had to be run by consensus and compromise, with a king working to gain the assent of top officials to his policy proposals, and the top officials sometimes forcing the king to adopt policies they favored rather than policies the king himself would have preferred.

As a result, the king's ministers came to exercise more power than they had been able to at the beginning of the dynasty. This meant that there was more at stake when bureaucrats vied for higher posts, and the jockeying among bureaucrats for those posts grew more heated. After the first dethroning, there were battles between merit subjects (those who gained access to high government office by siding with the winning side in a succession dispute) and scholar-officials (those who claimed the right to hold office because of their superior performance on civil service examinations). After the scholar-officials gained the upper hand, they discovered that there were more of them than there were powerful posts to be filled. They soon began fighting among themselves.

Historians usually trace the roots of eighteenth-century factionalism to the last quarter of the sixteenth century, when the opposing sides in a battle for control of the Ministry of Personnel coalesced into hereditary cliques. Since the leaders of those factions lived in different parts of Seoul, their followers became known as Easterners and Westerners, depending on where their allegiance lay. A decade and a half after the Easterners separated from the Westerners, the Easterners underwent fission once again, this time into the similarly named Southerners and Northerners. Almost a century later, when the Westerners could not agree on how long the queen dowager should mourn the recently deceased king, they ruptured as well, separating into hostile Old Doctrine and Young Doctrine camps.

As a result of these various disputes, the Choson dynasty entered the eighteenth century with four irreconcilable cliques differentiated not only by what their political positions were but also by what the political positions of their ancestors had been. These hereditary factions sought to place as many of their own members in high government posts as possible while excluding as many members of opposing factions as they possibly could. Kings naturally opposed this, since they would prefer to be surrounded by ministers inclined to follow the king's policy preferences rather than by ministers interested in promoting the narrow agenda of a particular faction.

The history of the eighteenth century is therefore a history of a constant struggle between the throne and the bureaucracy, with kings trying to claim supreme authority over their government but facing resistance from officials trying to bend the bureaucracy to serve factional interests.

Starting in 1720, the leverage Choson kings could exert against recalcitrant officials was weakened by questions about the legitimacy of three kings in a row: King Kyongjong (1720–1724), King Yongjo (1724–1776), and King Chongjo (1776–1800). King Kyongjong is reported to have suffered from serious health problems, both physical and mental. In fact, the leaders of the Old Doctrine faction were so concerned about his health, or so they said, that in the second year of his reign they tried to force him to delegate most of his authority to his younger half-brother, the prince who would later become King Yongjo. Kyongjong took offense at this challenge to his competency and had four Old Doctrine leaders executed. He may have been concerned that they were less worried about his health than they were about the fact that his mother had been condemned as a murderer and been ordered by his father to kill herself. Lady Chang, Kyongjong's mother, was believed to have used black magic to cause the death of one of her rivals for the king's affection, Queen Inhyon. This made Kyongjong the son of a criminal and thus in the eyes of some a less than legitimate claimant to the throne. Kyongjong, legitimate or not, was not on the throne for very long. He died in 1724, having come down with a severe bout of diarrhea shortly after eating some crabs pickled in soy sauce, which his half-brother, Crown Prince Yongjo, had sent him. Yongjo then became king, immediately raising suspicions that Kyongjong's death was not accidental. No one could prove that the pickled crabs were poisonous. However, some of Kyongjong's supporters remembered that the person who had first reported Lady Chang's use of black magic and thus was indirectly responsible for the death of Kyongjong's mother was the mother of Yongjo, which added to the suspicions about Yongjo and those crabs.

Yongjo thus ascended the throne with his legitimacy already compromised by rumors of fraternal regicide. Moreover, not only was his mother an informer, but she had been a lowly servant girl in the palace before she caught King Sukchong's eye. To the scholar-officials who put great stress on proper pedigree, her low social status made her an unacceptable mother for a king, and thus raised doubts about her son's right to claim the throne. Partially because of these doubts about Yongjo's legitimacy and partially because a few instigators felt threatened by the predominance of Old Doctrine officials in Yongjo's government, an armed attempt to unseat him broke out in 1728. Yongjo was able to muster enough military support to suppress that rebellion. Afterward, to broaden his base of support, he promoted a policy of Grand Harmony. Under this policy, the king claimed the authority to choose his officials from among the members of all major factions, ending the monopoly of one faction or another over high government posts. This policy, couched in the Confucian rhetoric of impartiality, was designed to encourage would-be officials to put loyalty to their king ahead of loyalty to their faction, since the king rather than a faction head would determine who held which government positions. Yongjo hoped this policy would allow him to become an "August Monarch," a north pole of politics around which all the lesser stars in his court revolved.

Yongjo had only limited success in breaking the grip of powerful factions over his bureaucracy. He was even less successful in another attempt to evade the constant efforts of his top officials to make him more a figurehead than a true ruler in his own right. In 1749 King Yongjo handed over many of his royal duties to his son, Crown Prince Sado, naming him regent in the hope that ambitious officials would cluster around the regent and allow the king to escape their constant attention. Unfortunately, despite the implications in this novel, the crown prince suffered from a mental disease that made him unsuitable for such a responsibility. In fact, he was so unsuitable that, since he was Yongjo's only surviving son, his survival threatened the survival of the dynasty itself. He began to engage in behavior that was not tolerated even in a king, including random acts of murder. Such behavior by a leading member of the royal family undermined the aura of virtue which the royal family needed in order to rule over the Confucian government of Korea. In order to save the royal family claim to the Choson throne, in 1762 King Yongjo ordered his son, Crown Prince Sado, sealed into a rice chest to die of dehydration. With this command, unfortunately, he not only caused the death of his only son, but he also caused two new factions to appear, the Flexible faction which supported the right of the son of that prince in the rice chest to ascend the throne, and the Intransigent faction which did not support it.

It was the son of the dead Crown Prince Sado who became the target of the factional intrigues portrayed in this novel. King Chongjo, like his grandfather Yongjo and his granduncle Kyongjong before him, ascended the throne under a cloud of doubts about the legitimacy of his claim to the throne.

Unlike his two predecessors, he was the son of a respectable mother from a family that had produced many top officials. Like his granduncle, however, he was the child of someone who had been condemned as a criminal. However, in his case, his parentage was more problematic than Kyongjong's, since patriarchal Korea was more interested in who someone's father was than in who that person's mother was. His father's death in that rice chest, and the conviction of many officials and scholars that Prince Sado's death was the inevitable and appropriate consequence of his unacceptable behavior, cast a shadow over Chongjo's claim to monarchial virtue. Like his grandfather, Chongjo tried to overcome that handicap of doubtful legitimacy by rising above factionalism and implementing a policy of Grand Harmony. By the middle of his reign, Chongjo had successfully forced the three most powerful factions—the Old Doctrine, the Young Doctrine, and the Southerners—to share the top ministerial posts.

In addition, Chongjo went further than his grandfather had, in trying to overcome the control top officials exercised over the mechanisms of government. He adopted a number of bold measures to weaken the traditional lines of bureaucratic authority and to create a separate group of officials more amenable to the royal will. For example, he created the Royal Library, modeled after the Imperial Library of Song China, and gave the young scholars who were employed there responsibility for administrative tasks in a number of government agencies. He also created a new military detachment, the Stout Braves Garrison, to take over many of the duties that had been the responsibility of military units under the control of leaders of powerful factions. He liberalized trade to weaken the grip of a few licensed shops on the sale of essential goods in the capital region. Besides all this, in a move that threatened the power of the elite families in Seoul more than anything else, he began preparing to move the capital south of Seoul, to a new walled city called Hwasong. There were even rumors that the king was planning on moving to Hwasong by himself, leaving the elite families of Seoul behind to deal with the crown prince, whom, rumors had it, King Chongjo intended to name as his regent.

The Intransigent faction, led by Shim Hwan-ji, was probably bothered more by Chongjo's attempt to gain supremacy over the entrenched power of high officials and elite families in Seoul than they were by his tainted ancestry. The Flexible faction, on the other hand, supported the king's strengthening of royal authority because a stronger king would mean more opportunities for scholars from weaker factions to advance through government ranks. The stage was thus set for factional battles. King Chongjo further exacerbated matters by insisting in the last year of his reign that, despite centuries of

Korean tradition, officials were supposed to obey their king, not argue with him. When Chongjo declared, as he did on the last day of May 1800, that he was the personification of Heavenly Principle on Earth, the August Monarch around whom government revolved, anger among the Intransigent faction reached unprecedented levels. When he went further and hinted that he might declare that their faction was responsible for the death of his father, they also began to fear that they would soon lose what little bureaucratic authority they had left.

It is no wonder that, when King Chongjo died less than a month after demanding unquestioning obedience from his officials, many suspected at the time that his death was no accident. (The fact that the physician who treated the King on his deathbed was related to Shim Hwan-ji appeared to some to be more than a coincidence.) It is also no wonder that once King Chongjo was dead and could no longer protect the Flexible faction, the full wrath of the Intransigent faction fell upon them.

The Flexible faction was rendered particularly vulnerable by the fact that among its ranks were the leaders of Korea's Catholic Church. Catholicism had appeared in Korea only fifteen years earlier, when a young member of the Southerner faction accompanied a diplomatic mission to Beijing and met some French missionaries there. Converted by those priests, he returned to Korea and began converting his friends and relatives. Within a decade there was an underground Catholic community on the peninsula several thousand strong. The Catholics in this community violated Korean law, refusing to mourn their dead in the prescribed Confucian manner because the Pope in Rome had told them Confucian mourning rituals were idolatrous. On top of this, they smuggled a foreigner, a Chinese Catholic priest, into Korea in 1794, and they tried to arrange for even more foreigners, including French troops, to come to Korea to force the Korean government to grant them religious freedom.

King Chongjo had tried to mitigate the persecution of Catholics, fearing that charges of Catholic connections would be wielded as a weapon by the Intransigent faction against the Flexible faction, stirring up the very factional fighting he was trying to put a stop to. Once he was dead, his fears were realized. The Intransigent faction seized control of the government and used its prosecutory authority to decimate the Flexible faction, killing those it could prove were active Catholics and exiling many others.

Everlasting Empire is a novel. The author is under no obligation to relate what actually happened in Korea in the year 1800. Instead, all he has to do is to weave a plausible story, one that can draw readers into the world it describes because the characters in it could have done what they did for the reasons the novelist says they did them. In this, he succeeds admirably. Most of the characters in this novel are based on actual individuals who were involved in the political struggles in King Chongjo's court. Moreover, the battles they wage in this novel resemble the actual battles that were fought there. As Korea moved from the eighteenth century into the nineteenth, King Chongjo argued with his officials over whether or not they were obligated to follow his orders. Shim Hwan-ji led resistance to many of King Chongjo's policy proposals, and to the growing influence of members of the Flexible faction. Chong Yag-yong maneuvered within the bureaucracy to support King Chongjo in his battles with Shim Hwan-ji and the rest of the Intransigent faction. Chong was also an early member of the Korean Catholic Church. Though he left the church after a few years, many of the other early converts did not and instead practiced their faith secretly, as did the Catholics in this novel.

It is sometimes said that historical novels offer their readers more faithful depictions of the past than do scholarly treatises on history. As much as it hurts me, a professional historian, to admit it, this may be an accurate statement. Though the events in this novel may not correspond to events that actually took place in January 1800, and though the narrator and a few other characters may be fictional, the overall political atmosphere in Seoul captured in this novel resembles what I have found in actual historical chronicles from this period. In fact, Yi In-hwa has captured the rivalries, cruelty, and treachery in Chongjo's Seoul with a vividness equaled by few historical records, or even historians' reconstructions. If one of the goals of the study of history is, and I believe it is, to open doors into the past so that we step back in time and experience the world of our predecessors on this planet, then *Everlasting Empire* is an effective door opener. I recommend it to anyone who wants to experience political intrigue on the Korea peninsula two centuries ago.

Don Baker
University of British Columbia

Translator's Note

This novel employs the device of a narrator who recounts what he has found in an old text. This text is said to be written in Chinese characters, which must be translated into contemporary Korean, and for this reason the narrator occasionally inserts himself into the text as the translator, sometimes subtly as he comments on historical facts, and other times more abruptly as he offers explanations in parentheses. While this does not pose any problem in the Korean original, it might cause confusion in the English translation. In the English edition, I have eliminated the parenthetical information to avoid confusion.

For the Romanization of the Korean alphabet, the McCune-Reischauer system was used, but the breve and the apostrophe were removed for technical and aesthetic reasons. For the Romanization of Chinese characters, the recent *pinyin* system was followed, as modified by the Chinese government in 1985; the English transliteration of the Chinese-Korean dictionary published by the Korean Culture Research Center, Korea University, was my guide.

For Korean government positions and other historical facts, I generally adopted the translated terms in *Korea Old and New: A History*, by Eckert et al., as well as *The Literati Purges: Political Conflict in Early Yi Korea* by Edward Wagner.

The Chinese philosophical terms used here are derived from some books on Chinese philosophy and history—notably *A Source Book in Chinese Philosophy*, by Wing-tsit Chan; *A Short History of Chinese Philosophy*, by Fung Yu-lan; and *China: A New History*, by John Fairbank. Donald Baker, professor of history at the University of British Columbia, also helped me a great deal with terms both Korean and Chinese.

I used the published translation of one poem: "The Owl," by Yang Xianyi et al. The other poems are my own translations.

References to Chinese classics play an important role in this novel; during the Choson dynasty (1392–1910), ruling-class men conducted official and private written business in Chinese characters. Naturally, these men were well versed in the Chinese classics, while women used the Korean alphabet for their letters and literature.

The drama of this story unfolds against the background of factional struggles. During King Chongjo's reign, the court was divided between two rival factions: the Southerners, who supported the ideal of strong monarchical rule, and the Old Doctrine members, who believed in the wisdom of power shared by the political literati, lay scholars, and the King. The Old Doctrine faction, consisting of the King's political opponents, dominated the administration. The Old Doctrine faction was further divided into two groups: the Principle (or Intransigent) and the Expediency (or Flexible).

Several specific rules of Choson dynasty etiquette are relevant to this novel. Upper-class men had more than one name. It was considered impolite to call a person by his given name, so his personal names and honorific names were used when addressing him or referring to him. In the story, for example, there is a man named Chae Hong-won, but he is almost always called I-suk or Chae I-suk. Another point that might interest the readers is the term "Teacher," which was used to indicate a degree of respect; a person was often addressed by the title "Teacher" plus his honorific name, as in "Teacher Pon-am."

Another point that may baffle readers is the Korean way of counting time. Korean counting includes the beginning day or year; for example, Korea was under Japanese colonial rule from 1910 to 1945, but Koreans say "thirty-six years of Japanese rule." To indicate the Western way of counting, people use the word "*man* (fully)" in front of numbers. Similarly, birthdays are not observed when people become one year older. Instead, everyone becomes a year older on New Year's Day, and a newborn baby is considered one year old at birth. Korean ages thus differ from Western ages by a year or two, depending on the person's actual date of birth. A good example is a baby born in December; it becomes two years old on New Year's Day.

A simple introduction to traditional Korean architecture will also help the reader to understand the novel. The houses of the ruling *yangban* class were divided into three parts: the women's quarters (inner quarters), which were far from outsiders' view; the men's quarters (outer quarters), where men lived and received guests; and the servants' quarters, near the gate. Normally the structures were a few feet above ground level. In the middle was a rectangular veranda that connected two rooms on either side with a latticed sliding door of mulberry paper, which were the main entrances to the rooms; in addition, each room generally had another door opening onto a narrow platform leading to the yard. People were required to take off their shoes before stepping up onto the veranda to enter the building. The rooms were heated by what is known as the *ondol* system. Flues were laid under the floor, and logs or charcoal were burned in an outside firebox to heat each room. People ate and slept on the floor, which was covered with shiny, lacquered paper. For meals a small tray with three or four short legs was brought in, laden with small dishes. Men usually ate by themselves, unless they had guests. When they slept, a folding mattress (similar to a futon), a quilt, and a pillow were taken out of the wardrobe.

To further facilitate readers' understanding, I have included a list of the characters and a glossary of Korean expressions.

Finally, I would like to express my thanks to those who have helped me in various ways. This translation was made possible by a generous grant from the Korea Literature Translation Institute. My sister, Young-mee Yu Cho, recommended *Everlasting Empire* for translation and supplied useful information on the Choson dynasty system and translations of Chinese classics. Yi In-hwa, the author of the novel, clarified many points for me and expressed his willingness to allow liberal editing. Elizabeth Lee provided me with the terms of government positions and other related details, as well as her enthusiasm. Diane Rudan pointed out many problems and solutions. Katie Wiltrout's keen eyes spotted many instances of awkwardness. Julie Pickering, Bruce Fulton, and Stephen Epstein edited parts of the manuscript. Janet Poole's editing also helped. Donald Baker provided authenticity by supplying correct terms and interpretations of some classical passages. Laura Nelson, my partner, was there from the beginning to the end; she provided me with encouragement and also edited the text several times.

References

Chinese-Korean Dictionary (Seoul: Korean Cultural Research Center, Korea University, 1989)

Korea Old and New: A History by Carter J. Eckert, Ki-baik Lee, Young Ick Lew, Michael Robinson, Edward Wagner (Seoul: Ilchhokak Publishers for Korea Institute, Harvard University, 1990)

The Literati Purge: Political Conflict in Early Yi Korea by Edward Wagner (Cambridge: East Asian Research Center and Harvard University Press, 1974)

A Source Book in Chinese Philosophy by Wing-tsit Chan (Princeton: Princeton University Press, 1963)

A Short History of Chinese Philosophy by Fung Yu-lan (New York: Free Press Paperback Edition, a division of Simon & Schuster, Inc. New York, 1966)

China: A New History by John King Fairbank (Cambridge: Belknap Press of Harvard University Press, 1992)

"The Owl" translated by Yang Xianyi in Selections from the *Book of Songs*, translated by Yang Xianyi, Gladys Yang, and Hu Shiguang (Beijing: Panda Books, Chinese Literature Press, 1983)

List of Characters

Chae Che-gong (Pon-am, posthumously given the name Duke Munsuk, 1720–1799): A celebrated high government official during the reigns of King Yongjo and King Chongjo. As the leader of the Southerners faction, he advocated mild treatment of persecuted Catholics.

Chae Hong-won (I-suk, 1762–1832): Son of Chae Che-gong. In the book, he is imprisoned and killed by the Old Doctrine faction in 1800, as they try to retrieve a secret book he has inherited from his celebrated father.

Chang Chong-o: A Rank 5A-book examiner of the Royal Library, who is an expert in epigraphy and skilled at copying any style of writing.

Chang-gon: A slave at In-mong's house.

Cho Hong-om: The sixth royal secretary.

Chong Chun-gyo: A messenger eunuch.

Chong Min-shi: Director of the Royal Library.

Chong-nae: A clerk at the Royal Library.

Chong Sang-u: The fourth royal secretary.

Chong Yag-yong (Ta-san, 1762–1836): One of the greatest Shirhak (Practical Learning School of Confucianism) scholars of the late Choson (1392–1910) period and a high government official. He was persecuted as a Catholic. In the book he is the third minister of the Board of Punishments.

Confucius (551–479 B.C.): The preeminent Chinese philosopher. Confucius advocated a system of rule based on moral principles. He believed in the perfectibility of all men, and offered as models the ancient sage-kings Yao, Shao, Wu, and Tang.

Crown Prince Sado: King Yongjo's son and King Chongjo's father.

Duke Munsuk: Chae Che-gong's posthumous title.

Duke of Zhou (d. 1094 B.C.): A historical figure in China, King Wen's brother in the Zhou dynasty (1100–256 B.C.). He laid a foundation for the royal family in support of his nephew King Cheng. He was said to be the author of The Rites of Zhou.

Fuxishi: A legendary emperor of ancient China, who is said to have ruled for a hundred and fifty years and to have been an enlightened ruler. He was also the creator of the eight hexagrams used for fortune telling.

Han Yu (768–824): A well-known literary figure during the Tang dynasty of China.

Hong Kug-yong (1748–1781): A high-level civil servant during the reigns of King Yongjo and King Chongjo. In particular, he exercised his authority over court officials during King Chongjo's reign. He died in banishment after it was revealed that he was engaged in a plot to assassinate the queen.

Hwang Po-chan: A Palace Guards commandant.

Hyon Sung-hon: A clerk under Librarian Yi In-mong.

Kae-dong's Father: Yi In-mong's neighbor, late in Yi's life.

Kim Chae-shin: The police chief.

Kim Cho-sun (1765–1831): The young leader of the Expediency group who became the father-in-law of King Sunjo, King Chongjo's son.

Kim Chong-su (1728–1799): The leader of the Old Doctrine faction during King Chongjo's reign.

Kim Il-gyong (1662–1724): The leader of the Young Doctrine faction during King Sukchong's reign. He was engaged in the purge of the Old Doctrine faction, but after King Yongjo's ascent, he was put to death.

Kim Kwan-ju: Queen Chongsun's brother and the virtual leader of the Principle group of the Old Doctrine faction.

Kim Pyong-yon (1807–1863): Known as Bamboo-Hatted Kim, he wandered the country writing satirical poems.

Kim Yu-jung: Yi In-mong's hometown friend.

King Cholchong (1831–1863, reign 1849–1863): The twenty-fifth king of the Choson dynasty. Banished to Kanghwa Island with his family due to his brother's imprisonment in 1844, he was living as an uneducated woodcutter until his ascent to the throne. He was reduced to a pawn in a power play by his wife's family.

King Chongjo (Hongjae, 1752–1800, reign 1777–1800): The twenty-second king of the Choson dynasty (1392–1910). As a son of Crown Prince Sado, who died tragically by the hand of his own father, he ascended to the throne following his grandfather, King Yongjo. He was responsible for the cultural golden age of the late Choson period in that he established the Royal Library and published numerous books, including Hongjae Collection. He promoted Shirhak (The Practical Learning School of Confucianism) instead of the more theoretical Neo-Confucianism.

King Honjong (1827–1849, reign 1834–1849): The twenty-fourth king of the Choson dynasty. Grandson of King Sunjo (reign 1801–1834).

King Sukchong (1661–1720, reign 1675–1720): The nineteenth king of the Choson dynasty (1392–1910). During his reign, factional fighting between the Westerners and the Southerners reached its peak.

King Tanjong (1441–1457, reign 1452–1455): The sixth king of the Choson dynasty. A child king, he was usurped by his uncle, Prince Suyang, who became King Sejo. King Tanjong was banished to a remote county and killed there.

King Yongjo (1694–1776, reign 1724–1776): The twenty-first king of the Choson dynasty (1392–1910): He introduced the policy of grand harmony in employing government officials as a way to suppress intense factional struggles. He is known to have been a strong king who attempted to strengthen the nation with the implementations of new systems. He killed his own son, Crown Prince Sado, by incarcerating him in a rice chest.

Ku Chae-gyom: Chief of the Special Cavalry Unit, he was the son of Ku Son-bok, a general who was put to death by King Chongjo for treason.

Kwon Chol-shin (1736–1801): A Catholic martyr who was executed with Yi Ka-hwan.

Madam Hong: Chong Yag-yong's wife.

Lady Oh: Chae Che-gong's wife and Chae I-suk's mother.

Madam Shin: Yu Chi-myong's wife.

Mencius (371–289 B.C.?): A professional philosopher and teacher who studied under the pupils of the grandson of Confucius. Like Confucius, he idolized the legendary sage-kings. Mencius declared that human nature is originally good and built his entire philosophy on this tenet. He was the first Chinese philosopher to do so.

Mok Man-jung : The censor-general.

Min Tae-hyok: The chief royal secretary.

Mun O-dok: A eunuch.

Nam Han-jo : A Southerners faction member.

Oh Sok-jung: The fifth councilor of the Office of Special Advisors. Yi In-mong's friend.

Pak Chi-won (Yon-am, posthumously given the name Mun-do, 1737–1805): A leading figure in the Northern Studies branch of the Old Doctrine faction. After his visit to Qing China, he wrote a travelogue that became renowned. Called *Jehol Diary*, it consisted of twenty-six volumes. His writing was well known even in China. He emphasized the importance of accepting the Practical Learning of Confucianism.

Pak Sang-hyo: Yi In-mong's pseudonym.

Park Chung Hee (1917–1979): The fourth president of the Republic of Korea (1961–1979). A soldier, he successfully staged a coup d'etat in 1961 and ruled the country until being assassinated by one of his own intelligence officers. He prolonged his presidency by changing the Constitution, notably in the October Restoration (yushin) of 1972.

Pyong-gu: A clerk at the Royal Library.

Queen Chongsun (1745–1805): The second wife of King Yongjo. Although she did not have a child of her own, she wielded enormous power in the court. She influenced King Yongjo's decision to kill his own son, Crown Prince Sado.

Ricci, Matteo (1552–1620): An Italian Jesuit missionary who gave the Chinese their first understanding of the West and provided Europeans with an accurate description of China. He lived in Bejing, the capital, from 1601 until his death in 1610. There he taught science to Chinese scholars, translated Christian works into Chinese, wrote books in Chinese, and gave Europe its first modern account of the Chinese Empire.

Sang-a: The wife of Yi In-mong, the protagonist.

Shim Hwan-ji (1730–1802): The Inflexible leader of the Principle group of the Old Doctrine faction and a staunch defender of Neo-Confucianism. Second state councilor.

So Yong-su: The minister of personnel.

So Yu-mun: The fifth royal secretary.

Song Hon (1535–1598): A Confucianist during King Sonjo's reign.

Song Shi-yol (1607–1689): A politician and scholar. He was the leader of the Westerners faction and later of the Old Doctrine faction. He was executed by poison by King Sukchong for infuriating the king on the matter of designating the crown prince.

So In-song: The director of the Eunuch Department, who closely cooperated with the Old Doctrine faction, the political opponents of King Chongjo.

So Yong-bo: The deputy director of the Royal Library.

Taewongun (1820–1898): The father of King Kojong (reign 1863–1907).

To Hak-sun: A coroner.

Yi Chae-hak: The minister of taxation.

Yi Cho-won (1735–1806): The minister of punishments.

Yi Han-pung: The chief commander of the Military Training Command.

Yi Hwang (Toe-gye, 1501–1570): A great Korean Confucian scholar during the reign of King Chungjong. He established one of the two major influential schools of thought, along with Yi I (Yul-gok).

Yi I (Yul-gok, 1536–1584): A great Korean Confucian scholar during the Choson dynasty. He was called "Confucius of the East," and his spirit tablet is kept at the Confucian Academy.

Yi In-jwa (? –1728): A rebel during King Yongjo's reign.

Yi In-mong: The protagonist of this novel; the librarian of the Royal Library.

Yi Ik (Song-ho, 1682–1763): A renowned scholar of Shirak (Practical Learning) during the reign of King Yongjo.

Yi Ik-un: The third royal secretary.

Yi Ka-hwan (Chong-jo, 1742–1801): A member of the Southerners faction and the grandson of Yi Ik, he was well known for his elegant writing, but was executed for being a Catholic.

Yi Kyong-chul: A eunuch.

Yi Kwan-gyu: The assistant section chief in the Board of Rites, who was a friend of Yi In-mong.

Yi Shi-su: The third state councilor and the director of the Royal Infirmary.

Yi So-gu: The second royal secretary.

Yi Sung-hun (1756–1801): The first baptized Korean. After being trained in China, returned to Korea in 1783 and did missionary work until he was executed in a large-scale Catholic persecution in 1801.

Yi Tok-mu (A-jong, 1741–1793): A great scholar during the reign of King Chongjo. He was considered one of the four great scholars of the recent modern period. Despite his scholarship, the only official positions he was allowed to hold were book examiner of the Royal Library and county magistrate, because he was of concubine lineage.

Yu Chi-myong (1777–1861): A civil servant and scholar during the reign of King Cholchong. In the book, he is a friend of Yi In-mong.

Yun Haeng-im (1762–1801): A civil servant during King Chongjo's reign. The leader of the Expediency (shipa) group, he was killed in a political purge after King Chongjo's death.

Yun Yu-il (1760–1795): A Catholic who was executed after the Failure of Arrest (1795) as an accomplice who helped the Chinese priest Zhou Wen Mo escape from Korea. In the book he is the brother of Sang-a.

Xiang Yu (232–202 B.C.): A Chinese military man who lived in the late Qin dynasty. Rugged and sturdy, he was known for his obstinacy.

Zhou Wenmo (1752–1802): A Chinese Catholic priest who came to Korea in secret by crossing the Yalu River in 1794 to proselytize. He was martyred in 1801, after surrendering himself to the authorities.

Zhu Xi (Chu Hsi; 1130–1200): A giant of Chinese Confucianism who influenced Chinese thought. He made Neo-Confucianism truly Confucian by stripping it of the Buddhist and Taoist influences that had been conspicuous in previous Neo-Confucian thought.

Author's Preface

I was eleven years-old when I first heard the tale of King Chongjo's death by poison. It was the winter of 1976, and I had accompanied my father to the first anniversary rite of the death of my father's aunt in Yean, Andong. I was a dull child. I was one of the worst students, who as a fifth-grader still made a wet map on my bedding at least once every three days. It was no wonder that my mother worried about my being so slow in everything. Yet I myself was not concerned; I threw down my book bag as soon as school was over, and I played with my friends, laughing and giggling. In a word, I was eleven. My blood boiled, my heart was bursting, and any new idea would tickle my head, which was shrouded in a sweet mist. Whenever I heard an interesting story, joy and longing, an affirmation of life, couldn't be prevented from spreading through me. I was like a sponge absorbing ink.

On that winter night, I was playing with some relatives of my age in a small corner room at a late hour, after we had paid our respects to the adult visitors. An aunt from Chongsong peeled chestnuts for us children and started to tell us about the "evil bastards who poisoned the king." Young as I was, I was overwhelmed by the tale. Although I was too young to understand what factional fighting was, the violent feelings, the hatreds, the repeated acts of vengeance, and the unbounded evil deeds struck me and ushered in an indescribable fear. I still remember vividly being so frightened that I couldn't venture out of the room, let alone to the dark outhouse. (That night's protagonist was Yi Ka-hwan. Perhaps it was the result of people's sympathy and folkloric empathy for Yi, who had died a terrible death.)

Since that day, the world has seemed like a threatening entity that can be viewed only with a sidelong glance. The story taught me the terrifying principle that most of a person's wishes are attained through competition with others, frustrating them and hurting their pride. After that winter, I stopped wetting my bedding.

Later, when I entered college and studied Korean language and literature, I learned that the story I had heard when I was eleven was a common tale in the southeastern region of Korea. An old professor who was born in Andong told me that he had heard the story from grown-ups when he was small. More peculiarly, Choe Ik-han (born in Uljin, Kyongsangbuk Province), the author of *Chong Ta-san and the Practical Learning Branch* (1955), a work said to be monumental among North Korean scholars, deals with King Chongjo's assassination plot in detail, using the phrase "according to handed-down words."

According to handed-down words? Whose words were they?

I began to imagine the first person who had told this tale. A young scholar with integrity and loyalty, who was by King Chongjo's side to help with his reform politics, who wouldn't forgive the king's political foes — nor his defeat and his miserable old age. That was how I composed the dreamlike incidents that this imaginary person experienced, over the course of one day and night, some months before King Chongjo's murder.

In short, I am a storyteller who is relaying this old tale in a new fashion. A novelist writes to express himself and to show off his uniqueness and the truth in himself, which is different from any other person's, but a storyteller lends his pen to recreate what has been handed down, rather than to expressing himself.

In order to avoid misunderstanding, I would like to add that this book is a work of fiction. I have attempted to reveal historical facts based on thorough research through the voice of a translator, and to approach the truth of this period in fiction and in the voice of Yi In-mong. For purposes of fictionalization I have used the methods of mystery novels, such as Umberto Eco's *The Name of the Rose*, Conan Doyle's *The Hound of the Baskervilles*, John Dickson Carr's *The Case of Constant Suicides*, and Robert Van Gulik's *Chinese Gold Murders*. The breathtaking events and the characters teeming in the twenty-four hour period covered by the novel are products of my imagination. To emphasize that some characters are fictional, I altered their names by changing the last syllables of their names, or the Chinese characters on which their Korean names are based. I would like to ask their descendants' forebearance.

Yi In-hwa
July 1993

The Book

It was June 1992.

My eyes happened to fall on an odd book entitled *The Encounter of the Stars* at the Toyo Bunko library in Tokyo. The book was handwritten in Chinese characters by one Yi In-mong, a Librarian of Rank 7A, who served during the reign of King Chongjo of the Choson dynasty. The book itself was written in King Honjong's first year on the throne, around 1835 by the Western calendar. I was amazed when I spotted it crammed among the mounds of books on the shelves.

"How on earth could such an ugly book exist?" I asked myself.

The tattered volume looked utterly out of place. It stank of rotting paper, and a number of pages toward the end were missing. Several sheets of leftover mulberry paper, soaked in water and then beaten with a laundry paddle, had been pasted together to form the cover; but over the years the portions that had received less paste had become detached. Those sections that had been paddled harder than the others had begun to crack. How pathetic this lone volume looked, surrounded by such august company as hard-covered personal booklets in multiple volumes, classified into poetry, memorials, formalized petitions to the throne, prefaces, and book reviews!

The author, whoever he was, had certainly left no descendants. If he had any, they would have at least left a copy on clean paper in proper calligraphy even if they hadn't been able to afford to publish a printed version. What could the title *The Encounter of the Stars* mean? A meeting of the stars? I assumed it had to refer to the myth describing how Altair and Vega meet once a year. . . . Hmmm, such an unusual title. . . . With pity and a modicum of curiosity, I began to leaf through the first few pages, but soon I became flabbergasted. My eyes caught such names as Chong Yag-yong, Yi Ok, Yi Hak-gyu, and Yi Chung-il. The contents seemed to have something to do with the restoration of literary style decreed by King Chongjo. This was related to the subject of my master's thesis!

I was hoping to shed light on the poets who had preceded Kim Pyong-yon, widely known as Kim Sakkat, or Bamboo-Hatted Kim, who ushered in a new literary epoch with Chinese poems of stunning creativity. In fact, I was staying in Tokyo to search for documentations of those poets who had composed unusual Chinese verses almost in the style of folk songs around the time of King Chongjo. This sudden good fortune made my pulse race.

Evidently no one had considered the book important: It had yet to be transferred to microfilm. While the Toyo Bunko library forbids the photocopying of books that have not been microfilmed, I didn't mind recording every single word in my notebook.

Yet this first flush of excitement was a mere taste of what would come.

It took me a week to finish reading the book, and Yi In-mong's story stunned me. The tale was unbelievable, a virtual mystery novel. Could it all possibly be true? How could such an incredible story remain hidden until now, for so many decades? Who was Yi In-mong? How had his book wound up in Japan? Such questions yielded only further riddles.

The Toyo Bunko, a specialized Asian Studies library, was established with more than 100,000 books that Japan had obtained in lieu of war reparation funds from Qing China, following its victory in the Sino-Japanese War in 1895. The library continued to grow throughout the Showa era, as an enormous number of books on East Asia were added, encompassing collections from China, Manchuria, Korea, and Indochina. *The Encounter of the Stars* was shelved in a room where Maema Kyosaku's collection was stored. The room was known as "Pavilion on the Mountains," according to Maema's honorific name. Many Korean researchers had visited this room. Was it really possible such an unusual book had escaped the notice of them all?

Upon returning to Seoul, I realized that my initial enthusiasm was absurd. If I quoted from the book in my thesis, my professors would wonder whether I had gone crazy. I was extremely distressed: There was no way to verify the contents of this book in any official accounts.

Who on earth was this Yi In-mong? He had evidently composed his work at age sixty-six to describe events he'd been involved in at the palace several decades earlier as a twenty-nine-year-old official. His name, however, didn't appear in the *Annals of the Royal Library*.

In the twenty-fourth year of King Chongjo's reign (1800), the librarian of Rank 7A was a man named Yi Chon-su. Yi, born in 1772, was therefore twenty-nine at that time, the same age as Yi In-mong, but his life could not have proceeded more differently. According to the *Official Roster of Civil Service Examination Passers*, Yi Chon-su was a member of a renowned clan that originated in Yonan. Yi belonged to the *shipa* (Expediency) group in the *noron* (Old Doctrine) faction. He was the grandson of Yi Chon-bo, a chief state councilor, and the son of Yi Mun-won, a head of a government board. Never in his life had he experienced exile or dismissal, practices quite common in those days, but rather he had been continually promoted. His meteoric rise included terms as minister of rites; minister of taxation; deputy director in the Office of Royal Decrees; third state councilor; and, finally, second state councilor. He died at the age of fifty-eight in the presence of his sons and grandsons. His life had been calm and fortunate, enough to elicit envy from anyone.

Then who was this Yi In-mong, purported librarian at the Royal Library in the first month of the twenty-fourth year of the reign of King Chongjo? Yi In-mong was either a pseudonym or a fictional character.

If "Yi In-mong" were indeed a fictional creation, the story of *The Encounter of the Stars* would be a work of imagination. Wouldn't it be a novel in that case? Ahh . . . had I been so stirred up by mere fiction? But it was too early to give up hope. As I read the book over and over again, I discovered several suggestive clues toward a solution. Yi tried not to reveal anything about his family history, and the introduction contained the following: "If this book falls into the wrong hands, the ruin of the entire clan will be inevitable. Members of the next generations who relate this information should be doubly cautious." Furthermore, a passage in Chapter 4 detailed the Revolt of Yi In-jwa.

The murder the book recounts took place in 1800. Soon afterward, King Chongjo passed away suddenly at age forty-eight, still in his prime. The author seems to insinuate a relationship between these two deaths. If the book had happened to fall into the "wrong hands," and consequently become known to the world, what would have happened? Years before, the Revolt of Yi In-jwa had taken place after rumors circulated that members of the Old Doctrine faction had murdered King Kyongjong to consolidate their power. Therefore, it was natural to assume that if the powerful Old Doctrine faction had become aware of the contents of this book, they would have made every effort possible to find the person who had revealed the story, even if it meant scouring the earth. It was not unlikely that the author would have fictionalized his identity.

A careful examination of the book turns up evidence that the identity of Yi In-mong, the "librarian of Rank 7A," was hastily concocted. For example, on the morning of the murder, Yi In-mong, running hither and thither in utter confusion, comes across Yi Kyong-chul, a eunuch who has entered the Royal Library without permission. Oddly, however, Yi Kyong-chul uses a respectful form of address at this point as if to an elder, while referring to himself in humble style. Yi Kyong-chul's position in the Department of Eunuchs was 7B, almost equal in status to Yi In-mong's. Even if eunuchs were not despised as a class, such highly respectful address definitely would have been out of order. Furthermore, King Chongjo, though he presides over thousands of courtiers and hundreds of civil servants, knows the personal name of Yi In-mong, a trifling official. Finally, Yi In-mong shows unexpected dignity and confidence as he orders his underlings around after the murder is discovered and he takes charge of settling the matter. These details hardly accord with a lowly position for Yi.

Once my thinking had progressed to this stage, I felt as though my chain of logic was gradually being sucked into some sort of mysterious cave with no apparent exit. I was being drawn into a historical spider's web spun by some fiendish writer. Except for the details about himself and the names of the major characters, however, Yi's facts were entirely consistent with other information about the Royal Library and court records. I surmised that he could have been an official at the library after all, but the level above librarian in Rank 7A was the deputy director of Rank 3A. When the incident took place, Yi In-mong was merely twenty-nine. A deputy director at the age of twenty-nine . . . impossible!

As questions followed one after another, my confusion grew. Without determining the writer's identity, it was impossible to judge the veracity of the account. If only I could figure out who Yi In-mong really was, I could establish the text as historical. As I lounged on the floor of my room, my head bursting with such thoughts, a few strange ideas bubbled forth.

I felt more and more like that poor barber in the legend who knows that the king has donkey's ears. How could I be the only one with knowledge of this unbelievable story?

One day I realized that I could use this story for a novel.

What if I gave up the claim that the events as described in Yi's book really took place and wrote a novel instead? A novel! Yes, what if I gave up my wish to analyze the book from a scholar's standpoint and escaped into a totally different realm, a realm where writing became amusement and I had limitless possibilities. That wouldn't be bad at all.

Nothing now exists to prove that the story in *The Encounter of the Stars* really happened. By the same token, nothing now could require me to identify the writer as a historical personage. It dawned on me that I should acquiesce in the author's will, since he had calculated every way he might be identified, and blocked precisely those parts which would give us a glimpse of him.

This is how I came to write *Everlasting Empire*. I can't predict the shape it will take. My one desire is to express complex, tangled events in a way readers will readily understand: the story of the death of Chang Chong-o, the book examiner; the questions concerning the death of King Chongjo; the political conflicts stemming from the interpretation of *The Book of Odes*; the "Notes on *Humble Thoughts on the Book of Odes*" that disappeared; and the tragic life of Yi In-mong and his wife Sang-a.

I have made some changes to the original text. The original book itself measures 15.5 cm by 27.0 cm, and contains 189 pages, each with fourteen lines of twenty characters. It would be both impossible and undesirable to translate it as is. The original was composed by an old man as memories occurred to him; hence, the temporal sequence is not chronological, and pages 35 and 36 as well as the pages from 165 to 182 are missing. One has to imagine what happened in these gaps.

I have reconstructed the events of a twenty-four hour period, from dawn of the nineteenth day of the first lunar month of 1800 to dawn of the twentieth day. In order to explain unique political circumstances and modes of thought difficult for contemporary readers to comprehend, I have changed from first to third person narrative and employed an omniscient point of view; in other words, I started sentences with "Yi In-mong. . . ." One should be as faithful to the original as possible, but I believe some alteration is appropriate for the reasons listed. I ask for my readers' understanding.

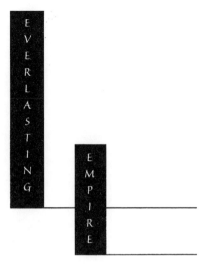

[*The* Book of Changes] *involves a certain curious principle which I have termed synchronicity, a concept that formulates a point of view diametrically opposed to that of causality. Since the latter is merely statistical truth and not absolute, it is a sort of working hypothesis of how events evolve one out of another, whereas synchronicity takes the coincidence of events in space and time as meaning something more than mere chance, namely, a peculiar interdependence of objective events among themselves as well as with the subjective (psychic) states of the observer or observers.*

— Karl Gustav Jung, from the Foreword to the *I Ching or Book of Changes* for the English edition.

1
The Board Game
Climbing the Ladder of Government Positions

Let us be together, dead or alive,
You and I promised firmly.
Let us grow old together till we die
With our hands joined fast.
Alas, we no longer are together,
Separated and far from each other.
Alas, far away from each other,
When can we ever keep our promise?

—"Beating the Drum (VI)," in "Odes of Pei"
From Confucius, *Book of Odes*

It was before the first light; dawn.

The north wind kicked Pukhan Mountain, growled and buffeted the hills above Waryong-dong, then flailed about like the edge of a sharp knife. Among the high pavilions and sleeping quarters that lined the hill, leaves swept into the darkness of the dawn. The leaves, covered with patches of frost that made them glisten like silver paper, were scattered as far as Tonhwa Gate.

The night duty office of the Royal Library was situated in the backcourt of Changdok Palace.

Librarian Yi In-mong heard a voice deep in his sleep. It came from behind him, far, far behind him where his eyes couldn't reach, from a mysterious darkness. It spouted from the dust of Time, and it flashed through him like lightning. His eyelids seemed weighed down by a thousand stones.

He turned toward the voice, as if someone tugged from behind.

At that very moment, he opened his eyes. A perplexed expression crossed his face. He lay in a room lined with shelves of old books. Dust and mildew permeated the air. Lying on his bedding stretched out on the floor, he looked up at the ceiling layered with pale wallpaper. Was he dreaming? A thin film of mist spread over his gaze.

"Sir!"

An actual voice.

"Sir! I brought you water to wash up with."

In-mong jerked upright and drank from the cup by his pillow. A gust of wind rustled the paper doors. The flapping sound echoed in In-mong's ears. The wind must have been whipping all night long.

"Sung-hon?"

"Yes, sir. You ordered me to wake you before *myoshi*, and . . ."

Still sitting, In-mong dragged himself to the doors and slid them open.

A chill mist rushed in, borne on the wind. Outside, Hyon Sung-hon, the library clerk, stood awkwardly before the narrow veranda that ran the length of the chamber. There he had placed a basin of water along with a cotton cloth and soap powder wrapped in a scrap of mulberry paper. It was still pitch-dark.

"You may go."

"Yes, sir."

It was the nineteeth day of the first lunar month of the twenty-fourth year in the reign of King Chongjo, 1800.

This was how Yi In-mong, who had turned twenty-nine with the new year, had met this fateful day. Even now, after many years and countless events, he still recalled that dawn with a sigh, and with deep regret and disquiet.

He slid the doors shut and rubbed his eyes, ignorant of the events about to unfold. In his sleepy daze, the small room where he had fallen asleep in the early morning hours, after having stayed on duty at the library, seemed oddly unfamiliar. It hadn't yet registered that he was not at home but in the grand palace. He looked around, his eyes bloodshot.

The bed he had just wriggled out of looked desolate without him.

He slept by himself whether at home or the palace. Leaning back against the high threshold, he stared at the bedding stretched out on the floor and felt a chill of pale loneliness deep within his heart.

He sat all alone in the darkness.

He had been alone for a long time. A long, long time. Not a year or two, but many, many years. A hundred years, two hundred years, perhaps more. Bewildered as a shaman whose spirit has departed by his own rites, he thought of the dream where his soul had rested until moments before. An icy tremor spread through his body. His head felt like it was whirling toward the ceiling.

He had been dreaming about his wife, the woman from whom he had been forced to separate.

What did the dream mean?

As he recalled the dream, everything in the room became unfamiliar. The quilt, the books, the bookshelves, the desk, even his own self. He rubbed his face and moaned to himself, "Sang-a . . ."

He felt as if he were submerged in water.

At the thought of his wife's name, tears welled in his eyes. He had expelled Sang-a from his house, commanded by a fate he considered irresistible. It was a memory he wished to escape, if possible. Nevertheless, he could not forget her face even after six long years. There it was, etched in black in his memory, like a tattoo. He would never be able to escape the memory of her face, no matter how long he lived.

"It will soon be light," he thought as he gazed at the small window.

Over the eastern hill behind the Sonhyang Chamber, warm sunlight would appear in a multicolored burst and the dream would vanish once more, swept up into the dust suspended in the air. Swept into blue-green

Time where it was neither dream nor reality. The dream would become a dark, fragile sorrow unable to withstand the bright light of day. He swallowed and pictured the face that would recede to the dark reaches of his memory.

The dream returned.

He was strolling in a familiar pine forest, on a path strewn with cones. A scarlet sunset, blood-red light filtering down hazily all around. Not a soul was visible. As he walked and walked on the seemingly endless path, he suddenly realized he was at the entrance to Itaewon, where he had lived before passing the national examination more than ten years earlier.

There was no reason he should be here. . . . "Ah, it's a dream," he thought. "I'm only dreaming." A sudden flurry of sights, scenes, and sounds rushed by. He could see the low hill he used to climb with Sang-a. There they would gaze at the sky as it turned red in the evening. The bamboo platform under the zelkova tree appeared, where he would improvise and recite poems, casually fanning himself. A cool breeze danced through lush and verdant forest, while cicadas screeched painfully.

Then he was walking along a dark alley lined with low thatch huts. The run-down huts were illuminated by dim lanterns. A melody from a "song of sorrows" drifted in the wind: "Make the spirit in your dream walk / make it leave traces. / Then half the pavement in front of the house / will crumble to sand. / Eh hey eee. . . . Can't live because I miss my love so much. . . ." In-mong walked on, surrounded by garbage—broken roof tiles, egg shells, putrid rat carcasses. . . . He passed through several narrow, wet, dark alleys, strewn with trash. As he turned a corner, an old thatched house came into view with a vegetable garden. He heard the worn thicket door rattle in the wind, and was overwhelmed with emotion.

His old house!

The scent of pine mingled with Chinese junipers and arbor vitae. A late spring evening, it seemed. There she was, passing from the kitchen to the courtyard. He glimpsed her through walls covered with vines and spindle trees.

His heart pounded with anxiety.

He found himself drawn inside the house as if by a cord. How was it possible? What kind of a dream was this? He shut his eyes. He heard footsteps and the rustling of a long skirt, then "Dear!" and a silky hand tugging at the loose end of his sleeve. In-mong opened his eyes wide and looked at his wife. She looked exactly as he remembered her.

My wife . . .

Everything came to a stop momentarily.

5

I . . . what did I do next? Was it something that happened in the dream, or something that had happened in real life? When I saw my wife . . . what did I do then? He rummaged through the details of his dream, oblivious to the growing light from the small window of his room. The songs of forgetfulness drew closer, like a voice in the mist.

In-mong recalled his wife's leading him inside by the hand. Then she warmed some wine and prepared some food to go with it. The next moment she was running into the kitchen, then out to the yard, her high voice as fresh as the chirping of a cricket. The moon rose over the reed fields that stretched to the river from his front gate.

Wine cup in hand, In-mong watched smoke coming from his neighbors' chimney as they cooked dinner.

His wife's arched eyebrows rippled and her eyes gazed into the dark night sky. Ah . . . that face. She was still beautiful—her ruddy cheeks blooming a perfect line from her nose curving down to her lips. Nothing had changed in ten years. When she fluttered her eyes slowly, she seemed to blossom with sensuality.

And then? Ah, we played "Climbing the Ladder of Government Positions." He recalled her youthful face as she pleaded with him, tugging at his sleeve and spreading out the game board like an innocent child. She had enjoyed that game since before they were married, asking him to play whenever they had spare time. But he detested it. . . . In his dream, though, he picked up the four sticks, compelled by the radiance of her face.

The game was similar to the more popular game of *yutmori*, except that it used a chart of government positions instead of the simpler *yutmori* board. He had always complained the game was for the ruling Old Doctrine faction, not for a humble scholar like him.

The four sticks were first tossed to determine your role as a player. Three heads and one tail meant the players became a foot soldier, while two heads and two tails meant becoming a low-level clerk for whom passing the national examinations was unnecessary. If one head and three tails came up, the player became a reclusive scholar whose government office was owed to his reputation. All tails, an official in the military class; all heads, a civil official. The player's ascent took place within these strict boundaries. This game saddened and dispirited In-mong, who in real life did not feel like tossing even for a foot soldier.

How many times had he cast the sticks in his dream?

A shriek from his wife jolted him out of his reverie. His marker had landed on the square "Poisoned by the Monarch." He suddenly felt a dark cloud overshadow the contentment he had been feeling with his wife. He pulled her toward him and embraced her. The musky fragrance of camellia oil rose from her hair. The smell reminded him of the air of a summer night dancing about, the smell of a drenching sweat mixed with mist. Then a thought struck him. What if this was real? He was torn by a feeling that he was deceiving her.

He shivered and said, "I'm sorry. I'm with you only in my dream. It's not real. We are in my dream. Once day breaks . . . we won't see each other again."

Sang-a pursed her lips and bowed her head. Her face looked ineffably sad. Her eyes appeared shaded with an undying loneliness. She closed them, and her lips, crushed flower petals, opened. Ah, those trembling, heavy-hearted words . . .

She said quietly, "Well, my dear, in fact, I'm dreaming, too. I'm with you only in my dream. When I wake . . . I won't be able to see you again, will I?"

What!

He separated from her, stunned—and that was when he heard the voice behind him, coming from somewhere he couldn't see, not behind him exactly, but from the side, way, way back. Was it Hyon's voice that had awakened him? No. It was the voice of this world, reverberating through his body like the beating of a drum. His dream ended.

What did it mean?

It felt like the prelude to a disaster.

Had Sang-a died? If she were still alive, was she suffering? Suffering unbearably?

She must be with the persecuted Catholics, pursued by government agents. Tonight, had she walked a long way, cooked rice in the wind, and slept under the dew? He pictured her gaunt face, and tears streamed from his eyes.

Who was the wife he met in his dream? Who was the wife who had said in such a frightened voice that it was a dream, that she was seeing him in her own dream? And who was he himself—who didn't know what to do?

People spoke of Zhuangzi's dream of the butterfly. Was he, the human being, dreaming the dream of butterflies? Or was he, the butterfly, dreaming the dream of a human being? What about the happy days that had passed? Had he gone over into his wife's dream? Or had his wife come into his?

Ah! Meetings in this world were not destined to last; they dispersed whirling into the distance, and it was difficult to grasp them again. The past had been hard to chase even in his dream, but that voice and face were now far away again. In the moment it took to look up then down, the past and present had traded places.

My heart trembling in the light. O my heart, left behind, lonely, after chasing the past all night. However hard I search, I can grasp nothing. Nakchon Pavilion, Hwayang Pavilion, Hungchon Temple. . . . Every spring the two of us went on an outing. We would spend the day eating flower cakes or playfully throwing arrows into a jar, and we would pray to the rising moon to remain husband and wife forever, even in death. Ah, the cruelty of Heaven! Before we could even worry about the other world, everything came to an end in this one.

In-mong bowed like a horse exhausted by a difficult journey.

Suddenly he realized that light was seeping into the room. The mulberry paper of the window facing east had become a pale blue. Ah. What were all those moving specks? In-mong was surprised at the sunlight—white, blue, and red—stealing in through the window and the papered doors. Illuminated, the dust particles in the air danced about as tiny specks of light.

Daybreak already!

Come to think of it, he might have heard the court bell announcing *myoshi* a while back. What disloyal behavior for a man who served His Majesty at close quarters! He kicked off his quilt and dressed quickly, knotting the ties around the bottoms of his pants. How could he have been so self-indulgent and forgotten his duty? That morning His Majesty would lecture on the *Book of Odes*. He had better go straight to the Main Hall of the Queen's Quarters to offer morning greetings to His Majesty, then prepare for the lecture.

He smoothed his forehead, checked his horsehair headband, and took a deep breath. This calmed him somewhat.

He slid open the doors and ventured out.

The water Sung-hon had brought was cold now, making it difficult to lather up with the soap powder. He soaped his face, rubbing carefully around his eyes to eliminate any trace of tears. For a winter losing its fierceness, it was unusually cold. He shuddered as he wiped his face, his breath visible in the chilly air.

He walked to the edge of the veranda and glanced up at the somber sky.

In fact, it was fortunate that the weather was this cold. The year before, a terrible epidemic had swept the country, killing 128,000 people. Victims fell hither and thither until the end of autumn. The epidemic had run its course only around this time of the year, thanks to the excruciating cold. How His Majesty had worried! Teacher Pon-am had died in that epidemic. "Hmm. Aren't the first anniversary rites of his death being held today?" In-mong mumbled, then turned and disappeared into his room.

At that moment, footsteps scampered closer, turning the corner around

Aeryon Pond.

In-mong peered out the still open door as he slipped the belt around his navy blue official uniform with the red silk insignia in front. Hyon, on duty in the other room, slid his doors open a crack to have a look.

"S . . . sir, mmm . . . Librarian. Librarian, sir!" His voice was frightened and breathless.

"What is it?"

Without tying his ankle straps, In-mong stepped outside. It was Mun O-dok, the eunuch on duty. His usually ashen face was flushed and the veins stood out. His flustered face gave In-mong a jolt. Had something happened during his brief sleep? What if a fire had broken out in the Royal Library? In-mong scowled with worry. He stepped down to the courtyard, without bothering to put on his shoes.

"Sir, the book . . . book examiner . . . Mr. Chang. . . . He . . . he . . ."

"Get a hold of yourself! Speak clearly. What about the book examiner?"

"He . . . he . . . I think he's dead."

"What!"

In-mong gasped, eyes wide. A sudden gust of wind sent a chill through his body, down his spine. The next moment, In-mong's eyebrows rose, and he grabbed the man's shoulders roughly as if he were about to punch him.

"What did you say?"

"Taeg . . . Taeg-yong discovered it. He was taking him a basin of water."

"Stop it. Don't act silly. You must have seen a ghost. He was up late on duty and he's probably sound asleep."

"No, sir. I checked his pulse. His body is cold . . . dead, sir."

Suddenly, there was murmuring all around, like a summer downpour. Sung-hon and some others had peeked out after hearing the flurry of footsteps and already they were in the courtyard, listening intently. In-mong, flustered, looked around. He saw Sung-hon, Pyong-gu, and Chong-nae.

"You . . ."

"Yes?"

"Don't make a fuss. . . . Don't talk, just follow me. Eunuch Mun, you too."

He scarcely remembered doing it, but somehow he had managed to put on his official silk hat and black shoes. In-mong ran, turning the corner of Aeryon Pond, passing by Chio Hall, the Kumma Gate, and Chewol Kwang-pung Pavilion. As he looked up at Chuhap Hall, the main office of the Royal Library, he shuddered in horror. The colorful designs under the eaves, minutely divided into vivid squares, didn't look as they usually did. Instead, he saw the game board of his dream: "Climbing the Ladder of Government Positions."

* * *

The news was like a bolt of lightning. Sweat ran into his eyes. He removed his hat and wiped his forehead with his sleeve. Although it was the middle of winter, the duty room was sweltering. The combination of heat from the *ondol* floor and his own excitement made In-mong's face flush. Gazing at Chang Chong-o's stiff body in this stuffy, modest-sized room, he felt he was losing his mind. A quilt half-covered Chang's body. Chang's pale face wore its usual absent expression. The wrinkles on Chang's brow were the first thing that came to mind when In-mong pictured him. Chang's eyes were shut as if he were sleeping comfortably. It was so peculiar. If In-mong hadn't touched his wrist, he would have thought Chang was dozing peacefully. In-mong flicked the man's eyelids, to no avail. The body was still a bit warm, but it was clear Chang had departed for the other world.

The mystery of it would have driven a ghost to distraction. In-mong wondered whether Chang could possibly have killed himself, but he could find no suicide note.

Chang appeared to have fallen asleep after reading and writing. The desks, one for an ink stone and the other usually holding a book to read, were cluttered with crumbly, tattered volumes. Under one of the desks lay an open notebook of mulberry paper sewn with hemp threads. Purple ink was still damp and its fragrance filled the room. In-mong glanced at the page and saw a poem of four stanzas in Chinese, which must have been written during the night.

> Owl, O Owl, hear my request,
> And do not, owl, destroy my nest
> You have taken my young,
> Though I over them hung,
> With the nursing of love and of care.
> Pity me, pity me! Hear my prayer.
> Ere the clouds the sky had obscured,
> The mulberry roots I secured.
> Door and window around
> Them so firmly I bound,
> That I said, casting downward my eyes,
> "Dare any of you my house despise?"

I tugged with my claws and I tore,
And my mouth and my claws were sore,
So the rushes I sought,
And all other things brought;
For to perfect the house I was bent,
And I grudged no toil with this intent.

My wings are deplorably torn,
And my tail is much injured and worn.
Tossed about by the wind,
While the rain beats unkind,
Oh! my house is in peril of harm,
And this note I scream out in alarm.

Without a second thought, In-mong shut the notebook, quickly noted the title on the cover, and placed it back beneath the desk. The poem was "The Owl" from the "Odes of *Pin*" in the *Book of Odes*. The cover said, "Notes on *Humble Thoughts on the Book of Odes*." Nothing to warrant suspicion.

He heaved a sigh, his shoulders drooping.

The dark room was silent save for the pounding of his heart. The sound, metallic to his ears, made him dizzy. He closed his eyes briefly, trying to calm himself, but the inescapable presence of the corpse next to him made him confused and panicky. The room seemed to tremble in shimmering waves with his fear.

He rose on numb knees and went outside.

The men lingering there approached, faces taut with tension. He gazed blankly at them, and collapsed on the stone embankment. His head pounded as if thousands of crows were shrieking relentlessly inside it.

How to explain it? No visible wound, no expression of agony; Chang lay dead as if asleep. His death could not have been caused by illness. Just last night they had chatted over dinner in the dining hall. Disease could not have struck within nine hours. Had someone poisoned him? In-mong's heart jumped like a dog hurtling itself against a fence. Who had done this? Why? He felt overcome with frustration and fear.

Whoever it was, the perpetrator had selected the precise time when In-mong was sharing night duty with Chang.

It hardly mattered whether Chang's death was the work of some fiend or simply one of fate's many cruel jokes; if some unknown force were determined to deal both of them a fatal blow, what could In-mong do? His skin prickled as he imagined the aftermath of Chang's death.

For a subject to die while on duty in the palace was not a light matter. In principle, only the king and his immediate family members possessed the right to die at court. If the ladies-in-waiting and the eunuchs who lived in the palace fell gravely ill, they were expected to report the news immediately. If they happened to die within the palace, their families were treated as traitors. Death, regardless of who suffered it, was an unpleasant, unpropitious matter, hardly something that should occur near the king.

Furthermore, Chang did not hold some trifling position like the ladies-in-waiting and the eunuchs; he was a book examiner of Rank 5A.

No one at the Royal Library, including In-mong, would escape blame. The high court officials frowned on the library as it was. How could In-mong distress His Majesty like this?

These thoughts caused In-mong's usually powdery white complexion to flush again. His large, clear eyes took on a confused look. His thin face and sharp chin made him look obstinate; similarly, his tight-lipped mouth suggested an inflexible, uncompromising personality.

He looked around, sad dismay in his eyes.

This sudden turn of events bewildered Pyong-gu and Chong-nae, still in their late twenties. Sung-hon, however, over forty, was deep in thought and his head was bowed. The strain of suppressing his anxiety and fear clouded his face. And then next to him . . .

In-mong saw one of the eunuchs scrambling toward the Royal Shrine.

"Eunuch Mun! Where are you going?"

Mun winced and turning to In-mong, implored him in a feeble voice. "Sir . . . I . . . sir . . . to the director of eunuchs, sir . . ."

"No! Wait."

"As you know, sir, my . . . my humble responsibility is to report what happens here to the director. If it's not done immediately, sir, I . . . I will lose my head, sir." When In-mong didn't respond right away, he continued, "So, sir, I will now —"

"Didn't I say to wait? Will the director still be in his office? It's well past the hour of *myoshi*, so he will likely be out on the archery range with His Majesty. I will go and report this myself. Don't worry about the details of rules."

"But, sir, I belong to the Eunuch Department, sir, and . . ."

Mun's frightened voice caused In-mong to regain his composure, as though someone had doused him with cold water. All kinds of possibilities began to occur him; the situation would only worsen if he dallied. He jumped to his feet and, straightening his hat, beckoned Hyon Sung-hon.

"Go to Teacher Sa-am's house as fast as you can. Inform him of this urgent matter and ask him to wait in his office for His Majesty's directions," he whispered.

"Do you mean Teacher Chong Yag-yong, the third minister of the Board of Punishments?"

"That's right. You must personally give him the message. Understand?"

The Board of Punishments examined all deaths of unknown cause. In-mong hoped Chong, who belonged to the Southerners faction, as did he himself, would take on the case, rather than any of the other officials, who were all of the Old Doctrine faction.

Sung-hon nodded and left.

In-mong ordered Pyong-gu to deliver the news to the dead man's family and then also report to Minister Chong Min-shi, director of the library. Chong-nae was ordered to cordon off the site with straw ropes.

In-mong then set off up the hill toward Chuhap Hall, with Eunuch Mun in tow.

"Sir . . . Sir . . . I should . . . ," Mun protested feebly.

In-mong halted abruptly near the wall below the Huiu Hall. He had heard quick footsteps and a rustling sound, almost like clothing brushing against grass, disappearing to the north. An unnerving thought came to him.

"Come here."

"Sir?"

Mun was trying to get away, but In-mong grabbed him, pushed him down roughly, and climbed up on his shoulders to peer over the wall. He thought he caught a glimpse of a dark blue shadow, but he couldn't be sure because the large trunks of pines blocked his view. The sound of hasty footsteps was still audible.

He climbed down from Mun's shoulders and sprinted to the raised flower garden leading to the Chuhap Hall. He opened the gate to the back garden of the Huiu Hall. There was no sound. He continued the pursuit down a little path leading to the north, but no one was there. Soon he was panting and his skin was crawling.

Whom had it been?

Whoever it was had disappeared in the blink of an eye. Who had entered the restricted Royal Library at this early hour? Why had he disappeared into the northern woods, where there was no path? In-mong looked about and opened his mouth. He wanted to summon someone, but there was no one to call and he realized it was better if he kept quiet.

Between early dawn and the arrival of morning a huge wave of emotion had swept over him, a mixture of confusion, anxiety, and fear. He felt he was in a nightmare. He looked back, but couldn't see Mun, who had stubbornly decided not to follow him. Heading for the archery range, he heaved a long sigh. Pity wrenched his heart as he thought of the dead Chang.

What a hapless fellow Chang had been! Though In-mong was overcome with emotion, he somehow remained dry-eyed.

Chang Chong-o, also known by his honorific name A-dam, had been thirty-three, four years older than In-mong. He was of the respected Chang clan of Andong, but of concubine lineage. In-mong had heard that Chang had a natural antipathy toward learning from others and so had studied on his own, without a mentor. As if being the descendant of a concubine and lacking academic connections were not enough, his personality was inflexible and he was incapable of ingratiating himself with others. It was crystal clear how his life would turn out. Until he had started working for the government as a special employee, a book examiner at the Royal Library, just a year ago, his life had been like a broken roof-tile.

In-mong had first met Chang at a poetry reading in 1791, the same year In-mong had passed the special civil examinations. Impressed by his honesty and integrity, In-mong had offered his friendship. As they became better acquainted, In-mong soon realized that Chang possessed an incomparable depth of learning. His wide knowledge of books past and present made even the best-versed scholars shake their heads in amazement. He was also conversant with the subject of rites. Most of all, he was an expert in epigraphy, the study of texts handed down on tombstones, ceremonial containers, and bells.

From an early age, Chang had dedicated his life to the study of epigraphy with unparalleled enthusiasm. Perhaps his enthusiasm resulted from his situation, for his status precluded the possibility of recognition in regular Confucian classical studies. He poured his efforts into calligraphy and what you might call the philosophy of calligraphy, the studies of ancient inscriptions on monuments. In the end, he could read and write not only the better-known styles of calligraphy — *zhuanshu, lishu, kaishu, xingshu,* and *caoshu* — but also the ancient and unusual styles of *qizi, zuoshu, mouzhuo,* and *xiazhuo,* with competent ease.

In-mong remembered gaping at a copy Chang had produced for the amusement of those at a gathering. When someone showed Chang a work of calligraphy, whether it was a free-flowing *caoshu* or a majestic *zhuanshu,* his eyes scanned it and he could produce an exact replica, in which not only the top and the bottom but every rise and every curve were precisely the same, as if it were a monument rubbing. He made it seem merely a pastime, but one could imagine the long and painstaking days Chang must have devoted to developing his talent.

In-mong had taken a strong liking to Chang on the day he first saw him make such a copy. When he learned that Chang shared a deep admiration for the great scholar Yi Tok-mu, whose honorific name was A-jong (Elegant Pavilion), In-mong bestowed the name A-dam (Elegant Pond) upon Chang. When Chang was appointed book examiner, In-mong was as elated as if he himself had been honored.

In-mong's own life had been far from easy.

He had become a government official at an exceptionally young age. Having passed the provincial examinations in 1788 and the special civil examinations in 1791, he started out as a third copyist in the Office of Diplomatic Correspondence. In the seventh month of 1793, he was arrested by the State Tribunal, resulting in the loss of his position and banishment to Yongwol in Kangwon Province, all because he had asserted that Kim Kwan-ju, the most powerful man in the *pyokpa* (Principle) group of the Old Doctrine faction, should be punished. The directive for In-mong's banishment was lifted after a year. Next came the agony of being forced to banish his wife against his wishes. In the tenth month of 1795 he was tortured because of an allegation that he was secretly propagating Catholicism, commonly known as Western Learning. In the third month of the twenty-second year of King Chongjo, five years after his position had been taken away, he was reinstated as a first diarist in the Office of Royal Decrees, and in the fifth month of the same year he was transferred to the Royal Library.

Was anyone more blind to the ways of the world than he?

These thoughts deflated In-mong further. He did not have enough fingers to count the occasions on which he had attracted criticism and provoked others, as a result of his constant desire to take the straight path and be true to himself. People said it was not good for an ordinary man to keep a jewel hidden under his shirt, near his heart. How could life be anything but exhausting if a trifling man like himself always tried to maintain loyalty to the king?

Chang's sudden misfortune took on a sinister hue in In-mong's mind as he approached the archery field and heard the distinct sound of willow-leaf arrowheads hitting the target. His Majesty was shooting the fifty arrows that constituted his chosen morning exercise routine.

In-mong bowed slightly to the royal guards at the entrance and strode directly to the platform from which the arrows were flying. Near the top of the steps, eunuchs armed with long swords stopped him. So In-song, director of the eunuchs, crouching in respect behind His Majesty, turned toward In-mong. As In-mong bowed to him slightly, So gestured with his chin to Chong Chun-gyo, the messenger eunuch.

Chong trotted up to In-mong. "Librarian Yi, you wish to offer a morning

15

greeting?" As he peered inquisitively at In-mong, a glint of displeasure appeared in his eyes.

The messenger eunuch, who was of Rank 3B, oversaw all communications between His Majesty and government officials high and low. During the reign of King Chongjo, the Royal Library officials reported directly to His Majesty. They greeted him personally after their night duty, reported on the progress of the work done during the night and the plans for the day, and generally shadowed His Majesty all day. Hence, they inevitably invaded the proper domains of the eunuchs, who acted as His Majesty's hands and feet. Chong must have been displeased, believing that the king's routine at the archery range was the purview of the eunuchs.

In-mong responded to Chong's question. "Something unfortunate occurred during the night and His Majesty's immediate instructions are required."

"What do you mean, 'something unfortunate'?"

In-mong had decided to reveal everything. He whispered the explanation from beginning to end.

Chong started. "That . . . that kind of matter cannot be my responsibility. Please report it directly to His Majesty."

"Yes, of course."

"Chong is easily startled," In-mong thought contemptuously. He went to a corner and waited, his expression stony. His Majesty had just let fly his fortieth arrow.

His Majesty bent and stuffed ten arrows into the holder on his thigh. He began to walk slowly to the left. It was his habit to fire the first forty shots while stationary, and the rest while walking. His waist had gained a considerable roll of flesh in recent years, but even now, at age forty-eight, King Chongjo's skills in martial arts were extraordinary; he was excellent with spear, club, knife, sword, and bow and arrow, and among these he was best at archery. The bow he was using now was not a small one of the sort that ordinary scholars used for practice, but a large one of the type used in real battles. The leaf-shaped arrowhead weighed ten ounces. He shot from a distance of a hundred and twenty paces. The target was smaller than the normal sort.

Today the arrows seemed particularly well aimed. Every time he shot, the flag was raised, indicating a bull's-eye.

In-mong peered at His Majesty. For the shots he fired while walking today, he paced six steps to the left, then turned and retraced two steps as he released the arrow. There was no jerky motion, and the balance between movement and pause was smooth and elegant. Even to In-mong, who was not knowledgeable about archery, His Majesty looked like someone who had reached the pinnacle of skill with bow and arrow. It was said that His Majesty had never skipped his fifty morning shots since his days as crown prince. This practice must have demanded severe discipline from a monarch made effete by a lifestyle excessively devoted to literary studies. True, he tended to expect similar discipline from everyone around him. In-mong thought that His Majesty, holding a bow, looked as virile as a bull or a stallion.

The king's thick beard gave his face an appearance of fullness. The shape of his mouth suggested strength and determination, and his narrow eyes gleamed sharply. Medium in height, but broad in the shoulders and with muscular forearms as thick as the thighs of ordinary officials, the king looked more like a wartime general than a peacetime monarch.

The forty-ninth arrow flew and the flag shot up again.

Amazingly, every one of today's forty-nine arrows had hit the bull's- eye.

King Chongjo gazed at the target with a stern look, then tossed aside the last arrow and thrust his bow into the arms of the director of the eunuchs. Everyone stood bewildered, wondering about the final arrow. Not until King Chongjo peeled off pigskin armguards from his arms did the eunuchs rush up to him, making a fuss, helping him put on his dragon-embroidered royal robe and black silk headgear.

"Your Majesty, won't you shoot the last arrow?" asked So In-song, director of the eunuchs, in an attempt to flatter the king and give him a chance to instruct his servants. But King Chongjo was not to be seduced by such a ruse. He gave no answer and appeared to be lost in thought as he allowed himself to be dressed in the dragon robe. The eunuch had lost face. A silence fell over the gathering.

All eyes were on King Chongjo as he put on his headgear. In-mong could see that His Majesty was not particularly angry or on the verge of venting anger. He always kept his servants in line with unfathomable silence rather than a show of anger.

The point was that he never allowed himself to shoot fifty bull's- eyes.

When he shot with his officials at archery competitions, the dramatic difference in skill between His Majesty and the others became obvious. After thirty shots, most civil servants had only managed to send their arrows to the ground; worse, some were unable to lift the bow. In order not to embarrass such servants, King Chongjo always sent his last arrow off target. When, like today, he was shooting by himself, he didn't use the fiftieth arrow at all.

According to His Majesty, it was not commendable to win every time one fought. From the king's point of view, to shoot fifty bull's-eyes would be excessive. He detested those who flaunted their talents. How then could he, patriarch of the people, conduct himself with such foolishness? His silence embodied this very principle.

At last, when the king had finished changing, he was told that In-mong was waiting to speak with him.

King Chongjo turned toward In-mong with a questioning look. In-mong approached, fell to his knees, bowed his head until it touched the ground, and delivered his morning greeting.

"Yes, but what brought you here so early, To-won? Why didn't you wait to see me in the Main Hall later?"

To-won was In-mong's personal name. His neck stiffened, as he bowed his head and answered hurriedly. "Your Majesty! My deep apologies for reporting this, but something unfortunate occurred at the Royal Library last night, and we wish to receive Your Majesty's instructions."

"What? 'Something unfortunate'?" King Chongjo's startled voice rang out. "What is this unfortunate thing?"

He snapped his head around and looked toward the Secret Garden, where the library was located. Although there was no agitation in his body, which remained as immobile as a stone lion, his face registered astonishment.

Alas, thought In-mong. He had made himself misunderstood. His Majesty must have imagined a fire. But once the words had spilled out, he couldn't gather them up again.

King Chongjo's reaction was natural enough. Fires erupted almost every other year in the palace. Once ignited, the palaces of medieval times often burned like dry straw. In the case of Changdok Palace, four major fires had almost wiped out the entire complex: in the twenty-fifth year of King Sonjo's reign (1592), the first year of King Injo's reign (1623), the thirty-third year of King Sunjo's reign (1833), and the sixth year of Taisho (1917).

"No, no, Your Majesty. It is . . . Book Examiner Chang died suddenly while on night duty."

"What? Chang Chong-o?"

"Yes. There is no wound and no trace of illness. It looks as if . . . he expired from overwork late into the night."

"Overwork?"

"Yes. I understand that Chang had been on duty three nights running, under Your Majesty's direction."

An incomprehensible expression darted across His Majesty's royal countenance. He appeared shocked by this death of a close subordinate, or rather it was as if he were confronted with some complicated matter.

In-mong kept his head bowed deeply. He didn't know where to look in his utter despondence. His spirit shriveled at the thought that he was disturbing His Majesty.

With a wave of the hand King Chongjo commanded the others around him to step back. The king squatted down next to In-mong and his graying hair and round stomach, which seemed to enhance his authority, appeared in In-mong's peripheral vision.

"To-won!"

"Yes? . . . Yes!"

He felt a chill sweat under his arms. In-mong knew that stern words could be expected when His Majesty addressed his servants in such a serious tone. King Chongjo lowered his voice further.

"This is bizarre. There are already complaints in the court about the special attentions I pay to the officials at the Royal Library. They say my actions are irregular, allowing not only officials but also clerks to stay on duty overnight. When a book examiner of Rank 5A dies on duty, the censors and inspectors will rise up like a swarm of bees, won't they?"

In-mong's distress became inexpressible.

"We, your servants, are to blame and deserve death," he finally muttered.

"And the circumstances? . . . Did Chang Chong-o happen to die of some contagious disease?"

"No. No, Your Majesty. Please understand. In this servant's opinion, that is not possible." Again In-mong broke out in a cold sweat.

The Royal Library personnel were obviously going to take the blame for Chang's death in the palace. But a contagious disease? If the charge of bringing a contagious disease close to the quarters of the king were added, Chang's family would be in danger.

"Ummm . . ."

King Chongjo rose, his brows deeply furrowed. He heaved a long sigh. He began to pace and appeared to be deep in thought. It seemed to In-mong that each step lasted many, many years.

"A postmortem must be conducted quickly. The matter should be settled by the end of this day," the king finally said. "Who should be called?"

"Apologies, Your Majesty, but Chong Yag-yong, the third minister of the Board of Punishments, will be waiting for Your Majesty's command in his office." In-mong could only muster a feeble response.

In-mong, fearful and uncomfortable, stole an embarrassed glance upward and met the king's stern gaze. His Majesty's eyes seemed to penetrate his innermost thoughts.

"That's idiotic! How can a mere third minister be given the responsibility for handling a book examiner's death, and one of Rank 5A at that? An official of higher standing should investigate. Otherwise complaints will surface afterward." The king tut-tutted. "Chun-gyo, are you there?"

"Yes, Your Majesty."

Chong Chun-gyo ran up from behind and crouched in respect.

"Write a summons to the second state councilor. Tell him the second state councilor should attend the postmortem and report the results to me. I have nothing else to add at the moment, so tell him to compose the report before he comes to see me. Is that clear?"

"Yes, Your Majesty."

"Also, send someone to the Board of Punishments and tell the third minister to hasten to the court with postmortem specialists."

"Your Majesty's command will be carried out promptly."

With his forehead still touching the ground, In-mong suppressed a cry of stunned dismay. Why in heaven's name did it have to be Shim Hwan-ji, the second state councilor? Why couldn't it be the minister of punishments and the chief magistrate of the State Tribunal? As he pictured Shim Hwan-ji's cold face, his heart sank. Shim was the leader of the Principle group of the Old Doctrine faction.

According to the criminal code, autopsies are to be conducted under the jurisdiction of the highest functionary of the place where the death occurred. Chong Min-shi, director of the Royal Library, was so ill that he was expected to depart for the other world any day. But why Shim Hwan-ji, the self-claimed Clean Current? Out of the entire Old Doctrine faction, Shim was the strictest adherent to formality. Instead of playing down the incident, he would transform it into a scandal.

In-mong couldn't fathom the king's intentions.

King Chongjo glanced quickly at the still motionless In-mong, and turned to Chong Chun-gyo.

"What are you waiting for, you idiot? Why haven't you started writing?" He stamped his foot.

"Yes? Oh, yes, yes."

He trembled, and sat folding his knees under him. Confusion ensued. People rushed up to the king. One gave Chong a document file, a second crouched in front of him to serve as a desk, a third picked up a bottle of ink and a thin brush from a portable writing kit. Chong made quick work of the summons and proffered it to the king. The king signed it hastily, his face clouded and veins in his forehead bulging.

As In-mong watched this flurry of activities, he was reminded of the lecture His Majesty planned to give that morning.

"What should we do about Your Majesty's lecture?"

"Lecture? Is there any reason besides Chang's death why it should be delayed?"

"It is not that, Your Majesty, but the hall is adjacent to where the postmortem will be performed, and it seems unpropitious."

"Umm . . . That's right. Even a commoner knows to treat his own body like a treasure, and to retire and die peacefully. Why can't you court officials take care of yourselves and avoid this trouble?" Then he added, "Postpone the lecture until tomorrow morning."

"Apologies, Your Majesty. Your servant will retire now."

"Wait!"

"Your Majesty?"

"Come closer." His Majesty lowered his voice again.

Back still bent, In-mong approached.

"My predecessor left a sacred piece of writing. I gave it to Chang Chong-o a few days ago so he could make notes. It concerns the *Book of Odes*, which I was going to talk about today. Take a good look around Chang's body and retrieve it. Bring it to me before you leave the palace today. Don't forget."

"Yes, Your Majesty."

"You may go."

"Yes, Your Majesty."

As he retreated from the king, he felt as if the ground were collapsing beneath him.

A piece of writing about the *Book of Odes*? Mocking, nightmarish laughter echoed in his ears.

* * *

The entourage of the king walked toward the Main Hall. Day had broken. In-mong made his way to the Royal Library alone, lost in thought. Something strange was going on. He couldn't put his finger on it, but there was something untoward about Chang's death. Even at first, sitting next to Chang's body, he had tried to identify it, but he had been unable to gather his thoughts. Later, as he reported the incident, his doubts had crystallized into a strong suspicion, which was unsettling him now.

Today His Majesty had planned to deliver a lecture on the *Book of Odes* in front of the Principle group of the Old Doctrine faction, his political opponents—and Chang had died while assisting His Majesty in his preparations for the lecture.

If someone had murdered Chang . . . why today? Was there any link between Chang's death and His Majesty's lecture? Next to his corpse lay

"Notes on *Humble Thoughts on the Book of Odes.*"

In-mong jerked to a halt. "Notes on *Humble Thoughts on the Book of Odes*"? His hitherto restless gaze fixed itself on a point in space. "Notes on *Humble Thoughts on the Book of Odes.*" Then a book with that title should have been somewhere nearby. The writings of the previous king that His Majesty had mentioned had to be *Humble Thoughts on the Book of Odes*. But In-mong had seen no such book in the room. Had he failed to notice it in his state of shock and confusion? No. All the books strewn about near Chang had been familiar. There had been no such book.

It dawned on him he shouldn't remain standing there, bewildered. Anxiety crept over him as he recalled the king's order to search carefully around the body. I should hurry and look for the book, he thought. He began walking again, with quickened steps, and soon he broke into a trot.

The path branched off in three directions: toward the Kyongchu Gate, Lotus Pond, and the Royal Library. Chong Chun-gyo emerged from behind some trees near where the paths joined, startling In-mong. Hadn't Chong followed the king?

Chong motioned to In-mong as he approached. "Librarian Yi, let me talk to you for a minute." Behind Chong were four brawny guard eunuchs holding swords. He gazed at Chong quizzically, an ominous presentiment stealing over him.

Chong, a squat man with sinister eyes, had rough, dark skin that made him look unhealthy. The harsh discipline and constant tension of court life had aged him prematurely; he looked well over sixty, but in fact was no more than fifty. His shoulders were stooped, his face a dead wooden mask. Wisps of white hair protruded from his silk headgear.

Chong drew near, an awkward smile playing on his lips. In-mong stopped himself form stepping back, feeling a strong aversion toward Chong. Chong apparently took no offense at In-mong's stiff expression. He gestured to the guard eunuchs behind him to withdraw a few paces.

As they moved away, Chong cleared his throat and spoke softly. "Librarian Yi. We see each other every morning and night, but we haven't had a chance to talk privately."

"That's true, now that you mention it . . ."

"Last night's incident was certainly inauspicious, but then again it was hardly your fault. I will make every effort to ensure that the blame doesn't fall on your shoulders. Don't worry."

"I don't know how to thank you enough."

"The reason you and I are on such uncomfortable terms is that His Majesty vowed to shun the eunuchs along with the queens' relatives when he took the throne. If we think about it, though, we all serve His Majesty at close quarters. Shouldn't we try to get along as well as fish in the pond?"

"Yes . . ."

"In my view, old as I am, His Majesty is not only intelligent, generous, and devoted to his parents, but he is also striving to rule this country well. Truly he is like the Chinese sage-rulers Yao, Shun, Yu, and Tang. We, his servants, should be of one mind and marshal all our loyalty so as not to sully His Majesty's grace . . ."

In-mong bowed his head to conceal the stiffening of his expression. He detected a hint of criticism of the king and the Royal Library, but a rash response would be inadvisable.

King Chongjo, from the beginning of his reign, had promoted two policies: first, to act in accordance with the previous king's intentions as well as the rules and precedents of antiquity, and second, to honor Confucian ideals and to respect Neo-Confucian scholarship. As time passed, the political significance of these two policies had become evident, and court officials had become ill at ease. Following the intent of the previous king meant that His Majesty would continue King Yongjo's policies for restraining factional struggles. Honoring Confucian ideals and respecting Taoism meant that His Majesty would take responsibility for national affairs, with the help of the literati. This could be interpreted to mean that he would shun the eunuchs and the queens' family members, who had opposed the exercise of strong sovereignty.

King Chongjo had founded the Royal Library precisely to promote these policies. In a few short years the library had become much more powerful. Not only had it assumed the functions of the Royal Secretariat and the Office of Royal Decrees, but it had also taken on the functions of the Office of Censor-General, detecting irregularities and corruption on the part of officials high and low. The Eunuch Department, to which Chong Chun-gyo belonged, had suffered most from the ascendance of the Royal Library. The eunuchs, who acted as a bridge between the cabinet and the queen's powerful relatives, had always been at the center of wheeling and dealing, but now they had no voice at all. Their discontent had manifested itself in a unanimous resignation, led by Secretarial Eunuch Kim Ung-so, in the fifth year of King Chongjo's reign.

Chong Chun-gyo was equivocating, at one moment insinuating criticism of the king's policy and in the next breath asserting that everyone should work together. One could hardly blame In-mong for being reserved and wondering what Chong would say next.

"As you may know, people in the capital are far from content. I'm sorry to say this to your face, but isn't it true that the Royal Library has been criticized by many high officials? As if that were not enough, His Majesty established that immense Royal Defense Garrison, and also had the new fortress erected in Hwasong as a detached palace. Everyone in the capital is worried because it looks as though there will be an upheaval sooner or later."

In-mong remained silent, and Chong continued. "Fear and anxiety have me at wit's end. There are rumors going around that His Majesty will hand over the throne to the Crown Prince sooner or later. That's no small matter. The very idea chills me to the bone . . ."

"Ah, Your Honor, it is indeed remarkable that you who stay inside the palace should know so much about the rumors circulating in the capital. How could I, a trifling low-level official, have such knowledge? All you have said is new to me."

With this implicit rebuke of the old man's impertinent and cunning remarks, In-mong nodded his head toward the Royal Library, a hint that In-mong wished to take his leave. There was the matter of Chang Chong-o's corpse. He bowed quickly in an attempt to leave.

The sly Chong could scarcely have missed this gesture, but he placed himself between In-mong and the library.

"Such humility!" he scoffed. "What young official is more appreciated by His Majesty than Librarian Yi? I am sure you understand His Majesty's thoughts better than anyone."

"What do you mean?"

"The matter of relinquishing the throne. When will he announce what he plans to do?"

"What are you talking about?" In-mong snapped, his eyes full of accusation.

Chong's intemperate reaction made In-mong realize he was no match for this seasoned survivor. The eunuch's words were inappropriate. It was a delicate matter; anyone, even an experienced minister, who ventured such remarks in a wrong setting did so at his peril. How could a mere eunuch waylay a passer-by on a palace path and speak in such a manner? In-mong's astonishment was readily comprehensible.

Had Chong really asked when His Majesty would relinquish the throne? What possessed him to speak so brazenly? Was he mad? If not, what was he getting at? He had not only intimated criticism of the Royal Library, but also implicated the Royal Defense Garrison.

King Chongjo had founded the Royal Defense Garrison as a successor to the Royal Guard. Before his ascent to the throne, the core of the Military

Training Command, a rough equivalent to today's Capital Security Command, had formed the core of the army. Most soldiers stationed in the capital fell under its jurisdiction, and the Military Training Command hosted the national military examinations and conducted the large-scale training that took place near Seoul in spring and autumn.

After the king learned that the influence of the queen's relatives and the Principle group had penetrated the Military Training Command and the Royal Guard, he decided to reduce them and instead restructure and expand the Royal Defense Garrison. In the meantime, four generals closely linked with the Principle group had been put to death. It had been alleged that, instigated by officials close to the king, the generals had attempted a revolt.

By the seventeenth year of his reign, in 1793, King Chongjo had expanded and restructured his personal bodyguard detachment, the Inner Palace Guards, and established a new army unit called the Royal Defense Garrison. King Chongjo restructured the Royal Guard from a mere three *cho* (a *cho* is equivalent to a company today) to twenty-five *cho* in the Inner Palace Guard under the direct command of the Palace, with additional units under the usual chain of command, including twenty *cho* in the Elite Defense Detachment and twenty-two *cho* in the Rear Guard. In other words, the Royal Guard had been upgraded to an army corps. In 1796, his twentieth year on the throne, having assumed supreme command, the king built a new city, which he called Hwasong. The outer headquarters of the Royal Defense Garrison were placed in the new city with the rationale of defending the capital and its environs.

After the new city was completed, a rumor spread widely among court officials and commoners that the king's escorts would revolt against the Principle group. The rumor was that King Chongjo would relinquish the throne to the crown prince at the time of his wedding. The king would then retire to the Hwasong Detached Palace but would retain control of the military, and would have his newly enthroned son issue a proclamation condemning the prosecution of the Principle group. The Grand Harmony branch of the Southerners faction masterminded this plan, which came to be known as royal punishment. Chae Che-gon, a renowned state councilor and the leader of this group, along with Yi Ka-hwan and Chong Yag-yong, supervised the construction of the fortress. Ordinarily such a responsibility would have fallen to the magistrate of Hwasong. Chong Yag-yong, then the fourth royal secretary, plunged himself into the project, neglecting the usual tasks of his position, and even inventing the first crane in Korea for the construction.

Spreading through the city were rumors about what would happen after the fortress was completed—rumors that would have been impossible to ignore. During the year and a half in which In-mong had been serving His Majesty, he had become more acutely aware than anyone that the crucial moment was drawing near. The Royal Defense Garrison, which the king had supported for the past eight years, had developed well; the crown prince had been announced; and in a few months Kim Cho-sun's daughter would be officially designated as the wife of the crown prince. Kim Cho-sun himself led the Expediency group.

The announcement that the king would abdicate might come any day now. In-mong's heart leapt with joy at the thought of restoration. Restoration! The Choson dynasty would renew the Mandate of Heaven at last! In-mong recalled how brave the Rear Guard of the Royal Defense Garrison had appeared, two springs earlier, when they marched in columns from the county Confucian academy in Shihung to the Noryangjin quay. An enormous change would soon be at hand. The entire privileged class, blinded by self-interest and greed, would be brought to justice. A new world without class discrimination would arise—a world where everyone was equal and happy under the monarch's wise rule, the ideal world of which Confucius himself had dreamed. No one could oppose such a noble cause. This was the way of the Exemplary Monarch, which would elevate the declining nation and its fraying systems.

In-mong studied Chong's face with inner complacency. At the same time he felt apprehensive, like a man hoarding a dazzling jewel beneath his shirt.

"Wait and see, you troublesome, cunning servants!" he thought. "You enemies who disparage the king and attempt to constrict him. The teachings of the sages leave people like you, who court Heaven's wrath, untouched. What remains for you but decapitation? The dream of the ideal past will soon be realized. It will bring a simple world, where the sage-king rules supreme over good subjects."

In-mong suppressed his rising elation and responded gravely to Chong's rash statements. "I cannot help but feel grateful for such generous favor. But perhaps it is inappropriate for us, his servants, to discuss His Majesty's plans. Furthermore, if the decision concerns so crucial a matter as the preservation of the throne, we should be more circumspect and cautious."

Chong laughed heartily. "You are right a hundred times over. Indeed you are brimming with intelligence. It is no wonder that you are a library official . . ."

A tremor of unease swept over In-mong. Chong was stealing glances at the Royal Library. His loud laughter was a cover. Why? Of course . . . he was delaying In-mong. Something was happening in the library, and Chong was on edge.

"Sir, it appears that you are holding it in with great difficulty. I shall take my leave."

"What . . . what do you mean?"

"You keep looking over there. I believe that nature calls and you seek the place of apricot blossoms and rain. Since I too must attend to my duties, I will take my leave now."

Chong was caught off guard. As In-mong bowed and turned to leave, Chong gestured to him to stop. "No, no. One moment, Librarian Yi. There is something important. Come here for a minute." Chong raked tensely at In-mong's sleeve.

In-mong politely removed the hand. "His Majesty's command is all-important. How can a lowly servant such as myself delay even a minute? I shall listen to your teachings later."

In-mong flew off, ignoring Chong's urgent calls. At the Huiu Gate of the Library, he braved a glance back. Chong had disappeared.

In-mong clucked his tongue ruefully, regretting his own rude behavior. Why was he so graceless, lacking any semblance of tact? He behaved so boorishly. It was no wonder that people took a dislike to him. He sighed, reflecting upon his stupidity—so extensive was it that the only excuse he had managed to come up with was visceral and childish.

Too late! In any case, he still had to find "Notes on *Humble Thoughts on the Book of Odes.*" He opened the gate at the highest point of the library grounds and entered the garden. As he gazed down at the buildings large and small, still shrouded in the morning mist, he felt a surge of emotion once more.

There stood the buildings of the Royal Library, one after another: Chuhap Hall, the inner quarters used for lectures and as a reading hall; the archives of Korean books; the archives for Chinese books; Kaeyuwa, King Chongjo's private library; the administration chamber; and the Royal Shrine where sacred writings of previous kings, including King Yongjo, were housed.

Every building contained mountains of rare books unavailable elsewhere. Within those faded tomes dwelled the chain of civilization, thousands of linked years. Some had been handed down from generation to generation; others Kim Chongjo had acquired without concern for expense, and they now numbered 100,187 volumes, with 10,730 miscellaneous documents. Twelve years before, in 1781, the director of the Royal Library had classified some 30,000 newly acquired books, adding summaries. Many sat in heaps, still unopened.

In-mong thought of the 100-volume *Hongjae Collection,* compiled the month before, and recalled Eunuch Chong's words. These volumes, now located in the administration building, constituted the complete work of King Chongjo. The librarians had compiled the writings of the monarch, peerless among all his predecessors, prompted by His Majesty's own enthusiastic encouragement. To In-mong, the publication appeared to be the final project the king had imposed on himself before the end of his rule. Would he relinquish the throne before the year was out, after all?

In-mong stood still and sighed. Then he heard the faint rustle of footwear on grass, the same sound he had heard on his way to report to His Majesty. What was it? His nerves prickled. In the western woods a gate creaked open and closed softly. In-mong felt a wave of shock. He recognized the sound of the Kongjin Gate. It was always locked, and he himself was the custodian of its key but someone had just left through that very gate.

In-mong opened the Huiu Gate and ran into the woods. "Who is it?" he yelled. Here was a clue that might unravel the tangle of the mysterious incidents that morning. He was elated. Several steps outside the Kongjin Gate, he saw a black shadow fleeing.

"Hey!"

In-mong flew after the man and grabbed him by the scruff of the neck, not realizing that a branch had torn his own robe.

"*Egugu!* . . . Why are you doing this, sir?"

The man yanked himself free and faced In-mong. He was an ugly eunuch with a dark complexion and prominent cheekbones. His eyebrows resembled two thick worms connected to each other.

"Aren't you Yi Kyong-chul of the Eunuch Department?"

"Ow, that hurts. Yes, sir, Elder. Why are you doing this to me at this ungodly hour?"

"You don't know? This is the Secret Garden, forbidden to outsiders. You should be in the Main Hall. What were you doing inside the Kongjin Gate?"

"Kong—Kongjin Gate? No, no, sir. Your humble servant was doing a Taoist morning exercise in the woods, sir."

"A Taoist exercise, you say?"

"Yes, sir. And last month I was transferred from the Main Hall to the management of the library garden."

In-mong glared. Grabbing the eunuch, In-mong whirled him around and passed his left hand across the man's backside.

"What in heaven's name are you doing, sir?"

"Ha! Are there Taoist exercises you can do standing up? If you were sitting in the woods, your rump should be wet with snow."

"Ah ... that ... that ... "

"You! Out with it! I saw you coming out of the Kongjin Gate. Do you still deny it?"

"That's nonsense! What proof do you have? You have no right to persecute a person this way."

"Be silent and follow me."

"No."

Yi Kyong-chul dug in his heels, his face red with exertion. A look of deadly determination came to his face. Unable to budge the eunuch, In-mong held on to his wrists and shouted over the gate.

"Chong-nae! Chong-nae! Are you there? Is anybody there?"

In-mong thought he heard a cold snort and at the same moment he gasped, feeling himself flying through the air. Yi had jerked his right hand from In-mong's grip, punched him in the chest, and kicked him in the groin. In the blink of an eye, In-mong found himself writhing in pain on the grass.

Grass blades bristled against his face, and a fierce kick landed in his armpit. He gasped again. The pain was severe. A shock wave spread throughout his body and his eyes blurred. He felt a pounding in his head and then he lost consciousness.

2
Another Death

*All were astonished and embarrassed, and left with
closed hearts,
And why would they want to be friends with me?
The bird-catching arrow is set up over me,
The bird net is spread under.
Catching me thus, they wish to please the king.
Try as I might to extricate myself, it is impossible
to avoid.*

—"Chanting in Regret," *Elegies of Chu*
(Chu Ci).

Hyon Sung-hon was walking along the street lined with the six board edifices, near Kyongbok Palace. Yi In-mong had asked him to deliver a message.

Sung-hon had not been able to find Chong Yag-yong, third minister of the Board of Punishments, at his Hyoehyon-dong house. His servant said that Chong had gone out in his official garb at the break of dawn. Sung-hon decided to visit the Board of Punishments, which stood across from Kyongbok Palace.

It was an unusually cold day. Every house was shut, and there wasn't a soul in the streets. Nothing moved beneath the icy sky except thin wisps of smoke emerging from the chimneys of frosty thatched-roof houses. Everything — streets, houses, roofs, bush clover walls — seemed to have frozen in deathly stillness.

As he walked along the thoroughfare, which offered a view of Kwanghwa Gate, Sung-hon began to feel intimidated. The gates leading to the government offices glistened cold and pale. Across from and to the right of the Kwanghwa Gate stood the offices of the State Council, the Board of Personnel, the Seoul Magistracy, and the Board of Taxation. To the left were the buildings of the Office of the Inspector-General, the Board of War, the Board of Punishments, and the Board of Public Works, all magnificent buildings with roofed gates soaring up to the sky.

At the gate of the Board of Punishments, Sung-hon approached a middle-aged guard sporting a loose hat and asked for an interview with Chong Yag-yong.

"Hyon Sung-hon, clerk from the Royal Library. I wish to see the third minister, under the order of the drafter-librarian."

"Ah, you're working hard even before breakfast. Hey, Chun-sam! Show this gentleman to the third minister and be quick about it."

"Thank you," Sung-hon said.

Chun-sam was a big-boned young soldier who still had youthful fuzz on his face. "Follow me, please." Leaving the compound, he strode down the thoroughfare. Sung-hon was surprised; he had assumed Chong Yag-yong would be in the main office building.

Chun-sam walked south for a considerable distance, what is now Sejong

Avenue, turned left at the crossroads from which Unhyon Palace was visible in the distance, and arrived at the jail in Sorinbang. Only then did the young man look back at Sung-hon and point at the dark, dingy building. This jail held important prisoners incarcerated under the jurisdiction of the Board of Punishments.

"The third minister left a while ago to come here. Follow me, please."

"All right."

Sung-hon's forehead wrinkled at a whiff of the stench: A stale smell made up of mildew, sweat, rotting fish, and feces stung his nose. The odor seemed to have transformed itself from a smell into a thick liquid that flowed into his nostrils. He suppressed nausea, feeling that he might vomit any moment.

Sung-hon hesitated at the gate. Wasn't the third minister an official of Rank 3A? What on earth was such a high official doing in this pigsty? A sudden shriek came from the building.

"You deserve death! What reason is there for this delay? Didn't you hear the third minister? Run and fetch a brazier now!"

The jail gate burst open with a clatter and several guards flew out hatless, their topknots in full view, as if fleeing a fire. They crashed into Sung-hon.

"Hey, what do you . . . ," Sung-hon started to complain, his eyes bulging with accusation. He rubbed the numb ridge of his battered nose. Without so much as a glance at him, the guards scurried away. Chun-sam ran after them, perplexed. Sung-hon, left alone, turned his attention to what was going on inside.

A voice, different from the first, rang out. "You! Listen to me, Chief Jailor!"

"Yes, sir."

"Since ancient times, those who engage in economic activities to serve the king are called the 'masses,' and those who take care of them are called 'government officials.' Anyone in the government, whether high or low, is a cultivator and thus must care for the masses. Even prisoners belong to the masses. The prisoners in this jail are members of the masses brought under your care, isn't that so? You, as the official responsible for their well-being, left them to freeze to death. What punishment, then, do you deserve?"

"My guilt is worthy of death, but the guards have gone to get coal and braziers. If you can wait a bit, we might be able to revive these people by thawing their frozen bodies, sir."

"What are you saying? Braziers? We can't do anything for those who have died, but these two people still have breath in their bodies. They should be moved to my room immediately."

"We cannot do that, sir! These are suspects who were brought here on the charge of spreading the Catholic Doctrines. The minister himself ordered us to torture them to find out where their ringleader, Father Zhou Wenmo, is hiding. We cannot lay these people out in the main administration office. That is a thousand times impossible, sir."

"Enough!"

"Sir!"

The sound of scuffling could be heard, and the gate opened again. Sung-hon was astonished to see a middle-aged man emerge. The man was dressed in an official robe embroidered with a hawk and wore a third minister's red hat. He was huffing and puffing, carrying a blood-soaked form on his back.

Sung-hon was amazed not only by the unusual sight, but also by the realization that the official, who had a flowing beard and a benevolent expression, was none other than Sa-am Chong Yag-yong. It would be many more years before he achieved his enduring reputation, more closely associated with his pen name Ta-san, or Tea Mountain. Yet even at that time he was already well known, for without any strong political backing he had ascended to Rank 3A in his early thirties, and Sung-hon, the clerk at the Royal Library, of course knew about him. Chong Yag-yong glimpsed Sung-hon standing agape. Judging from Sung-hon's outfit that he was a government clerk, Chong jerked his chin toward the jail.

"Listen. A woman has almost frozen to death in there. Carry her out."

"Sir?"

"Hush! Go now. She's dying."

"Yes, yes, sir." Sung-hon entered the jail amid the confusion of the moment. There he encountered a military official wearing a fierce scowl. Sung-hon assumed the official was the chief jailor. His hat, which had a large-beaded string that drooped down around his chin, made him appear to be at least a director of the Jurisdiction Chamber. He had long sideburns. Sung-hon hesitated, eyeing him. The official glared at him briefly, then hawked and spat before stomping into the inner quarters.

Sung-hon waited for his eyes to adjust to the darkness. His legs trembled. The scene was dreadful beyond description. On either side of a hallway running through the middle of the building were two cells with iron bars as thick as a child's arm. Further along, at the end of the building, was a rectangular room. The structure of the building resembled a T. What Sung-hon saw on the wall at the end made his legs grow numb. There hung iron picks for severing the Achilles' tendon, boards for twisting legs, sticks for thrashing suspects, and a huge flatiron for scorching prisoners' skin.

That was not all. As he peered into a cell with its doors flung open, he saw three blood-drenched corpses laid out side by side. A patch of straw mat covered them.

Fear gripped his heart. He averted his eyes, only to discover a woman lying on a plank in the cell opposite. The young woman, who seemed to be in her mid-twenties, was lying on her side, her body curled up like a shrimp, covered by a small mat of rice stalks, inadequate to protect her from the cold. A suffocating stench arose from the mat, which had rotted because of the snow and rain beating in through the cracks around the window, and which was soaked with blood, urine, feces, and pus. The face peeking out from under the stalks was blue; the tops of the woman's hands had tiny frostbite cracks like fish scales.

What crime had she committed to deserve such treatment?

The prisoners covered with thatch must have died during the night. This woman and the man Chong had carried out on his back seemed barely alive.

Choson dynasty law was generous, in that prisoners were usually sent home when the cold weather became unbearable and imprisoned again when a thaw came along. The prisoners still left in the jail must have committed hideous crimes. There had been talk about the spreading of the Catholic Doctrines. Catholic Doctrines?

"Why are you dawdling? Bring her out immediately!" Chong's angry voice rang in Sung-hon's ears.

"*Aigu.* Yes, yes. I'm coming."

Sung-hon realized there was no way out. He had to flee from this jail, from this gloomy den where ghosts might jump out any moment. He shut his eyes and lifted the woman to his back. She reeked so badly of filth that he wished he didn't have to touch her.

As Sung-hon came out the door, Chong, who had been waiting with the other prisoner on his back, turned sharply without a word and started walking. The nearby guards pleaded to be allowed to carry the prisoner, but Chong showed no sign of hearing them. The woman Sung-hon carried was unconscious and her limbs were limp, but the male prisoner remained conscious despite exhaustion. He must have been beaten severely; wounds oozing blood and pus could be seen through the tattered clothes on his trunk and arms, but the lower part of his body looked comparatively sound. Sung-hon believed the prisoner could have walked. He thought it strange that Chong was personally carrying him, and was sorry to see him doing it.

By now it had grown completely light. Passers-by on the thoroughfare leading to the Kwanghwa Gate looked wide-eyed at the official who was walking along with a blood-covered prisoner on his back, followed by several guards. Upon reaching the gate of the Board of Punishments, Chong shouted at the guards who were awkwardly trailing behind him to go back to the jail. He signaled to Sung-hon to follow him in. The soldiers at the gate surrounded them in astonishment.

The Board of Punishments compound consisted of an administration hall in the center flanked by buildings on either side. Included were the appeals office which dealt with criminal cases sent by the eight provinces; the Bureau of Legal Research, which handled the proclamation and examination of law; the Bureau of Prohibitions; and the Bureau of Slave Administration. A little farther off was the building where the soldiers stood guard.

Chong strode across the courtyard to the main hall, glanced back at Sung-hon and the soldiers, and spoke in a voice devoid of emotion. "Lay that woman down in the room on the left, the one with the overhead wood decorations. Chun-sam, O-sang! Fetch some boiling water, and stoke the fires to heat the floors of both rooms."

"Yes, sir."

Chong entered the large room to the left, and the soldiers darted away.

Sung-hon was left alone, exasperated. Yi In-mong would be waiting impatiently at the Royal Library, but Sung-hon had yet to open his mouth to deliver the message. The limp body on his back felt as heavy as a large sack of rice. He felt sorrier and sorrier for himself.

Sung-hon remembered a saying that describes someone with miserable luck: "Your journey falls on a market day and your friend is not at home." Of all days to experience such complications! If things continued this way, nothing would be accomplished. He should lay this woman down and then see the third minister. He looked around. Two four-tier bookcases stood side by side on one wall. Opposite was a decorative stand that held a white porcelain jar with blue-glaze design. The framed work of calligraphy hanging above the jar contributed to the impression that the room was for receiving guests. Sung-hon noticed that there was no wardrobe for holding blankets. He laid the woman on the floor and waited. Soon the soldiers came in with an old cotton blanket, along with a basin of hot water. Sung-hon seized the opportunity and escaped from the room.

Now he had to see the third minister.

The large central administrative building, facing south, housed the offices of the minister, the second minister, and the third minister. There was a wooden veranda in the center, and to the east was a small room framed by an overhead wood decoration and stone pillars. Nearby was another small room, presumably for the administrative clerks. To the west was a large room that seemed to occupy almost a third of the building. Sung-hon stood in the central veranda, trying to gather his thoughts.

Why had Librarian Yi told him to go and see Chong Yag-yong, of all people? He must have thought the matter could be settled at the level of Chong. Book Examiner Chang's death could be considered grave, but on the other hand it could be deemed ordinary.

Deaths within the palace were usually not investigated too closely. Not only were the capital punishments of eunuchs and ladies-in-waiting glossed over, but so too were the questionable deaths of queens and kings' concubines. They don't know what to do with this case, Sung-hon realized, because a court official who lives outside the court hardly ever dies on duty. But there had certainly been enough instances of people dying when the cause of death was unknown. Perhaps they really did need Chong's help. Perhaps only Chong could persuade the king, using the results of the postmortem the Board of Punishments would supervise, to minimize the aftershock on Yi's behalf.

After all, Librarian Yi also belonged to the Southerners faction, didn't he?

Sung-hon reflected over this unavoidable fact and clucked his tongue. A cough coming from the large room jolted him from his reverie.

"Look here, Sa-am!"

Whose voice was that? The prisoner's? Did he say, "Look here, Sa-am"? Did he know the third minister that well? Sung-hon's ears pricked up, and he eavesdropped on the low conversation drifting out of the room.

"Look here, Sa-am. If you take care of me like this, you are putting your neck in their noose. Don't be stubborn — send me back to jail. I urge you."

"That won't do. I can't just allow such outrageous treatment. Don't worry, I-suk. I'll confront the minister of punishments. What crime did you commit? Did you burn up ancestral tablets like the others, or did you fail to perform ancestral rites? Or did you show contempt for the king? The so-called crime they have fabricated . . ."

"How can you say I am not guilty? My crime is being a follower of Western Learning. Not only did I myself believe in the evil teaching of the foreign devils. . . . Many innocent people . . . have been tainted by my immoral ways. . . . I am a criminal."

With a self-mocking laugh, the voice — a dying voice that the prisoner seemed to squeeze from deep within — continued feebly. His curiosity piqued, Sung-hon stepped closer.

Korean houses were certainly not designed with secrecy in mind. Carrying on a serious, urgent discussion in private was impossible: The walls were thin, the windows were as big as doors, and the doors themselves were covered by flimsy paper sheets through which a finger could easily poke holes. Sitting in such a room, one could hear women doing laundry and the racket of neighborhood children. Furthermore, people could burst inside at any moment.

In his agitation, Chong must have forgotten how open and insecure the structure was. His voice rang out through the paper door.

"What do you mean? Immoral ways? Who dared say such a thing? How can people behave this way? It's only now that I understand the saying that true fidelity is demonstrated in bad times. When Teacher Pon-am was alive, people held your hand and smiled, ready to give their own organs for you, but today no one shows his face around you. No one told me you had been taken to jail the day before last or that you almost froze to death. When there was no trouble, people were glad to see you. They invited you to drinking parties and poetry readings, they offered wine, made forced jokes, and claimed that they would be at your side dead or alive. Where have they all gone? They say scholars will even offer their own heads for the sake of their friends. For you to be thrown in prison as an immoral thug just because you have a copy of *A True Disputation About the Lord of Heaven* is absurd. That can't be. I'll be dead and my eyes filled with dirt before I stand for such a thing."

The sound of Chong's intermittent sobs, bursting from between his clamped teeth, wafted from the room.

Sung-hon grew feverish. He felt sweat in his armpits. Good reputations are not built on false foundations, he thought. Chong was truly special! Sung-hon had heard the rumor that only Chong Yag-yong could become the leader of the Southerners faction, but he had scoffed at it. He had pictured Chong to be no different from Yi In-mong, a bookish scholar, just a little older perhaps. Now he realized that was not true. Chong was risking his own life, something small-minded people would not do. The prisoner must be I-suk Chae Hong-won, a former royal secretary and the son of Chae Che-gong. He had heard that Chae Hong-won and Chong Yag-yong were the same age, good friends who had studied together.

Chae Che-gong had been third state councilor, second state councilor, and chief state councilor over an unbroken period of ten years, from the twelfth year to the twenty-second year of King Chongjo. The sole official from the Southerners faction, he had led the government, filled with the Principle group of the Old Doctrine faction, supporting the king with great competence. He had died only a year before. The tide of the world had changed its course, and now his only son had been thrown in prison, falsely accused of being a Catholic. A wave of fear passed over Sung-hon at the thought of living in such a world.

A cough was heard again, followed by the prisoner's voice. "What happened to the woman imprisoned with us?"

"What? Ah, we laid her down in the room across the veranda. Should I bring her over here?"

What? Bring the woman over? Sung-hon backed away hurriedly, on tiptoe. He perched on the shoe ledge, in his stocking feet, a step down from the veranda. The conversation continued in an undertone. He couldn't hear as clearly as before.

"No. Look, Sa-am! I'm entrusting her to you. I don't matter, but she has to be set free."

"Who is she? Is she your daughter-in-law?"

"No. Actually, she is a guest who came all the way from Chonjinam."

Chonjinam! Chong couldn't help but stiffen. Chonjinam was a temple located on Aengja Mountain in Kwangju County. The students of Kwon Chol-shin and Yi Ik had assembled there in Kyonggi Province to learn and study Western Learning, particularly Catholicism. Recently, Catholics all over the country had secretly begun gathering there as well, and it had become their de facto headquarters. Chong had stopped going, although he had visited several times to meet Kwon and his students.

"That woman is the wife of the current librarian, Yi In-mong, the fellow from Andong. She was expelled because she is a Catholic."

"Then . . . that woman is Yun Yu-il's . . ."

"Yes, she's his younger sister."

"Then you are really a Catholic too . . ."

"No. That's not true. Look, Sa-am, there's something you should know. Soldiers from the Board of Punishments burst in on us the other night under the pretext of arresting that woman, but it was really just an excuse to search my house. Only after they turned my study upside down did I begin to suspect that they were not looking for Catholic books like *A True Disputation About the Lord of Heaven* or *Seven Victories*. Do you understand, Sa-am? The book they were looking for was written by the previous king, the one called 'the metal-bound' . . ."

"Hey! Is anyone there? Look, I-suk, pull yourself together. I-suk . . ." Chong's voice rang out in fear.

As Sung-hon craned his neck to hear better, the door flung open and Chong rushed out. Sung-hon felt guilty about eavesdropping. Unable to look Chong in the face, he bowed deeply in deference. He heard the soldiers scrambling out of their room.

"Listen. The prisoner fainted and is having trouble breathing. Go get a doctor. Hurry!"

"Yes, sir."

"And you over there. Who are you? You don't look like a clerk of our board. Why are you loitering here?"

Chong seemed to have noticed Sung-hon for the first time. His eyes gleamed with suspicion.

"Sir, this is Hyon Sung-hon, a clerk at the Royal Library. He has some urgent words to convey to you from Librarian Yi In-mong."

"Yi In-mong? Yi In-mong sent you?" Chong appeared shaken as he heard the name. "Mmm. I thought you were a new clerk at the board. I apologize for having asked you to perform such an unpleasant chore. But . . . someone needs our help at the moment. I'll listen to your message later." He spun around to return to the prisoner.

"Uh . . . Third Minister, sir!" Sung-hon blurted out.

The emotions he had felt while eavesdropping still overwhelmed him. A blind impulse to do anything to help Chong sprang from deep within.

"Third Minister, sir! The prisoner seems gravely ill. It will take some time for the doctor to arrive. I happen to have some *chongshimhwan* tablets, and am wondering whether they might be of use."

"Ahh, have you? Good! Don't hesitate—come up here."

"Thank you, sir."

Sung-hon grew worried upon entering the room. Bookshelves lined the long walls. A filing cabinet with a red padlock and a Qing-style table indicated the official nature of this room. It was more than a little incongruous that a prisoner, his long, flowing hair in disarray, lay on bedding in this room.

Third Minister Chong's actions were admirable, but he would not be able to endure the consequences. Sung-hon stole a quick glance at Chong. Even if he was the third minister, the second minister and the minister remained above him. They often stayed in court to serve the king instead of coming to their own offices. Although the official in charge of everyday affairs at the board was indeed the third minister, Sung-hon began to fret about whether Chong could handle this case as he pleased within such a chain of command.

It was impossible to tell whether Chong was aware of Sung-hon's anxiety. The minister's impatient eyes urged him to work quickly. Sung-hon lifted the quilt from the sick prisoner and was assaulted by a stench. The man's headband was torn; his topknot was unraveled; and his long, tangled hair covered half his face. Sung-hon brushed the hair aside and studied the prisoner's face: withered, dark brown skin; hollow cheeks still smeared with congealed rivulets of blood; wrinkles around the mouth; cold sweat was dripping down the gaunt neck. He lay as if already dead, a ghost in this dim room fetid with perspiration, human waste, and blood.

Sung-hon placed a finger under the prisoner's nostrils. The situation appeared grave: the prisoner's breathing came in spasmodic gasps.

Sung-hon's worry increased when he checked the prisoner's pulse. He started to regret having stepped forward and suggesting the medicine. What he had heard had given him no idea that the prisoner would be this far gone. He had thought the prisoner had lost consciousness because his weakened body couldn't tolerate the sudden transition from the frozen jail to the warm room.

"It looks as if the tablet won't help him, sir."

"Why?"

"The elder hasn't simply lost consciousness. His complexion was rather dark even before this, wasn't it?"

"Yes, I think so."

"He is in a hepatic coma. His liver was not in good condition to begin with, and then while he was suffering in jail, ammonia from his waste spread to his liver and brain. Judging from his breathing, his life is in danger."

"What do we do then?"

"An enema should be given to purge him of all fecal matter and let him rest completely. And he should be treated with ginseng . . . but there's not a second to lose. He's having a hard time breathing as it is. . . . He needs acupuncture to open his respiratory system . . ."

"Wait. You are a clerk serving under Librarian Yi. How is it you are so knowledgeable about medicine? I have read many medical books, but I am at a loss."

"It's nothing. It's just what I have overheard in my family." Sung-hon shook his head vigorously. He realized he had displayed too much knowledge. Chong, however, refused to accept his vague response.

"What you have overheard in your family? You said your name is Hyon Sung-hon. Hyon Sung-hon? Hyon Sung-hon . . . Are you related to Hyon Chu-hon, the physician of Rank 6B at the Royal Infirmary?"

Sung-hon's expression turned sour. Chong's trouble was he knew too much.

"He is my younger brother."

"Ah, is that so? You're Physician Hyon's brother. I am sorry. Then you are of the renowned Hyon family of Chungin."

The Chungin class was below the *yangban* and above the commoners. It encompassed such technocrats as medical doctors, translators, and legal secretaries as well as various administrative clerks of local and central governments. The Hyon clan of Chonnyong was the most renowned of the class.

The topic of family enveloped Sung-hon's heart in dark, dense clouds. An enormous difference in status existed between himself and his brother: His younger sibling had become a physician at the Royal Infirmary, whereas he himself had repeatedly failed the medical examinations and ended up as a lowly clerk at the Royal Library. Doctors held the highest status in the Chungin class, being able to advance as far as Rank 3. By contrast, clerks, the lowest of Chungin, normally had no rank. In the rare cases when they entered the ranks, the highest they could aspire to was Rank 7. The different fates derived from differing talents. He couldn't help but feel shame. Chong's speech had begun to shift from the lowest form of respect to the next higher form, but Sung-hon was not pleased with the sudden change of tone.

"As you are Physician Sung-hon's brother, you too must have learned medicine. It was handed down from generation to generation in your family. You are not just any healer in a marketplace. I entrust this man to you. Please save him. If you need an acupuncture needle, I will have it brought right away."

"No, please don't. I am not confident about this."

"By saying you lack confidence, you're admitting you know how to perform acupuncture."

"That's not true. How could I know such a thing? In principle, acupuncture is not used when the patient is very weak or hungry, or in cold weather. This elder's condition doesn't allow treatment. How can I perform upon a patient whose life is in danger?"

"Yet . . . I know how to read a patient's condition a little. . . . If we don't do anything, he's unlikely to survive for more than half an hour. Isn't that so?" Chong asked.

A heavy silence ensued.

Sung-hon involuntarily touched his chest, feeling through his undershirt for his acupuncture needle holder and the round tablet box hanging from his neck. These represented the dreams of his youth, now all withered. He had grown up believing that his destiny and family traditions would lead him to work in the palace as a physician; but perhaps he was unlucky with examinations. He had failed the medical examinations four years running, but had given up after the fourth year when his younger brother breezed through on his first try. Sung-hon's youth had faded as he spent it aimlessly playing *mahjong* and flower cards. When he entered his thirties, he had been fortunate to land a job at the Royal Library, and now he rarely used the acupuncture needle except as an occasional pastime to cure children of colds. How could a quack like him attempt such a difficult procedure?

Even so, as he met Chong's fiery eyes, Sung-hon felt the ambition of his youthful days revive. His hand gripped the needle box.

"All right, sir. I will do everything I can. Please pass me some water."

"Thank you. I sincerely thank you."

Sung-hon spread out a piece of clean cotton cloth and placed the needles on it. He began by crushing a *chongshimhwan* tablet in the water bowl. All of a sudden, busy footsteps sounded in the courtyard and an angry voice called for Chong.

"Sa-am, Sa-am! Where are you? Come out right now!"

Sung-hon's hand stopped.

"Don't worry. Continue," Chong said in a resolute voice and pressed down encouragingly on Sung-hon's shoulders.

The sliding doors flew open as if about to break, and a giant of a man appeared. He looked to be in his forties. He was almost seven feet tall and his beard flowed freely. Sung-hon looked up in surprise and caught sight of a silk robe embroidered with clouds and cranes, indicating an official of Rank 2A.

It was Yi Cho-won, the minister of punishments.

"Sa-am! Have you gone completely mad? What is this outrage?"

When Chong did not reply, he continued, "How can you remove a prisoner from jail and lay him out in the main office of a government building? Don't you have an iota of respect for the law? If the Office of the Inspector-General gets wind of this, you will certainly be impeached and lose your position. Quickly now, hand the prisoner over."

Chong remained as immobile as a stone Buddha.

"Aren't you moving yet? Hey, Chief Jailor!"

"Yes, Your Honor, I am waiting for your command." The person who presented himself in a flash before the door was none other than the officer with the sideburns, who had been at the jail. He must have tattled to the minister.

Chong Yag-yong's eyes blazed with fury.

"What is your hesitation? Hurry up and tie the prisoner . . ."

"Your Excellency!" Chong pounded the floor with his palm and sprang to his feet.

This thunderclap left the minister speechless. Chong stepped toward the minister, his bloodshot eyes glaring as if they would pierce him. The minister retreated, overwhelmed by the fury of his inferior.

Sung-hon, witnessing this exchange, instinctively swallowed.

"Your Excellency! Will you accept responsibility for persecuting and beating worthy scholars to death? Do you realize that this man is the son of the former Chief State Councilor Pon-am? You have illegally jailed a scholar from a well-respected family, Your Excellency. Three people from his household have died after two days in prison as a result of torture and the bitter weather, and this man is hovering on the brink of death. This is simply a private vendetta carried out in the name of government authority. A vendetta, I say! Does Your Excellency take the law so lightly?"

"How dare you! . . . Such impudence! What in the world? . . . They found those icons, whatever they are called . . . crosses and *A True Disputation About the Lord of Heaven* in his home. . . . Do you wish to protect the followers of Western Learning, which is prohibited by national law?"

A True Disputation About the Lord of Heaven was a Catholic catechism. Matteo Ricci, a Jesuit missionary and peerless scholar of Chinese studies, had composed it as a conversation between a Chinese Confucian scholar and a Western missionary, showing extensive knowledge and understanding of Confucianism. It was as engaging as a work of fiction, and was read widely in China, Korea, Japan, and Vietnam.

"No one knows yet whether the icons you refer to belong to this elder, or to the men who died in jail, or to someone else, for that matter. For the sake of argument, let's presume that the book belonged to this elder. It has been two hundred years since Matteo Ricci's book was introduced to Korea, and almost every scholar inside and outside the government has read it. Even His Majesty read it when he was the crown prince, and he commented that it was wonderful that a Western devil could be such a good scholar of the knowledge and arts of the Middle Kingdom. Ever since Yun and the others set fire to the ancestral tablets at Chinsan, angry opinions have prevailed and for that reason the book has been forbidden. But is it a crime that deserves death? Should a member of the family of the late respected minister, who served the king closely, die in jail just because of a book? I shall go and ask His Majesty's opinion right away."

"Sa-am! Wait."

"Let me go!"

"Sa-am! Calm down. Don't get carried away. Let's discuss this point by point."

"Let me go. And please leave. The healer is feeling for a pulse now."

The minister had been restraining Chong Yag-yong, but Chong shrugged him off and stormed out. Confounded, the minister glanced at Sung-hon who was crushing the tablet in the water, and followed Chong out of the room.

Quiet descended on the room, as if a tornado had just swept past. Sung-hon stood up to shut the door and sighed in relief. That was close. Judging from the minister's look of fear, it seemed unlikely he would insist on sending the patient back to jail.

Sung-hon leaned on the door as if to bar anyone from entering, and his eyes rested on the file cabinet with the red padlock, and then crept up to the sliding window pasted with thin, pale paper. He was startled when a shadow darted from the corner of the window and disappeared. Someone had been spying.

Sung-hon stepped around the patient, pushed aside the furniture, and opened the window over the file cabinet. The small courtyard was empty. He craned his neck and looked out. Nothing. Not a sound.

Had he imagined it? He couldn't help but feel perturbed.

If someone had been spying, no one was safe. Sung-hon should do what he needed and hurry off.

He sat by the patient's head, and pried his mouth open with a wooden chopstick. Sung-hon studied the patient's coloring after the medicine he spooned into the patient's mouth had trickled down his throat.

The patient groaned, then grew quiet. Sung-hon took a large needle and pricked the pressure points under the knees and under the joint of the arm, twisting the needle three times up and down and to the left and right. Using a needle on the head would be more effective, but the method he chose was safer, given the patient's exceedingly weak state.

When he had finished treatment, he waited for some time, long enough for a person to drink a hot cup of tea.

The patient's breathing quickened, and his eyes snapped open. Sung-hon, delighted at the improvement, stopped kneading the patient's limbs and brought his face near the patient's eyes. A hand gripped the scruff of Sung-hon's neck. This feeble patient possessed such force? Astonishing. Sung-hon was equally startled by the patient's diluted pupils. It looked like he was now in the brief interlude of semiconsciousness given to a dying man, a state in which sights and sounds do not register.

"Sir! . . . sir!" Sung-hon called out.

"Look, Sa-am."

"Sir, I am not the third minister."

"Listen to what I have to say. What I am telling you . . . the destiny of the Southerners . . . no, His Majesty's very life depends on it. The arrow that pierces birds is above us, and the bird net is below. . . . Are we guaranteed to survive? But His Majesty must avoid the poisonous ha — hand. Sa . . . Sa-am, I'm talking about the previous king's tale of the metal-bound coffer. It's a story only my late father and I have known about. In the year of *imo*, 1762 . . ."

The voice droned although growing softer and softer, as he mustered his dying strength to convey the story. What a heartbreaking sight he was! Sung-hon, in the vise of the dying man's grip, trembled like an aspen shaking in the wind.

It seemed more than an hour had passed to Sung-hon, who had endured the agony of the terrifying tale. The veranda reverberated with footsteps, and Chong Yag-yong appeared.

"Everything is fine now. The minister has issued a command that this elder and the woman be released."

Sung-hon was quiet.

"Why, is he . . . ?"

"He has just passed away."

3
Mightier Than Fate

When King Wu died, Uncle Guan, supported by his younger brothers, said that the Duke of Zhou would aim for the throne and maliciously harm his nephew some day. When he heard this, the Duke of Zhou commented to Duke Shao and Duke Tai that if he did not cease being regent and go far away, internal upheaval would ensue, in which case he would lose face before the former kings. He took refuge in the east. That was how he acquired for himself the reputation of a guilty man. Two years later, the Duke of Zhou wrote a poem entitled "The Owl" and presented it to the king, and the king dared not scold him.

—*Book of History*, from Zhou, fourth section of The Metal-Bound Coffer.

"Minister, sir, others' lives are a mere spectacle. People are born with their fates fixed, aren't they?"

The third minister gave no reply.

"Everyone dies at his own time; the best death is sudden. It is much better than dragging on or lingering. What's the use of living a few more years? Life is but a fleeting dream, as the saying goes. A long life only means more useless worries."

Still no answer.

"Minister, sir, you did all you could for him. No one in this world could have done more . . ."

"That's enough!" Chong Yag-yong snapped.

To Hak-sun scratched idly at his sideburns. The two young coroners managed to suppress smiles. Hyon Sung-hon, walking a few steps behind them, was submerged in deep thought. His face betrayed myriad emotions.

They were at the gate leading to the backcourt of Changdok Palace.

To Hak-sun, a squat old man, had worked at the Board of Punishments more than thirty years. In order to promote expertise, the Board of Punishments had its own doctors, selected by special examinations distinct from those administered by the Royal Infirmary. Although To Hak-sun was the most experienced member of the postmortem team, he commanded little respect. He never refused a drink, hence his nose and the flesh around his eyes were always red. He generally wore the half-closed-eyes look of a dozing man. His nonsensical opinions, readily volunteered, met with frequent ridicule.

He had meant to comfort Chong Yag-yong, but before long his words had misfired.

When Chong had realized Chae I-suk was indeed dead, he embraced the body and wept unashamedly until he fainted. Teacher Pon-am had always supported and encouraged Chong, and now Chong had let his teacher's only son die in his own office.

"He always trusted me and was loyal to the end!" Chong wailed when he came to. "He was a good man!"

Chae had always wished Chong luck. Now Chong felt as if someone had carved up his heart. Others had rushed to assist him, massaging his limbs and spraying him with water, but he wasn't himself. He mumbled a few words, wept, stopped, and then resumed weeping. Finally the soldiers sent from the palace made Chong pull himself together.

A royal command had arrived. Chong was to report to the palace immediately with a team of coroners. Only when heading for the Tonhwa Gate of Changdok Palace, leading his group from the Board through Anguk-dong, did he appear to regain composure.

He heard from Sung-hon what had happened, and knew of Yi In-mong's hope that Chong would handle the situation and spare the Royal Library undue difficulties. Chong asked Sung-hon, who had seen Chang Chong-o last, how he had appeared at that time. Deep regret and fury were etched in Chong's blood-shot eyes; everyone around him was uneasy.

The team showed their passes to the sentries at the gate, walked the lane passing by the Main Hall and the Royal Infirmary, and reached the back garden where the Royal Library was located. Passage into the garden was restricted. Immediately after taking the throne, King Chongjo had decreed the library off limits except to those with business there, and even they had to be escorted by a library official. It was around this time that the garden at the back of the palace had begun to be called the Secret Garden.

Now they were waiting for a guide. Eventually the gate opened and Librarian Yi appeared.

Sung-hon was surprised by Yi's face, which looked as white as a sheet. Yi tottered awkwardly as he led them to the library, and Chong asked him if he felt sick. In-mong responded negatively, but his voice was frail.

The building where Chang Chong-o had died was cordoned off at the pillars. Upon arrival, Chong and To went in briefly to have a look at the body. Soon To and the two assistants began to busy themselves: They unwrapped their instruments, set out a wooden frame in the backcourt for the corpse, and fetched hot bean-boiled water from the huge, bubbling cauldron in the dining hall.

Chong exchanged several words with In-mong. Then, deep in thought, he left for Chuhap Hall.

"Sir . . . Librarian, sir." Sung-hon and In-mong were alone at last in front of the building, and Sung-hon had been seeking an opportunity, like a dog waiting for a chance to go to the bathroom.

"Yes?"

"Uh . . . what is 'the tale of the metal-bound coffer,' sir?"

"The tale of the metal-bound coffer" was what Chae had said. Sung-hon, with his limited classical learning, could only guess that Chae's words meant something serious. He couldn't ask Chong Yag-yong for an explanation, so he went to In-mong, with whom he felt comfortable.

"'The tale of the metal-bound coffer'? Haven't you read the *Book of History*?"

"No, I wasn't interested in such studies. I barely finished the beginners' reader."

"It is the story of the great virtues of the Duke of Zhou, who lived in China a long time ago. The Duke of Zhou, the younger brother of King Wu, not only contributed decisively when Zhou conquered the House of Yin and unified all the kingdoms, but also he was highly regarded by the people. When King Wu died, young King Cheng ascended to the throne and ruled the country under Duke of Zhou's regency; but King Wu had three more brothers named Guan, Cai, and Huo. They were jealous of the duke's advancement in the world and began to spread rumors that he would usurp the throne. When the duke heard this, he was sorely tormented and couldn't sleep. He decided to resign, and left for the east on the pretext of conquering foreign devils, and people wrongly thought the rumor was true and that his leaving reflected his guilt."

In-mong heaved a long sigh. His pallid face looked gloomier. Eyes downcast, he appeared preoccupied but went on with the story.

"Sometime later there were a series of natural disasters. In order to fathom their cause, court officials opened the metal-bound coffer that held accounts of special happenings of days past. Inside was a document revealing that when King Wu was deathly ill, the duke had secretly prayed to the gods to take his own life instead of his brother's. When King Cheng saw this he wept, saying he had not understood the truth because he had been so young, even though he had seen for himself the dedication of his uncle working in his father's court. He said he regretted that he had been suspicious of an elder who had wished to sacrifice his own life for the royal family. He then reinstated the duke."

"Is that all?"

In-mong simply nodded.

"Sir, . . . was there something like that in our court, too? What is meant by 'the previous king's tale of the metal-bound coffer'?"

In-mong's face registered surprise. He looked around, his eyes alert with tension. He tugged at Sung-hon's sleeve. They hastened to a pine tree nearby almost as if being pursued.

"Where did you hear that?"

"I just heard about it by accident. I don't remember who . . . I only asked because I wanted to broaden my knowledge."

"I am not interested in the details. It's just . . . you'd better not tell anyone else. The previous king's tale of the metal-bound coffer is such a delicate matter that I don't know the details of it myself. The topic is avoided at court. All I know is that the whole court was in turmoil seven years ago and State Councilors Chae Che-gong and Kim Chong-su were dismissed the same day because of that matter. You'd better not invite any harm to yourself by talking about it."

"Yes, of course."

"You may go home now. You have worked long and hard after your night duty. Go."

In-mong's eyes followed Sung-hon as he hurried off. He sighed again.

After experiencing shock after shock, even the act of breathing had become exhausting.

After his beating by Yi Kyong-chul, In-mong had been rescued by Chong-nae, who had run out upon hearing his shouts. When he regained consciousness, he found himself lying in the duty room of the administration chamber. He rose quickly and rushed to the building where Chang's body lay. His hunch proved right. Not only *Humble Thoughts on the Book of Odes*, whose existence he had inferred, but also the "Notes on *Humble Thoughts on the Book of Odes*," which he had indeed seen, were missing. Someone must have made off with it, most likely that thug near Konjim Gate.

In-mong reported the incident to Min Tae-hyok, Chief Royal Secretary, and sent a messenger to the Palace Guards Headquarters to request Yi Kyong-chul's arrest. Chong-nae, who had delivered In-mong's report, came back in puzzlement after his meeting with the Palace Guards commandant.

"Sir, Yi is no longer in the Eunuch Department."

"What do you mean?"

"He's dead. The director of the eunuchs became furious and beheaded him because he had strayed from his duty area without permission this morning. This was reported by the Eunuch Department a short while ago, and the Palace Guards have already performed the postmortem. They must have removed his body by now."

In-mong was so shocked that words failed him.

Only with the beheading of Yi did he begin to sense some enormous force encircling Chang's corpse in the room, a force beyond the reach of Yi Kyong-chul or anyone like himself.

In-mong was gripped with violent anxiety. Fragmented images oscillated in a tempest of disquiet: Chang Chong-o's body, the king's eyes as he ordered In-mong to retrieve Chang's document, the fluttering gestures of Chong Chun-gyo, and Yi Kyong-chul gritting his teeth as he fought back with all his might.

It is no longer possible to settle this quietly, he thought. A book examiner had died in the palace, and a sacred text belonging to the previous king had disappeared—not just any document, but the very one His Majesty had ordered In-mong to bring him. There was no way he could avoid blame and punishment.

Was it fair to foist all responsibilities for these calamities on In-mong's doorstep? The death of Chang Chong-o was not his fault, and the outsider's invasion of the library had been Chang's responsibility—but would they take these facts into account? Didn't people hide their own faults as though guarding their hands while playing flower cards, but reveal others' faults as though peeling off tangerine skins?

In-mong was utterly distraught, not because he feared the voices of controversy that would rise up around him like a cloud of dust, but because His Majesty gave meaning to his existence. Fidelity to the king was the only satisfaction in his life. He had endured everything for the sake of the king, divorcing his beloved wife, and remained in Seoul despite all kinds of insults when he lost his position years before. He had lived on the meager salary of a poor civil servant attending the king closely, never once asking for a lucrative position outside the capital. His eyes stung at the idea that all his efforts would come to naught as a result of this preposterous affair.

Even so, In-mong had felt strange comfort when he was recounting the story of the Duke of Zhou. The duke had lived 2,500 years ago—more than that—2,900 years ago. Defiled by an irrefutable allegation, the honorable and righteous regent had groaned under the world's contempt, but his story taught that something mightier than fate existed in the world: the courage to accept the burden of fate unblinkingly.

Some things cannot be avoided in the course of life: I might plead with them, In-mong thought, I might grovel, I might avoid them, but I can't get away from people who wish me dead. Like the *Book of History* that told of the Duke of Zhou's innocence, perhaps a book in the future will reveal my own purity, he told himself. Perhaps In-mong could write it himself. Yes, destiny showed determined people the way; it didn't drag them by their clothing. The virtue and innocence of the Duke of Zhou survived 2,900 years.

In the distant future, today's matters would become an old lesson. If In-mong faced his fate with courage and fortitude, his could become an instructive story. The eternal value of ancient times comforts the people of today who live in the grip of constant change.

Perhaps the brilliant age of King Wen, King Wu, and the Duke of Zhou was only fiction, but it did not matter; the important thing was that human dreams beautified antiquity. Visions of an ideal past age brought dignity to life and filled it with beauty. People believed they were restoring the high moral principles of the old days or rectifying the bad customs of the past even when they were inventing a new social system. People believed the Duke of Zhou's extraordinary courage had enabled him to endure destiny and survive; they believed in the perfection of ancient times, and drew on these beliefs, in order to take comfort in the fleeting nature of the present and to imbue it with meaning. The present allowed the past to be fulfilled.

"To-won, you look pensive."

In-mong suddenly realized Chong Yag-yong was standing in front of him.

While In-mong felt drained, Chong Yag-yong, tormented, felt as heavy as a huge pile of drenched cotton.

"Let us talk later. The second state councilor has arrived."

"I see." In-mong quickly dismissed his daydream and went out to the front of the building.

From the path behind Yonghwa Hall, Second State Councilor Shim's entourage, guided by the deputy director of the library, was walking by Puyong Pond. Yi In-mong and Chong Yag-yong quickly approached and offered deep bows.

"How is the postmortem coming along?"

"We have not begun yet. Your Excellency, we were waiting for your arrival."

Shim turned his eyes to Chong. They were narrow and bright, but expressionless. The furrows of his forehead were as deep as scars, his gray eyebrows were frosty, and the slits of his small eyes blinked slowly, as if at any moment they would become buried in the wrinkles surrounding them. His advanced age, over seventy, seemed to have twisted his mouth, and the skin around it twitched intermittently, but his eyes had a bright glint. Those eyes seemed to be absent of all emotion. Undying ambition alone remained under those wrinkles.

"If he died from a contagious disease, this is a grave matter, indeed. Start right away."

"Yes, Your Excellency."

"Who saw Chang Chong-o last?"

"I did, Your Excellency." In-mong stepped forward. "We dined together, then I remained on duty in the administration chamber while Book Examiner Chang went into the book room."

"Hmm."

"He looked no different from any other time when we had dinner. He did not appear unwell. In fact, he laughed more than usual and finished two bowls of rice."

"Then you would say his death was not due to disease?"

"My apologies, sir, . . . but we could not find the cause of his death. It is true, though, that he appeared very healthy until last night."

"Is that so?" Shim's piercing eyes flashed at In-mong. His lips formed a strange smile, but whether from satisfaction or contempt was hard to tell. In-mong bent in deference, not daring to meet Shim's eyes. The second state councilor's eyes seemed to imply some bestial threat, an evil power that could instantly transform other people's happiness into an ordeal.

Shim approached the book room. He was a man of few words, rarely uttering more than a sentence at a time. He preferred short, vague phrases that seemed solemn and dignified, or a few words capable of throwing an interlocutor off balance. His silence contrasted with his slowly blinking eyes and his large, twisted mouth reminiscent of a catfish. His demeanor exuded a singular tension.

His old face resembled the mask of one of the main characters of the Hahoe mask play *Choraeng-i*, but his taciturn demeanor and upright posture fit that comic face poorly. His overpowering silence terrified others, and when that catfish mouth of his exploded in diatribe, arrests and bloodbaths inevitably resulted.

The postmortem commenced upon Shim's arrival at the back courtyard. To Hak-sun and his two assistants rolled up their sleeves and began to rub the body with the still-hot bean-boiled water brought in earlier. This method of cleaning a body revealed wounds that one could not normally see.

The backyard was a tiny space between the book room and the wall, several paces wide on each side. By the time the three coroners, Chong Yag-yong, Shim's entourage, and Yi In-mong squeezed in around the wooden doorframe on which the corpse lay, there was no room left. Although it was a frosty day, steam from the boiled water and the heat of so many tense people crammed together warmed the area.

After the corpse had been washed, To examined it with a teacup-sized magnifying glass. As he finished each section, he reported whether there was anything out of the ordinary. A young coroner jotted down To's pronouncements on the official form.

The postmortem procedure of the Choson dynasty was renowned for its thoroughness and exactitude. Officials used a form, first published in the *Coroner's Guide to Avoid Grievances* during the reign of King Sejong, to record the condition of seventy-six sites observable by the naked eye. Then they measured the size of wounds and sketched the shape of the body. Two examinations were required, and for a mysterious murder or for a body buried surreptitiously, the official in charge of the particular district had to be present. If that person neglected his duty and left the postmortem to his subordinates, he was stripped of his position and could not be reemployed by the government.

To Hak-sun peered inside the throat for a long time, then straightened up. He turned to Shim.

"Your Excellency, he did not die from a contagious disease."

"Are you certain?"

"It is neither typhoid fever nor smallpox. The throat is not swollen, there is no inflammation of the head, and nothing indicates that he suffered a febrile disease. Please look at this complexion. There are some spots that have appeared since his death, but the face itself is pale. It could not have been a contagious disease."

Shim turned to the physicians who had accompanied him. They had watched To's every movement, standing right next to him, and they now nodded.

"Then what caused his death?" Shim asked.

"Well, . . . that. . . ." An awkward expression appeared on To's face. He displayed a thin, flat silver piece attached to a string that he had just retrieved from the corpse's throat. The pure silver hadn't changed color.

"As you can see, sir, it was not poison. Seventy-six points of the body were examined as minutely as if we were searching for lice, but there is no wound either."

The veins on Shim's forehead pulsed. "Then did a ghost take him? What do you expect me to write in the report?"

The coroner winced and answered in a diminishing voice. "There is nothing left but to do an autopsy. Will that be all right?"

Shim scowled. He looked at Yi Shi-su, the third state councilor, and So Yong-bo, the deputy director of the Royal Library. They also looked ill at ease and made no reply.

In principle, when the cause of death could not be determined by the first and second investigations, the examiners would perform third and fourth tests, and then, if necessary, fifth and even sixth examinations, continuing until all doubt was dispelled. During this procedure, a buried body could be exhumed, and even an autopsy might be unavoidable, although cutting into a body with a knife was no light matter. The regulations governing these procedures, though, were for ordinary people. In the case of a mid-level government official like Chang Chong-o, an autopsy might not be undertaken because the act defiled the body. This particular postmortem had been initiated by a royal command, but if the examiners went ahead with an autopsy, there was no knowing what bitter, resentful words Chang's family would launch at them.

Shim's lips twitched. "An autopsy seems excessive," he said in a low voice. "Third Minister Chong!"

"Yes, sir."

"Having attended the procedure thus far, we old folks will retire to the administration chamber. From this point on, I want you to take charge of the procedure. Prepare a report and send it to me. And General Yi, since they report that no contagious disease was present, it looks like there is nothing for the Military Training Command to do. You may leave the palace and resume your duties."

General Yi's face brightened. The Military Training Command had devoted an enormous amount of work to preventive measures when an epidemic had rampaged through the country two years earlier. With an apologetic expression, General Yi murmured encouragement to Chong Yag-yong before making a quick exit. The deputy director of library led the second and third state councilors to the warm administration chamber.

Chong Yag-yong, Yi In-mong, the coroners, and the physicians remained. The thorny decision of the autopsy had been left to Chong. He stroked his chin for a few minutes.

"Putting a knife to the body of a book examiner is problematic, but there is no way to determine the cause of death if we don't. In view of His Majesty's command, we can't stop where we are. We can't treat the body like a slaughtered animal, but it may be all right to draw some blood from an arm or a leg. What do you think, Librarian Yi?"

"That seems acceptable, sir."

"Then, Coroner To, begin by drawing some blood."

"Yes, sir."

To, sweating profusely, turned the corpse's wrist so the veins were showing. Chang's body was beginning to stiffen, indicating Chang must have been dead for six hours. In principle, the autopsy was to be performed twenty-four hours after death, when the body was relaxed and had started to emit a rotting smell characteristic of decomposition. To grumbled to himself at this inconvenient, premature autopsy procedure. He used a sharp five-inch knife to make an incision in the wrist.

The coroner caught the dripping blood in a silver bowl and observed it for some time. Then he asked his assistant to prepare some vinegar residue. The young man soaked a long cotton bandage with the residue and handed it to To, who wrapped it tightly about the mouth and neck of the corpse. To Hak-sun looked at the blood in the bowl a second time and then examined the body's forehead with his magnifying glass. Next, with his hand on its forehead, he turned the body and inserted the fingers of his other hand in the anus. After this, a long time passed while the examiners attended to various other details.

It was already past noon, and In-mong felt the tension, which had intensified since early morning, gradually decrease. It was difficult for him to remain on his feet, because his stomach hurt and he was painfully thirsty. He had yet to have even a sip of water. The stench of vinegar from the bandage around the corpse's neck was overwhelming; In-mong's eyes watered and he couldn't breathe. He willed his drooping eyelids to stay open and stole a glance at Chong, standing next to him.

Chong had his back to the corpse, and was gazing at the *ondol* firebox facing the backyard. His face wore a suspicious frown. The young assistant unfurled the bandage and whispered something into To's ear.

"Third Minister, sir, it certainly looks like asphyxiation," the coroner announced evenly, after looking at the bowl for a third time and testing the blood with his finger.

"Asphyxiation, you say."

"The blood has a strong blue-green tinge and it won't coagulate; that is how someone who has suffocated usually looks. But . . . it does not seem that his mouth or nose was muffled with a towel, or that someone strangled him."

"How can you tell?"

"According to *The Guide to Official Procedures*, strangulation is indicated by five characteristics. First, blue spots appear like sores on the face. Second, when the area of impact is treated with vinegar residue, it turns red. Third, feces are expelled right before death. Fourth, the tongue shows teeth marks. Fifth, the forehead becomes stiff from top to bottom and therefore hard to the touch. But this body exhibits none of these characteristics."

Chong groaned.

"So the man had a long-term illness, suddenly lost consciousness, and died from asphyxiation. It is such a pity," said the coroner.

"A long-term illness?" Chong appeared dubious.

Paek Song-il, one of the physicians from the Royal Infirmary, interposed. "Minister, sir, it is very common. Some have epileptic seizures and food obstructs the breathing tract, while others lose consciousness from palsy with their faces buried in their mattresses, and still others die suddenly because the palsy occurs in the back of the brain, right behind the cerebrum. Such causes produce symptoms similar to death from asphyxiation."

Chong's eyes glinted. He straightened his shoulders and nodded gently. Did a cold smile pass Chong's lips or had In-mong merely imagined it?

"Ah, that makes sense," Chong said. "Then the postmortem will end here. Coroner To, go inside and write up a draft report. Physicians, thank you both. Librarian Yi, please remain here."

The two physicians immediately bowed and left. Coroner To seemed relieved. He tied a tourniquet soaked in thistle juice to stanch the blood flowing from the wrist and then fled to the warmth of the room. His assistants started to gather the instruments and materials and fold the reed mat.

"It's all right," Chong said. "You'll have to dress the corpse and attend to many other matters. First go inside and thaw out. You can resume later. I will ask the eunuchs to bring something to eat from the dining hall."

"Yes, sir."

After shooing everyone away in this manner, he called to In-mong in an undertone.

"That is the firebox feeding the room where Chang died, is it not?"

In-mong had thought the postmortem had come to an end. He looked in the direction Chong had pointed and saw in the middle of the wall a firebox that showed no indication of fire.

Changdok Palace utilized an *ondol* system of closed fireboxes, each protected by a wall, rather than the protruding ones common outside the palace. Wrought-iron doors with intricate designs specially produced for the palace covered all holes, so that their interiors were not visible from the outside. In-mong looked at the firebox, and agreed with Chong that it was for the room where Chang had died.

Chong picked up a wooden poker and tapped the door open. In-mong crouched and peered into the firebox and saw sand. Chong-nae, the man in charge of the area, must have extinguished the fire, lest the body decompose too rapidly. Chong poked the sand covered with ash, and then jumped down to the front of the firebox, which was located below ground level.

"What is it, Teacher?"

"Look." Chong picked up a sooty lump that had not burned completely.

At first In-mong was baffled, but when he examined the object in Chong's outstretched hand, he realized that it was not wood. The black lump resembled dirt or soft stone, but it was obviously not ordinary baked wood.

Chong caught a look of realization on In-mong's face, then lifted the lump to his nose and sniffed.

"What is that, Teacher?"

"Perhaps you don't know, because you've always worked in the capital. It is coal, produced in places like Kilju in Hamgyong Province."

"Coal?"

"A stone strewn about in the fields and mountains. It produces more heat than wood, so it is used in common households. When I went out as a welcoming official for the Chinese envoys last year, I discovered that some houses in Pyongan Province also use it. But . . ."

"But?"

"But it has one fatal disadvantage, and that is why it is not distributed widely. It produces toxic fumes with no color and no smell. No one confined in a sealed room for two hours could withstand it. Even the strongest man, like General Xiang Yu of China, would be asphyxiated."

"Really?"

"Smell this."

"Isn't that . . . ?"

"Yes, sulfur. Someone covered this lump of coal with sulfur and created a poison. Chang must have died within an hour."

In-mong gaped at the lump. He couldn't move, couldn't speak. So toxic fumes had killed A-dam? In-mong's limbs grew icily numb, but his head felt as if it were burning with heat from the strange object.

He finally managed to croak, "Then someone . . . then someone . . ."

"Yes. This is a poisoning, cunningly disguised."

In-mong's face grew pale. The horrible foreboding, casting a mysterious anxiety over him, finally had become reality. He felt the singular mixture of worry and torment one experiences when a troublesome suspicion is finally confirmed.

"Calm down. Let's walk."

Chong led In-mong by the arm down the narrow path to the Royal Shrine. In-mong, still trembling with fright and shock, was harboring a new suspicion. Thick clouds of anxiety billowed out from this new, shapeless apprehension and enclosed him.

How had Chong solved the mystery so easily? Was it natural for a cunning murder to be detected by simple reasoning? In-mong couldn't breathe. He tried to curb his runaway imagination.

In-mong and Chong were very close. Although Chong was only ten years older, he was a father figure to In-mong. In-mong had been treated as an elder ever since he began his career as a civil servant, and he had no teacher to speak of except for Chong. Chong had taught In-mong everything he knew, and In-mong did not hesitate to do whatever this teacher asked of him.

Between them, though, there was one difference that could not be bridged, one point on which they could not sympathize with each other. Although both belonged to the Southerners faction, Chong's branch was from the central region, which advocated coexistence with other factions whether they liked them or not. In-mong, however, was of the Southerners faction from the southeastern region and had grown up believing that the Old Doctrine faction members were incorrigible devils. Yet Chong cherished In-mong and In-mong respected Chong's profound learning. Without Chong's full backing, In-mong could not have ascended to his current important position. How could he suspect his teacher?

"What was your clue?"

"Two years ago, when I was magistrate of Koksan, I attended a postmortem very similar to this one. That was where I learned that people could die from coal fumes. When I went into the book room, the memory of that corpse came back to me. The papered floor where Chang lay was deep brown, darker than usual. I touched it, and the bean oil from the paper was seeping out. It was evident that a very recent fire had caused the dark color. Ordinary charcoal will not cause paper to burn to that extent, so I became curious about the firebox."

In-mong could only listen raptly.

"When I came back to the capital and began to frequent the palace, I briefly entertained the notion of replacing the expensive charcoal in the court with coal. Ordinary household fireboxes are not sealed well, so toxic gas seeps out. I thought, though, that coal might work in the palace, since Seoul's celebrated artisans made the stone slabs covering the flues of the heating system under the floors; but I learned through careful testing that this would not work. The problem was the ventilation. Ordinary chimneys are attached to the wall, and the smoke escapes easily because the seal between the firebox and the chimney is not airtight. But look over there!"

He pointed at the tall brick chimneys.

"Because of aesthetic considerations, they make the pipes pass underground through the backyard to the chimneys on the other side of the wall. The pipes are long and the holes are big, with complex joints between the pipes. This presents no problem with charcoal, but the toxic particles from coal are so much finer than wood smoke that they easily filter through the floor, even if it's well sealed."

"Then who killed A-dam?"

"That's what I would like to ask you. Do you have any inkling?"

"Well, actually . . ."

In-mong stammered out an explanation of the incident with Yi Kyong-chul and the disappearance of "Notes on *Humble Thoughts on the Book of Odes.*" He added that Yi had been executed by the Eunuch Department.

Chong was stunned by this news, but he listened to In-mong without interrupting.

"Then what was Chang Chong-o doing last night?" Chong asked.

"He had been working on some secret project for three nights running. We don't know what he was doing. We only know that he was working under His Majesty's special command. Chang had his meals brought to his room, and no one was allowed in the building that he was in charge of. Last night Chang joined me for supper in the dining hall. It was the first time I had seen him in three days."

"What did he talk about?"

"We talked mostly about his private affairs. He said it was hard to live in his house in Namji because it was so drafty. He also said he always felt guilty not having an heir to take care of the ancestral rites because his only child had died. He said he wouldn't mind becoming a hungry ghost himself and wandering around, but the idea that no one would take over the ancestral rites worried him so much that it gave him insomnia. He thought he should adopt a son, and yet . . . ."

"All right. Was there anything particularly strange or suspicious besides that?"

"No, nothing. He seemed happy last night, as if some heavy load had been taken off his mind, and he talked a lot, too. After eating, we parted in front of the dining hall. That was the last time I saw him alive."

"He looked like someone who was freed from heavy burden, you said? At any rate, you are in a difficult position. His Majesty gave you a strict order, so you had better find that book, *Humble Thoughts on the Book of Odes*. Go and search the Royal Shrine, where the previous king's manuscripts are kept. If Chang looked relieved, maybe he replaced it after he had finished whatever he was doing."

"Yes. Then . . . ."

"Ah, wait a minute." He stopped In-mong, who had already started hurrying away.

"There is something we must do first. We should go and see the second state councilor at the administration chamber with the postmortem report. Coroner To should have drafted it by now. And there is the issue of . . . whether we should report what we have discovered to the state councilor."

"We should not."

"No?"

"No. Many people in the Eunuch Department, including the director, are confidants of State Councilor Shim. Evidently the Eunuch Department had something to do with Chang's death. Why should we reveal our findings to the state councilor? Considering the circumstances, this matter should be reported directly to His Majesty."

"No, no. That won't do. We have barely caught the end of a thread. How can we report to the king? A poisoning in the court is hardly an everyday affair. We'll be stirring up a tempest before we can even grab the hem of the murderer's robe. This matter should be treated with the utmost caution," Chong warned gravely.

In-mong was unhappy, but could only nod in agreement.

* * *

"According to this postmortem report, the death of Chang Chon-o is not to be brushed aside lightly." Shim Hwan-ji put the report down on the desk.

In-mong, sitting in a respectful crouch, hands in front of him, turned in surprise toward Chong Yag-yong. Chong sat stony-faced, his eyes half closed. They were in the duty room in the administration chamber. Shim Hwan-ji and Yi Shi-su, the third state councilor, sat with proper dignity.

"Granted, he was working on a secret mission under royal orders," Shim continued, "Nonetheless solemn rules take precedence. We cannot gloss over his culpability in dying with his four limbs so rudely sprawled about in His Majesty's residence. It is proper that his family be punished for that. What do you think, Third State Councilor? Even if we elders were not to discuss punishment, the young ones at the Office of the Inspector-General would not tolerate this incident." Shim gave the third state councilor a sidelong glance, a firm expression set on his face.

"Yes, in principle that is correct. . . ." Yi Shi-su scratched his white sideburns in embarrassment. He looked calm and gentle with his beard flowing down to his chest. "But such a procedure seems too punctilious. At the time of disaster, he was on duty following an order of His Majesty, even though he was not feeling well. He committed his error because he was loyal to a fault. It could be said that he was a victim of duty."

"How can you say that? A victim of duty?" asked Shim. "From time to time a scholar estimates the hour of his death and prepares for a tranquil death because he fears Heaven and is mindful of posterity. This was brash behavior for a man who had ascended to the middle ranks thanks to His Majesty's bountiful grace! I recognized Chang's lowly origins early on. Only good roots sprout shoots of the right color. Can the origins of a humble concubine be concealed? The palace steps are so lofty that neither sky nor earth can diminish them. How dare he leave his dirty corpse in such a place? His behavior should be treated as disloyal, and his parents and brothers should be punished."

"Your . . . Your Highness is right." Overwhelmed by Shim's frostiness, Yi abandoned all efforts at opposition.

In-mong felt his blood rage from head to toe. "You . . . you damn fossil," he thought. "You deserve to be torn to pieces. What? Punish his family?"

"Please forgive me for venturing my humble opinion, sir, but . . ."

The quaver in In-mong's voice would have dismayed any listener. His lack of restraint made his true feelings obvious. He swallowed and clenched his fists before continuing. "How can life and death be at human whim? Book Examiner Chang's death has an element that cannot be regarded as his fault alone. Isn't there more than one kind of death by asphyxiation?" As In-mong made these insinuations, he looked the elder Shim in the eye.

Shim closed his eyes without answering. He tilted back his white-tinged hair and inhaled deeply. His thoughts were impossible to read; maybe something had reached him, but maybe not.

"What are you trying to say?" Yi Shi-su, an affable man, looked puzzled.

In-mong thrust himself forward impetuously, but Chong poked him, signaling with his eyes that In-mong should stop.

Just at that moment, Shim opened his eyes and spoke loudly. "You are right. How can such a disaster be Chang's fault alone? Bizarre events in the palace have taken place for no other reason than that the laws of the former kings were treated lightly. Look around Changdok Palace. If the former kings' teachings had been respected, would such a disaster have happened? The palace was constructed according to the *Book of Changes*, was it not? I am sure the earth demon emerged because the 9 side of divination sign 45 has been shaken."

Shim's cunning maneuver left Yi In-mong speechless: By proffering the theory of *feng shui* from the *Book of Changes*, he had discounted In-mong's hint of murder. Closer consideration even suggested that he was pinning the blame on the revolutionary politics of King Chongjo, in which the Royal Library played an important role.

Shim's mention of divination sign 45 was an oblique reference to the emergence of a turtle from the Loshui River when King Yu was attempting to control a flood. This sign is the origin of the Great Plan in the *Book of History* and is also the basic structure of the eight trigrams of the *Book of Changes*, along with the Ten Symbols in the River Chart. It is a square composed of the following numbers:

$$
\begin{array}{ccc}
4 & 9 & 2 \\
3 & 5 & 7 \\
8 & 1 & 6
\end{array}
$$

Adding three numbers in any direction—horizontally, vertically, or diagonally—produces 15. Each of the nine numbers is different, and this structure allows spirits from three places to coexist with the most stability possible. In China, from time immemorial, the number 3 has been considered supremely stable. Accordingly, the magic square, in which the number 3 can be arranged with the most stability, is held to underline the basic structure of the universe and the foundation of all architecture.

Changdok Palace too could be understood in light of the magic square. The number 1 in the bottom row would correspond to the Main Hall, where government conferences took place. Therefore, this row would indicate the administration buildings aligned between Tonhwa Gate and Huijong Hall (Bright Government Hall). The middle row would correspond to the sleeping quarters, such as the Main Hall of the Queen's Quarters and Kyonghun Pavilion. The top row would indicate the space in the back garden, including Chuhap Hall. Then what did Shim mean by referring to number 9 of divination sign 45?

Needless to say, the position of number 9 was held by the Royal Library.

King Chongjo had initiated the building of the library, he said, in order to house his predecessors' manuscripts; but this was only an excuse to avoid the expected opposition of his government. Once the library had been built, King Chongjo expanded it, adding one building after another—the Royal Shrine, the administration chamber, the Chinese Archives, and the book room. Ultimately he bestowed upon it concentrated power in both substance and appearance, and thus the library, the "9 side," could not be kept in line.

Shim's sudden shifting of the conversation with this unwarranted accusation against King Chongjo's politics left In-mong with his mouth agape. He looked like a fish that had swallowed the bait.

Obliquely eyeing him, Shim lowered his voice. "I was only talking about principles. One cannot dare claim Chang was innocent. Still, his fault derived from unflinching, single-minded loyalty, and he should be treated gently. As you said, decisions of life and death are not at human whim."

In-mong made no response, and Shim added, "Then let us conclude the matter. I will take the report to His Majesty. As for the corpse, leave it here until evening to avoid curious eyes. Then have a casket delivered from the Palace Supply Office and remove the body. Third Minister and Librarian Yi! Thank you for your efforts. You may go now."

In-mong and Chong looked at each other, astonished. What a dramatic retreat on Shim's part! Now he had completely set aside the sinister tirade about divination sign 45 and the earth demon, replacing it with a resolution to which In-mong and Chong had no objection.

"As you wish, Your Excellency."

After the two left, Shim gave a light cough that seemed to indicate displeasure. The expression on his face was still mysterious. It changed from smile to sneer from moment to moment, and was impossible to read. He questioned Yi Shi-su in detail about In-mong's background. Then the two men stood up and left the room. Shim was carrying the report. After he parted from Yi Shi-su in front of the library, he marched to the Main Hall of the Queen's Quarters without looking back.

Shim's audience with the king in the Queen's Quarters ended shortly. He went next to the Royal Infirmary, located to the left of the Huijong Hall. He went directly to the room of the somber head physician, sat with dignity, and slid open the side door to the adjoining room.

Facing the darkness of that room, he mumbled, as if to himself, "How did the affair at the Board of Punishments go?"

A face, half-hidden by the shadows of the door, appeared. Short, fat caterpillar eyebrows and leathery skin came into view briefly and then disappeared into the shadows again.

"Chae I-suk died without saying anything."

"Too bad!"

"Chong Yag-yong came to the jail and removed Chae early this morning, as we had predicted, but Chae died soon afterward. Minister Yi intervened and so the two men did not have a chance to talk to each other at length. But one thing bothers us. . . . A clerk from the Royal Library stayed with him until the very end, taking care of him."

"A clerk from the library?"

"Yes, a clerk named Hyon Sung-hon."

"What did the inspector-general say?"

"He said it turned out better than expected."

"Is that so? That's very lucky then. That Yi In-mong you were talking about . . ."

Shim leaned toward the other man and whispered, remaining vigilant even in this secluded place. When the whispering ended, he added, "As for that clerk . . . arrest him and take him to the Constabulary on the Left. I am on my way to the State Council. Tell the minister of personnel to come and see me right away."

"Yes, sir."

When the man took leave of Shim and opened the door, sunlight revealed Chong Chun-gyo, the messenger eunuch.

* * *

So Yong-su, the minister of personnel, frowned deeply when he received a summons to the State Council.

"One of the old men must be furious again," he thought.

So Yong-su also served as an associate director of the Royal Infirmary under Yi Shi-su, the third state councilor who simultaneously held the position of the deputy director of the Royal Infirmary. He had overslept this morning and was unaware of the postmortem at the palace.

Last night he had taken in Ok-nan, the *kisaeng* from Poun, as his concubine. Her soft, coquettish manner had so entranced him that he lost track of time. When he woke, the sun was already high in the sky. To his dismay and embarrassment, he soon learned that State Councilor Yi Shi-su, an old man going on sixty, had had to attend the postmortem in his stead.

"Still, someone could be late once in a while, right? What did they want from me now?" he asked himself. "Even if I was absent, they were supposed to carry on as best as they could."

So Yong-su muttered, hawked, and spat. The buildings of the Board of Personnel and the State Council faced each other, with a thoroughfare between them. Still, qualms were inevitable. Officially, only a single rank's difference separated the minister of personnel and the state councilors at the State Council, but in reality the gulf was greater. Yi Pyong-mo, the chief state councilor, and Shim Hwan-ji, the second state councilor, were both in their seventies, and So Yong-su was a youthful forty-four, still green. Furthermore, these old men were like younger grandfathers or elder uncles within academic hierarchy.

What if these inflexible old men ordered him to roll up his pant legs for a whipping?

So Yong-su already had a grandson, but he fretted in this unbecoming way as he entered the compound. As he approached the state councilor's quarters, a middle-aged servant opened his mouth, prepared to bark, "The minister of personnel has come!" in the direction of the main room. So Yong-su stopped him hurriedly, with a wave of his arm, before he could speak, and sent him away.

"I have come at your command, sir."

"Enter!" It was the voice of Shim Hwan-ji. State Councilor Shim. "Today's luck was getting worse," thought So Yong-su. So and Shim both belonged to the Principle group, but they were hardly on friendly terms. So Yong-su still recalled bitterly that he had been turned away from Shim's doorstep about ten years ago, right before the reshuffle of government positions. This incident was not the sole reason for So's dislike for Shim, and So did not hesitate to criticize Shim in the company of his contemporaries.

"One should know what life is all about," So would begin. "Shim is the second councilor and yet he still lives in a leaky thatched-roof house in Stone Bridge Valley. Is that appropriate for a respected party elder? He has risen high enough. What more glory does he hope to gain by pretending such austerity? A person cannot hope to live an unblemished life. As the world goes, so goes life. When one person washes his hands of troublesome affairs, the next person has to do all the dirty work. Isn't this the way the world works?"

Not for a moment, not even in the lucrative posts of magistrate of Sangju and Kaesong and governor of Kyonggi Province, had So been spared of the burden of funding for his own group. Now, as the minister of personnel, he was in charge of political funds for the entire Old Doctrine faction, and his fund-raising headaches had grown more acute. For this reason, he instinctively recoiled from anyone who flaunted his morality. The Old Doctrine faction had first assumed absolute power seventy years ago, and at present virtually the entire nation was in the hands of a few celebrated Old Doctrine clans. In the era of peace and prosperity, Shim considered himself the only clean civil servant and projected the life of a poor man.

"That old man blackens all of our faces," thought So.

These days Shim seemed engaged in some conspiracy, judging from the bustle around him. He was surrounded by such figures as Yi Chae-hak, the minister of taxation; Han Yong-gu, the minister of rites; Yi Cho-won, the minister of punishments; and top military officials, such as the general of the Military Training Command and the police chief, and, further, division and regimental commanders. A conspiracy involving so many, however, would necessitate large sums of money.

"He always makes a show of fastidiousness, but when the time comes, he will open his palm to me," thought So Yong-su. "Damned old man!"

So Yong-su entered Shim's chamber with pursed lips. He found the old man reading an official document by the light of a candle perched on a holder embossed with dragons. It was just after *mishi*, but even in the midday brightness Shim was squinting, perhaps because he was farsighted.

So Yong-su stood quietly, his hands folded in front of him deferentially, in order not to disturb Shim's reading. Shim did not invite him to sit down. So Yong-su did not know where to look; he gazed absently at the ceiling with square designs and then at the sliding door with its geometric patterns. Finally he decided to prostrate himself with a deep bow and offer a greeting.

"Your Excellency, how are you, sir?"

"Tut . . . It must be time for this sender to die," Shim muttered. "He used to have such handsome handwriting, but now look at this feeble scrawl. . ." With a leisurely brush stroke, he signed.

Shim pushed the document aside and retrieved another from the file box. After he had finished with two documents, he nudged away the little desk in front of him and sipped at the sweetened arrowroot tea placed on top of the document drawers.

"Listen, Yo-jung."

"Yes, sir."

"Life lasts one hundred years at best, but it is merely a lamp in a gust of wind. We can never be at ease. A man should shut his doors and stay at home, and become acquainted with the *komungo* music and drink. If one enters the road of officialdom and is later burdened with a heavy workload, he suffers physically and mentally until the day he dies."

So Yong-su swallowed and sat nervously. He had never heard Shim utter such pathetic sentiments. He seemed to be rambling to himself, offering the complaints of a man who has everything. So Yong-su had nothing to say. Gradually Shim's tone became critical.

"Here I am sullying the position of state councilor in the midst of youngsters, picking out white hairs in front of the mirror. Do you think I keep at this work because I like it? If I had my way, I would go back to my hometown and spend the rest of my days fishing. Do you know why I remain here? I shall tell you. What you people are doing is so precarious that I do not dare retire. Look at the way affairs proceed in the court. It is as though people are jumping into a fire with hay on their backs. I'm old and should have gone to my grave long ago. I no longer have energy, nor am I familiar with current ways. If something dreadful happens, I cannot be of any use. People like you are the ones who should handle the high, strong tides that will come in the future. But what are you people doing these days? How can you be so impudent as to shut yourselves in at home and pretend nothing touches you!"

"My humble apologies, sir. But what do you mean by high tides coming in the future?" So lifted his head and looked at Shim.

Shim rose with a stony expression and flung open the latticed window to the yard. Some innocent clerk must have been standing around. Shim thundered at him to leave and came back to his seat. He brought up phlegm with vehemence and spat in the spittoon.

"Don't you realize that the imminent royal marriage is a grave matter?"

"Yes. I do not approve of it, either, but how can we stand in the way of the crown prince's choice?" So Yong-su feigned gravity, but he could not help scoffing silently. The old man was apparently not in the mood to disparage So this morning. The royal marriage? So Yong-su could make excuse after excuse about that.

He had surmised that Shim was displeased with the marriage. Shim Hwan-ji had attempted to influence Queen Hong of Haegyonggung, the birth mother of King Chongjo, and persuaded the court women to push the daughter of Yi Chae-hak, the minister of taxation, as a marriage candidate. Nonetheless the daughter of Kim Cho-sun, the young leader of the Expediency group, had been selected as bride, although no official announcement had been made yet. The eleven-year-old crown prince had astonished the court by saying a formal selection process was unnecessary: either he would marry the daughter of Kim Cho-sun, or he would not marry at all. It was revealed that last year the crown prince had visited Kim Cho-sun's house on his way home from bidding farewell to the Qing China envoys. He had seen the girl, a year older than he, and had fallen in love with her at first sight.

What could they do? The crown prince was the apple of His Majesty's eye. The king, after endless difficulties, had finally sired a son at age thiry-seven. For civil servants to oppose the match would be fruitless. So Yong-su entertained these thoughts and then silently laughed them away.

Shim had other ideas, though. "Aha. You do not know the entire story," he retorted. "Although the crown prince chose Kim Cho-sun's daughter, His Majesty rushed the procedure as if impatient for the announcement of his son's preference. No, His Majesty has other intentions."

"Other intentions, sir?"

"Crown Prince Sado, His Majesty's father, was killed because he was considered a lunatic, because he criticized us, the Principle group. If you think about it, His Majesty and our group are mortal enemies. Nevertheless, instead of ruining us he embraced us and let us play a role in his government. Why do you think that was? Because of the queens' relatives. In order to eliminate them, he needed us. . . . Do you understand? With one arm he embraced us, and with the other he spurned the queens' relatives by poisoning Hong In-han, Chong Hu-gyun, Kim Ha-jae, Hong Sang-gan, and Yun Yang-no, and by banishing Kim Ku-ju and Hong Nag-im. After that he needed us in order to suppress the literati outside the government. While we have allowed him to use our name, the court has been transformed from a public tool to a private party that dances to the tune of His Majesty's wishes. His Majesty may have accorded strong authority to the three state councilors Kim Chong-su, Yun Shi-dong, and Chae Che-gong over the past twenty years, but the Confucian scholars have become mere puppets. Where do you think His Majesty will aim next?"

"So . . . you mean it is our turn next time."

"Yes! And the royal marriage is the proof of it. He used to criticize the concentration of power in queens' families and their tyranny, so why would he choose to forge a tie with the Kims of Andong? The clan is the mightiest of the celebrated households. As it is, they have wielded enormous power for more than a hundred years, ever since the days of Kim Sang-hon. He will give them wings by making one of them the father-in-law of the crown prince. This is the trick of catching a dragon by inviting in a tiger."

"I find that hard to comprehend. . . . Not that I haven't heard such rumors, but how can they be true? His Majesty has to take into account what the people think, not to mention the opinions of the literati who are impartial. If the king attacks in this way, he will be criticized as immoral for forgetting and betraying his ancestors. It chills me to say this, . . . but a revolt would break out right away. Seven or eight out of the ten high court officials belong to our group."

"That's very shortsighted of you! It is precisely because we have been lulled time and again into counting heads that things have come to this unfortunate state. Open your eyes and look around. What power do we have now? The Military Command Headquarters, including the Military Training Command, is a mere husk of its former self; the real power lies in the Royal Defense Garrison. When the time comes, the Garrison's Palace Unit will disarm the Military Training Command and escort the royal carriage, and the Rear Guard will lay siege to the entire capital and skewer those who flee as if they were a string of dried fish. The literati with impartial opinions? You speak like a frog living in a dark, tiny well. Does every scholar belong to the Old Doctrine faction? If a secret edict were sent to the Tosan Academy, as happened during King Sukchong's reign, Confucian scholars would come up to Seoul by the hundreds petitioning the king to eradicate us. At such times, what happens to morality?"

"But Your Excellency! What wrong did we do? There is no cause." So was still refusing to retreat.

"'What wrong did we do?'" Confronted with such narrow, unyielding thinking, Shim turned away and heaved a sigh. His discontent with these youngsters began to sizzle anew deep in his heart.

"How can you say there is no cause? Do you mean you have already forgotten the memorial Chae Che-gong wrote? Have you forgotten his demand for the full disclosure of the Disaster of 1762, when Crown Prince Sado was locked in a rice chest until he suffocated to death? Don't you remember how he demanded that the enemies behind the incident be annihilated?"

"That cannot be used as a pretext! King Yongjo issued a strict command that His Majesty not take revenge in that matter. First of all, King Yongjo removed His Majesty's name from Crown Prince Sado's family registry and transferred it to his elder brother Crown Prince Hyojang's. Second, he made His Majesty vow that he would not even mention his birth father, let alone restore his name and avenge him, and he announced that if His Majesty violated that vow he would incur the reputation of one who has forgotten and betrayed his ancestors. Third, he made Hong Pong-han, His Majesty's maternal grandfather, acknowledge that the blame for the death of Crown Prince Sado lay partially with himself. Fourth, he nominated Queen Chongsun as an elder of the court, so that even after his death, he could be sure she would protect our Principle group. Would His Majesty disobey such strict orders and do something disloyal? On that point, at least, you need not worry."

"*Eit!* What a dolt! How can you be so obtuse? Would His Majesty have scruples about something like that? Does His Majesty appear sane to you? Haven't you heard him disparage the profound truths of Teacher Nong-am, Kim Chang-hyop, as vulgar Confucianism, and instead praise the convoluted writing of the likes of So-gye Pak Se-dang? It gives me the shivers just thinking about it."

"But that is fundamentally different."

"Not at all! I recognized early on that His Majesty's scholarship was immature, shadowed by heresy. He ignores the Four Books canonized by Zhu Xi and claims instead that the Six Classics are scholarship's foundation, and remains furious with us for patronizing vulgar studies. He brings up ancient times to deprecate wise scholars and to disdain the classics, and still he does not realize how mistaken he is, nor does he heed what he is doing. His Majesty is insane, I tell you! He's the son of the former crown prince, isn't he? Like father, like son."

The official position of the Old Doctrine faction was that Crown Prince Sado died because of insanity. So Yong-su blanched at the impudence of Shim's word.

"Your . . . Your Excellency. You have gone too far, sir."

"Do not interrupt me. The teachings of the two wise men, Chengzi and Zhu Xi, are in grave danger. Why should I listen to your leisurely talk? This world is divided into Yin and Yang: Exemplary men are balanced by the petty; orthodoxy must exist with heresy. How can we distinguish right and wrong when the king has grown stronger than his servants? As a result, exemplary men and orthodoxy have become weak, while small men and heresy have gained strength. But this kind of confusion cannot last long."

"You . . . Your Excellency. . . . What if someone overhears us?"

Shim had by now lowered his voice to something resembling a hiss, but his eyes glistened like a knife blade. How could he intimate so clearly that the king would not last long? Listening to this relentless vehemence, So, normally of a daring mind, felt his hands begin to tremble.

Fear of Shim Hwan-ji was even stronger in his own faction than among the Southerners. Shim always planned ahead and schemed with utmost care for his goals; when the time came to implement a plan he moved swiftly, wasting no opportunity, pushing ahead ceaselessly, as if crazed. He habitually drove his faction to extremes.

Kim Chong-su and Yun Shi-dong, two other leading figures in the Expediency group, had possessed endearing, humane qualities and the sagacity to flow with the tide. Shim, however, fundamentally lacked such a temperament. Since Kim and Yun had died, Shim had become the official voice of their faction, and that was an extraordinarily disturbing development.

Perhaps the above reasons have caused Shim to be depicted as a villain in today's popular historical novels. Every one of them accuses him of self-righteousness and insanity because he directed the persecution of the Southerners and the merciless massacre of Catholics in 1801.

But I, the translator of *The Encounter of the Stars*, have a different view: Those faults of Shim's which are condemned by posterity originated in his enthusiasm for preserving orthodox ideology. In fact, he dedicated his life to Neo-Confucian orthodoxy in the face of myriad heresies demanding a new epoch. As difficult as this may be for modern readers, Shim's convictions that Western Learning was heresy and that those who learned heresies were traitors were the consensus of the literati of the era, deeply submerged as they were in Neo-Confucianism. The literati of the entire country must have watched Shim's triumphs and persecutions in the name of orthodoxy, and he must have believed that in this task lay his sole joy and fruition, his sole obligation and glory.

Of course, we cannot say that Shim excelled beyond other eminent scholars who led the Old Doctrine faction. His scholarship, in both breadth and depth, was far inferior not only to that of his predecessors, such as Song Shi-yol and Yi Chae, but also to the scholarship of his contemporaries, such as Kim Chong-su and Yun Shi-dong. His rough and unrefined writing could never be compared to elegant compositions directed to the king, nor to the instructions penned by the likes of Yi Chon-bo and Yu Chok-gi, famous state councilors.

Shim had passed the civil examination at the mature age of forty-two. Since then he had suffered four banishments and countless impeachments, and had become embroiled in numerous controversies. His late debut and the numerous storms he had encountered had endowed him with patience, superior political sensibility, and an understanding of how to deal with the world. His clear, steady eyes took in the endlessly changing political scene. He never failed to grasp decisive moments that were invisible to others. Perhaps the present situation was a prime example.

With his gravelly senescent voice, Shim had been pointing out the exact moments when King Chongjo and his faction had clashed, and in this way predicted the king's imminent elimination of the Old Doctrine faction. The conflict between the king and the Old Doctrine was based on a disagreement over the Six Classics or the Four Books.

"To consider the Six Classics [*Book of Odes, Book of History, Book of Changes, Spring and Autumn Annals, Book of Rites, Book of Music*] as orthodox is rubbish! Two thousand years ago the First Emperor of Qin burned all the books, and the Six Classics were destroyed without a trace. Today's Six Classics are forgeries patched together by Han dynasty scholars. Any babbling child knows this. It is absurd for His Majesty to contend that scholarship that searches for the truth must have as its foundation the Six Classics. Such a comment is fit for a blind cur. How could it drift out of His Majesty's Office?

"Han dynasty scholars were not conversant with the fundamentals of the Tao, so they went along with the claim that it predicted destiny, or else they immersed themselves in the game of telling fortunes. Their words teach nothing about how to train oneself and how to rule the world. These were the charlatans who patched together the Six Classics and annotated them with silly commentaries. How can we say these are genuine vestiges of the sage-kings of ancient times? No matter what people claim, the true path to scholarship was revealed during the Song dynasty when one wise person after another emerged and scholarship finally blossomed with Zhu Xi's complete compilation."

"You are right, of course, sir." So had no choice but to agree.

"Zhu Xi found the clue to our rediscovery of a heritage lost for a thousand years. He established as the foundation of scholarship the suppression of one's emotions to return to one's true nature; he established as the basis of governance the Plumbing Principle and the Investigation of Things. He defined the Mindfulness as persevering in one path and not meandering; he defined Benevolence as rational thought and an uncorrupted mind. His teaching emanated truly from his heart, and he eliminated all doubts by carefully examining the ancient times and rectifying errors. Zhu Xi eliminated impure doctrines and swept heresies aside; he illuminated hidden truths. His contributions match those of King Yu. The teaching of Zhu Xi is the beginning and the end, the one and all. The peace of this world depends on whether we defend these teachings. Do you understand?"

With this, Shim fell quiet and closed his eyes

Shim's words, filled with the missionary zeal of an old scholar trying to defend Neo-Confucian orthodoxy, silenced So Yong-su for a while. He had much to think about.

People commonly speak of the Four Books and the Three Classics in one breath, but these works differ in character. The Three Classics — *Book of Odes, Book of History,* and *Book of Changes* — are handed down from the distant Zhou dynasty, the golden age of ancient China. But the Four Books — *Great Learning, Analects, Book of Mencius,* and *Doctrine of the Mean* — were canonized by Zhu Xi during the Song dynasty. Consequently, only much later did they become accepted textbooks.

The import of the Three Classics lies in their confirmation of the existence of sage-kings. All three works praise the wise rule of ancient emperors such as Yao, Shun, Yu, Tang, Wen of Zhou, and Wu of Zhou. They consider the brilliance of royal sovereignty the only transcendence in the secular world, as it realizes the Mandate of Heaven, always just and never influenced by personal feelings.

The Four Books expand that transcendence to a more general and metaphysical model; instead of focusing on the practical aspects of the king's absolute authority, a philosophical ideology was introduced to explain the fundamentals of the universe and human nature as *li* (principle) and *qi* (material force).

These differences gave rise to conflicts between those who believed in absolute royal authority and those who denied the fundamental difference between the king and the literati, believing both to be under the influence of the universal law of rites. The conflicts between King Chongjo and the Old Doctrine faction were a prime example.

The basic assumptions of So Yong-su, a member of the Old Doctrine faction, differed little from those of Shim Hwan-ji. King Chongjo's reverence for antiquity was certainly extreme; his criticism of younger civil servants who used a refined new style led to a restoration of more traditional modes of expression; he banished these younger writers, insisting that the crude and rough style of antiquity remain standard. King Chongjo brought up the depiction of the sage kings in the *Book of Odes* at every opportunity, and argued that his country, now in decline, must restore the Mandate of Heaven.

So Yong-su had often snorted at this idea. People always tend to believe their own era to be the most difficult, most corrupt, most imperfect, and most tragic. Likewise, they believe that ancient times—the epoch of the ancient sage-kings of Yao, Shun, Yu, Tang, Wen, and Wu, and the Duke of Zhou— were perfect, clean, and righteous. How childish! Times have been always difficult, always corrupt, always imperfect, and always tragic. Such is the nature of the world. The era of sage-kings had never existed and never would. The world had never been perfect, was not perfect, and would never be perfect. It was obvious. The ancient era was only a vague, moral cause, and life in any era is a shabby cowshed. How could a king not be able to distinguish between reality and fiction?

So thought the king's fanatic enthusiasm had nothing to do with the matter at hand. If he had been a man of ordinary strength and will power, assassins would have seen to it that he became a ghost in the Royal Ancestral Shrine.

When King Chongjo had ascended the throne more than twenty years before, few thought the son of Crown Prince Sado would hold power for so long. For more than a decade, would-be killers climbed over the palace wall every year; treacherous conspiracies, large and small, came to light; the criticisms of the literati grew steadily more vociferous. His Majesty escaped this difficult period by using both carrot and stick. Soon after assuming the throne, he paid homage at Song Shi-yol's tomb to obtain the Old Doctrine faction's sympathy, and he relentlessly eliminated political foes at the mildest sign of treason, using his confidante Hong Kug-yong as his point man. In order to placate the Principle group, when Hong became the target of their enmity, the king forced him to retire prematurely in a show of brilliant political manipulation.

Eventually, So ventured a reply to Shim's comments. But, "Your Excellency," he said, "this is not the time to blame His Majesty. In my humble opinion, His Majesty is no inferior man. If he wanted to carry out such a lawless plan, he would need evidence that the previous king's strict command was not what it appears to be. Your Excellency is so concerned. . . . Perhaps you mean that His Majesty has such evidence? Please explain in detail."

So's words hit home. He sometimes feigned a lack of understanding, but, in fact, he was no fool. He had more political savvy than any of his contemporaries who were poised to take over the leadership of the group. He had sensed a grave conflict behind Shim's unprecedentedly vehement words.

Shim had been locked in silent contemplation, but his eyes fluttered and his lips twitched. "Evidence. . . . Yes, His Majesty has definite evidence, evidence that could identify us as traitors and cost us our heads."

4
The Book in Question

This servant has for decades been tormented with aching pain and has lost all sense of life's joy. The evil and cunning group who falsely and maliciously accused Crown Prince Sado were traitors whose behavior cannot be tolerated in any age, and yet this servant has failed to open his belly and carve out his liver in order to speak publicly about what is right and wrong, to inform the whole world for a thousand years to come. Therefore how can it be said that the situation is not urgent? Even if Your Majesty does not listen because it is impossible to listen, and this servant does not tell because it is impossible to tell, it would truly be good if the world knew Your Majesty's heart and this person's heart. Defying death, this foolish servant expresses his thoughts: If the evil and cunning group's crime was concealed and the revelation was not made, on what would the hundredth generation from now rely for truth?

— Chae Che-gong, "A Memorial from Hwasong in Appreciation of Receiving the Post of Chief State Councilor," *The Veritable Records of King Chongjo*, the fifth month of the seventeenth year, *kimi* section, *Pon-am Collection*, Book 26.

"Your Excellencies, may I offer you your luncheon tray?"

Chu Chong-nae, a clerk at the Royal Library, peered about the Royal Shrine, craning his neck in every direction, looking for Chong Yag-yong and Yi In-mong. A lady-in-waiting followed with a tray from the dining hall.

The two men had disappeared like water ghosts

Chong-nae was annoyed. He himself could not eat until he found the librarian and his companion. The two clerks on duty with Chong-nae the night before had gone home even before the postmortem had commenced. The second councilor and the third councilor had left, and the coroners had eaten and departed. Librarian Yi had singled out Chong-nae and instructed him to wait, and now at this late lunchtime the librarian was nowhere in sight.

Librarian Yi lived alone with his children, deprived of his wife's assistance in raising them and running the household. Perhaps this was why he did not seem eager to go home. Just like the Water Ghost! Because he was like that, he thought everyone else was the same. When he could wait no longer, Chong-nae had arranged for the lady-in-waiting to bring the lunch.

From the vicinity of the Royal Shrine Chong-nae heard rustling sounds and low voices.

"Librarian, sir. Your luncheon tray . . ."

The paper doors of the main room clattered open. Chong-nae's eyes widened at the sight of In-mong. The librarian had removed his official hat and rolled up his sleeves, and his arms and shoulders were covered with spider webs. He looked anxious and exhausted. "Whatever has he been doing?" wondered Chong-nae.

The Royal Shrine, where the books and sacred writings of the previous king were stored, was accessible to only a handful of people. It was an archive but also the shrine where the king and the crown prince performed the ancestral rites every spring and autumn. Chong-nae was understandably taken aback at the sight of In-mong in such a solemn, secret place in shirt-sleeves, with his topknot brazenly bared.

"It's good that you are here. Enter, please. I have something to ask you." In-mong beckoned to the clerk but dismissed the woman, saying he was not hungry.

Chong-nae stood awkwardly at the foot of the shoe ledge, an embarrassed look on his face.

"But Librarian, sir, . . . I am not allowed to enter this revered place."

"It doesn't matter. Come in for a moment."

"Sir, this is where the rite for the previous king takes place. How can I . . . where his holy spirit resides . . ."

The corners of In-mong's eyes arched upward.

It sounded to him as if Chong-nae's reluctance stemmed from more than simply fear of violating a sacred place. The man's words reminded In-mong of the rumor his enemies whispered among themselves—that Yi In-mong was an abominable Catholic. Was he implying that In-mong did not honor this sacred place of rites? In-mong suffered greatly on account of this rumor, and now a sense of shame encroached upon his heart.

When In-mong spoke, his voice quivered. "Look here. You imagine the Royal Shrine as something like a village shrine where various spirits are honored. As Confucius said in the chapter on ghosts and spirits in the sixteenth section of the *Doctrine of the Mean,* "The approaches of the Spirits you cannot surmise—and can you treat them with indifference!" The ghost connotes *yin* and the spirit connotes *yang*. They cannot be dealt with separately; rather, it is nature's own harmony that the two material forces (*qi*) of *yin* and *yang* bring about. So if this shrine is not the den of sundry spirits, how can the spirit of the previous king dwell here?"

"I do not understand, sir. If the previous king's spirit does not reside in this place, why would His Majesty come here every spring and autumn to conduct the rites?"

"Spiritual communication at the time of the rite does not depend on the place, but on the integrity of the person who performs the rite. Therefore, Confucius taught, at the end of the ghosts and spirits section, "Such is the manifestation of the subtle. Such is the impossibility of hiding the real." If the person who performs the rite concentrates with reverence and sincerity, the one that receives—that is, the spirit's *li*—converges and flows and moves, so that the shapeless takes shape, the soundless takes sound, and the heartless takes heart."

"Does the *li* of the spirit flow and move? I do not have great learning, but I know this much: *Li* is unmoving; it is the basic principle, the law of all things. *Qi* has concrete aspects and form; it is born, it moves and it dies. How can you say there is no *li* in the ghosts, and yet at the same time claim that *li* rises up and moves about?"

In-mong laughed. "So, the argument about the *li-qi* theory. Admirable. But the argument that *li* is immobile and *qi* is mobile and that one cannot function without the other is a syllogism, constructed by those who revere Yi Yul-gok. If only *qi* moves, the *li* that is the source of all things cannot be differentiated from sterile emptiness. *Li* and *qi* are different: The four instinctive feelings originate from *li* and the seven emotions come from *qi*. Do you understand?"

"Now that I listen to you . . ."

"If you understand, speak no more. Just come in."

Chong-nae could refuse no longer. Scowling, he entered.

The musty smell of mildew spores from old books stung his nose. The room had no windows and was gloomy and cold.

In the middle of the room were several reading desks, each bearing a mountain of books. Large book cabinets surrounded them, four each to the right and left, with one end set against the wall. Beyond the reading desks, two padlocked bookcases stood against the wall facing the door; two official hats and robes belonging to In-mong and Chong Yag-yong rested on top of them. Chong, squatting in the corner to the left, glanced up at Chong-nae, then returned to the book.

Chong-nae was puzzled. "Do you recall," In-mong asked in an undertone, "that this morning I ordered you to cordon off the building and keep an eye on it?"

"Yes, of course, sir."

"You remained there after I left."

"Yes . . . pretty much, yes."

In-mong's pale face stiffened.

"What do you mean? I'm not accusing you. I'm just inquiring, so tell the truth."

"Actually . . . there was no straw rope nearby. So after you left, I went up to the Storage Bureau and borrowed some. Then I cordoned the place off, and put out the fire because I thought it would be bad for the body. I was scared to go into the building, so I stayed outside. Then I heard you calling from a distance. So I hurried out and saw you lying unconscious. It shocked me. I carried you on my back to the administration chamber and I massaged your arms and legs . . ."

"Yes, I thank you for that. Without you, I don't know what would have happened, . . . but you watched the building only long enough for a person to drink hot tea."

"Yes . . . that is . . . that is right."

"How unfortunate . . ."

In-mong's face, almost as pretty as a woman's, showed anguish and exhaustion. His complexion, once as fair as a cloud so that his thin, dark eyebrows and his large eyes stood out, was now sallow. His long eyelashes almost touched the ridge of his nose and his nose cast a deep shadow across the right side of his face. His small mouth curved slightly in a way that lent sincerity to his face.

"During the three days that Teacher Chang was on secret duty, did he say anything unusual?" In-mong asked nonchalantly.

"*Aigu*. Do I have time to listen to the book examiner? My responsibility is to take care of the officials' meals and supply the materials needed for their work. And the book examiner, as you know, stayed in the book room all by himself. . . . Ah, but there was something. I remember now." He lowered his voice, suddenly conscious of Chong Yag-yong. "When I brought his dinner three days ago, the book examiner asked what we, Chungin, thought of the late crown prince."

"Crown Prince Sado?"

"Yes, sir."

At that moment Chong Yag-yong stood up and approached, his face tense, and proceeded to dismiss Chong-nae. Chong-nae eyed In-mong, who merely nodded, his gaze fixed in space.

"Sirs, your luncheon . . ."

"We have no appetite. Forget it."

Sensing something unusual about the mood of the two men, Chong-nae hastened to leave. The sliding doors in the main hall closed softly, and the sound of Chong-nae's footsteps receded.

The former crown prince . . . In-mong lowered his head in despair. This dark room seemed no different from the internal maze through which In-mong was wandering. He saw only one dark path after another.

Something mysterious was happening, but In-mong had no idea what it was. He only sensed a force behind this incident, a force that had darted away like lightning. The death of Chang Chong-o; the death of Yi Kyong-chul, which quickly followed; the death of Chae I-suk, which Chong Yag-yong had told him about. . . . In-mong imagined a single arrow piercing all three deaths. Now the death of the crown prince thirty years earlier had arisen.

Most shocking to In-mong was Chae I-suk's death.

He had heard that two nights ago, soldiers had burst into Chae's house by order of Yi Cho-won, the minister of punishments, and had made arrests. This morning Chae had died from bitter cold and torture.

This was no ordinary matter. The rites marking the first anniversary of Chae Che-gong's death had not yet been performed, and causing the chief mourner to die in jail was an unthinkable act of violence. In-mong remembered Chae's funeral, a Confucian Scholars' Funeral almost as elaborate as a national mourning rite. His Majesty was a strong monarch, and there were literati who had respected State Councilor Chae both in and outside the court. They had arrested the chief mourner and killed him before Chae's casket dried out.

Was the Old Doctrine faction digging its own grave? Chae I-suk's death could not have been conceived and carried out at the level of the minister of punishments. If the Old Doctrine faction had had to resort to such extremes, they must have had a serious motive. Could Chae's death possibly be related to the deaths of Chang Chong-o and Yi Kyong-chul?

In-mong quaked at the suspicious, almost unreal circumstances that seemed to encompass the three deaths. He was feeling the sort of terror that accompanies the sensation of being tricked but not knowing exactly how.

Chong Yag-yong tapped In-mong on the shoulder.

"To-won, look at this."

In-mong turned to find Chong holding out to him Book Seven of the *Chronicle of King Yongjo,* one of nine books that recorded Yongjo achievements and writings as king. Book Seven contained the records from the fortieth year (1764) to the forty-third year (1767) of King Yongjo's reign. Puzzled, In-mong read the passage Chong indicated.

"*Sulshi,* on the fifteenth day of the ninth month of the forty-third year of King Yongjo. His Majesty carefully read the *Book of Odes* and personally composed *Humble Thoughts on the Book of Odes.*"

"So, there really is such a book!"

"Well . . ." Ignoring In-mong's enthusiastic outcry, Chong frowned and continued to stare at the passage. "Something is wrong." His expression was clouded

"What do you mean?"

"I have looked everywhere, and there is no such record in *The Veritable Records of King Yongjo* or in the *Records of the Royal Secretariat* for that day. Possibly, *Humble Thoughts on the Book of Odes* was a very personal composition. But look here."

"Ah, yes. *A List of Works Personally Written by King Yongjo.*"

"Indeed. This was made by the Veritable Records Office when the *Veritable Records of King Yongjo* was compiled. No book entitled *Humble Thoughts on the Book of Odes* here, either."

Only then did In-mong realize what Chong was driving at. Their eyes met. In-mong felt a spark of recognition. The two men slid open the door and hurried out, intending to examine the calligraphy of the *Chronicle of King Yongjo.*

The courtyard was bathed in sunlight. In-mong opened the book and held it up over his head, as if offering a sacrifice to the sun. He shut one eye and squinted at the passage starting with "His Majesty carefully read the *Book of Odes*." The sun, the opened page, and In-mong's eye aligned.

Yes, indeed!

"Are they floating?"

"Yes, they appear to be."

Characters written with thick traditional ink on mulberry paper are absorbed, as the years go by. If someone adds to the existing text, the new writing, by comparison, appears more distinct. Philologists describe such a phenomenon as "floating." Even if the second writer uses ink ground long ago, and no matter how similar the script, floating is taken as irrefutable proof of an unoriginal text.

How was this possible?

In-mong again compared the twelve Chinese characters "His Majesty carefully read the *Book of Odes* and personally composed *Humble Thoughts on the Book of Odes*" with other characters. However meticulously he examined them, they appeared to have been written by the same hand. It would have looked the same even if he had used a magnifying glass. It was evident that someone had added the phrase in a blank space, or that someone had cleverly washed out the existing characters in order to replace them. Among the people In-mong knew, only one was capable of doing this.

Chang Chong-o.

"Teacher, perhaps it was Chang who did this?"

"You think so, too?"

In-mong drew a deep breath. He and Chong exchanged surprised looks.

Why would Chang have done something like this? How could he dare tamper with the chronicles of the previous king? It was an extremely serious offense, and even if Chang could have been hanged ten times over, he still could not have paid the price. And what about His Majesty? What had he meant that morning? Did he mean that In-mong should locate a fictional book, a book that had never existed?

"I think," Chong said, "that perhaps *Humble Thoughts on the Book of Odes* is one of the secret texts that have been handed down solely for the eyes of the king's descendants. It's extraordinary."

"But if that were the case, why was that passage added to the *Chronicle of King Yongjo*? And the title itself is strange. If we were considering notes on books that focus on governance, such as the *Great Learning* or the *Book of Rites*, they might be a secret text, but why should someone go to such lengths to pass on annotations on a book of literature?"

"That is hard to say. But it was serious enough to prompt a murder."

Chong turned back to the building. "At any rate, let us return everything and leave this place. It is useless to search the shrine. If there really was such a book as *Humble Thoughts on the Book of Odes*, it disappeared when Chang was murdered. As you guessed, Yi Kyong-chul could have taken it."

"Then how do you explain the death of Yi Kyong-chul?"

"In general, people commit crimes not because they are hungry but because their stomachs are too full. It is not people who desire something but people who do not want to lose something who most easily commit murder. Those who have taken the book may be endangered by its existence. When you discovered Yi Kyong-chul, they were afraid that the matter would escalate beyond their control, so they shut him up by killing him."

In-mong nodded and followed Chong inside. With a gloomy face, he replaced the books and donned his official robe. He and Chong then sat down on the stools in front of the desk. In-mong passed his tongue over his lips and discovered that they were chapped from dehydration.

An uneasy sense of resignation seeped into his heart.

There was no way out. Yi Kyong-chul could not return from the dead to be interrogated. . . . All that was left was for In-mong to prostrate himself in front of His Majesty and await his punishment. How could In-mong explain to the king that the book His Majesty wanted couldn't be found?

Then he was struck by a suspicion.

"Teacher! There is something I forgot. When I went in to check on Chang Chong-o the first time, I saw no book entitled *Humble Thoughts on the Book of Odes*. There was only "Notes on *Humble Thoughts on the Book of Odes*," from which Chang Chong-o had been taking notes. There were other books scattered around the desks, but I recognized all of them immediately. They were interpretations of the *Book of Odes*, books you and I would know in our sleep, such as *Collected Commentaries on the Book of Odes* by Zhu Xi, *Mao's Version of the Book of Odes* by Zheng Xuan of the Han dynasty, *Commentary on Mao's Version of the Book of Odes* by Kong Yingda of the Tang dynasty, *The Correct Reading of Mao's Version of the Book of Odes* by Cheng Baiyu, and *Thoughts on the Book of Odes* by Wang Yinglin of the Song dynasty. So the previous king's composition disappeared before the discovery of Chang's death and the confusion that ensued."

"So?"

"Then why did Yi Kyong-chul return to the library? If they already had the book they were looking for, why did they come back for the notebook and risk being seen?"

"Yes, that is indeed bizarre."

"It was clear from Yi Kyong-chul's behavior that he had something to do

89

with what happened at the library. But even if he killed Chang, it is possible that someone else took the book and the notebook. Yi came back because *Humble Thoughts on the Book of Odes* was not the book they had expected."

"What are you getting at?"

"They had someone take the *Humble Thoughts on the Book of Odes* as soon as Chang died, before *myoshi*. They examined it, but didn't find what they were looking for. They thought there must be some other document and they sent Yi to fetch it. That would be the notebook that disappeared after I left to see His Majesty. If I had known things would turn out this way, I would have read through the notebook. . . . All I did was glance at the page where 'The Owl' was copied."

"The owl?"

"I mean the poem 'The Owl' in the *Book of Odes*. The one the Duke of Zhou is said to have written about his experience of injustice, when he exiled himself to the east after his brother Guan brought false charges against him. It's the poem recorded in the section on the tale of the metal-bound coffer in the *Book of History*. Heavens!"

"What?"

"Oh, it's nothing. This morning, a clerk under my authority inquired about the previous king's tale of the metal-bound coffer. What a coincidence!"

"Oh? You don't mean Hyon Sung-hon? The elder brother of Hyon Chu-hon, the physician at the Royal Infirmary?"

"Yes, it was he."

"How unfortunate!" Chong's face took on the bewildered look of a child who has just realized that he made an enormous mistake. His eyes were fixed in space as he recalled the events of several hours before.

"What is the matter, Teacher?"

"This morning when I laid my friend I-suk in the office, he mumbled something about 'metal-bound' before he fainted. I was frightened by his appearance, for it seemed he would stop breathing any moment, and I rushed out without giving his words a second thought. I saw Hyon Sung-hon standing outside. He seemed to know some acupuncture, so I asked him to help my friend. Then Minister Yi Cho-won came in and I had to accompany him to the main office. I had to argue with him for half an hour, and when I came back I discovered that I-suk had died. During that half hour, I-suk and Hyon Sung-hon were all alone."

"Then you mean . . ."

"I-suk must have said something before he died."

"About the previous king's tale of the metal-bound coffer? Teacher, what exactly is that all about? All I know is that one is not supposed to mention it, and when it was discussed in 1793 the entire court was in turmoil, and Teacher Pon-am and State Councilor Kim Chong-su were dismissed, and . . ."

In-mong lapsed into silence, awaiting Chong's reaction.

Chong nodded perfunctorily, an involuntary frown crossing his forehead.

In-mong sat quietly, scarcely daring to speak. Finally, Chong let out a sigh.

"The past seems to flow away like a river, but it comes back again and again like migrating birds. Who can avoid evil, which is inevitable in human life? In this wretched hut of existence, people execute others again and again in the name of honoring the dead. The previous king's tale of the metal-bound coffer is truly sad and complex. There is no knowing when it will spawn a new bloodbath. How fortunate if it could remain buried in the deep silence of the years!"

Chong's mild and affable face was shadowed by a somber despondency.

Looking at his teacher's weary expression, In-mong grew more curious. The tale must indeed be sinister. Whenever In-mong had been in trouble, the teacher had always comforted him, either calming him with sympathetic silence or enlightening him with heartfelt wisdom. In-mong's eyes burned with curiosity and ardor. His mind raced and his pulse quickened.

Prompted by In-mong's fervent eyes, Chong began the story, his voice muted.

"It is a tale about the crown prince who passed away. It can't be explained in a word or two. In fact, the story starts as far back as two hundred years ago. But of course, you know all that."

Chong began to review the history behind his tale, and In-mong settled in to listen.

"Two hundred years before, during the reigns of King Myongjong and King Sonjo, court officials were divided into the Easterners and Westerners, which in turn splintered into the Southerners, the Northerners, the Old Doctrine, and the Young Doctrine. Vicious conflicts among these various factions ensued. This situation owed to the administration's adoption of the political parties of Song China as its ideal system. The underlying influence on this system was Neo-Confucianism, which had attained absolute ideological authority in Song China.

"In this system the literati were divided into factions based on their political views and monarchical rule was subject to checks and balances. Such was the ideal, anyway.

"In Korea the ideal was soon forgotten in the midst of ever-intensifying factional fighting. Politics degenerated into vendettas. After numerous disputes, condemnations, conspiracies, and veiled struggles, a preeminent force had emerged by the end of King Sukchong's reign. To the surprise of many, that force was the Old Doctrine faction.

"How had the members of the Old Doctrine survived and taken control amid the rough seas and tumult of court politics, despite their frequent conflicts with the kings?

"Their slogan, 'Respect the rustic literati and lose no opportunity for a royal marriage,' worked for them at every turn. The rustic literati were the scholars outside the political system who stayed on in Confucian academies. Their support was vital. The Old Doctrine faction also concentrated on providing candidates for queen from their families, thereby creating a strongly protective cocoon in court. When the daughters of Old Doctrine members occupied the highest position among the palace women, the eunuchs naturally fell into their hands, for they lived and died at the whim of high-placed women. The faction gained access to every political drama played out around the king. It was as easy as reading one's palm.

"But a hundred and eleven years before, in the sixteenth year of King Sukchong's reign (1689), an incident had taken place—the Reversal of Situation of 1689—that had decisively frustrated the calculations of the Old Doctrine faction.

"King Sukchong, age twenty-eight, acting with a fearless, youthful exuberance, expelled Queen Inhyon, daughter of Min Yu-jong, who was an enthusiastic follower of Song Shi-yol, a giant of the Old Doctrine faction. The king ordered death by poison for the eighty-three year-old Song, then accomplished the unbelievable feat of promoting Concubine Chang, the daughter of a trifling translator, to Principal Queen. A large-scale purge followed and the Southerners seized power. Thus was the Old Doctrine presented with its first and only crisis.

"The Southerners had a fundamentally different political philosophy.

"Seeing the king's authority weakened by passionate factional fighting and realizing that politics became the means to carry out vendettas, the Southerners rejected the very idea of party politics. Their logic was as follows:

"What was the politics Confucius had dreamed of, the politics of ancient times? It was not party politics, but the concentration of power in a good and wise king, such as King Wen or King Wu of Zhou. The monarchal ideal was realized by the king's teachings—in other words, rule by sage-kings. How far had things gone astray in the present court? The king should be trusted and power should be given to him. If the king's authority was stripped to a nominal level, then politics degenerated into condemnation, conspiracy, and ugly fighting over slices of the pie. Under such circumstances, how could the court look after the people and repel foreign enemies?

"To those who shared the Southerners' philosophy, the Old Doctrine faction, the students of Song Shi-yol, were unpardonable, treacherous civil servants who denied any fundamental difference between the king and the literati in terms of the knowledge of rites. They were extremists who believed in the universality of Neo-Confucianism, and who openly interfered in the affairs of the royal family, both large and small. On the other hand, to the Old Doctrine faction, the Southerners were fawning servants who flattered the king, uncivilized footmen who failed to heed the impartial opinions of the court officials, deceptive sycophants who neglected to ask questions even when they were aware of the king's mistakes. After all, according to the Old Doctrine faction, the literati must be wary of royal dictatorship and must lead the king to a fair consensus with the literati outside the government.

"The Reversal of Situation of 1689 was the watershed event in the intellectual history of the dynasty's middle period. It revealed the uncompromising conflict between the Southerners and the Old Doctrine faction, a conflict between original Confucianism and Neo-Confucianism.

"The Reversal of Situation of 1689 was followed by the Revolt of Yi In-jwa.

"In the forty-third year of King Sukchong's reign, the question of the king's successor arose. By that time Queen Inhyon had been reinstated and Concubine Chang executed. To the Old Doctrine faction, who had suffered a bloodbath on the concubine's account, Chang was the consummate witch, an evil creature without precedent. They all agreed that the son of such a witch should not be allowed to ascend to the throne.

"They supported Prince Yoning (later King Yongjo) instead of the crown prince (later King Kyongjong), who was the son of Concubine Chang. The crown prince was gentle and bright, but he was often sick and had not been successful in producing a son even though he was almost thirty. King Sukchong, concerned about the crown prince's future, preemptively attacked the Old Doctrine in what was known as the Exclusive Interview of 1716.

"The king sent off the scribes for historical records and dismissed the ministers, then proceeded to privately interview Yi I-myong, an Old Doctrine elder. He began by asking Yi if Prince Yoning should replace the crown prince. Yi was taken by surprise and lacked the courage to say it was a reasonable idea. He tried to hedge by saying it did not seem humane to discard a crown prince of almost thirty years. King Sukchong immediately agreed with him wholeheartedly, then announced that the entire court accepted Yi's willingness to confirm the crown prince as his successor. He even asked Yi to keep a solicitous eye on the crown prince in the future.

Finally, he restored honor to the descendants of Crown Prince Sohyon (King Hyojong's brother), who had been ordered to take poison as a result of the accusations of the Old Doctrine faction (called the Westerners back then). Thus the king opened a way for the crown prince to adopt an heir from among the descendants of Crown Prince Sohyon.

"Subsequent to King Sukchong's dedicated efforts, the crown prince succeeded him and became King Kyongjong.

"The Old Doctrine faction was shaken by this critical development, and many thought the nightmare of 1689 was recurring.

"Greatly alarmed, Old Doctrine members remonstrated with the king, who had been on the throne less than a month, arguing that Prince Yoning should be designated the successor with due haste. The king, who loved his younger brother dearly, assented, decreeing Prince Yoning as the crown prince; but the Old Doctrine faction was not to be satisfied. They demanded, after only two months, that since the king was not in good health, the crown prince should rule the country as regent in his stead. This was equivalent to suggesting that the king abdicate.

"Then . . . a man named Kim Il-kyong emerged."

At this point in his tale, Chong Yag-yong sighed and glanced at In-mong. In-mong smiled awkwardly and lowered his head.

A-gye Kim Il-kyong, of the Young Doctrine faction, was a figure about whom there was little agreement, even within his own faction. Had he been a hero or a villain? There were people such as Chong Yag-yong, who despised him as a conniving, relentless power monger, as well as those, such as In-mong, who admired him as a civil servant whose loyalty would be rare in any age. A few years earlier, In-mong and Chong had argued heatedly over this historical figure. After they finished dinner, the topic had somehow drifted to events during King Kyongjong's reign. They had become angry enough with each other to consider severing their friendship. Now both men were recalling that episode.

While they were still pouring each other drinks and enjoying themselves. In-mong had asked, "Yi In-jwa's revolt had its roots in King Kyongjong's reign, didn't it?"

"Certainly. This is because there was so much bloodshed during that period. The mistake of one man, Kim Il-kyong, hamstrung the freedom of the Young Doctrine faction and the Southerners."

In-mong's face had stiffened. Chong was well aware of In-mong's temperament and his thoughts on the subject, but he didn't back down. "You have expressed a different opinion of him, but if only he had desisted from his merciless and fatal imprisonments!"

"How can you say that?" In-mong asked. "The nation can be a nation only when there is loyalty between the king and his subjects. The king is king and subjects are subjects, no matter what. What did Teacher Kim Il-kyong do wrong? Think of the Old Doctrine faction in those days. They were subjects, but they interfered with the royal succession—it was insolent through and through. Did they not attempt to intimidate the nation's patriarch into abdicating, almost as he soon as he had ascended? The new king had just been announced to the Royal Ancestral Shrine when mountains of wicked memorials demanding his abdication began to appear daily. No one had the courage to prostrate himself before the king or speak honestly. Finally Kim Il-kyong, the sixth royal secretary, boldly stood up, approached the king, and pleaded with him in tears. Kim was almost sixty years old and ill, but he voiced his thoughts, punished those with evil motives, and prevented a crisis that would have shaken the dynasty and toppled the court. How can you disparage his actions, saying they were merciless and based on private vengeance? You sound like some feeble woman."

"And how can you view the matter so narrowly?" Chang asked. Confucius said in the *Analects* that a person's faults depend on his political party, and by looking at his faults one can judge his character. Since the time our government was divided into factions, people born into the Southerners faction see and hear only one viewpoint, and people born into the Old Doctrine faction are just the same. What the other factions do is characterized as evil, even when their goodness is apparent to anyone. On the other hand, people consider their own faction's actions good, even when its wickedness is obvious. Since fathers teach their sons and older brothers guide younger brothers, these distorted views are handed down to each new generation. So how can there be an end to the fighting? Lift your eyes beyond the narrow vision of your faction and reflect on benevolence. You know that those who are removed from benevolence are in utter conflict with the ways of Heaven. How, then, can anyone say that Kim Il-kyong did the right thing by wiping the four celebrated clans from the face of the earth? Even babies at the breast were slaughtered!"

"That is an erroneous notion, Teacher. Governance depends on the mood of the times; can one strive to be benevolent when it comes to eliminating traitors? Confucius said in *Gongyang Commentary on the Spring and Autumn Annals* that when a person serving a king begins to have other ambitions, he should lose his head. If Kim Il-kyong had not killed each and every one of the four major ministers of the Old Doctrine faction and exterminated their paternal and maternal families' seed as well as that of their wives' families, the people and the nation would have turned rebellious and the result would have been ruinous. The course of action caused great sadness, but there was no other way. Teacher Kim attacked those shameless traitors and the following year he executed the remaining 170 co-conspirators. This was how he purified the court. If not for him, those corrupt deceivers would not have known that Heaven existed above them."

Chong had been listening closely. "Then how do you explain the facts that such a loyal servant died a miserable death from torture and that even now, eighty years later, he is considered a traitor? You mistrust the judgment of history."

"*Ai* . . . I cannot talk with you. Eighty years? Unbending loyalty endures a hundred generations. How can you make such frivolous statements?"

In-mong had exploded in youthful passion and rushed out of the room like a raging fire. Since then the two men had guarded their words and avoided sensitive topics. This time was no different. Chong made no further mention of Kim Il-kyong and proceeded directly to an account of the Revolt of Yi In-jwa.

"In 1724, only four years after his ascent, King Kyongjong died a sudden death.

"Shim Yu-hyon, the younger brother of Queen Shim, was present at the king's deathbed, and he later testified that the king had been poisoned: Unnaturally dark blood had poured out of the king's nine orifices and his face had turned black. Shim's words spawned endless waves of fury.

"As soon as King Yongjo took the throne, leaflets about the former king's death appeared all over the country and a rebellious army openly recruited men in Chungchong and Pyong-an provinces. Astonished, King Yongjo issued an emergency decree to the Three Army Commands to protect the capital. He tried to assuage the masses by driving out the Old Doctrine faction, which had become the target of the people's hatred, in favor of the Young Doctrine faction. This became known to history as the Reversal of the Situation of 1727. The next year, in the third month of the fourth year of King Yongjo's reign, Young Doctrine men and Southerners joined forces to occupy Chongju Fortress and the revolt began.

"This was the Revolt of Yi In-jwa.

"The occupying forces, announcing that they sought revenge for the death of their previous patriarch, demanded the extermination of the traitors. They placed King Kyongjong's spirit tablet in their barracks, and the entire army paid its respects morning and evening with ritual wailing. The rebels sent a manifesto to every part of the country, entreating the people to rise up with them as a righteous army to annul the ascent of King Yongjo and to elevate Prince Milpung to the throne. The prince was the great-grandson of

Prince Sohyon, who had been expected to be adopted as the crown prince by King Kyongjong. In the southeastern region, Kochang, Anum, Hapchon, Hamyang, and Sangju in Kyongsang Province and Taein in Cholla Province joined; in the north, Yi Sa-song, the military commander of Pyongan Province, rose up with an army; in Seoul, Nam Tae-jing, the Royal Guards commandant in charge of Changdok Palace, joined as well.

"The rebels advanced north from Chongju by way of Mokchon, Chongan, and Chinchon, and at Ansong they clashed with the government army led by Oh Myong-hang, the minister of war. On the twenty-fourth day of the third month after a violent battle that lasted a day and a night, the rebels were completely defeated. The government army advanced with amazing spirit and eradicated the remnants of the revolutionary army in Kochang. The revolt was over.

"But the shock waves were enormous," Chong continued. "The rebels' manifesto had spread all over the country, and it contained a detailed account of the embarrassing incidents surrounding the death of King Kyongjong and the ascent of King Yongjo. It also described why King Sukchong protected the crown prince, although his mother was Concubine Chang, and why he had not taken a liking to Prince Yoning. These matters continued to burden King Yongjo until his death at eighty."

Chong had measured his words all during his account of the Revolt of Yi In-jwa. After all, King Yongjo was the grandfather of His Majesty, whom both In-mong and Chong venerated.

"King Sukchong disliked King Yongjo," Chong went on, "but not simply because the woman Choe who gave birth to his son was a laundress for court ladies. King Sukchong had thought she was a virgin, but after he had slept with her he learned she had been recently widowed. The issue of her origins aside, it was unprecedented that a widow had become a king's concubine.

"Yi In-jwa's followers argued that King Yongjo was not King Sukchong's son, but rather the seed of the laundress's former husband. The lie was groundless, considering the timing of Choe's arrival at the court, but the rumors about his mother had dealt King Yongjo a wound to his heart that was never to heal.

"At any rate, the revolt was suppressed and the Old Doctrine faction returned to power.

"Kim Il-kyong, who had resisted the Old Doctrine faction's plot to switch sovereigns, was first banished and then put to death by poison, along with his son. The honor of the four ministers who had died during King Kyongjong's reign was restored. For the next twenty years, members of the Old Doctrine faction considered themselves the most loyal of the servants who had brought

King Yongjo to the throne. These were, for them, triumphant years.

"In an effort to check and balance the power of the Old Doctrine faction, King Yongjo strove to implement a policy of grand harmony by employing people regardless of their affiliation, but the strategy proved ineffective. In short, the policy ended up reinforcing the tyranny of the Old Doctrine faction. Whenever the king tried to curb their power, the Old Doctrine members cornered him by arguing that they were the ones who had supported him at the time of his ascent, and if not for them no one would have provided a defense against the false accusations about King Kyongjong's death.

"This was the so-called Debt of Gratitude of Shin-Im — 'Shin' indicating the year of King Kyongjong's ascent and 'Im' indicating the following year.

"Who was it, the Old Doctrine members had asked rhetorically, that had protected King Yongjo in the first and the second year of King Kyongjong's ascent, braving persecution so that he could be king today? If the traitors had not been distinguished from the loyal servants, what defense would have been possible against the false charges of King Kyongjong's death, so widely spread by the rebels? To justify the succession of King Yongjo, they reasoned, Young Doctrine members and Southerners who had disseminated rumors about the former king's death should be put to death. Where was the legitimacy in a policy of grand harmony? How could His Majesty even conceive such a naive plan?

"But in 1749, the twenty-fifth year of King Yongjo's reign, the Old Doctrine faction suddenly realized that a formidable foe had emerged. The king proclaimed that the crown prince, posthumously called Sado, would rule the country as regent. The crown prince was truly fearless and open-minded, as well as determined," Chong said.

Listening to his teacher's words of longing, In-mong felt his eyes become moist with tears.

"What an outstanding man Sado had been!" Chong went on, "governing the country as crown prince! His rule as regent began at the tender age of fourteen, but then he didn't hesitate to storm at Kim Chae-ro, chief state councilor. He exhibited a strong sense of filial piety from an early age, and the king trusted him fully. It was said that if he heard one thing he grasped the meaning of ten things; he was that intelligent.

"The Old Doctrine faction set a trap: they falsely accused the crown prince and had him killed. They then fabricated fantastic lies about him and spread them among the people. They claimed that he possessed superhuman strength, that he was prone to violence, that he was insane. He killed court ladies and eunuchs at will, and when the king could tolerate this behavior no longer, he had him incarcerated in a rice chest and left him there to die."

In-mong shuddered with furious hatred as he reflected on those horrible lies. It was like killing the dead all over again. If no one ever corrected this misinformation, who would know the virtues of the dead crown prince?

Chong resumed his story. "A year before the current king took the throne, the documents concerning the death of the crown prince in the rice chest in 1762, which had been kept for fifteen years, had all been burned. Still, the Old Doctrine people were not satisfied; they proceeded to expunge each and every brush stroke in the official documents, including the *Records of the Royal Secretariat*, that had anything to do with Sado's death. Now where were the texts that could attest to the true character of the crown prince?"

Large teardrops flowed from In-mong's eyes.

"You must be aware of the rumors spread in the streets about the crown prince's death," said Chong. "When I think of the miserable lies they made up, I am ashamed to be alive. They said that the crown prince's mental illness worsened around the sixth month of the thirtieth year of King Yongjo's reign, in 1754, and that he began to behave irrationally. But the crown prince handled all manners of national affairs for thirteen years in his father's stead, from the twenty-fifth year to the thirty-eighth year of the reign. What is the court after all? Would the court have allowed an insane person to govern the country? From the moment he rises in the morning to the hour he goes to bed, the regent's schedule is crammed with official duties. If his insanity had lasted that long, his erratic behavior must have been recorded incidentally in documents about lectures, conferences on personnel, or interviews with his administrators. On the contrary, though, all of his statements set down in such documents are wise and intelligent."

"Of course, about that there is no dispute." Chong's eyes, like In-mong's, were bright with heartfelt longing. "He was too intelligent; that was the crown prince's problem.

"As soon as he started his regency he knew instinctively that the Debt of Gratitude of Shin-Im had bound his father to the Old Doctrine faction. The crown prince reacted by criticizing the Old Doctrine's unbridled tyranny and by absolutely refusing to allow political revenge to be taken on the Young Doctrine faction or the Southerners faction. Gradually, he began to take a critical stance toward his father's policy of grand harmony, which had resulted in the willy-nilly employment of moderates, thus increasing political confusion. The crown prince conceived a policy featuring a powerful king and administrators who believed in the creeds of their own factions.

"Designed to check established power while remaining faithful to the ideal described in the Great Plan, the Zhou part in the *Book of History*, the policy aimed at grand harmony and thereby the stability of royal power. Soon government officials, impressed by the crown prince's passion, gathered around him: Pak Mun-su of the Young Doctrine faction, who had suppressed the Revolt of Yi In-jwa and gained fame as a secret royal inspector; Chae Che-gong of the Southerners faction; Cho Hyon-myong of the Old Doctrine faction. The Old Doctrine faction split into the Principle group, which argued that the crown prince should not be allowed to do as he pleased, and the Expediency group, which admired the crown prince's outstanding abilities and character.

"The Old Doctrine faction could not hide their shock as they watched members of different factions gather under the wing of the crown prince, awaiting an opportunity for a comeback. They decided to alienate King Yongjo from the crown prince, who until then had been so close to his father. The two were said to sit together beside a single candle, reading books and talking long into the night.

"Kim Ku-ju and Hong Ke-hui mobilized subordinates in their party to make false accusations, claiming that the crown prince had failed to comprehend the utmost importance of the Debt of Gratitude of Shin-Im to the Old Doctrine faction. At first King Yongjo did not believe these groundless accusations, and he criticized their underlying designs. But constant raindrops drill a hole in a boulder: King Yongjo's ears were pummeled by a constant barrage of alleged abominations on the part of his son, and gradually he began to suspect the crown prince. The crown prince, having an open, incautious character, could not tolerate his father's suspicions, and animosity between father and son grew to threatening proportions.

"Finally, on the day of the full moon in the fifth month of the thirty-eighth year (1762), the crown prince was brought to his furious father and was caged in a rice chest in the scorching heat of midsummer. The crown prince, screaming and wailing from hunger, thirst, and the steamy heat for six days, breathed his last on the twenty-first day. He was only twenty-eight.

"But the falsity of the charges against the crown prince could not be concealed forever. In less than a year's time, King Yongjo discovered the truth. How can one describe the bitterness of a father who, deceived by malicious advisers, had killed his own innocent son? King Yongjo's sorrow for his son's wrongful death peaked in 1764, when a tomb was built for his son."

It was after all this, In-mong knew, that the incident of the tale of the metal-bound coffer finally took place. Few people had witnessed the incident, and now for the first time, In-mong would hear the story.

"In the ninth month of that year . . . it was a dark autumn night," said Chong. "The king sent away his secretaries, scribes, and eunuchs, and had an interview alone with Pon-am, Chae Che-gong. The king entrusted to him a poem about how he mourned the crown prince. He then dictated his motivations for writing the poem. He instructed Pon-am to keep the poem and the document secret until the son of the late crown prince ascended to the throne. In this, he was following the example of the old tale of the Duke of Zhou, as recorded in the tale of the metal latch section of the Zhou part of the *Book of History*."

"That would have been thirty-six years ago. So what happened to the poem and the accompanying document?" asked In-mong.

"The secret was well kept for almost thirty years. Then, around the sixth month of 1793, certain things happened that provoked Teacher Chae." Chong was referring here to the conflicts following the Commercial Equalization Act of 1791.

"Around that time, Kim Chong-su of the Principle group resigned from his post as third state councilor in order to properly mourn his mother. With the post of chief state councilor also vacant, it was left to Chae Che-gong of the Southerners faction to single-handedly lead the court officials. In the autumn of 1790, goods were so scarce in the walled capital that people could not get rice and fruit for the Harvest Moon Festival. This was because Kim Mun-sun, the minister of taxation and a member of the Principle group, had been cornering the market and hoarding goods as a way to undermine Chae's administration. In the second month of the following year, Chae surprised his opponents by announcing a commercial policy, the Commercial Equalization Act of 1791, that abolished monopoly privileges for the merchants in the capital.

"For Chae, this was the manifestation of his long-held belief that national wealth should be developed by encouraging commerce and industry. In response, criticism and harassment from the conservative Old Doctrine faction grew intolerably strong. Chae Che-gong left Seoul on the pretext of supervising the construction of Hwasong Fortress, and while at Hwasong, he received a royal edict appointing him chief state councilor.

"Had the time finally come? Chae thought so. He hosted a memorial service for Crown Prince Sado at Hwasong Fortress. And for the occasion he wrote the famous memorial urging the king that the time had come to tell the previous king's tale of the metal-bound coffer, and that the enemies of the late crown prince should be eliminated, one and all. This was the Memorial from Hwasong in Appreciation of Receiving the Post of Chief State Councilor.

"It wreaked havoc in the court," Chong explained. "You may not be familiar with the details, because you were in exile at Yongwol at the time. State Councilors Kim Chong-su and Shim Hwan-ji prostrated themselves in the Royal Library courtyard day in and day out, entreating the king to take the head of Chae Che-gong. His Majesty anguished over the situation. But the incident came to a sudden end. On the fourth night after the arrival of the memorial, His Majesty summoned Kim Chong-su, Shim Hwan-ji, and Chae Che-gong. No one knows what he said, and the three men kept silent about the interview. The curious thing is . . . while I was going through Teacher Pon-am's writings after his death last year, I happened to see a secret letter he had written to some leading scholars in the southern region. In the letter I was surprised to find the poem that is part of the previous king's tale of the metal-bound coffer, together with the document he had dictated. The poem is called 'The Song of the Blood-stained Hemp and the Mourning Staff,' and it tells of how he misses the crown prince's filial piety and how he laments his death."

In-mong was incredulous. "You mean to say he revealed the poem and related documents, which the previous king had entrusted to him, to some southern scholars? I can't believe he would do anything of the sort."

"Well, no," answered Chong. "There must have been some reason we don't know of. Something must have happened that night when the three state councilors were summoned to His Majesty."

"What do you mean by 'some reason we don't know of'?"

"I think that evening His Majesty showed them the poem and—I am reluctant to use the expression, may His Majesty pardon me—he seems to have threatened the two state councilors of the Old Doctrine faction. Teacher Pon-am thought the poem was already in circulation among the Old Doctrine faction, and perhaps he thought he should let the Southerners, his colleagues in the southeast region, know about it."

"A threat? . . . "In-mong was puzzled.

"Think of the import of the tale of the metal-bound coffer for a minute. The king gave his own poem to Teacher Pon-am in the fashion of the Duke of Zhou. Didn't an anonymous scribe record that the Duke of Zhou had wished to sacrifice his life for King Wu? And was that record not kept in a metal-bound coffer for posterity? So the most important thing is the previous king's confession about Crown Prince Sado's death in 1762, which Teacher Pon-am had recorded. Now it is the nature of poetry that it expresses reality through figures of speech and allusions; it doesn't allow for detailed explanation. But a dictated record is different. It is prose, and it is possible that the document dictated to Teacher Pon-am makes concrete mention of the perpetrators. Especially now, since all the official documents have been burned, it is the only evidence concerning what happened in 1762. I am sure that His Majesty showed only the poem to the state councilors and then threatened them with drastic action—the publication of decisive documentation."

"Then . . . what is 'The Song of the Blood-Stained Hemp and the

Mourning Staff'?"

"The content of that poem is. . . . Shall I recite it? It is so short and unusual that I still remember it.

> Mourning clothes soaked in blood, mourning clothes soaked in blood
> The mourning staff, the mourning staff, whose was it?
> If it were kept for a thousand years in a metal-bound coffer
> I would feel regret wherever rites are held in this world.

That is all."

"I am sorry to say this . . . but it sounds like a shaman's chant. And what on earth is the meaning of this riddle?"

"It refers to the fateful events that provoked the king to execute the crown prince. That spring the relationship between father and son couldn't have been worse. One day the king heard from his beloved concubine Mun that the crown prince had prepared a make-believe mourning nook to pray for his father's death. Furious, the king sent his night-duty soldiers to search the crown prince's quarters. Believe it or not, in his bedroom they found mourning clothes and the staff the head mourner holds during the ancestral rite. It was then that the king decided on the horrible execution."

"It is true, then, that the crown prince actually committed this unforgivable sin?"

"Not at all! It was a cunning fabrication. The mourning clothes and the staff were not for his father. They were the ones used during the mourning period in 1757 for Queen Chongsong, King Yongjo's principal queen. She had loved the crown prince with the greatest affection and care, even though he was not her son. She stood by him in the face of every accusation brought against him by the Old Doctrine faction. When such a person dies, how does one express sorrow? Wasn't the crown prince born with filial piety bestowed by Heaven? During the national funeral he could not tear himself away from the casket. Nobody was unmoved by his heartfelt loss. He cried and wailed until his clothes were soaked with his tears.

"After the death of Queen Chongsong, the women remaining in the court were all of the Principle group of the Old Doctrine. Queen Chongsun, daughter of that malignancy Kim Han-gu, became the principal queen. And that sniveling woman Hong of Hyegyong Palace betrayed every little weakness of the crown prince—her own husband, mind you!—to those conspiring relatives of hers. It is no wonder that His Majesty, as soon as he took the throne, slaughtered all of his own mother's family save for one cousin to perform the ancestral memorial services for the family.

"With things in this state, you can imagine how the crown prince missed the late queen. When the mourning period was over, he could not bring himself to part with the tear-stained mourning clothes and staff. They should have been burned or buried, but he kept them as a tearful means of sustenance for whenever he was wrongfully accused. Evil creatures from inside and out joined forces to create the impression of a crime, and even a superior king could not help being deceived. The poem was written after the king realized the truth. He was so shocked and bitter that he tore his clothes and wept while writing it."

"Ah! So that is the story."

At that very moment they heard the approach of running footsteps.

"Librarian, sir! Librarian, sir! His Majesty is summoning you."

The two men tidied their robes and rushed out.

It was Chae-dong, the chamber keeper of the library. "A eunuch from the Main Hall delivered a message. His Majesty commands you to come directly with the material he directed you to bring."

"Where is His Majesty?"

"In Huijong Hall, sir."

"Very well."

Finally.

In-mong felt his hair stand on end. Brushing dust from his robe, he looked at Chong Yag-yong.

"What are you going to do if His Majesty asks you about *Humble Thoughts on the Book of Odes*?" Chong asked with a look of foreboding.

"What can I do? If we Southerners were to be compared with trees, we would be but vines, weakly rooted and easily plucked. There is no wall to support us. We exist in a tiny plot only under the munificence of His Majesty. Whatever happens to me, I cannot report anything but the truth. I will tell His Majesty everything, and follow his orders. If he punishes me, I will accept it gladly."

"That is most brave of you!"

"And you, Teacher, you will . . ."

"I will go and see Hyon Sung-hon. I-suk may have said something to him."

"Please do so."

"To-won, . . . have you heard from your estranged wife?"

"Ah, no. She used to come to see the children behind my back, but not for a few years now. Why do you ask?"

"No matter. How can we have leisurely talk about a thousand matters in one day? We will speak later."

"Well . . . then. I will take my leave, sir."

In-mong scooped snow from the flower garden in front of the building and cleaned his hands, then turned and briskly walked away. Chong, following him with his eyes, tsk-tsked in spite of himself.

Chong Yag-yong was well versed in the *Book of Changes*. He criticized artifices steeped in mysticism, but he was the very person who had revived the old-style *Book of Changes*, based on the ancient Chinese numerology of Yin-Yang and the Five Elements Theory. Equipped with such academic knowledge, he had observed glories and declines, fortunes and disasters, and longevity in the court. He had developed a talent for discerning people's fates through their physiognomies.

According to his observations, In-mong's face contained some frighteningly unpropitious elements. His features were strong, but his nose was sharp and fleshless, which showed that he would never attain the authority that comes with power. His chin was not round, which indicated that his life would end in defeat and failure. He looked handsome, but the impression of his face as a whole was weak. The body concealed by the loose robe must be slight, too. A thin, delicate body, fit for nothing but the act of reading.

"Should I have told him about his wife?" Chong asked himself.

The woman who had been released that morning, her face pitiable beyond description: At first Chong had not recognized that face, which he had seen only one time at In-mong's house seven years earlier. How could he have guessed that the dying woman with the dirty face and disheveled hair was In-mong's wife?

He thought about what he knew of In-mong's background. His hometown was Andong. His family must have been quite well off, Chong Yag-yong thought, for they sent him to Seoul at an early age, and later they married him into the Yun family of Haenam, who lived in Seoul. This marriage must have been a reflection of In-mong's family's ambition, perhaps passed from generation to generation, to have the sons advance in the world; but something had happened to douse the clan's expectations. In-mong's wife's family, tainted by Western Learning, had become Catholics. This had happened after In-mong's wife gave birth to two sons. Chong had heard rumors that In-mong had banished his wife in fury.

Until then, they had been a loving couple, or so he had heard. There was an old saying that you shouldn't marry your daughter to a loyal civil servant, and old sayings were never wrong. The husband could follow the noble cause of abiding by the law of the nation, but the wife lost a pillar to lean on.

In Chong Yag-yong's eyes, In-mong was a narrow and abrupt person in both words and action. He would not attend to what the world said, instead clinging single-mindedly to his loyalty to the king. He trusted only his heart and tried to walk a straight line, but society shunned him and would not trust him.

It was true: In-mong had ungenerously banished his wife to prove his own innocence, but this had not spared him from rumors that he was a Catholic. In 1795, the year he banished his wife, the head of her family was executed and their wealth was confiscated, on the charge that they had helped Father Zhou Wenmo escape. In-mong was then investigated by the State Tribunal on suspicion of being a Catholic. What a rough path In-mong had been traveling, Chong thought, as he walked to the administration chamber to look for someone who knew where Hyon Sung-hon lived.

* * *

At that time, Hyon Sung-hon was at his house in Chongga, near the Constabulary on the Left. It was well past *shinshi*. He had just waked from a leisurely nap he had begun upon returning from the palace. He was fixing his loosened shirt ties and straightening his horsehair headband when his daughter-in-law came in with a small meal tray.

She had married into his family only the month before.

Pollack and egg drop soup, *kimchi*, pickled radish cubes, and the special dish of the day—boiled conch with soy sauce seasoning. This painstaking tray made the father-in-law feel childishly happy and at the same time guilty. The rice was freshly cooked, steam wafted up from the bowl.

Sung-hon imagined the young woman running tirelessly to the men's quarters to see if her father-in-law had waked from his long nap. Picking up his spoon, he stole a glance at her face.

"Little one, you don't get enough sleep, do you?"

"It is all right, sir."

"We are not a fussy *yangban* family, so you needn't perform the morning and night greetings any more. Particularly at dawn, when you have to be out in the kitchen and then clean the house—I can't imagine it's easy to wash, change into a good outfit, and make a formal greeting to your parents-in-law before light. As for me, I spend many nights like last night at the palace. So really, etiquette is not important—in fact it's a bother. Starting tomorrow, you have yourself a nice, sound sleep until *myoshi*."

"Oh, no, I couldn't."

"What do you mean, no? Your face has become so thin and it's not even been a month. Your parents will blame us, eh? . . . I will tell Grandma later."

The daughter-in-law was silent.

"Where is your husband?"

"At the elder uncle's house, sir. He went to help them with the expansion of the servants' quarters."

"Again? They did that only last year. It looks as if their fortune is rising like a fire."

His son had been visiting Sung-hon's brother, the one who had opened an herb clinic, to learn medicine. Sung-hon heard that his brother's house in Pirun-dong was crammed to the doorway with patients from dawn to dusk. Sung-hon squinted as he slurped his soup, thinking of his brother's house. Then he caught sight of his daughter-in-law sitting in the far corner and he scolded her gently.

"Why are you watching me? You may go about your business. There's no need for a daughter-in-law to keep an eye on an elder while he's eating. Our house doesn't abide by such empty formalities, didn't I tell you?"

"Yes, sir." She stepped aside, head bowed, and disappeared.

A new bride was expected to wear a yellow blouse and red skirt for one year and to whiten her face with face powder softened in water. This new child was the apple of his eye—a common sentiment, he realized—but he felt so sorry for her.

However well one raised them, daughters were supposed to be a punishment. But was it their fault that they were born female? A daughter left her family to go to a stranger's house and serve his parents. For this reason she could never repay what her parents had done for her.

Sung-hon emptied a big bowl of rice, pushed away the tray, and picked up his long pipe. His daughter-in-law returned to serve him a bowl of warm rice-boiled water and to remove the tray. She noticed the pipe and, shuffling closer on her knees, filled it with tobacco and lit it for him. Smoking left his nose with a pleasant sting, but desolate thoughts crept into his mind.

Now that he had a daughter-in-law, wasn't it time for him to retire from his trifling work?

What glory could he see at his age, working at the palace? If he practiced acupuncture at his brother's house, he wouldn't have to worry about food, or anything else for that matter. Learned people had more problems, or so the saying went. The cause of it all was that he had studied literature a bit more than his brothers. Around the age of thirty, he had become absorbed with Chinese Tang poems and had frequented a poetry reading group called the Jade Valley Poetry Society, whose members came from the Chungin class. There he had caught the eye of Yi Ho-min, the sixth state councilor and the society's sponsor. State Councilor Yi had been instrumental in securing Sung-hon's position at the library. Now more than ten years had passed.

Of course, it had been exciting, and he had felt a sense of accomplishment too. He had seen His Majesty, although from a distance, and he felt grateful that in general he had been treated well by ministers, writers, and scholars. But . . . this morning's incident made him feel like throwing up his meal.

Involvement in such a thing could easily lead to the abbreviation of your allotted life span, Sung-hon thought, squinting at the smoke filling the room. If he had known that the matter would become so complicated and serious, he would have discouraged Yi In-mong when he insisted on reporting Chang's death.

In fact, Sung-hon had wanted to dissuade him from the beginning. It was an unfortunate event, one that he wished had not happened. But since it had happened, one didn't have to abide by the rules so closely. They could have bribed the men at the Palace Guards Headquarters and had the corpse carried out through the back gate. After the body was taken home, they could have said he had died there after returning from work. Wasn't that simple enough? He had been concerned, though, about the eyes of others and rumors that might spread from the lips of the bereaved, so he had followed In-mong's directions without offering his advice.

The death had become a public matter, requiring a postmortem, which must have been finished by now. Yes, it had surely been finished . . . and yet it was no ordinary death. The vague premonition of disaster, looming over Sung-hon since that morning, had taken definite shape after he heard the dying man's words.

Two nights before, soldiers had burst into Chae I-suk's house, by order of the minister of punishments, and had arrested him and some others. Chae had died this morning after terrible torture and exposure to the cold. His death had looked like an accident — until Sung-hon heard his last words.

And early this morning, Chang Chong-o had been found dead of unknown causes at the Royal Library in the palace. At that time neither Sung-hon nor anyone else had known the cause of his death. But if one took Chae's death into account, then Chang Chong-o's passing must have been connected with some strange plot.

Ai, he lamented, ignorance is medicine and knowledge is illness.

Should he convey to Chong Yag-yong what he had heard from Chae I-suk? What if it went wrong from there? Chae I-suk, the one who had revealed the secret, had died. In the end, he was the only witness. . . . Sung-hon pictured in his mind the tortures inflicted to draw out confessions: burning the flesh with a flatiron, crunching every leg joint with a press. He had seen those horrid instruments of torture at the jail. Ugh. Just thinking of them . . .

his blood flowed to his head, he felt a stifling sensation, and his teeth clattered like an alarm bell.

Chae I-suk had mistaken him for Chong Yag-yong . . . so it was only ethical to tell Chong . . . Third Minister Chong was a good man.

Here Sung-hon checked himself. There was no man in this world who was good to the end. Actually, there were only two kinds of good people: the dead and the unborn. The rest were a headache, for no one knew what kind of demons would attach themselves to a man, or when they would do so.

Loyalty and treachery? Right and wrong?

Aigo, he didn't have an ounce of intention to risk his life for such notions. Those questions were decided by others, people like the king and the *yangban*. He hoped they would make good decisions, but even if they made the wrong decision, he would continue to stand on the safe side, forever.

When he was young, it had been his habit to childishly criticize such attitudes; but now he wouldn't get involved, not even if someone prodded him with academic ideas about good versus evil or the noble cause versus the wrong cause. He had arrived at an age when he realized that the Way of Human Life was loftier and more practical than mere wordplay. In other words, he was an adult in appearance and also in substance.

People strived to live responsibly whatever position they held.

How could different perople's feelings and hearts possibly be the same? What was goodness to one person could be an abomination to others. One couldn't deny that everyone wanted to lead a better life. Be humble, strive to live better, aid others with compassion and within the limit of one's power— this was the Way of Human Life.

Sung-hon had now acquired this realization, a gift the years presented to those who lived long enough. Why make an effort to defend some principles, fuzzy though they might be, while attacking others? Others should be treated with appropriate concern and due politeness, as dictated by one's practical interests. What goes around comes around.

Wasn't that better?

Of course, there were occasionally people who disparaged this attitude and vehemently asserted their own beliefs, always pushing the academic noble cause. The *yangban*. They were the ones who believed that arguing their case should guarantee them a comfortable life.

How could those fantasy-wrought people not degenerate? Was it any wonder that they attached themselves to the mighty, were obsessed with factions, fawned and flattered the powerful, and spent the rest of their time scheming to live an easy life and fattening themselves? So removed were they from the reality of the Way of Human Life.

Their false rituals, empty morality, and studies of rites brimmed with hypocrisy. The essence of their life was vanity and pitiful narcissism — the narcissism of those who could never start a fight, but who announced triumph from under a quilt.

Suddenly, a noise came from the gate, a rude shaking. Then shouting, and then the quick approach of his daughter-in-law's footsteps.

"Father. Father. People from the Constabulary on the Left." Her thin voice trembled.

Surprised, Sung-hon jerked himself to his knees and slid open the door. His daughter-in-law's distraught face appeared below the shoe ledge.

"What? What business do they have in our house?"

"They are looking for you, Father."

Sung-hon grumbled. "How odd."

Sung-hon was only of Chungin, but his sense of etiquette was no different from a literati's. In particular, he was careful to appear presentable before receiving a guest. He hurriedly located his pale green coat, and put on his headgear.

Suddenly, a wave of fear washed over him; but he could hesitate no longer. Impatient shouting summoned him. He hastily stepped down from his room and ventured out to the servants' quarters. The gates had been flung open, and a tall, sturdy officer in blue uniform, sword in hand, stood in the courtyard glaring at Sung-hon. Two constables waited outside.

"What is the meaning of this?"

"Are you Clerk Hyon who works at the Royal Library?"

"Yes, but . . ."

The officer turned to his men and shouted, "Hey, you! Bind this rascal!"

Sung-hon winced. The two constables hurriedly approached and began to tie him up.

"What lawless behavior is this? What crime have I committed and why are you trifling with me?"

The officer thrust an arrest warrant under his nose: "Directive: Board of Personnel."

"You imbecile!" he roared, "Don't you realize the wrong you have committed? There is a message from the Palace Supply Office that you falsified an official seal to divert polished rice to the branch office in Kanghwa. Come with us and be quick about it. The high officials from the Military Command Headquarters have arrived to investigate you."

"Wha . . . what?"

Rice diverted to the branch office in Kanghwa? What wild notion was this? Sung-hon's mind went blank and he began to tremble like a man afflicted with malaria. Before he could protest, the muscular hand of one of the brawny constables yanked on the rope that bound Sung-hon and dragged him through the gate. His wife came running out of the women's quarters in her stocking feet.

"*Aigo*, sirs! What is the meaning of this violence! What in heaven's name has my husband done?"

She grabbed the officer's sleeve, her eyes as wide as a rabbit's. Her presence helped Sung-hon to gather his thoughts. Seizing the opportunity, he hurriedly whispered in her ear: He didn't know what this was all about, so she should inform everyone: the sixth state councilor, whose residence was in Chae-dong; his elder brother; and Librarian Yi, whose residence was in Namsan-gol.

Then he was dragged out to the alley, and thence to the Constabulary on the Left, only a stone's throw from his home.

The constabulary was located on the edge of Chongsonbang in Chongga, in the area commonly called "Midtown." Everyone in the neighborhood had some connection with government officials, and Sung-hon had never heard of any of his neighbors being arrested by constabulary officials. Distraught though he was, he felt his face burn with shame at the thought that his neighbors might witness this sudden humiliation.

The constables pushed aside his wife and daughter-in-law, who had been clinging to them and wailing as if the sky had fallen, then shut the gate. They took Sung-hon directly to the administration building, and when he saw beneath an awning a plaque reading "Office of Military Affairs," he began to feel something was amiss. If it were thought that he had swindled rice from the Palace Supply Office, he should have been taken to the State Tribunal or the Board of Punishments. Why was he at the Constabulary on the Left, where common burglars were taken? It didn't make sense.

No sooner had these thoughts occurred to him than a hexagonal club was swung down on his head. "You criminal! Where do you think you are? Why are you standing so proudly? Your eyes must be at the back of your head, not in front!" A kick landed in his belly. His old body could not stand this. He rolled on the ground and coughed profusely. At first he thought the violence was routine, a way to threaten the accused. But no, several constables spilled out of the building, flinging abusive remarks.

"Hey, look at this, a gentleman's coat! You're in good hands now."

"They say he's a Chungin and he lives in this neighborhood."

"You, a Chungin daring to wear a pale green gentleman's coat? That's like a horseshoe on a dog's paw. You scoundrel!"

Asking no questions, they clubbed him, kicked him, stomped on him, and crushed him. Blood flowed from Sung-hon's head and his coat was torn to rags.

"Mercy, oh mercy, someone help me!" His shriek was muffled by the bloody mess in his mouth.

Objects became blurry. He felt he was hovering above the path to the Other World. Because he had never harmed anyone and had never experienced anything particularly unpleasant, the abuse was all the more difficult to endure. Another kick jabbed deep into his neck.

Sung-hon gasped. His eyes rolled back, showing only the whites, and he began to lose consciousness.

Just then a high official sauntered out from the office. He wore a dark-blue civil servant's robe and his belt was embroidered with a cloud-crane design.

"You scoundrels! The ancient rules mandate that torture should be conducted only after an investigation. Who authorized you to thrash him as you please?"

The constables eyed one another, puzzled by this upbraiding. The official's garb and appearance indicated he was very highly placed, but his words were at odds with their superior's instructions.

Then, from behind the official there appeared a brawny man over six feet tall, dressed in a gentleman's coat and a wide-brimmed horsehair hat.

This second man was extraordinary. His eyes shone as if a rainbow would arch from them. A murderous look seemed to lurk within them, a look meant for anyone who stared at him. He was obviously a man of the martial arts. One arm placed against his chest held something long—perhaps five feet long—wrapped in a scarf. A Seven-Star Sword?

"You thugs! How dare you gawk? This elder is the minister of personnel."

The constables quickly bowed, awed by the cold, weighty ring of the man's voice. Slowly the realization dawned on them that the minister of personnel was the direct superior of the head of the Constabulary on the Left. Their backs bent farther, realizing that they could be in hot water. Yes, the man on the veranda was none other than So Yong-su.

Observing the constables' newfound deference, So asked in a mild voice, "Is he dead?"

"No, Your Excellency. He is merely faking. We would not kill a suspect without permission."

"Revive him and bring him in."

"Sir? He is covered with dirt."

The martial artist intervened. "Just do what you're told. No more mindless babbling from you!"

"Damn! You yourself look like someone with a bandit's past," the constables silently retorted. Each tried to recall whether if he had had an unpropitious dream the night before—something that might explain the minister of personnel's unexpected appearance.

The men muttered under their breath, their mouths pouting as big as South Mountain; but what choice did they have? A gourd of cold water was produced and one of the constables poured it over Sung-hon's face. Sung-hon's stiff body quaked and a low moan escaped his lips. The men seized Sung-hon roughly by his arms and legs, carried him onto the veranda, and deposited him in front of the large room out of which the minister had come.

The tall official called out, and three men in similar outfits and sideburns came out of the room. The tall man signaled to them with his eyes, and they carried Sung-hon into the room.

So Yong-su looked at the constables. "Good. Now you may go. Forbid anyone to come near."

"Yes, yes, sir."

Sung-hon opened his eyes, suddenly aware that it was eerily silent. His body felt as limp as a water-drenched wad of cotton.

The room in which he found himself, more than ten long paces from one end to the other, was very dark. The walls were lined with layer upon layer of drapes, perhaps to prevent a draft, and there were wall screens all around. The window was covered by a dark gray cloth embroidered with black designs. The ceiling was also draped. In this heavily insulated room, three men sat in total silence.

Sung-hon willed his drooping eyelids to stay open. He looked at the men.

The man sitting nearest him was Yi Cho-won, the minister of punishments. This was a surprise. Next to him was a white-haired general dressed in a military official's deep-blue robe and hat. Occupying the seat of honor was an old man in a jade silk gentleman's coat and an exquisite horsehair hat from Tongyong. His face was not visible against the light from the window, but Sung-hon could feel the man's penetrating gaze fixed on him.

Then the official who had saved him from the beating entered the room.

Only then did Sung-hon realize that this man was So Yong-su, the minister of personnel. He cocked his head to have a look at So Yong-su, then noticed four giants standing behind him. They were armed with long rods wrapped in cloth, and their eyes stared down at him with piercing intensity. Sung-hon sensed a deathly mood and shifted his gaze.

So Yong-su took a seat to the right of the minister of punishments.

One of the four tall men pulled Sung-hon to his feet.

Finally the minister of punishments craned his neck toward Sung-hon. "Are you Hyon Sung-hon, clerk at the Royal Library?"

"That is correct, sir."

"Is this a document you have composed?"

Documents sent between government offices were drafted by the clerks. Sung-hon approached the minister, almost crawling, trying to steady his trembling arms. The paper held an astounding message. "From the polished rice allotted by the Palace Supply Office for the use of the Royal Library, forty sacks are to be delivered to the branch office in Kanghwa Island as of the first day of the first lunar month. The Chief of the Horse Transportation Section of the Palace Supply Office is advised to transfer the above item to the clerk at the branch office in Kanghwa." The drafter's name was Sung-hon, and the document also bore the official seal of the director and the signature of the deputy director. The document was genuine in every respect.

The amazing thing was Sung-hon had never seen it before, let alone written it.

Yi Cho-won read the consternation on Sung-hon's face, but he remained stern. "There is more proof," he snapped, throwing a fist-sized object toward Sung-hon.

Sung-hon felt a shock wave, imagining it was a dead rat. The object was oval-shaped, partly earth-brown and party gray. One end was cut with a knife, revealing dense-looking flesh. It was light and not as hard as a rock, so perhaps it was some kind of a root, like a radish. Sung-hon had never seen such an object before.

"That potato was found on your desk in the library. Will you still pretend that you don't know about it?"

"Sir? This . . . this is a potato?"

"Aha! You deny it still?"

A chill went down Sung-hon's spine. He broke out in a cold sweat.

These events occurred in the first month of 1800, thirty years before the potato was introduced to Korea in a few select books, like *Notes and Musings on Myriad Topics by O-ju Yi Kyu-gyong*. Envoys had sometimes brought a bag of potatoes from Yanjing, China, but nobody considered the things edible. Not until almost one hundred and twenty years after that winter morning would potatoes be cultivated all over the country. Thus it was not surprising that Sung-hon did not recognize the one that had been thrown at him.

At that time, the potato was still a rarity, something grown in China and used to forge seals, because its oil had an ingredient similar to red sealing ink.

In forgery, the potato was first steamed and one end was sliced off. The flesh was then pressed to the seal of a document to absorb its red ink. Pressure was applied for about half the duration of a meal. Then, the potato was removed and placed over a lit candle until it became hot. When the image of the seal began to gather moisture, the potato was applied to a forged document and pressed for the same length of time as when extracting the seal. This method transferred the seal to the forged document, producing so authentic looking an image that no one would know the difference.

The moment Yi Cho-won had tossed him the potato, Sung-hon's teeth had started clattering. He now realized this was not a misunderstanding or a mistake but a trap that had been laid for him. But why? His head was a jumble of shock and fright. He felt he might explode in panic.

"It is now revealed in broad daylight, thanks to the report from the Palace Supply Office, that you have attempted to steal the Library's property by scheming with a clerk at Kanghwa. You must realize that the crime of forging an official seal by a government employee is punishable by decapitation."

"Minister, sir. Please give this matter more consideration. I have heard of the potato, but I have never seen one before, and have never seen or heard of this document. How can a thing like this . . . ?"

"Silence, you conniving scoundrel! The clerk at Kanghwa made a full confession. Do you think you will be able to extricate yourself at this point?"

"Who . . . who in heaven's name is this clerk you speak of? I implore you. Please let me see him. Who could . . . ? This inconceivable document . . ."

"Were he alive, would we lower ourselves to argue with you? The clerk who produced this document was thrashed to death yesterday during the investigation. You could not have committed corruption of this magnitude on your own. Who made you do it? Tell the truth!"

"Your Excellency, this accusation is false, sir."

"You rogue! Do you still deny it?" Yi shouted furiously, eyes bulging. "Look here, Chief Kim," he called to the general wearing the military hat. Sung-hon thought this must be Kim Chae-shin, the police chief. "It appears from this recalcitrant attitude that he will not confess easily. Please order your subordinates to prepare a rack and the leg-twisting board at the jail."

Sung-hon plunged into inarticulate despair.

"Yes, sir," said Chief Kim.

"One moment!" So Yong-su straightened himself. "Kyong-hon (Yi Cho-won's personal name) is impatient. . . . It will not be too late if the torture follows a detailed interrogation. Is it not strange that a person who composed a false document would leave his name there? Perhaps the dead clerk at

Kanghwa made a spurious confession. The customs of today have become so complex and heartless that it is difficult to accept people's words at face value. There are countless cases in which tricks have been played to incriminate innocent people. How can we say definitely that this man was not entrapped? Clerk Hyon, is that not the case?"

Sung-hon could not suppress his surging gratitude as he listened to So's gentle voice defending him. So Yong-su was like a Buddha one might encounter in hell's mountain of daggers and swords.

Sung-hon burst into tears. "That is the truth, sir. That is the truth. Unless this humble person has gone crazy, why would he have done something that would bring certain death?"

"Yes, yes. Those are my thoughts, too. But the minister of punishments mentioned that when he heard your name he was not surprised. We heard you are close to the undesirable elements of the Southerners faction. You went to see Chong Yag-yong and Chae I-suk at the Board of Punishments this morning, did you not? So, it would appear that your actions might have been instigated by those elements."

"Oh, no. That is not true, sir. I met Third Minister Chong for the first time today. I went there on an errand, and Minister Chae was in such critical condition that I took care of him briefly."

"Is that so? Then that is a different story. Chief Kim, Minister of Punishments! The Palace Supply Office is under my board, so I am responsible in this matter. I would like to speak with this man in the next room about the incident. Is that acceptable, Minister of Punishments?"

"As you prefer. But take care that you are not taken in by this rogue's shrewd deceptions."

So Yong-su supported Sung-hon, slid open the small doors to the side veranda, and escorted him into the next room. Sung-hon was deeply touched. Respect for the minister bubbled up inside him like boiling water. This minister had never seen him before, but he had grasped the situation at a glance and was attempting to save him, lowly person that he was. Was this not an exemplary person full of benevolence?

The side room was a small space of about twelve square yards, with no furniture except a clothes rack.

Sung-hon sat down in the corner and wept. "Your Excellency, looking down on this humble person with such grace and brightness will never be forgotten. Even in death, I will repay you. I will follow your orders, even if Your Excellency says to jump into a fire with a haystack strapped to my back."

"That is quite all right. It is nothing much." So Yong-su waved his hands in a gesture of self-deprecation, and sat down. "Try to think who could possibly have borne false witness against you. Oh, and. . . . " So's face had turned embarrassed and sorrowful. He heaved a long sigh.

Sung-hon gazed at the minister with anxious, wondering eyes.

So Yong-su continued, his words barely audible. "I did not tell the truth in the other room, for I am all too aware of the eyes and ears of the world. I was very close to Chae I-suk, despite our different affiliations. How is it possible . . . ? A friend who had such a bright future, dying after becoming a Catholic. . . ." Tears gathered in So's eyes.

Pangs of fiery emotion warmed Sung-hon's chest. They say exemplary people have exemplary friends, and indeed good people have good friends. By now Sung-hon completely trusted So.

"And by the way . . . did he leave any last words? For his wife or son? What did he say about his family? Did he not ask that someone look out for them? Is that not so?"

"Yes . . . I mean . . . that is. . . ." Something inexplicable told Sung-hon that he should never reveal his secret.

So Yong-su quickly read the hesitation. "Also his father was chief state councilor, and he was once third royal secretary, so he must have had something important to say about the nation. If that's the case, then I should be informed. Among all the civil servants, I am the only one who could appreciate Chae I-suk's loyalty. If you tell me, might it not be possible that you could be freed of this false allegation — if what you tell me is the right sort of thing? I believe I am a good judge of people. I see that you are not the kind of person who would accept a paltry amount for some foolish motive."

His last pronouncement stung. Sung-hon winced, looked at the minister, and leaned forward. "I will tell you, sir. I will tell you, sir. I realize that I can trust Your Excellency, sir."

So Yong-su nodded deeply. He pretended to be relaxed, offering an encouraging smile, but his face grew so tense that he failed to blink as he waited for Sung-hon's next words.

"Minister Chae was not completely conscious, and he thought that I was Third Minister Chong. He said that the distinction between loyalty and treachery would become clear in what he had to say and that His Majesty's life depended on it. He said it had something to do with 'the tale of the metal-bound coffer' and he asked that His Majesty be informed of the following: 'Under Your Majesty's strict orders, I have been safeguarding the original of the tale of the metal-bound coffer until recently, but my house has become unsafe recently and even my humble life could not be saved. Under these circumstances I felt I had to deliver it to some colleagues hiding in

117

Chonjinam, and for that purpose I gave it to someone trustworthy. My inability to abide by Your Majesty's sacred command cannot be atoned for even in the Other World.' And then . . ."

"And?" The veins on So's forehead bulged. He broke out in a cold sweat.

"He said, 'The husband-less Yun who was imprisoned with me knows the whereabouts of the original. His Majesty should search for that woman,' and . . ."

"Yun . . husband-less Yun. . . . And then what?"

"His last words were so feeble that it was hard to catch them entirely. 'The previous king's tale of the metal-bound coffer is the very thing we all knew. . . . I think I heard that much. He breathed his last."

"'The previous king's tale of the metal-bound coffer is the very thing we all knew' . . ."

"Yes, it was clear up to that point."

"Hmmm." With difficulty So Yong-su suppressed a groan. His face turned pale.

Sung-hon's heart wrenched. "Ah, it really is something grave," he thought. Fear for the future rushed in.

"It was good of you to tell me," So said, "I promise you will receive good treatment. But you realize that because of the magnitude of this matter, I cannot release you immediately. We will make a show of confining you in the jail and pretend to interrogate you, so even if you are cold and inconvenient, bear with it, won't you?"

"Thank you, Your Excellency." Sung-hon bowed several times.

So Yong-su stood up and was about to open the door, but some doubts remained.

"Did you . . . by any chance . . . tell Third Minister Chong about this?"

"Oh, no, no. There was no time, sir. Right after escorting the third minister to the palace, I left the palace, sir."

Sung-hon didn't see the cold sneer flitting on So's lips.

"That is very well. Excellent. I would advise you to keep silent. For the time being it will be best if only you and I know about it."

"Yes, yes. Of course, sir."

So Yong-su, as he closed the door, signaled with his eyes to the man with the sideburns to keep a good watch over the prisoner. When he reentered the large room, his face had transformed completely.

He sat with a grave, confused expression, bent in deference, and, creeping on his knees, approached the old man. This was none other than Shim Hwan-ji. The old man sat in the darkest shadows with his eyes closed, either dozing or deep in thought, leaning into the shadows. As So Yong-su approached him, Shim beckoned to the other two men, signalling that they too should come near.

Speaking in tense whispers, So repeated what Sung-hon had told him.

"What! Husband-less Yun?" exclaimed Yi Cho-won.

"Yes. She is still in jail, isn't she?"

"No, no. That Chong Yag-yong person made such a fuss that . . . I released her this morning, along with Chae's body."

"You did? Then you don't know where she is now?"

"Well, how can I . . ."

"Who is that woman? Why would Chae entrust such an important book to a mere woman? Is it not strange?"

"Well, I do not know. I concentrated my attention on . . . I did not look at the woman's investigation papers, but how can one trust such papers anyway? Being a woman, of course she did not have an identification plaque, and all we know about her is what she told us in her confession. I believe I heard she is a widow living in Yangju, Kyonggi Province . . ."

"Are you serious?"

"Stop it!" Shim scolded them, frowning deeply. The stone Buddha had spoken.

So Yong-su reddened and looked away, stifling a moan. Yi's head jerked down as if something had been dropped onto his crotch.

A heavy silence descended. Not a breath could be heard from the three ministers who surrounded Shim Hwan-ji, nor from the four brawny guards who stood by respectfully.

Shim clutched a square bamboo pillow with his gnarled hand, and put it on his back. His joints cracked. Breathing deeply, he noticed the sweat pouring down Yi's forehead.

These younger men were cowardly. Look at how confused and flustered they were. No wonder their faction was in such trouble. Each generation was pettier than the last, and each generation's intelligence grew shoddier.

If only Mong-o Kim Chong-su were alive . . .

Shim's old eyes envisioned those brave, intelligent souls who, together with him, had formed the secret society known as Clean Name. Shim's memories were crowded with their graves. "A human being is a slave to the past," he thought. "As one ages, one gazes at the ghosts inside him and behind him."

At this difficult juncture, Shim missed the dauntless, heroic demeanor of his comrades.

In 1793, when Chae Che-gong, recently honored with the post of chief state councilor, had sent a memorial urging the king to eliminate the enemies of Crown Prince Sado, Shim Hwan-ji had been confronted with a dark future. He felt as if his mind and spirit had been pulverized. It was not only Shim who felt this way. Others who had been involved in the death of the crown prince had withdrawn into a desperate silence.

It was then that Kim Chong-su had sprung into action, encouraging Shim.

The two men wrote a memorial to the king, demanding that the evil thief Chae Che-gong be decapitated, on the grounds that he had confused the fundamentals of loyalty and treachery and had slandered innocent court officials. They awaited His Majesty's answer for two days and two nights, refusing food and water, and prostrating themselves in the courtyard of Yonghwa Hall of the Royal Library. His Majesty denied them an audience.

On the third morning they heard the king's response: Kim Chong-su and Shim Hwan-ji would be discharged from their positions. The two had been exposed to a bamboo-thick, pelting monsoon downpour all through the night. When Shim learned that the end had come, he felt as if the sky had fallen upon his head. The earth seemed to have caved in beneath his feet.

Now, trying to quell the recurring emotions of those days, Shim picked up his long pipe. Mong-o had been dignified even then. Shim could still hear his words, "Look here, Man-po," he said, taking Shim by the shoulders and shaking him. "The integrity of the scholars is the fundamental force of the nation. From days of old, many are those who have been killed as traitors after volunteering loyal advice to the king. What is there to be afraid of? Will our death not be meaningful if we die to help distinguish between loyalty and treachery? Scholars across the nation will approve of our administration. Otherwise this administration would remain corrupt, for appearance and substance have been alienated."

They had expected imminent arrest by officials from the State Tribunal and direct interrogation by His Majesty.

Instead, toward evening they learned of His Majesty's directive that Chae Che-gong be relieved of his post as well. His Majesty had changed his mind after observing the mood of his court for a day. Late that night, the king summoned the three ministers. That was when they heard about "the previous king's tale of the metal-bound coffer." Now, in the absence of his comrade, Shim alone had to carry the destiny of their nation on his shoulders. Who could guess the indelible memories in his heart?

After a respectful pause, So Yong-su interrupted Shim's reverie. "Your Excellency, our situation has become very difficult, but perhaps not absolutely hopeless. Upon careful reflection, I see two possible solutions."

"Hmm."

"The first is to comb the walled capital inside and out, and get rid of that Yun woman and the book. The second is to eliminate the Southerners faction from court. Otherwise they will attack us now that they have this new weapon at their disposal These two means used together will reduce our worries, even if His Majesty has other intentions, for one needs two palms to make a sound."

"What a foolish idea!"

"Sir?"

Shim Hwan-ji turned away from So, and slammed his pipe on the ashtray. The sound penetrated So's spine.

"His Majesty will be standing around with his arms folded? By now His Majesty must have heard of Chae I-suk's death. He will disguise himself and go directly to the Thinking of the Bright King Manor in Myongdok-dong, the house of Chae Chae-gong, escorted by the Royal Guard Unit of the Royal Defense Garrison. And if that woman is already there, will she fall into your hands so easily? Today is the first anniversary of Chae Che-gong's death. His house will be bursting at the seams with Southerners from all over the country. Will you go there brandishing your swords and ask them to hand over that woman? If His Majesty's entourage were to arrive when you were there, you would be thrashed to death on the spot."

"Apologies for interrupting your statement, sir," said Yi, the minister of punishments, "but events will not unfold that way. From what one saw this morning, that woman was half dead from cold and torture. It would take a strong man half a day to travel from here to Myongdok-dong. She could not have arrived already. Moreover, the Special Cavalry Unit is concealed along every path to Chae's house, watching who come and go. If we give the order, they will make certain that woman does not reach it."

"Mmm." Shim's narrow eyes glinted like sunlight on a knife blade. Again his pipe knocked against the ashtray.

"Chae-gyom?" Shim asked.

"Yes, sir." One of the guards crept forward on his knees.

"How is the Special Cavalry Unit disposed?"

"We have about sixty men near Chae I-suk's house on Surak Mountain. Another thirty are stationed in a safe house near Changdok Palace awaiting word from the palace. Sixty are waiting in a safe house in Tabang-gol."

"The minister of punishments will give you a sketch of that woman. Search everywhere within the city walls. Keep watch over the houses of those belonging to the Kyongshin Society, that secret society of Southerners, and check who comes and goes. Begin immediately."

"Yes, sir."

"Chief Kim!"

"Yes, sir."

"Send out men from the Constabulary on the Left to watch the four city gates and reinforce the regular sentinels. Tell them to shut the doors firmly at *sulshi*."

"Yes, sir."

"Minister of Punishments, send someone to bring Coroner To Hak-sun. He may have overheard something about that Yun woman. Minister of Personnel, go to Tabang-gol, stay there, and implement any necessary measures as the situation changes. I will wait here in this office tonight."

"Yes, sir."

Shim's orders had been issued as quickly as flowing water, and the room suddenly grew lively. Kim Chae-shin adjusted his military hat and left. One of the guards standing near the door rushed out to find a painter from the Art Office who could sketch the woman.

The man called Chae-gyom, as he was about to stand, tilted his head toward So Yong-su.

"Your Excellency, what should we do about the man in the other room?"

So's eyes took on a look of indecision. Like ripples from a stone dropped into a calm well, a troubled expression spread from his eyes to every part of his face. Presently, he bowed his graying head and sighed.

"There is no grain that does not need night soil for fertilizer, and there is no noble cause that is not helped along by vice. Kill him, but leave no visible wounds. Then cut his tongue out, so it would appear he killed himself by biting it off and bleeding to death. There will be a use for the body later on, so keep it here for the time being. People from the Office of the Censor-General and the Office of the Inspector-General will come and fetch it."

5
The Dragon Moves

Ah. This unfilial son has reached today without dying, harboring a vengeance that reaches up to the sky and to the ends of the earth, but the past is far away, looking like an immoveable boulder. My father's birth was Heaven's granting the wish of our nation. What dare I write here? Only after writing about the existence of my father can it be revealed to posterity that this humble person was born of him. Therefore I hold a brush and write with anguished tears in front of the tomb holding my father's casket that his memorial name was Hyon, his personal name was Yun-gwan, he was the grandson of King Sukchong and the son of King Yongjo.

—King Chongjo, "Writing at the Tomb of Crown Prince Sado (1789)," vol. 16, *Hongjae Collection* (Royal Archives).

The ditch was frozen, crammed with refuse.

Warmed by the meager sunlight of a winter afternoon, the sour odor of rotting food and the stench of feces and urine wafted into the air. Next to the ditch stood houses with low chimneys. Mangy, fur-shedding dogs and giggling children with oozing eyes, the dirt flaking off their faces and hands, frolicked together. The children's eyes grew wide at the sight of So Yong-su and Yi Cho-won in the blinding grandeur of their official silk robes.

This was an alley between Hap-dong and Tabang-gol.

The two men reached the safe house at the alley's dead end and were ushered into the main room. Cavaliers of the Military Training Command, disguised in ordinary clothes and waiting in absolute silence, could be seen in the servants' and the women's quarters.

The two men tried to look as if nothing had gone amiss; once they sat in the room, a tense silence enveloped them.

"That old beggar!" So Yong-su finally growled, glaring the air.

"Who?" asked Yi Cho-won, grinning.

"You know who."

After this brief exchange, the men sat in silence.

"That old man has sucked in all sweet taste with his cohorts, and now he wants the rest of us to face catastrophe together, like a water ghost," So Yong-su thought, but he didn't speak his thoughts. He felt resentment against Shim Hwan-ji surge in his throat. Ten years after the death of Crown Prince Sado, when King Chongjo was about to take the throne, every man of the Old Doctrine faction had been seized with a sense of crisis. The leaders who had been involved in the crown prince's death decided to organize a secret society called the Clean Name, excluding the masterminds who had already been revealed, such as Hong Kye-hui and Kim Ku-ju, and they pledged to live and die together.

After his ascent, King Chongjo executed a few men, including Hong and Kim, but he could not touch the Clean Name, although its members had schemed for Crown Prince Sado's death. Now King Chongjo seemed ready to strike the Clean Name. The surviving members of the group were Yi Pyong-mo and Shim Hwan-ji. Shim was fretting so much because his neck was in danger now.

So Yong-su was deep in thought: "Those old crooks! This is why one should refrain from getting involved in a royal succession. They were the source of disaster, bringing up the ideas of the Clean Will and the Wind of the Scholars and so forth just as they pleased, and now they blame us younger ones! Should we secretly report those oldsters as traitors, and extricate ourselves? Ah . . . it is no easy matter by any measure. Any young man who had a degree of power is connected to the Clean Name as a relative, in-law, or student. The sparks of imprisonment would catch fire far and wide if we tipped off the authorities."

The same anxiety whirled in Yi Cho-won's heart. He was numb. "There is a saying," he thought, "that one who travels on a high sedan under a parasol has greater worries, and it is just so: As soon as I became a minister, this had to happen.

The silence continued, heavy and prolonged

Suddenly, a gong sounded from close by, and bang, bang went a drum.

So Yong-su almost let out a shriek; he jumped to his feet and flung open the window looking out on the alley. Where were they? He thought the Royal Guards were coming. The face of Yi, who rushed to the window with So, was bloodless.

The oppressive tension dissipated quickly. The men soon realized that the drum did not belong to the army but was playing the twelve-beat rhythm of a shaman's rite. Soon a bell rang, and then a shaman's hat and her raised pale brown sleeves holding fans came into view. The procession was visible over a low clover bush wall that was visible from the room where the two men waited. A shamanistic ceremony was about to begin in a house several doors down the alley.

So Yong-su turned away from the window and spoke to Yi.

"Kyong-hon, have you seen the shrines to the Rice Chest King?"

"What?" Yi cocked his head at this sudden question.

"I have heard that lately, in the areas of Samgye and Yongsan, shrines to the Rice Chest King are sprouting up, honoring him as a shamanistic god. In other words, the masses worship him as a god-king, like King Kongmin and King Tanjong. The foolish people believe that the ghosts of those who died a wrongful death have more spiritual power because they have a stronger spirit of vengeance. In addition to satisfying their appetites, apparently they wish to console the wronged spirit of Crown Prince Sado."

Yi remained silent.

"On top of that, it will be announced that the true villains who made the false charge against the late crown prince have been found, and that a royal command will be issued to punish those lawless traitors. This is how things will develop."

"Yo-jung, are you saying that if His Majesty prosecutes us, the public will not object because they pity Crown Prince Sado?"

"What do you mean by 'object'? Rather, they will be happy, calling it justice."

"Mmm. Yo-jung, what do you think we should do?"

"At this point there is no choice. What do you think about extricating ourselves from this situation, as if carving out a boil before it reaches a head?"

"What are you saying?

"The Introduction to the Symbols in the *Book of Changes* says that the existence of the king and his subjects precedes the high and the low, and then after the distinction between the high and the low comes propriety. The distinction between the king and his subjects is ever so important, so what can we do as his subjects? We must follow His Majesty's intentions. It would be another matter if His Majesty were a dark king—evil, violent, decadent. But he is not like that at all. Since he took power, the nation has grown wealthier and the masses are better off. He enriched the financial holdings of the royal family by mining gold in the northwestern region; he had reservoirs repaired, doubling the size of rice paddies and fields in every village in the three southern regions; and he caused the markets to thrive with the Commercial Equalization Act. Naturally, the people look up to him as they would a father, so . . ."

"Shut up, you stuffy idiot!"

So Yong-su winced in surprise. He had never seen Yi lose his temper. Yi's face was flushed with anger. His flowing beard was trembling.

"Aren't you going too far?" So protested.

"Absolutely not. What? The people look up to His Majesty like a father? Since his ascent, nine powerful families out of ten have been unable to avoid terrible persecutions. As if that were not enough, now His Majesty is intending to discipline us court officials. Haven't we served him well, concealing our complaints? He is a tyrant. How can you say the masses look up to that despot?"

So Yong-su was silent.

"What is the king? On the one hand, he should respect the wishes of the founder of his dynasty, and on the other, he should understand what the public desires. He should govern diligently, with fear and caution. Now this king intends to protect himself, so he has abolished the laws of his predecessors. He collects the fruits of the people's hard labor, and he is generous when he should be sparing, but he is parsimonious when he should be generous. Just because Crown Prince Sado was his birth father, he harbors the intention of honoring him. Using that as an excuse, he will drive our Principle group extinct. When His Majesty's confusion has reached this far, how dare you think of saving your own skin? Will you run up to His Majesty and disclose everything? How can a high-ranking scholar say something like that? I ask you how!"

So's fury had reached a peak also. "Then what is your plan? To look for a needle on the banks of the Han River, do you mean to try to find that woman? If His Majesty ends up getting his hands on that book, what will you do? Will you commit regicide?"

Yi Cho-won's face blanched.

So Yong-su felt as stunned as if he had been struck by lightening. He was astonished by his own words. He had spat them out without thinking, but now goose bumps covered his body and drops of cold sweat oozed from the thin band of his headgear. Regicide! It was a word never to be uttered. Not that they were afraid of the consequences. From the time they had first opened their eyes to the world, they had been exposed to such an education.

But words could turn into reality.

They grew more nervous, because it might become a reality. Regicide was possible, and they could picture such a frightful, terrible event.

Yi softened his expression and apologized. "I am sorry. I went too far. Be generous with me."

"No, no. It is I who should say that. Please forget what I just said."

"Hmm. It is all His Majesty's fault. He decides all the national affairs at the Royal Library without even publishing them in the official gazette. Even a trifling librarian walks in His Majesty's shadow and expresses his opinions, but we, the ministers of the government, have a hard time catching a view of him. I have not had an audience in almost a month."

"You can say that again."

"So, about what you said . . . please don't even think about it. This matter is not simple enough to be solved by secret reports."

"Well . . . all right." So Yong-su nodded.

"Yi might be right," he thought. "Would His Majesty's ambitions stop at dispensing with a few high-level administrators?"

His Majesty, from early childhood, had enjoyed reciting the section of King Wen in the Book of Odes: "King Wen is on high / Zhou is an old people / But its charge is new." For a long time His Majesty had cherished the dream of revitalizing his nation, which was declining day by day, by solving the problems of the old system.

How could one achieve revitalization?

The answer lay in the king's foreword to *On an Exemplary Monarch*

(1790), asserting the establishment of a powerful exemplary monarchy. The term "exemplary monarch" invoked a passage in the *Book of History* indicating that a strong royal authority could restrain a nation's factional squabbles and conflict.

The emergence of a strong royal authority: King Chongjo asserted that it was the only way to root out chronic problems and stabilize the daily lives of the commoners. The people were equal under the king. He wished to punish the groups that ruled over the people, disguising their ambitions for power with such titles as the Clean Name, Unbiased Opinions, and so forth.

From the Old Doctrine's point of view, however, this was no more than fanciful sophism.

In principle, what was the division of factions? Zhu Xi taught that exemplary people had exemplary companions, while insignificant people had factions of insignificance. The division into factions was inevitable, and it could not be abolished by human effort. In Korea, King Sonjo had said, "Yi I is an exemplary person, so it is not worrisome that his faction exists, rather it is worrisome that there are so few factions. I will follow the teachings of Zhu Xi and join the faction of Song Hon."

The present king did not distinguish between exemplary men and petty men, between orthodoxy and heresy; he simply attempted to reinforce the royal authority, and in doing so turned his back on his predecessors and ignored unbiased opinions. He temporized on the discussion of right and wrong, not differentiating loyalty from perfidy. In short, his actions amounted to tyranny. He was preoccupied with the consolidation of his power base, silencing his subjects in the name of grand harmony, and luring scholars with the bait of vested rights and government positions.

So Yong-su was reminded of Yi Taek-ching, an elder minister, who had vented his anger in front of the king a few years earlier.

"Your Majesty!" Yi Taek-ching exclaimed. "Is this country yours alone? Is this dynasty yours only? No. It is the literati who have maintained this four-hundred-year-old dynasty. At calamitous moments after the catastrophic Japanese and Chinese invasions, who was responsible for keeping the dynasty intact? It was the literati with integrity, who have accepted the teachings of Zhu Xi, who considered the Just Cause more important than worldly honors, and who threw away their lives as lightly as the feathers of a wild goose.

"Your Majesty distances yourself from the unbiased opinions of such literati and settles all national matters after discussing them with the Royal Library. The officials at the library, basking in Your Majesty's trust, exceed their authority. This servant says this, risking death. The library is Your

Majesty's private administration, and not the public administration of the nation, and the library officials have become Your Majesty's private servants, no longer officials of the court. Please understand the situation with wisdom."

"All this notwithstanding . . . what gives His Majesty the confidence to behave that way?" So wondered silently.

The abolishment of discrimination between the offspring of the lawful wife and the concubines. The repeal of the slave system. The complete revision of the government examinations. The promotion of commerce and industry. Finally, the fundamental reform of taxation. All these policies advocated by the king had invariably met the court officials' staunch opposition at every turn. Yet, the moves of royal revival had appeared one after another since the dawn of the New Year. One needn't even mention the hurried decision on the crown prince's marriage. A few days earlier the king had expressed his wishes that His Majesty himself would supervise and implement the abolition of discrimination against children of concubines as well as the slave system. What gave His Majesty such confidence? Again, was it naturally connected with the previous king's tale of the metal-bound coffer?

A sudden flurry of approaching footsteps was heard.

So and Yi winced.

"Your Excellency, this is Chae-gyom, sir," said a manly voice as the door opened.

The man who knelt at the door, supporting his weight with one hand, was none other than the large-boned martial artist who had been at the Constabulary on the Left. As the man sat with a knee drawn to his chest, So's eyes were at the same level as the man's ribs. The way he had ventured into the room without waiting for permission, combined with his imposing bulk, indicated a daring nature. It is said that one who knows tactics does not hesitate as he moves and does not show any sign of restraint in his actions. "Did he say his name was Ku Chae-gyom?" So Yong-su asked himself, studying the features of this unusual man.

Yi, the minister of punishments, seemed to know him well, for he addressed him familiarly.

"What happened to that woman?"

"Our boys are searching within the walled city with the sketch. We have asked for the cooperation of the jailers and patrols, with the order that she should be arrested immediately because she is an agent of the Catholics. And we have placed a spy at each of the Kyongshin Society ring's house."

"Hmm. . . . Any message from the palace?"

"It is supposed to come to this house."

"You've worked hard. Minister of Personnel, you haven't met this youth yet, have you? Chae-gyom, meet this elder formally."

Yi waited until the giant rose and bowed deeply before he introduced the young man to So.

"I have mentioned this briefly at the Constabulary on the Left, but this youngster is Chae-gyom, a descendant of the Ku family from Nungsong. Now he is the head of the Special Cavalry Unit of the Military Training Command, and no one is better than he for a secret mission. Please give him your assistance in the future."

"Of the Ku clan of Nungsong. . . . Then, by any chance . . . ?"

"That's right. This is the son of the late Ku Son-bok, the former general of the Military Training Command."

"Huh, . . ." So Yong-su swallowed.

The Ku family of Nungsong was the most renowned military family in all Korea; they had produced a general from each generation for two hundred years, since the Restoration of King Injo. During the reign of King Yongjo, sons of this clan had become a police chief, a provincial army commander, a navy commander, and a commandant of the Palace Guards Headquarters; their influence in the military was far reaching and their martial arts skills, handed down in the family, were outstanding. Then, fourteen years ago, King Chongjo had attempted to destroy the family's influence by linking Ku Son-bok and his nephew Myong-gyom to a treason conspiracy masterminded by Chief State Councilor Kim Sang-chol. Both uncle and nephew had been thrashed to death.

The clan itself, though, had not been wiped from the face of the earth with one blow. The family web spun over generations could not be obliterated by King Chongjo alone. Shin Tae-gyom, the commander of the Royal Defense Garrison, whom the king trusted wholeheartedly, was none other than a son-in-law of Ku Song-ik, the uncle of the late Ku Son-bok. And wasn't the son of a traitor, Ku Chae-gyom himself, the head of the Special Cavalry Unit?

The Special Cavalry Unit, directly under the Military Training Command, had been created after the Revolt of Yi In-jwa. It was composed of special warriors, accomplished martial artists selected by special military national examinations, separate from the regular military examinations. While the ordinary military official selection process was based chiefly on archery, the candidates for these special examinations were tested in four types of equestrian skills, Chinese swordsmanship, the pear-blossom lance skill, and two-handed knife fighting.

The land of Korea was so mountainous and so densely inhabited that martial arts other than archery were not developed. However dexterous a person was with a knife, a sword, a lance, or a club, he could not defeat an enemy who took advantage of tree branches and rocks as he shot arrows in retreat. For this reason, it was the Special Cavalry Unit to which Korea's handful of martial arts experts applied for positions.

The unit, however, had lost King Chongjo's trust, because it had often been involved in the treasonous conspiracies of powerful ministers. Though it used to patrol the palace wall perimeter, it had been demoted to a patrol unit for the city walls, stationed outside the Hungnye Gate. The powerful Old Doctrine faction made use of the unit's discontent and employed its members in political espionage. Palace information reached the Old Doctrine's ears through the Eunuch Department, while the Special Cavalry Unit conveyed information from outside the palace.

After a lengthy pause, So Yong-su muttered, "He looks like a person fit for a great task. So how old are you, young man?"

"Twenty-nine, sir."

"I am proud of you. You have turned out well. I am moved. I feel as if I were in the dignified presence of the late General Ku. According to the 'Summary of the Rules of Propriety' of the *Book of Rites*, 'One should not live under the same sky as one's father's enemy,' so you must have mixed feelings."

So Yong-su, known as an adroit tactician, threw the bait. Contrary to his expectations, however, Ku responded nonchalantly, like the lid of a rice pot when tapped.

"No, sir. It may sound presumptuous, but it is said that a true man refrains from allowing his private anger to turn into public indignation. My father was guilty in the eyes of the nation. How could I harbor other thoughts because of my family's private grudge?"

The mood of the room chilled. So Yong-su, taken aback by such an unexpected response, felt his temple tighten, and turned to look at Yi Cho-won. Yi's face also registered shock, his mouth agape. Their eyes returned to Ku. A smile spread over Ku's face as he continued with dignity.

"But . . ."

"But?"

"When one humbly thinks about the nation, how can one not fret with concern? Recently His Majesty has been busy pushing away exemplary people and showing respect to those who are fawning and petty. He has destroyed renowned loyal clans that served kings for generations, and he has disregarded the unbiased opinions of rustic literati. This has led to a breach of trust between the king and his servants. Those impudent knaves who enjoy royal favor ignore the teachings of Zhu Xi and embrace heretic ways, inviting foreign humiliation and trouble. How could a nation be more imperiled than ours?"

Yi slapped his thigh in enthusiastic agreement with this admirable logic. So's face took on an approving look. Ku continued as if he hadn't noticed a thing.

"To prevent the dynasty from falling into danger, the source of the danger should be eliminated first. There is a saying that a human being exists for a generation, but the dynasty lasts for ten thousand generations. My apologies for saying this, but . . ."

"Well, well, that's enough," So cried out, waving his hand. "I understand what you mean. Such talk is premature. We shouldn't put the cart before the horse. Now, it is important to find that Yun woman and get the tale of the metal-bound coffer. If things turn out otherwise, only then . . ."

A human being exists for one generation, but the dynasty lasts for ten thousand generations. It sounded as neat as cutting a bamboo stalk from top to bottom. This Ku Cha-gyom, though military, was extraordinary. The two ministers looked at each other with implicit understanding. The troubles that had made them tense throughout the afternoon didn't seem so insurmountable after all. Ku, reading their expressions, spoke.

"In fact, I came here to ask some questions concerning this matter. Do the two ministers have any inkling as to the identity of that woman?"

"Well . . . that's a blind spot of our criminal law. We investigate only the personal and family history of men who carry identity plaques, and women are always treated as accomplices. When things like this happen, it is like searching for a needle on the banks of the Han River. The late Chae I-suk took advantage of such a hole in the law."

"According to the report on the investigation conducted in the jail, she is in the records as Widow Min Kan-nan, a commoner living in Kwangju, Kyonggi Province," Ku said. "An underling was dispatched to Kwangju on horseback, but it is obvious that this was a lie. Would Chae entrust such an important book to the hands of the widow of some nameless commoner? She must be from a good family of the Western Learning group of the Southerners faction. According to what Chae said before his death, her family name must be Yun, not Min. Do you ministers happen to know a Yun family among the Catholics of the Southerners faction?"

"Yun . . . Yun . . ."

"She was half-dead when she was released in the morning. Where could she have gone in such a state? She has nowhere to go but to a family friend, so if we just knew her identity, finding her would be as simple as turning over one's palm."

Despite Ku's confident tone, So's forehead was still furrowed. "But among the well-known Yun families, there are quite a handful tainted by Western Learning. Yun from Haenam, Yun from Papyong, Yun from Haman. There must be more than ten people who were contaminated while they frequented Song-ho Yi Ik's house. Yun Tong-kyu, Yun Hung-so, Yun Chi-bom, Yun Chi-nul, Yun Yong-hui. And Yun Chi-chung who died because of the Chinsan incident, and Yun Yu-il who died in 1795 because he refused to reveal Father Zhou's whereabouts, . . . and . . ."

"Your Excellency. The answer might not be that difficult after all. Feeling a foreboding of bodily threat, Chae tried to send the original book to Chonjinam, the hiding place of the Kyongshin Society. This husband-less Yun is a messenger, so she is not from a family that is merely acquainted with the Catholics, but from a most trusted family who can come and go at any time."

"That makes sense." So was deep in thought, cradling his chin with his hand. He stared at the floor, searching for a clue that might have been passed over until then.

Nevertheless, he could not pinpoint any suspect, and he lifted his head and gazed out the window that was still open. Outside, dusk was already descending. A voice came closer, calling for Ku.

"Chief, sir. Chief, sir. There is a message from the second state councilor."

"What is it?" Ku flung open the door.

The man was one of the three who had been with Ku at the Constabulary on the Left. At a glance one could tell he was intemperate, with a wiry, stiff beard sprouting from his droopy cheeks. His eyes shifted from the ministers to Ku as he whispered.

"We found out who that Yun woman is. Old To Hak-sun of the Board of Punishments eavesdropped on the exchange between Chae I-suk and Chong Yag-yong. She is the former wife of Yi In-mong. She was banished because she believed in Catholicism and has not been heard from since."

"Yi In-mong's former wife? Then, . . ." So leaned forward. "Then isn't she the younger sister of Yun Yu-il, who was put to death during the Father Zhou Wenmo incident?"

"That is right, sir."

"Is that so?" So said, "I have heard that Catholics have high esteem for those who die defending their beliefs, calling them martyrs. Since Yun Yu-il is what they call a martyr, his family must be highly regarded by the Catholics, and because many of them used to hold government positions, it must have been easy to be engaged in secret communications with Chae. Chae-gyom, don't stay here idly. Go to the Board of Punishments and look into Yun Yu-il's records. Since he was prosecuted as a traitor, you should be able to find his family history and his family members' addresses. Search carefully for every household that is related to that woman."

Ku nodded.

Yi Cho-won fished the official seal out of the red silk pouch hanging from his waistband and tossed it to Ku.

"Take this and go see the investigation chief at the Board of Punishments. He will show you the papers concerning Yun Yu-il."

"Yes, sir." Ku threw his usual sharp glance at the two ministers before he picked up the pouch and left.

"So that is Ku Son-bok's son," So muttered to himself, stroking the skin around his thin lips. A glimmer fleeted in his dark pupils under the thick eyelids.

Yi fretted. "What do you think? Shouldn't we go to the Constabulary on the Left?"

"No, not yet. We should watch the movements of the dragon. More important. . . ." So didn't continue but stared at the lacquered floor. He was grave. Yi couldn't comprehend what troubled his friend, so he began to feel anxious.

"About Chae I-suk's last words. . . ." So began.

Yi's eyes widened in question.

"Do you remember what Chae is supposed to have said? He died saying 'The previous king's tale of the metal-bound coffer is what we all knew. . . .' "

"And?"

"What does that mean?"

"Of course it has to do with the contents of the tale of the metal-bound coffer. But who would know? No one has heard it to the end."

"Right. It has to do with the contents of the tale of the metal-bound coffer. Why didn't we think of that?"

"What? What exactly do you mean? Don't try my patience."

"Consider how Ku acted a little while ago. He is a mere military man, but when he talked about a private grudge, he prettified it by throwing up a smoke screen and beating around the bush, pretending he felt public indignation for the nation. When it comes to the patriarch of the nation, the previous king, what more is there to explain?"

"And?"

"The contents of the book must be different from what we have assumed. How could the king spell out the names—a Shim, a Kim—to order that they be punished for having committed offenses? However heartbroken he was by the incident of Crown Prince Sado, and however great his rage against those who trapped his son, he would never have voiced his feelings outright."

"Hmm."

"'The previous king's tale of the metal-bound coffer is what we all knew.'. . . What comes next?"

"'What we all knew'. . . 'what we all knew'. . ."

Yi spat out, "Yo-jung. Do we have to understand that at this very moment?"

"Of course! Look here, Kyong-hon. We are overlooking an important possibility now because we are overwrought with worries and anxiety. Maybe . . . maybe the book is simply a bundle of white pages with nothing written on them."

"What? What do you mean by that?"

"From the beginning nothing was known about the book. When Chae Che-gong's memorial caused a shock wave in 1791, the king summoned Chae along with our councilors Kim Chong-su and Shim Hwan-ji. He showed them a poem called "The Song of the Blood-Stained Hemp and the Mourning Staff" and told them about the book. That night, His Majesty took out the poem from underneath Queen Chongsong's spiritual tablet, and said there was another record, a dictated documentation concerning Crown Prince Sado's death. But all we have is His Majesty's word. After all, who has seen it?"

"Then . . ."

"Perhaps His Majesty's aim is not the book itself, but the anxiety he has caused in us with the threat that the book will be made public."

"Our anxiety?"

"Torn by anxiety, we might launch a premature attack. It would give His Majesty an excuse to crush his foes."

Yi seemed frozen, his back straight and his eyes wide open. Was their anxiety His Majesty's aim? "The previous king's tale of the metal-bound coffer is what we all knew.". . . What now?

Yi might have let out a scream had he not been trained from childhood to obey the precept that a good Confucian scholar never loses his calm. For a moment he seemed to have forgotten to breathe. Then he sprang to his feet.

"We can't idle away our time now. Yo . . . Yo-jung. I am returning to the palace."

"What is the matter?"

"I think I finally understand what 'the previous king's tale of the metal-bound coffer' is. And . . . but, but the book. That book . . ."

Yi rushed out without completing his sentence.

* * *

The front court of Huijong Hall in Changdok Palace looked as if it had been bleached by snowflakes. His Majesty stood straight, his left hand stuck in the band around his waist , which was embroidered with flowers. He was looking at the refreshing scenery through a wide-open sliding window, watching his white breath float up and then disappear, and listening to his officials reading the memorials.

His Majesty had studied day and night since boyhood, and his eyes had grown weak. He had started wearing a pair of French-made magnifying glasses the year before, but, even with the glasses, his eyes hurt and dimmed only after an hour of reading. He had no choice but to have his officials read aloud to him all ordinary memorials and routine official reports sent by special envoys from country towns.

Sitting next to the king, Yi In-mong exerted himself summarizing the memorials as best he could. Concurrently with his library position he held a position as a drafter of state records. He had been summoned from the Royal Shrine to read the texts, and he was still at it at this hour, after *kyongshi*.

"This is a memorial from To Chae-gil," he announced, "a former third inspector in the Office of the Inspector-General." He then read the memorial aloud, as he did.

> It is the foundation of the Confucian system that all children of the lawful wife belong to the proper line and those of concubines belong to the concubines' line. Our ceremonial rules for adult rites, weddings, funerals, and memorial services follow these distinctions. Why has Your Majesty enacted a sacrilegious law that allows the employment of concubines' children in government positions, and announced that Your Majesty will erase the distinction between the proper line and the concubine's line? This will bring, in the future . . .

"Received!" The king pronounced gloomily, his eyes still glued to the view outside.

In-mong handed over the memorial to Hong Sok-ju, a copyist. Hong wrote "Received" in red ink on the royal reply at the top of the memorial before handing the reply over to Min Tae-hyok, the first royal secretary. Min pressed the royal seal on the reply. In this manner, the memorials were read and disposed of, one by one.

As he read aloud, In-mong kept picking up a piece of coal he had wrapped in silk and putting it down again. As soon as he arrived, he had been ordered to read the memorials. Now more than an hour had passed. He had been looking for a private chance to report the incident in the Royal Library, but His Majesty didn't show any inclination to take a break. In-mong couldn't hope for a chance to see the king alone, yet he felt there were too many officials around — five royal secretaries; two copyists; and Chong Chun-gyo, the messenger eunuch. Furthermore, other secretaries came and went continually, bringing in the documents and taking out the royal directives.

What should he do? In-mong noticed that the first royal secretary was eyeing him with disapproval. In-mong hurriedly picked up the next memorial and glanced through it until he found the part with the main argument.

"This is from Yang Hyon-gi, a lay scholar from Hoedok."

> Since the announcement that the concubine's line be incorporated into the proper line, there have been continuous disputes over inheritance between the children of proper wives and those of concubines here in Hoedok Small County. Your Majesty has asserted that the current system is a bad law and is not found in China, but our case is different. Unlike China, where families live together and share property, we have long followed the custom of setting up separate families and dividing property when the sons marry. Even now, when the principle of favoring the proper first son is firmly established, we see many arguments, fights, and lawsuits. Furthermore, the wealth intended to fund the performance of ancestral rites in the first proper son's household is insufficient as it is. If the distinction between the proper line and the concubine's line is abolished . . .

"Not right!" King Chongjo interrupted In-mong's reading.

His voice was tinged with anger, and those present became nervous. Some officials had been dozing, sitting at small desks lined up before the king, but now they straightened themselves: First Royal Secretary Min Tae-hyok, Second Royal Secretary Yi So-gu, Third Royal Secretary Yi Ik-un, Fourth Royal Secretary Chong Sang-u, and Fifth Royal Secretary So Yu-mun.

They were all exhausted after a long day's work. The memorials were particularly uninspiring because all of them were in opposition to King Chongjo's royal directives.

The reforms King Chongjo had confirmed in this first lunar month contained two concrete plans. The first was the revision of the articles dealing with the state examination system found in the statues and regulations of the Board of Rites section of the National Administrative Code that had barred concubines' sons from applying; now they were guaranteed an opportunity to advance in the government hierarchy. The second was the emancipation of sixty-six thousand public slaves working in palaces and administrative offices in the walled city by setting fire to their certificates of indenture. Since the day of the announcement, memorials had poured in not only from the Old Doctrine faction in the court but also from the rustic literati.

The royal words reached the ears of the officials.

"There cannot be discrimination when employing talented people in the court. The ability of each person should be respected, and a person should be employed according to his talent. What does using people in court regardless of their origins have to do with family inheritance? And if it were related, have I ever said to give priority to concubines' sons over proper eldest sons? I just said when there is no son in the proper line, it is better for a concubine's son to continue the line than to adopt a son from a distant relative."

The king paused briefly. His eyes were fixed on a distant point, and his breathing was loud. He was angry with the scholars who didn't attempt to understand his intentions, and with the country people who were so obstinate that they couldn't be made to come around.

Copyist Hong's brush flew as he wrote down the king's response. "The court employs people strictly according to their talents. The affairs of court are different from those of private households."

In-mong was embarrassed to read the next memorial, having just seen Hong's text, because it used the same words to oppose the king's proclamation. Over a mountain came a bigger mountain. The characters danced before his eyes. He looked up at the king's bloodshot eyes with sympathy and began to read the last memorial.

"This is from Kim U-gyong, the seventh state councilor at the State Council.

> The affairs of court are different from those of private households. Your Majesty's three directives concerning the abolition of the distinction between the proper line and the concubines' line should follow the above logic. First, Your Majesty has said that the concubines' children can call their father "Father" and their older brother "Older Brother," but this was never prohibited. Each family should decide this matter. Second, Your Majesty has said that when there is no heir in the proper family line, a concubine's son can be treated as the eldest, but again each family should decide the matter. Third, Your Majesty has said that the concubines' children should not be deterred from advancement in the government, but this is not something that needs to be brought up again, because Your Majesty already so directed at the launch of your rule.

"What?" King Chongjo's eyes shone with a dangerous gleam.

Do not bring it up again because His Majesty had so directed at the launch of his rule? What impertinence!

King Chongjo had lowered himself to reannounce the directive because it had not been practiced at all for the twenty years since its proclamation. Since the first directive in the first year of his reign, he had urged the practice of the new system almost every year. But the Old Doctrine faction, administrators of practical matters, had either ignored it or, when pressured, had created ridiculous-sounding positions, such as Provisional Rank 4 or Provisional Rank 5 for the concubines' descendants. Fully aware of the situation, Kim U-gyong was purposely taunting the exasperated king.

"Continue."

"Your Majesty?"

"There must be more. Read what comes next." The king's pursed lips twitched.

In-mong's hands and feet grew cold and his whole body tensed as he looked up at the royal countenance. In-mong's eyes fell on a phrase starting, "Your Majesty's court is truly pathetic." He felt as if a thorn or a knife had been thrust into his eyes.

"It . . . it will be continued, Your Majesty."

> Your Majesty's court is truly pathetic. The so-called ministers, in an attempt to save their own positions, do not dare speak their minds although this matter might endanger the very discipline of the country. Braving death, this servant says that the abolition of the discrimination against the concubines' line is not a matter of justice but is a disaster that would shake the very foundation of this country. It was not only the concubines' lines that the former kings prohibited from applying for national examinations. If Your Majesty opens the gates of permission to them, everyone—not only the northwesterners, the residents of the capital of the previous dynasty, and the Chungin class, but also the slaves who scoop up feces and the butchers who slaughter oxen—will come forward pleading the unfairness of their status. How does Your Majesty expect to withstand such chaos?

In-mong heard a sudden slap and raised his head. The king had struck the surface of a stationery chest with his palm.

"Disaster? Disaster? That old fossil dares to say our policy is a disaster? Who is he, feeling entitled to utter such impudence?"

The king's burning eyes were on Min Tae-hyok, the first royal secretary.

Min had seemed ill at ease, but now he hung his head. He was related to the memorial's author by their children's marriage. The king bit his trembling lips and shut his eyes. They could have heard a pin drop.

Finally, the king asked, "What is the king after all? The universe is composed of three elements: Heaven, Earth, and Humanity. Those three elements correspond to the three powers: the Indeterminate Ultimate, the August Ultimate, and the Supreme Ultimate. All things originate from the Indeterminate Ultimate, and the culmination of the transformations that produces Heaven and Earth is Humanity, the Supreme Ultimate. The Supreme Ultimate takes ten steps back and one step forward and becomes the August Ultimate, and so a king appears in the world. A king is none other than the personification of the August Ultimate, a person who reveals the laws of Earth.

"The person who becomes the king restrains the strong and supports the weak to uphold the impartial principles. If the king is not fit for this position, and if the strong always wield their tyrannical power, gained from generations of privilege, and the weak continue to shed tears, forever downtrodden, what is the use of having a king and how can one discuss the true order of the world? Ah! As the world deteriorates, the powerful become more chaotic, and false justice and false order reach their climax. Aren't the distinctions between the proper line and the concubines' line, and between the *yangban* and the slaves, good examples of this? Then did that old goat say that it was not only concubines' lines that the former kings denied application rights to examinations? Even long-lived, beautiful laws should be amended if they do not fit current customs and sentiments. How dare he babble about an ugly precedent?"

"My apologies, Your Majesty." Min Tae-hyok bowed further and his body trembled as His Majesty's fiery gaze was again directed at him.

Others felt a chill in their hearts. Again there would be rumors of heresy all over town. His Majesty's thoughts, in both the past and the present, were in direct opposition to the party politics of Yi I, the philosophical leader of the Old Doctrine faction.

Yi I, Yul-gok, was a renowned scholar going back several generations, highly respected as the Zhu Xi of the East, as was his contemporary Yi Toe-gye. How can I, merely the translator of this story, *The Encounter of the Stars,* and a student at the end of the totem pole years later, discuss the factional differences between these two giants? Although it is humbling, I should mention the differences between these two masters to help explain this story, which was written from a typical Southerners' point of view.

Yul-gok's view of politics is shown in "On the Kingly Way," in Book 15 of the *Complete Works of Yulgok*. He criticized Emperor Shenzong of Song China as a dark ruler. Why was he a dark ruler when he consolidated the throne and attempted strong reform politics according to the principle of recovering the ideals of the "Three Dynasties," with Wang Anshih as his point man? It was because he temporarily suppressed the discussion of right and wrong with the logic of grand harmony, as King Chongjo has just described, and he did not distinguish between exemplary and petty people. According to Yul-gok, the king should distinguish between those who are exemplary and those who are petty, and then he should join forces with the exemplary people. This philosophy was systematized into "A Seven-Article Proposal for Dealing with Urgent Tasks."

Yul-gok's seven-article proposal, hinting at the superiority of Confucian scholars over their monarch, was opposed to Toe-gye's Six-Article Memorial, presented in 1568. In the fourth article, Toe-gye explained the relationship between the throne and his servants as *li* (Principle) and *qi* (Material Force), in parallel to the relationship between the Way and people's minds, asserting that people's minds should follow the Way at all times and on all occasions. The Way and people's minds should never be confused or their roles reversed; if that happened, he warned, the result would be the destruction of social ethics and the corruption of politics.

Toe-gye's duality of *li* and *qi* was well suited to the political philosophy of a strong monarchal power. His thoughts were adopted as the national philosophy by the Japanese *Tokugawa* regime (*kimon* school) and later helped Kusumoto and Motoda develop the *Meiji* Restoration in the nineteenth century, propelled by its concept of a strong monarch.

The idea of the fair and just way of the August Ultimate, explicated by King Chongjo, followed the Toe-gye school's interpretation of the Great Plan section of the Zhou part of the *Book of History*.

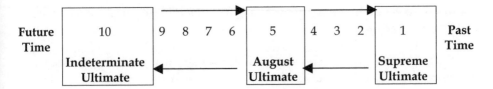

The left is the future and the right is the past. The future and the past are unified in the extant present of the five—the August Ultimate. Who is the master of the August Ultimate, who makes use of all things according to the present circumstances by revealing the past and predicting the future? According to Commentary on the Appended Phrases in the *Book of Changes*, it is the sage-king, namely the ruler, who is aware of the laws of Heaven

Then what happens when the August Ultimate is diminished because there is no sage-king? The epoch governed by Hexagram 12, the hexagram of Obstruction, dawns when the good fortune of the world dries up and the leadership of the times passes from the king to a new force that divines the Way of Heaven. It is inevitable, then, that a revolution comes to transform the epoch of obstruction into the epoch governed by Hexagram 11, the hexagram of Peace. This was what happened sixty years after the end of King Chongjo's reign, when Choe Che-u, the leader of the Tonghak (Eastern Learning) Uprising, rose up under the banner of the Great Transformation of the Latter Heaven, and stained the whole country with blood.

Officials sitting before King Chongjo had no idea that such a horrible collapse awaited their country. The dynasty was enjoying a healthy, prosperous era, in which the country was foremost in the world in terms of its literacy rate, the number of its publications, the independence of its national finance, and its government services for protecting people and dealing with their complaints. Domestically, people were proud and confident that Korea was the center of culture; diplomatically, it was a peaceful time because of the success of the policy called Serving the Great and Being Friendly with Neighboring Countries. Over the sea, far off to the west, reportedly there was huge earth-shaking trouble, according to an envoy who had been to Yanjing. It was said that hungry people had become violent and chopped off the heads of their own king and queen, and a massacre, difficult for the human eye to witness, had occurred, with blood washed by rivers of new blood.

In this peaceful time, King Chongjo's impatient wish to institute reform often appeared irrational even to his close officials, as if he were stirring up a calm sea for no obvious reason. Who could have dreamed at this point that such an advanced country would degenerate into a backward one only one hundred years after the death of King Chongjo? After the king's death came the Old Doctrine's political monopoly and ultimately Japanese colonization

.

Why couldn't His Majesty restrain himself? The frown on the face of Chong Sang-u, the fourth royal secretary, who belonged to the circle closest to the king, seemed to reveal this thought. The king, who was so cautious in real politics, often became excitable about academic matters; it was as if he were a totally different person. Regardless of his officials' worries, he would challenge established, accepted notions. Chong Sang-u silently lamented, thinking that it was all because His Majesty was intellectually arrogant, overconfident about his own academic achievements.

Only In-mong looked up at the king's gleaming eyes. He looked like a man who had fallen head over heels for a woman.

"Oh, is there another king like this in the entire world?" he thought.

King Sejong, renowned for his love of studies, was not said to have exceeded his scholar-officials at the Hall of Worthies, except perhaps in the field of phonetics. The level of King Chongjo's learning, however, was so high that his civil servants could not compete with him. His understanding of the thirteen classical books was peerless, and his comprehension of administrative practices such as law and finance was beyond that of any official; furthermore, he was conversant with military arts and medical science.

That was why the royal lectures had changed during the reign of King Chongjo. Until then a learned official gave a lecture to the king. They used to drag the sleeping king out of a concubine's chamber after a night of debauched abandon. He more often than not sat with his eyes glazed over, and soon enough he would doze off. King Chongjo had changed the custom and would teach young officials in their twenties and thirties. The change took place in the fifth year of his reign, 1781.

The king was a demanding teacher. The amount of homework he assigned was so huge that the officials could barely read the books on the reading list if they stayed up all night. The king himself had read all the books carefully, and did not tolerate either complaints about the amount of work or attempts at deception. On the day of the lecture, eight out of ten officials came to class without finishing their assignments, or wrote their examinations so poorly that they were scolded until they were on the verge of tears. In this drastic and fierce fashion, King Chongjo chiseled his authority onto a court that was dominated by the Old Doctrine faction.

"He is a true sage-king, one who appears in this world every thousand years," thought In-mong, filled with wholehearted admiration. "I could be dismissed by this king for having made a mistake." In-mong gazed at the coal wrapped in cloth. His heart brimmed with indescribable torment. He hoped His Majesty would speak for a long time. Perhaps this would be In-mong's last opportunity to listen to a royal speech made to the officials. As early as the next day, there would be a discussion of disciplinary measures for In-mong. He felt a strong urge to bury the reality that troubled him greatly. His

Majesty's words were heading toward a conclusion.

"Was there such relentless shackling of the classes in the epoch of the sage-kings of Yao, Shun, Yu, Tang, King Wen, King Wu, and the Duke of Zhou? In my eyes there is no great difference between the proper son and the concubine's son, between the *yangban* class and the slaves. The distinction between the king and his subjects is enough for the ruler and the ruled. If you court officials and the heads of the factions become the rulers and if all your subordinates behave like rulers, how can the powerless carry on with their lives?"

"Your grace is boundless, Your Majesty," said one of the officials.

"A king is his people's Heaven," the King continued. "The will of Heaven is to allow everything to live and grow. Does Heaven not always brighten the shade and dampen dry earth? It is humans who busy themselves with making distinctions between the privileged and the humble. Heaven speaks with one voice, based on a person's virtue. The discrimination against Chungin, concubines' children, and the northwesterners exists only in our country, and it has never been my belief. Whatever others say, you should understand that I absolutely do not accept it."

When he was done speaking, King Chongjo regained his calm. Only then did he notice the visibly exhausted faces of his secretaries, who had been working under tense conditions all day. Yi Ik-un, the third royal secretary, had a sleepy look on his full, good-natured face.

"Is this the last memorial concerning the emancipation of slaves and the opening of opportunities to concubines' lines? Then you may retire to the Secretariat to rest and come back at *sulshi*. Now I will prepare orders for the Royal Defense Garrison. The first royal secretary and the fourth royal secretary will kindly stay on."

The king turned toward the main room. Huijong Hall had a reception hall of twenty-four square yards, where the king discussed politics with his officials, and two inner rooms of fourteen square yards each, where His Majesty handled private affairs. Except for related personnel, the secretaries were not present when military orders were handled. On such occasions, the first and the fourth royal secretaries were the only ones who could be with the king. The other secretaries stood up, made their deep bows, and left.

In-mong spoke timidly to the king. "Your Majesty!"

"What is it?"

"There is something I would like to report privately about Chang's death, about what Your Majesty ordered me to do this morning."

"Ah, yes, about Chang Chong-o. Good that you reminded me. Wait a moment until I finish with the order."

"Yes, Your Majesty."

In-mong bent his back as His Majesty headed for the main room. His Majesty's low voice drifted out of the room, sometimes audible, sometimes inaudible, as he dictated an order to the fourth royal secretary.

"I commend the soldiers' efforts during my visit to Crown Prince Sado's tomb yesterday. The Royal Defense Garrison, from the general down to the soldiers who are entrusted with the important responsibility of protecting the king and the capital, has been the object of my great interest and expectation, and will continue to be. At the same time, please keep in mind that I always pay attention to the conditions and morale of the Royal Defense Garrison. As I saw yesterday during my visit to the tomb . . ."

* * *

"What? Died of poison?"

A thin yellow notebook fell from the king's fingers. It was an account book on the rice tax for the Royal Defense Garrison, prepared by the Equal Service Office. His Majesty had taken off his glasses, and his flushed face registered disbelief. He stood still next to a table piled with taxation account books for the Royal Defense Garrison.

"Poison? What do you mean? Then what about the postmortem report submitted by the second state councilor?"

"It is a matter of such importance that I have not told the second state councilor yet, and firm evidence was discovered only after the report was completed."

"Then what did Chang Chong-o eat and who gave it to him? I will not be tolerant if you are just spreading groundless rumors."

"This humble servant would not dream of speaking falsely before Your Majesty. Chang did not die from poisoned food."

In-mong unfolded the cloth and shuffled toward His Majesty, and then handed the bundle over to Min Tae-hyok. In-mong caught sight of a tense expression on the face of the first royal secretary as he proffered the bundle to the king.

In the cloth lay the coal from the furnace of the duty room. In-mong explained what he had learned about the fatal smoke from Chong Yag-yong. Next he added a description of the incident with Yi Kyong-chul in the morning, saying that Yi had been spotted slipping out of the Royal Library but had managed to get away, and that right afterward he had been executed. Min Tae-hyok confirmed that In-Mong had requested Yi Kyong-chul's arrest that morning.

In-Mong continued: "So . . . I am deeply ashamed to report this, but the previous king's composition could not be found. It is believed to have been stolen at the moment Chang was poisoned, but it is my fault for not having been alert as a person in charge, a fault that deserves one thousand deaths. I wish that Your Majesty would send me to the organs of justice for severe punishment."

The room grew so quiet that no breath could be heard. This room, the large room on the right, was filled with eerie sunlight filtering through the paper door. The light reflecting off the glistening papered floor shone on the king's pursed lips.

His Majesty was calm. The stern face above the well-developed shoulders had already regained its calm, albeit concealing tension that might erupt any time. His eyes were locked as he followed a certain train of thought. Was there a smile on His Majesty's face as he lowered his head?

In-mong soon forgot about that strange smile. His heart was full of mixed feelings. He glanced up at the thick, graying hair under the blue-green crown, and then shut his eyes. He felt completely defeated. Behind the purple darkness of his eyes, images of every corner of this palace, the late Chae Che-gong's face, and his own banished wife flashed. He heard His Majesty's voice.

"First Royal Secretary!"

"Yes, Your Majesty."

"Who executed Yi Kyong-chul?"

"The director of the eunuchs, Your Majesty. The director has the authority to reward or punish eunuchs according to disciplinary policies."

"Director of the Eunuchs! Are you out there? Come in!" His Majesty's voice suddenly took on a sharp edge that shook the paper of the sliding doors as if it might tear them.

The first and the fourth royal secretaries trembled. Next to them, Yi Ik-un, the third royal secretary, and Chong Chun-gyo, the messenger eunuch, looked nervous as well. Even In-mong, who was completely resigned, felt something heavy weighing upon him. His Majesty was terrifying. When he fell into a rage, all officials, high and low, shook in fear. His fierce and intense countenance revealed his suspicion.

So In-song opened the door, entered, and prostrated himself. He must have perceived the mood of the room because he had been standing on the other side of the paper doors, but his face was tranquil and expressionless. Beneath the curve of his deeply hunched shoulders, his eyes were alert.

"Director! Did you thrash Yi Kyong-chul to death?"

"That is correct, Your Majesty."

"Why did you do it?"

"He was on duty at the Main Hall, and he had been warned and punished many times for shirking his duties and abandoning his post. Yet this morning he was absent from his post and did not return until after *sashi*. How can such behavior be tolerated in the Eunuch Department that serves His Majesty? It was as clear as daylight that if such things were ignored, moral discipline would collapse and the superiors could not control their juniors. Therefore I punished him to teach others a lesson; it did not originate from any personal anger. Please grant your understanding, Your Majesty."

In-mong was agape at his eloquence.

Even eunuchs were not allowed into the Royal Library without permission, so it made sense that they could not find Yi Kyong-chul anywhere. So In-song sat calmly, as if nothing unusual had happened. Nevertheless, His Majesty was no fool.

"That is hard to accept. Unless he was crazy, why would he do something so outrageous, knowing that it would bring him death?"

"As Your Majesty has mentioned, Yi Kyong-chul was not entirely normal in the head, so we had often considered dismissing him."

"How could such a person be allowed to take care of the Main Hall as a Rank 7B official? This is even more difficult to understand. The director, normally so strict, sometimes grants special favors, eh?"

"My apologies, Your Majesty. He said he had nowhere to go if he were fired, and I felt sorry for him."

"All right. If Yi Kyong-chul was looking after the Main Hall, who oversaw the heating of the Royal Library yesterday?"

"Apologies, Your Majesty. I supervise more than four hundred eunuchs, so I am not sure who is on duty at a certain place on a given day. I will find out immediately, Your Majesty." So In-song raised himself, looking really embarrassed.

"Wait!"

So's face registered a bewildered look as His Majesty ordered him not to leave. In-mong's silk bundle was tossed to So.

"That won't be necessary. Librarian Yi has already reported the information. Eunuch Mun O-dok heated the room, and that piece of coal coated with sulfur was found in the firebox. Book Examiner Chang died of poisonous fumes. What do you think of this turn of events, Director?"

His Majesty's energy, emanating from all over his body, was directed at So. This energy might be called a murderous spirit, and it sprang from the King's every pore like so many needles.

In-mong felt as if a long time passed, but it was only a brief moment— the moment it took the lump of coal to fall from the cloth, roll toward a corner, and stop.

So In-song's loud voice broke the momentary silence.

"A false incrimination, Your Majesty! All the fireboxes in the palace use charcoal provided by the Royal Supply Office. This is the first time I saw this so-called coal. It was not brought in by eunuchs, and some sinister personage must have staged this incident. Your Majesty, have mercy and please reconsider. Why on earth would we poison the book examiner? There has never been any conflict between the book examiner and ourselves." So's trembling voice and expression made an impression, and his words were logical.

His Majesty was unmoved. "That might not be so." His voice was chilly.

"Your Majesty?"

"The day before yesterday, I went to the library and entrusted some books wrapped in cloth to the book examiner. I told him to make notes before I returned from Hwasong Detached Palace — and I said something significant, that these books constitute the previous king's tale of the metal-bound coffer. There was no one with me — no one except you, Director of the Eunuchs!"

"I . . . I have no recollection of . . ."

In-mong and the others couldn't believe their eyes. His Majesty kicked So savagely on the chin. His body rolled like a squirrel's. His lips were torn and bloody.

"You bastard!" thundered His Majesty. "The principle of the King's Law is as clear as the sun and the moon. How dare you attempt to lie? Do you know why I hand-picked you to be the director when the former Director Kim Hon died? It was because I knew you were conspiring with cowardly individuals in the Queen Dowager's quarters, and because I knew you were plotting with disloyal groups outside the court. I have kept you near me just so the traitors would jump into my royal net. What I said to the book examiner the day before yesterday was for your ears. Do you think you can extricate yourself from this catastrophe?"

"Ahhh! . . ." So In-song's face turned ashen.

The director of the eunuchs was not the only one who was jolted. In-mong's heart burst into a thousand pieces like a wave hitting against a rock and bursting into fine spray.

"Then . . . His Majesty? . . . " In-Mong wondered ruefully.

He remembered Chong Yag-yong's warning. "To-won, don't trust His Majesty. I know, because I was the fifth royal secretary. He gives the impression to all around him that he trusts them wholeheartedly — but he doesn't trust anyone. He never does. Look at what happened to Hong Kug-yong, who had feared neither fire nor water on His Majesty's behalf. His

Majesty promotes a man, but at the same time looks for weaknesses, so he can remove the man later. He promotes the person's rival so as to impeach him someday. He is that kind of person. If he were not, he might not still be here in this world."

His Majesty was indeed fearsome.

His Majesty's resounding voice pounded against In-mong's ears.

"Listen now. Palace Guards! Commandants! Come and hear my commands!"

Immediately, noisy footsteps rushed into the courtyard. His Majesty strode to the sliding doors and opened them with his own hands.

"Ready for your command, sir!" The three Inner Palace Guards Battalion Commandants—Hwang Po-chan, Kim Hyong-gyun, and Yi Chang-uk—ran toward a flower bed filled with crawling staff trees and prostrated themselves before the stone ledge. They were wearing scarlet robes and yellow straw hats with tiger's hair, symbolizing the special detachment of the Palace Guards. They had been waiting at the gate since the first shouts rang out from the hall.

"Tie up this rascal and put him in the brig on the grounds of the Royal Defense Garrison in Hwasong."

"Your command will be obeyed, Your Majesty!"

"Fourth Royal Secretary, I appoint you the investigator. Investigate him thoroughly and discover the truth about the deaths of Chang Chong-o and Yi Kyong-chul. Find out the people who instigated the murders. This is a grave crime concerning the monarchy. Show him no sympathy."

"Yes, Your Majesty."

Chong Sang-u, the fourth royal secretary, stepped forward to follow the royal command.

In-mong glimpsed a look of determination flitting through So In-song's eyes as he remained prostrate, his face miserable. Though his eyes revealed fear of the imminent torture, what was even more evident was burning fury. His Majesty's eyes were on the fourth royal secretary. So In-song raised his torso, his knees still on the floor, his eyes fixed on His Majesty.

In-Mong was reminded of a cockfight he had seen a long time ago. When the cock bent himself and ducked his neck, his feathers rose to an almost vertical position and turned from copper to brown. When the cock relaxed his neck and straightened up, his feathers lay down and turned bright copper. He then fluttered those copper feathers, circling the enemy with his claws outstretched, looking for a chance to scratch. Protruding claws on wrinkled wavy feet. A sudden fear chilled In-mong's spine.

So In-song made a circle on the floor with the ends of his loose sleeves. When the straps attached to the daggers hidden around his wrists were unwound, So In-song felt a sudden heat, as if all the hairs on his body were on fire. "Now that His Majesty has trapped me," he thought, "I have no hope of being spared. Rather than being thrashed to death after a horrifying series of tortures. . . . The Queen Dowager will arrange for my family to adopt a son who will take care of them."

"Heavenly Retribution!" shrieked So.

Steely glints flew from both sleeves toward His Majesty, who was standing only eight steps from So—but the daggers narrowly missed their target. In-mong had leapt up and rammed himself against So In-song's waist and shoulders.

The flashes—two daggers—flew past the king's neck and broke the sliding door on his right. Simultaneously, So In-song fell to the floor on the left side of the room. It was not that any logical thought had occurred to In-mong. A glimpse of So's tensed lips was enough to induce In-mong to throw himself.

Even after he felled So, In-mong couldn't see what So had thrown. Holding So's arm, In-mong struggled to pin him down, but So could not be held down by someone like In-mong. Both the dead Yi Kyong-chul and So were experts at martial arts and both were former guard eunuchs. So's elbow hit a vital point on In-mong's forehead. A sharp pain coursed through In-Mong's body, and he couldn't open his eyes.

So scrambled up and drew his right hand back as if he were pulling something in, while his left hand swung rapidly. At the next moment, So, his back to the wall, was holding two strange-looking daggers—Three-Skill Daggers—tied to leather straps.

From the handle of a Three-Skill Dagger, below the main blade, protruded a smaller blade, like a deer's antler. A strap, threaded through a hole in the handle, was tied to the thrower's wrist. The Three-Skill Dagger took advantage of the same principle as the fist that was pulled before a punch. The large blade would pass through the target and the smaller blade would enlarge the wound. The strap made it possible to withdraw such a dagger and throw it again, any number of times.

The witnesses to this scene doubted their eyes, unable to bring themselves to believe what was happening. The director of the eunuchs, who looked after the king in the closest quarters, was now attempting to kill the king. His Majesty hurriedly flung himself toward the opposite wall. The three secretaries almost unconsciously stepped backward, protecting the king. They seemed frozen in their positions.

"Traitor!" shouted the commandants Hwang Po-chan and Kim Hyong-gyun, rushing into the room and blocking So In-song. They looked fierce, with their swords drawn and their straw hats thrown back around their necks. They thrust their swords immediately toward So's shoulder.

"Heh!" So In-song snorted and jumped back a step. So In-song's hands, moved in two arcs, releasing the daggers too fast to be discerned by the eye. This time he had thrown the daggers from a stable posture.

The right dagger went through Hwang Po-chan's right chest, and the left dagger struck Kim Hyong-gyun just above his right knee. The wounds should not have been fatal, because the knives did not travel far enough to pick up speed,but the moment the daggers dug into their targets, So twisted his wrists. The knives whirled in a circle in the victims' flesh, carving wounds as big as soup bowls, before returning to So's hands.

The two commandants helplessly rolled on the floor, shrieking. Blood gushed out. The other men in the room didn't have time to take a good look at the commandants. So's two daggers next flew directly at King Chongjo's neck and chest. The men surrounding him, including Third Royal Secretary Yi Ik-un, spread out their arms, their faces ashen, to block the blades.

Another commandant, Yi Chang-uk, burst in, breaking the paper door. So stepped aside quickly to avoid the commandant's sword, hurriedly reclaiming the daggers that would have gone through Yi Ik-un. Now the situation had changed. Commander Yi's sword sliced the air from top to bottom, cornering So In-song, and in the blink of an eye hit the daggers several times.

The clanging between the blades continued. Cornered against a wall, So felt pain as severe as if burning charcoal had been spilled on his right arm and his left waist. He was badly wounded. He groaned in pain, and his face bore a look of despair. He felt every single element of his body — veins, flesh, nails, hair, even eyelashes — convulse, attempting a final grasp at life. He gritted his teeth, threw his body to the left, knelt on his left knee, and lashed out with his left hand in an attempt to stab Yi Chang-uk's waist — but Yi's sword, which had been held high above his head, was already falling swiftly.

A dull thud was heard, as if a folding mattress on a laundry line was being beaten with a paddle. There was no shriek. So's body had been sliced through from the right side of the neck to the left side of the chest. His head fell toward the broken door, blood spurting to the ceiling. Gushing blood soaked the lacquered floor and splashed as far as In-mong, who was lying motionless near the wall.

Complete silence descended.

The sounds of urgency disappeared with a diminishing echo like an auditory hallucination. In-mong felt as if his limbs had melted into water and were absorbed by the floor.

Everyone was paralyzed—everyone except one man: His Majesty, whose expressive face looked surreal among the frozen grimaces that surrounded him. His Majesty stepped out from behind the human barrier. His white socks drenched in blood, His Majesty strode forward and stood in front of So's body. His Majesty looked shocked, and yet his face was in control.

"Did . . . you kill him?" Disappointment could be detected in his first words, but he immediately took on a solemn expression and issued a command. "Shut the doors of the Huijong Gate and the Sonpyong Gate. First Royal Secretary, take a list of the names of who have been in the compounds of Huijong Hall, and order them not to breathe a word about this. If the news spreads outside before I give the order otherwise, all on the list will be beheaded, no matter who revealed it. Take the wounded commandants to the Royal Infirmary right away. Paper this room over. Only the eunuchs and the palace matrons who have been present can do the work. Until it is redecorated, national affairs will be administered in the Main Hall. Secretaries, gather the documents and move them there."

Only then did Commandant Yi Chang-uk, as if awakening from sleep, throw his sword and prostrate himself on the bloody floor. "Your Majesty! Put me to death! It is my fault that Your Majesty saw a traitor's blade. Put me to death, Your Majesty!" he pleaded.

"Your Majesty, put us to death!" The officials prostrated themselves one by one to take the blame. In-mong heard the words as if in a dream. He tottered forward and prostrated himself at the feet of His Majesty.

* * *

"You are a subject of such loyalty as is rarely found throughout the generations," Yi Ik-un, the third royal secretary, rubbed his hands together and smiled broadly. "To-won, this is really an opportunity one can only hope for." He could not conceal his glee.

The two officials were in Yi's office in the Royal Secretariat, right in front of the Tonhwa Gate. The sun was still up, but near the door a candle had been lit on the stick embossed with butterflies.

"What an admirable feat! You have just saved His Majesty from evil people attempting regicide. It is undeniably the perfect chance to push the renewal His Majesty has been pondering all along."

In-mong was silent.

"First, all the eunuchs must be rounded up so as to find the cohorts of that enemy, So In-song. Excepting those who are assigned to offices involved with construction or with supplying food, clothing, or other necessities to the palace, that's some two hundred eunuchs alone. Also, the powerful officials who incited those eunuch knaves must be ferreted out and a widespread investigation must be immediately undertaken in the palace."

"Someone might overhear you, sir."

"If they want, let them listen. This was an attempted regicide. Will the likes of them have a hole to escape into unless they can fly up to the sky or disappear under the earth?" Yi exclaimed in a loud voice, shaking his full head of gray hair.

Yi Ik-un was fifty-three. Chae Che-gong had taken Yi under his wing and had taught him at his own house. Because of his age and his appearance, he was an important figure among the Southerners. His weakness was that he was too affable and too emotional to be a good politician. In the sixth year of King Chongjo's reign (1782), he had let loose a river of abuse at the Principle group members who were then attacking Chae. As a result, he had been stripped of his position. Later he had exhibited disorderly, drunken behavior at a party where the king was present, and for that he had been banished to Huksan Island. It was said that King Chongjo had joked about why he had kept him at the Royal Secretariat starting in the eighteenth year (1794): "Ke-su (Yi Ik-un's personal name) should be kept near me. Otherwise I cannot feel relaxed about him."

In-mong adored Yi Ik-un for his fierce loyalty and his lack of greed, but, for some reason, he didn't feel like agreeing with him today. Perhaps he was angry — his forehead wrinkled — on account of his elder's simplicity.

In-mong bowed his head. He had a splitting headache from So In-song's blow. Melting into the pain, In-mong's consciousness perceived reality as a dream. Bizarre occurrences, previously unimaginable in his not-so-short life, had been taking place since early morning. And the incident of So In-song . . .

Loyalty to the king, righteousness and fidelity, devotion. . . . The very foundations of life's sacred laws of cause and effect were being shaken. When In-Mong made his report to the king about the death of Chang Chong-o and the disappearance of *Humble Thoughts on the Book of Odes*, he had been ready to receive any punishment. "The king is sacred and wise, and I deserve death." He had recited Han Yu's words and had no other thoughts. Now it turned out that everything that had happened was the result of His Majesty's schemes and orchestrations. In-mong shuddered with displeasure, as if he had imbibed fouled water.

It was so ugly.

His eyes stung and tears gathered. What had he been living for until now? He had hoped to lead a beautiful life. He had wished to devote himself to the good king and to live a beautiful life, but now his dream was a fallen leaf. He had never anticipated the abyss of life that he was to cross today. Filthy people had shown their filthiness to His Majesty, and His Majesty had become unclean. If he remained loyal to the sullied king, In-mong too would become dirty.

His Majesty's absurd appearance, kicking So In-song's chin . . . So In-song's pursed lips as he threw the daggers at His majesty . . . and His Majesty's words, "I have kept you near me just so the traitors would jump into my royal net." The ugly conniving. . . . Then what was the difference between His Majesty and the Old Doctrine faction? In-mong bit his nails. His face was distorted.

"I can't help but be worried about His Majesty," Yi Ik-un continued, ignoring In-mong's agitation.

"What do you mean?"

'The throne is higher than anything, so it is perilous and difficult to maintain.   When the king in such a position takes the initiative and seeks reforms, the threat of assassination always follows. This is on the same principle as when you poke at a beehive: The bees swarm over you. Therefore, the king should never take on the responsibility of being the principal reformer. He should hand over that hateful role to a trustworthy official, and he himself should always assume the role of a wise ruler who advises his officials gently and dispenses benevolence—in other words, a relationship like the one Emperor Shenzong of Song China had with Wang Anshi, or the one Korean King Chungjong had with Cho Kwang-jo. But what about our king now? Chae Che-gong has died, and Minister Chong Min-shi is dying. Yi Ka-hwan was accused of being a Catholic and has lost power, and Kim Cho-sun is too young to have a solid basis. As his surroundings are so weak, His Majesty has taken matters into his own hands. Today's incident is but a single hair among the numerous hairs of many oxen. Something grave may happen in the near future."

In-mong did not reply.

"This is a rare opportunity for His Majesty. He should root out his enemies and revamp the court completely to place his friends near him."

"But the matter . . . is not so simple," In-mong said. "Let's assume the eunuchs were rounded up and they were forced to name the enemies. . . . So In-song has died, and there is no evidence about his conspirators. How can you arrest all the adversaries on suspicion? Such an action would be fruitless, no more effective than simply poking the beehive. Queen Dowager Kim would go into a frenzy, saying the loyal officials from the previous reign were being persecuted unfairly, and then she would threaten to move out to private quarters, saying she could not suffer such injustice. Then the Old Doctrine faction would go further, saying His Majesty was attempting to exile his own grandmother, and memorials would flood in from rustic literati, finding fault with his Majesty's unfilial behavior toward his own ancestors. Haven't we already experienced this? For instance, with the incident of Yi Chae-gan, the chief magistrate of the State Tribunal, and the incident of Prince Unon?"

"Hmm."

"It seems this is why His Majesty, considering such consequences, prohibited discussion of today's attempt. His Majesty must have some plan, so we had better wait and see."

"What do you mean by a plan? Do you have any idea?"

"No, sir. I am just a lowly civil servant. It is just that a thought occurred to me while talking to Chong Yag-yong this morning. It appears that His Majesty is thinking about his father."

"The former crown prince?"

"The people have sympathy for the former crown prince, who met such a violent death. His Majesty will reveal that the allegations against the crown prince were false, and posthumously declare him king. And then he will pursue all Principle group members as the masterminds of that regicide. In my limited perspective . . . the renewal His Majesty emphasizes is a reform that will come from the king. If he wants to implement the renewal in an environment where almost all the court officials are against the idea, he has no choice but to call upon the people's sympathy and take advantage of their opinions. Then also the problem is . . . "

In-Mong here interjected his own thoughts about Yi Ik-un's predictions: "It is now quite well known that the allegations against the late crown prince were fabricated, but would it be possible to declare him monarch posthumously when the previous king pronounced him a traitor to the dynasty and prohibited anyone from mentioning his name?"

"It appears, however, that it is not impossible. In fact, there was a discussion of the previous king's tale of the metal-bound coffer this morning, and . . . "

Yi In-mong leaned toward the other man, planning to divulge a secret, but just then an impatient voice was heard from outside, accompanied by noisy footsteps.

"Librarian Yi, Librarian Yi! Are you here?" The voice belonged to Chong Sang-u, the fourth royal secretary.

Yi Ik-un and In-mong rose in surprise. Yi Ik-un opened the door, and they stepped out to the veranda.

In-Mong responded to the secretary's calls. "Right here, sir. What is the matter?"

"Ah, Librarian Yi. Quickly, come to the Main Hall."

"Yes?"

"His Majesty summons you." Chong's face was pale, and his eyes conveyed sympathy.

Sensing Chong's uneasiness, Yi Ik-un prompted him. "Po-jong (Chong's personal name), what is going on?   Has something happened to His Majesty?"

"No. The first royal secretary has delivered the memorials from the Office of the Censor-General and Office of the Inspector-General and His Majesty has read them."

"What? Is he crazy? When an assassin was just killed, is it time to hand in memorials? The whole dynasty depends on His Majesty's sacred body. He must go into his quarters to calm his nerves and compose his precious personage, and now what memorials? And how can memorials go directly to His Majesty without any discussion at the Royal Secretariat?"

"The memorials from the Office of the Censor-General and the Office of the Inspector-General do not go through the Secretariat, do they? Sir, this is not a time to talk about such things. Librarian Yi, please, let us go."

Chong Sang-u took hold of In-mong's wrist, pulled him impatiently to the edge of the veranda, and urged him to put on his shoes quickly. In-mong slipped his feet into his shoes, and Chong opened the small gate leading to the Main Hall and urged him to hurry up. The western quarters outside the main office were wrapped in solemn silence.

As In-mong walked along the path toward the Main Hall, he noticed that the air felt oppressive, as if a fire were burning nearby. His lungs labored in fatigue. The surroundings gave off a strong, poisonous smell. The air was so thin that he felt he would suffocate. Now what wind would blow him over? The sun was about to descend, and it was dusk. He had never been called to the Main Hall at such a late hour. He pictured a boat with a broken mast proceeding toward a sunken rock and inevitable disaster.

What was the matter? In-mong pulled on Chong's sleeve as they approached the end of the path, planning to ask about the reason for his summons; but a voice growled out from the Main Hall.

"Call the commander of the Palace Guards Regiment!" It was His Majesty.

The middle door was flung open and His Majesty, in leather slippers, descended to the shoe ledge.

Looking up at His Majesty, In-mong gasped in surprise and fear. The King's face was flushed with anger—but In-mong was not sure who was the target. His Majesty's lips were pursed, and his cheekbones and eyes were red, as if he were inebriated. His furious eyes were fixed on some distant point, and he didn't see In-mong standing right in front of him.

"Living Quarters Matron!" His Majesty's voice boomed.

In-mong's heart was choked with anxiety. Palace Matron Han, who was standing on the right side of the shoe ledge, all but rolled over.

"Prepare a military outfit, horse, bow, and sword!"

Palace Matron Han winced at the unexpected command, but ran to the inner quarters without a word, having sensed the strange atmosphere. Flurries of activity spread out in concentric circles around the king. In-mong stood with Chong Sang-u in the center not understanding what was going on. Before he could hazard a guess, a red-robed military commander darted in from the main gate, his sword's sheath clanging against his gold waistband. He seemed to fly over the stone pavement.

"Ready for Your Majesty's command!"

The commander bent before the king, kneeling on his right knee with his right hand on the ground, like a collapsing mountain. He was Kwon O-sang, who was the veritable commander of the Royal Defense Garrison because he was the commander of the Dragon and Tiger Regiment. His shoulders shook; he had sprinted from his post near the Tonhwa Gate.

"Order Kang Ho-un, cavalry chief, to arrest Yi Cho-won, the minister of punishments; Kim Myong-ik, the second minister of punishments; and Chong Yag-yong, the third minister of punishments!"

"Your command will be obeyed, sir!"

"Also, pick thirty cavalry men from the duty cavalry detachment of the Royal Defense Garrison. Feed them and their horses, and have them waiting at the Kumho Gate by *sulshi*."

"Then where will you go, Your Majesty?"

"To Chae I-suk's house on Myondok Mountain. Go and get ready!"

Kwon O-sang stuck out his chest as he looked up at His Majesty, and said, "Ready for Your Majesty's Command!" He sprang up and disappeared.

In-mong looked back at Chong Sang-u, but Chong's expression indicated that he was in the dark as well. Only then did His Majesty realize In-mong was waiting.

"Drafter!"

"Yes, Your Majesty!"

His Majesty's face was dark and grave. It was rare for him to call In-mong by his official title.

"Follow me."

"Yes, Your Majesty."

Palace Matron Han and some other palace women came into the

courtyard through the east gate. They were holding a bundle, containing His Majesty's russet military outfit and robe, as well as the royal sword and the royal bow, high in front of them. His Majesty glanced at their procession and turned to the main office.

In the office were only three officials: Min Tae-hyok, the first royal secretary; Yi So-gu, the second royal secretary; and Cho Hung-um, the sixth royal secretary. There were no eunuchs or scribes. When His Majesty signaled with his eyes, the sixth royal secretary carried to In-Mong a red tray bearing a memorial. It was an unusual memorial, judging from its volume for it was not a letter in an envelope, but a scroll. This meant it had probably been signed by many people and therefore it concerned a serious matter.

In-mong looked up at His Majesty in bewilderment, and His Majesty gestured to indicate that In-Mong should read the memorial.

In-mong knelt at His Majesty's right side, grasped the edge that said "Please Open Before His Majesty," and unfurled the roll. He felt as if burning coals had been spilled on his back. He hastily straightened himself. His eyes grew as large as an oil lamp's saucer, and his feminine, thin, white fingers shook.

This was no wonder, because the memorial had the title "A Memorial Requesting an Intensive Investigation of Chong Yag-yong and Yi In-mong." In-mong's face was as white as a sheet; he began to read.

> The Office of the Inspector-General and the Office of the Censor-General report this with joined forces. A nation is a proper nation when there is law and order. When there is law and order, a nation prospers. When law and order shakes, the nation declines. Therefore the wise in the past emphasized the importance of law and order time and again.
>
> Since the time when this dynasty was founded on the principle of civil administration, prosperity and cultural excellence, the generations of kings were such that it seemed like the capital of Zhou Confucius envisioned. Unfortunately, however, ethics have deteriorated and heresies and pernicious studies have risen. As a result, it is hard to determine what is law and what is order in this country.
>
> Ahh! It is indeed lamentable. How many times have our two offices submitted memorials recommending the rejection of heresies and pernicious studies? The royal net is truly sparse; the question of punishments was raised and then dropped for several years, and not an enemy was prosecuted. Now poisonous teeth gnaw at the law and order of the court.
>
> We, lowly servants, have heard that today Chong Yag-yong

took away Chae I-suk, who had been arrested by order of the minister of punishments, and murdered him with premeditation. Yi In-mong, currently with the Royal Library, is involved in this matter. How can these people so wantonly and immorally commit this evil crime of heresy? This group, which does not respect the importance of law and order and the significance of the king's law, is rooted in pernicious heretical theories. Therefore we are fearful; our breath comes short and we feel timorous. . . .

In-Mong felt as if a bolt of lightning had struck him.

Who in the world had written this frightful memorial? With fearful eyes, In-mong gazed at His Majesty, but His Majesty was not looking at him. He had taken off the crown and the dragon robe, and was putting on the military garb the court women had brought, while listening to the argument of the fourth royal secretary.

"Your Majesty, you should not do this. Night will fall soon. It is perilous for Your Royal Highness to go to a far-away mountain at this late hour. Besides, there was the appalling conspiracy of that enemy So. And Your Majesty intends to venture out secretly with only thirty escorts. It is a command issued lightly, indeed. Please reconsider, and cancel it."

Another official echoed the plea: "Your Majesty, the fourth royal secretary is right. Please cancel your command."

His Majesty was impatient. "Don't waste words. There is something at Chae I-suk's house that must be investigated without delay."

Again the fourth royal secretary pleaded, "Please cancel your command, Your Majesty."

"Enough!"

Though the king spoke firmly and decisively, the discussion between him and his servants didn't seem likely to end soon. In-mong's wavering eyes fell again on the memorial.

Yag-yong and In-mong are tainted with heresy. Thousands of their cunning ways and tens of thousands of their wicked schemes cannot be recorded on a humble piece of paper. Yag-yong's household is the den of evil studies, and the whole world knows it. Yun Chi-chung, the most immoral person in the world, who burned up his own mother's spiritual tablet and terminated her ancestral ceremony in Chinsan in 1791, was Yag-yong's first cousin on his mother's side. Yi Sung-hun, the evil leader of the heresy who was baptized in Qing China, is Yag-yong's brother-in-law. The fact that his brothers are followers of heresy and that Yag-yong himself was once a follower has been revealed time and time again by impeachments. Swept by the currents of the times, Yag-yong excuses himself, saying that he has severed his ties with the heresy, but it is an evil lie. The whole country observes that because Yag-yong's group exists, incitement of the heresies and pernicious studies do not stop.

When Chae I-suk was arrested and his true colors were about to be revealed, Yag-yong took him away, and taking the advantage of his position killed him off. According to an intelligence report sent from the jail to the Board of Punishments, Yag-yong threatened the chief jailor, and carried the suspect on his own back to the main room of the Board office. He did not allow anyone to come in except for a clerk sent by Yi In-mong. Soon Yag-yong ran out pronouncing Chae's death, but no one saw how he died so suddenly, for he had been in good health only minutes before. If this is not an attempt on the part of Yag-yong and In-mong to seal his mouth, what other explanation is possible?

Ah . . . How great are His Majesty's favor and concern for Yag-yong, and how high a position he holds! Nevertheless, he has committed an appalling crime resorting to evil and dirty scheming, his eyes set on his own promotion. Even so, His Majesty's heavenly mirror reflects as brightly as the sun and the moon, so how is it possible that his betrayal and ruse would remain concealed?

As for the matter of In-mong, words cannot be spared.

The woman incarcerated with Chae I-suk, a Yun Sang-a, who was released by Yag-yong's tricks, was In-mong's former wife. The bond between husband and wife, having faced disasters and happiness together, is second to none; is there any better way to know In-mong inside and out than through his wife? The woman has disappeared since her release this morning, and so it is clear that In-mong and Yag-yong conspired for her liberation. How can such a thing have happened? We have heard of no more bizarre occurrence since the foundation of this dynasty four hundred years ago.

In-mong's wife's family members are all heretics. Yun Yu-il was In-mong's brother-in-law. Yun helped the escape of the Catholic priest by deceiving police with the use of evil methods in 1795 when the court pursued them to their dens. The court arrested Yun Yu-il, Choe In-gil, and Chi Hwang to interrogate them as to the whereabouts of the Western Religion's monk, but they died at the same hour of the same day in jail. As Your Majesty knows, that was why we failed to obtain the rabble's list. Their mouths were sealed with poison by their superiors—Yi Sung-hun, Yi Ka-hwan, and Chong Yag-yong under the direction of Chae Che-gong. If they had not died simultaneously and had instead revealed the truth, how would a person like In-mong have avoided punishment?

We humble servants prostrate ourselves and look around, but among the young officials in the court, no other person deceives Your Majesty and turns his back to the nation for his own personal ambitions as much as In-mong does. Judging from In-mong's actions, it is crystal clear that he encouraged Yag-yong to commit crime with cunning methods, and incited his own clerk to kill Chae I-suk.

In general, In-mong's deceptive, cunning actions have a thousand faces. In-mong was originally a nameless scholar from an impoverished country home, and none of his ancestors contributed a mote to the improvement of the dynasty. Such a man advanced along the path of government positions, having memorized a mosquito-leg-sized body of learning, all thanks to his wife's family in Seoul. In-mong wholeheartedly submitted to the heresies, abandoning what little he had learned. He socialized with the heresy's rabble in Kangnam and criticized the royal court and tried to harm the Queen Dowager with premeditation, all in the name of His Majesty. Yet he was not put to death, only banished, all because His Majesty, whose virtue is as vast as the sea, pitied the tender youth.

Even during his banishment, In-mong did not discard his wickedness; while discussing the ways of the legendary Three Dynasties in public, he harbored the heresies in his heart. The police guessed his designs and attempted to arrest him again, but In-mong divorced his wife to hide his true face, and began to say that he had severed his ties with his wife's family, who were tainted with heresy. How can a human being be so abominable?

Those out there tainted with the heresies are easily arrested and punished for they do not fear death, but those in the court, like In-mong, conceal their true colors for the sake of their own promotion, so it is difficult to identify them. There have already been worries and concerns about these concealed individuals, but His Majesty placed people like In-mong, characters already known, near him and allowed their cunning shoots to grow.

No epoch can possibly be free from the words that dazzle and deceive the people and blot out benevolence, but nothing is more wretched than the heresies of the West. If Your Majesty does not show a strong will to kill all the heretics according to the laws of a country, there is no way to root them out, for they will sprout up like radish seeds in the sand, the younger following the older, the son following the father.

Their heaven-shaking crimes have been revealed one by one. If Your Majesty does not weed them out and punish them, we believe there will not be another chance to destroy the dens of these heretics. Your Majesty, please interrogate and punish Yag-yong and In-mong according to the laws of the country, and let these traitors know the power of Heaven, for they, contaminated by heresies, do not respect morals and ethics. We prostrate ourselves before you and wait for your sacred direction.

In-mong's mind reeled.

The memorial rattled him, and sent him into a whirl of confusion. He could not move an inch. To confound him further, Sang-a . . . Sang-a. She was in Seoul, then. They said Chong Yag-yong killed Chae I-suk. And he himself. . . . Death seemed to shake him by the hair. Confused emotions echoed in his heart.

If he had been alone, he would have flailed his arms and vented his fury against this heartless world, or he would have wailed in pain until he lost consciousness. Instead, he only stared at the scroll with a blank expression. His spirit seemed to have drifted away. Frightened and cowering, it could have been frozen, like the snowflakes now falling outside the window.

Yi Ik-un, the third royal secretary, was approaching him. In-mong had not been aware of his presence. Ik-un picked up the scroll and began to read. He gasped.

"Drafter!" His Majesty called. He had changed into his military garb.

To In-mong, His Majesty's words sounded like a far-off noise. In-Mong's tongue would not move. Terror and fury swept over him. His Majesty was standing before In-mong. He had a determined air. His arms were folded and his legs wide apart.

"Drafter!"

"Yes, Your Majesty!"

"What do you say to this?" His voice was low and wretched, like a groan.

In-mong's face stiffened more. "Your Majesty! This is not true at all! It is slander, Your Majesty!"

"Then, what about the clerk they say you sent to the Board of Punishments this morning?"

"He was sent to inform the Board of Punishments of Chang Chong-o's death. This humble servant did not know at that time that Chae I-suk had been arrested and jailed, Your Majesty!" In-mong's voice was shaking pathetically.

Yi Ik-un defended In-mong, his bull-like body crouching. "Your Majesty, Librarian Yi is right. It is not possible. How could Yag-yong or Librarian Yi conspire to murder the son of Teacher Pon-am? They are not the kind of people who would do such a thing; they would rather let their entire clans die."

His Majesty, however, continued harshly. "Third Royal Secretary, you stay out of this. You simply cannot say it would not have been possible. I personally sent the Palace Guards to call the coroners, so why did you have to send someone else to the Board of Punishments?"

In-mong could not respond. Clearly, though, it was not the time to keep anything from His Majesty.

"Your Majesty, please understand. I sent the clerk to give word to Yag-yong personally. He does not go to the office very frequently since he was impeached last year. I thought if he was not informed, another official would investigate Chang's death. As the person who was on duty last night, I hoped that the matter would be solved smoothly—and hoped Yag-yong would take on the responsibility."

In-mong's anguished excuses stopped there. Oh, how ugly it was! Spilling out cowardly excuses! In-mong pitied himself. Life had all kinds of shapes! Why had he been born destined to be trapped by others? How could each of his awkward actions invite hatred, envy, contempt, and mockery of the worst kind? Once again sullied by groundless suspicion, he felt the events in his life were mistakes or foolish conduct. Others developed insight into life as they aged, but he had been a simpleton, providing fodder for such tricks. The result of his life was excruciating pain.

In-mong clenched his teeth, suppressing a cry that yearned to burst out. The past that had been distorted in the memorial flooded back into his memory, exacerbating his bitter wounds.

King Chongjo frowned, observing how dazed In-mong looked. "I will ask one more thing. Did you know that Chae I-suk had died in the Board of Punishments?"

"I did not know the details, but heard the news from Chong Yag-yong when he came to conduct Chang's postmortem."

"Why did you not tell me? Do you not know what is important and what is not? You should have reported Chae's death, above everything else."

"My shortcoming deserves death . . ."

"You worms! What have you been doing? What have you been doing while my trusted one, who is like my own limb, died in jail, and no one knew about it?"

His Majesty was now addressing the royal secretaries—Min Tae-hyok, Yi So-gu, Yi Ik-un, Chang Sang-u, and Cho Hong-um—who were standing on either side of him. They shook in fear, like aspen leaves. The six royal secretaries were responsible for the six boards. The first royal secretary oversaw the Board of Personnel, the second royal secretary the Board of

Taxation, the third royal secretary the Board of Rites, the fourth royal secretary the Board of War, the fifth royal secretary the Board of Punishments, and the sixth royal secretary the Board of Public Works. The responsibility for reporting Chae I-suk's death was that of So Yu-mun, the fifth royal secretary, but he was nowhere in sight. In-mong didn't know that Yu-mun had already left the palace to get the investigation report from the Board of Punishments, after His Majesty reprimanded him.

In-Mong said, "Your Majesty, my apologies . . ."

"That's enough! How is it possible that I learned about Chae I-suk's imprisonment only after reading this memorial? Who arrested him? Who jailed him? Second Royal Secretary, you cannot say you did not know about it, can you?"

His Majesty made his point well.

It was indeed strange that His Majesty had not known about it. Yi So-gu held an additional post, as deputy director of the Office of Incarceration. Why hadn't he reported Chae's arrest to His Majesty? Although the incident had occurred while His Majesty was away at Hwasong Fortress for three days, at least His Majesty should have been informed this morning.

"Please punish me harshly," Yi So-gu volunteered. "I have not yet checked the reports from the Office of Incarceration. This laziness deserves a hundred deaths."

In-mong felt a chill run down his spine as he looked at the man who volunteered to assume all responsibility. Was he too a villain?

In-mong was afraid of the enemies lurking behind all these incidents. In-mong had guessed vaguely that those who had imprisoned Chae I-suk and put him to death were ultra-conservatives, with Second State Councilor Shim Hwan-ji at the core. But now . . . it seemed as though the range of enemies was not as limited as In-mong had guessed.

Inside the Principle group of the Old Doctrine faction, there were three branches: ultra-conservatives, such as Chief State Councilor Yi Pyong-mo, Second State Councilor Shim, Minister of War Cho Om-gwan, Minister of Taxation Yi Chae-hak, and Minister of Punishments Yi Cho-won; mild conservatives who were ready to compromise with His Majesty's reforms, including Third State Councilor Yi Shi-su, Minister of Personnel So Yong-su, and Minister of Public Works Hong Ok; the so-called Northern Learning branch, which was eager to participate in reforms, including the celebrated Yon-am Pak Chi-won.

Second Royal Secretary Yi So-gu was at the core of the Northern Learning branch along with Pak Che-ga, general of the Five Guards Divisions of the Royal Defense Garrison, but now the second royal secretary was attempting to conceal the true nature of the incident, blaming it on his laziness. So did the Northern Learning branch have something to do with it? Yes, the three branches must have conspired together, In-mong thought.

In-mong was truly one of the Southerners.

It is said that if there is a shadow of doubt in one's heart, delusions grow. Shocked and confused, In-mong now regarded every one of the Old Doctrine faction members as an enemy who would destroy him. Was it possible that even the Northern Learning branch acted as an arm of the ultra-conservatives? In-mong's suspicion was not completely groundless.

The Northern Learning branch had participated in His Majesty's reforms on the surface, asserting that various institutions should be improved by accepting China's advanced civilization. The members of the Northern Learning branch were truly privileged; they had been completely intoxicated by the sweetness of power from the time of their birth. They had all been able to go to Yanjing, the capital of China, for their families were at the core of the Principle group. Therefore, the reforms they had in mind were fundamentally different from His Majesty's restoration. His Majesty wanted rule by the sage-king, in which he himself would be the driving force for reforms as a wise monarch, like Yao, Shun, and Yu of ancient times.

The Northern Learning branch had a different idea. Times were changing. Now it seemed that the world was becoming a place where moneyed commoners prevailed. There were countless cases of powerful families who had been high officials until the previous generation but were now reduced to farming or itinerant peddling. In Cart Knoll and Bean Fluff Port, people who had been slaves only a few years back had now purchased genealogies and were claiming to be Confucian scholars who had passed the preliminary government examinations. Few officials paid attention to this problem. In a turbulent period like this, the only way to maintain the monarchy was for the powerful literati to intervene between the king and affluent commoners.

In other words, they believed that reforms should be undertaken according to the times, but they themselves wanted to be the protagonists of change, for they had been at the center of power in the capital for generations. Against this backdrop, it was only natural that In-mong regarded the Northern Learning branch with suspicion. To In-mong, it was as if someone who had been tarred and feathered was now venturing out to reform someone in the stocks—the object of reform wishing to be the force of the reform.

In-mong could understand the radical elements in the Southerners faction, who were willing to embrace even Catholicism in the name of reformation, but the Northern Learning branch claimed that they could reform the country without a strong monarch, the source of current authority, and without Catholicism, with its religious appeal. How would they manage reform, and on what power would they rely? Those cunning conservatives wearing the mask of reformation . . . In-mong winced.

His Majesty didn't continue interrogating Yi So-gu, the second royal secretary. He became preoccupied and dropped the matter. In-mong had never seen His Majesty so shaken up as he was today. When Chae I-suk's name had been brought up, his face had become gloomy.

"I cannot stand the sight of you. Get out, all of you!"

The officials, including the first royal secretary, gathered up their documents in a hurry and retreated on tiptoe. His Majesty remained immobile.

"Why haven't you gone yet?" His Majesty roared at In-mong, who was still prostrated.

Go? Go where? Literal-minded In-mong didn't know what to do. He felt like crying. Hadn't His Majesty ordered the arrest of Chong Yag-yong, Yi Cho-won, and Kim Myong-ik? Wasn't he in the same boat as Chong Yag-yong? Did His Majesty mean he could go home?

"Denounced by the two inspection offices, I should await investigation. Your Majesty should hand me over to a judge for an interrogation."

Only then did an inscrutable expression appear on His Majesty's face. The furrow between his eyebrows twitched and formed an arc. Looking up at his Majesty's face, In-mong felt his heart fill with emotions. This was indeed the end, he feared. Whether he would be punished or acquitted, he could remain no longer in the court, after such an accusation.

"Defamation of this servant has peaked with the memorial submitted by the two offices. My honor has been trampled on and torn apart, and now it has become sullied waste. The weak, sad, dying voice of this servant is shameful even to his own ears. What more excuses can I make before His Majesty?

"I am by nature solitary, lowly, and useless. I realize that I cannot compromise with the times because of my narrow, deficient temperament. Yet, Your Majesty did not consider me useless — although I do not know what Your Majesty saw in me — and placed me nearby. This vessel is unworthy of your benevolence. Even if I whittle my bone and chafe my flesh with my meager loyalty, I will never be able to repay Your Majesty's grace, as vast as a sea.

"Through the false accusations of today, I have inflicted harm on your Sacred Grace, and such presumption adds to my offense. I deserve death.

167

Please imprison this servant along with Chong Yag-yong, and punish us both severely according to the unbiased opinions of the court. I deserve to starve to death. I will await execution, and if by any chance my life is saved, I will leave the capital and eat what I have tilled, drink from a well I have dug, and forever remain a recluse in a good world."

In-mong's forehead knocked against the floor, without his realizing it. He tried to say, "Please look down and have mercy," but the plea died in his mouth and became a wail.

"Stop it! A scholar's heart should be wide, large, firm, and strong. What is this ugly behavior? In the *Analects*, Confucius says that a scholar's responsibility is heavy and he has a long way to travel. A scholar's duty is to behave in a humane manner, and that is why his responsibility is heavy. He can be rid of his duty only with death and that is why he has a long way to travel. How dare you wail noisily, as if the world has come to an end? Leave the palace today. It would be advisable to prepare an explanation, in writing, for your interrogation by the State Tribunal tomorrow. Suspicions about you are so overwhelming that I cannot do anything about them."

"My apologies, Your Majesty!"

6
Bitter Memories

*Today's scholars are more and more corrupt, and
literary style is distorted further every day. In the
case of the literati, they copy the style of fiction,
treating the profundity of the classics as useless.
The fictitious style is light, shallow, strange,
bizarre, completely different from the old standards.
Also it is sorrowful, dismal, frivolous, never the
voice of government. . . . If there is even one Chinese
character in the fictitious style on a test paper for
the National Academy examinations, reject it, even
if the test is otherwise filled with precious gems.
Such a writer should not be forgiven at all; his name
should be made public and he should be forever
prohibited from sitting for national civil service
examinations.*

— King Chongjo, "Directions on the Question
of Literary Style" (1792), *The Veritable Records
of King Chongjo*, in the tenth month of the
sixteenth year.

*[Since His Majesty's restoration of literary style] if
there is a small phrase with a shade of newness or a
character out of the ordinary, His Majesty suddenly
asks if there is such an expression in the old records.
If the answer is no, he becomes angry and asks how
dare one write that way. Alas, if the same phrase
existed in an old piece of writing, why would I
repeat it?*

— Pak Chi-won, quoting Yi So-gu's words in
"Introduction to the *Nokchong-gwan*
Collection," vol. 7, Yon-am Collection.

When In-mong went out through the Tonhwa Gate, the sky was already dusky. The last rays of the day remained on the edge of the western sky like a folding screen. In-mong was walking along the walls of the Royal Ancestral Shrine toward the Pajo Bridge, but he suddenly stopped in his tracks and put up his sleeves before his face. A cold wind, gusting around him, was pushing the hazy, sandy dust toward the sky. A brown leaf, half decomposed, circled around and around, and flew over the decorated walls of a house with a magnificent gate.

In-mong felt a fever creeping up from his neck to the top of his head. A violent cough started. Controlling his shaky ankles, he seized a tree. His whole body shook and he felt a chill. He realized he had not eaten or drunk all day. Was he coming down with a cold? As he looked down, he saw his own pathetic shadow dancing past the tall shadow of a tree stretching over the wall of the Royal Ancestral Shrine. A fallen leaf rustled into the shadows. A leaf rolling in the fierce wind . . . a leaf struggling in the dust-filled world.

What would happen to this nation? Those who deceived the king didn't care how frightening Heaven would be. Didn't they say In-mong had killed the son of Teacher Pon-am? How could they lie so boldly? Yet when dirt flew, it defiled white outfits. Even if it were revealed later to have been a false accusation, how could he face the world again?

In-mong felt as if he were in a depressing dream. The swirling memories. At the end of these waves, his wife's face floated vaguely. Poor thing, she had been imprisoned in this cold. In this harsh weather . . . if he had been with her. . . . no, it would have made no difference.

"My love, I am sorry," he thought. "It looks really hopeless. It would have been better if I had continued studying, instead of entering the world of government positions! The life of rustic literati is a wise abandonment of reality, giving in to the destiny of the learned. They worry about the royal family and society, but give up their duties goodheartedly in order to roam about the world of the Six Classics. If I had done that, I wouldn't have been parted from you. Since the day I joined the civil service, has there been a day without worries and concerns? The burden has been too heavy for my deficient abilities, and in the end I am haplessly collapsing. However hard I have tried to be on guard, it has never been enough."

In-mong lifted his head and looked at the street. Lights were coming on one by one, near and far. At last, he shuffled along, leaving the tree behind.

The street was deserted in the twilight. Only his pale shadow floated along. By the time he arrived at his home near the Southern Military Encampment in Chonghak-dong, it would be completely dark. All he could see were winter shadows, which would disappear soon enough. The tree branches were trembling in the harsh north wind, and the falling leaves looked desolate. This evening street was familiar. It was a portrait of himself. His life was like the winter dusk. Dreams of dawn! The morning sky of a translucent spring day! Those things seemed so far away!

In-mong coughed intermittently as he trudged along, eyes downcast. Suddenly he heard a frightening wail in the sky. He looked up in surprise, and saw an ugly owl on the branch of a tree in the Royal Ancestral Shrine. Its screech sounded like the cry of a ghost from hell — or the howl of a devil as it tore flesh from a dead body and consumed it.

An owl!

How could that ill-omened bird be in the shrine? Weren't owls caught as soon as they were sighted within the town walls? In-mong's teeth chattered. Had he grown weak? Vague sensations passed through his head. "The Appearance of Spirits" by Yi Ha, which he had read as a child, buzzed in his ears.

> When the sun goes down and dusk descends, ghosts come. . . . Swept by the wind, riding horses, kicking at clouds. Music rises up from the earth, the sound of strings as if weeping and sobbing, the sound of the flute. The shaman dances, rustling her long skirt against the floor, the leaves of cinnamon trees tremble in the wind, their fruits fall, the wildcats wail, vomiting blood, and foxes die from fear . . . As the rain god goes into the pond, riding a dragon painted on a wall, the dragon twisting its golden tail. . . . The hundred year-old owl becomes a ghost. . . . Dismal ghosts living in old trees. . . . Its crying sound, its blue eyes, it is ominous for the nests.

To In-mong, his own shadow gradually merging into the darkness looked spooky.

From the darkness came a whiff of rotting fish from an alley market. It was a pathetic odor, wavering and melting in the darkness, smelly, sad, miserable. "When the sun goes down and dusk descends, ghosts come . . . Swept by the wind, riding horses, kicking at clouds. Music rises up from the earth . . . weeping and sobbing. . . . When the sun goes down and dusk descends, ghosts come. Swept by the wind . . ." The words echoed in his head.

In-mong's thoughts were rushing toward a certain realization. What was this unfathomable fright that shackled him, interfering with his reasoning? Fear and trembling billowed up like mist, almost palpable. Owl . . . owl . . . owl!

"The Owl" written in Chang's notebook. *Humble Thoughts on the Book of Odes*. Chang must have seen this work, written by the previous king. The king must have referred to the poem in some way. The previous king and "The Owl"? The previous king and "The Owl." In his head, In-mong gently turned the pages of the *Book of Odes* to the second poem of the "Odes of *Pin*" section. He was startled by what he found. "Do not, owl, destroy my nest . . ./ you have taken my young, . . . / The mulberry roots I secured / Door and window around / Them so firmly I bound . . . / 'Dare any of you my house despise?'"

How could it be? Wasn't "The Owl" like the previous king's life? In-Mong recited the entire poem in his head.

> Owl, O owl, hear my request,
> And do not, owl, destroy my nest.
> You have taken my young,
> Though I over them hung,
> With the nursing of love and of care.
> Pity me, pity me! Hear my prayer.
>
> Ere the clouds the sky had obscured,
> The mulberry roots I secured.
> Door and window around
> Them so firmly I bound,
> That I said, casting downward my eyes,
> "Dare any of you my house despise?"
>
> I tugged with my claws and I tore,
> And my mouth and my claws were sore,
> So the rushes I sought,
> And all other things brought;
> For to perfect the house I was bent,
> And grudged no toil with this intent.
>
> My wings are deplorably torn,
> And my tail is much injured and worn.
> Tossed about by the wind,
> While the rain beats unkind,
> Oh! My house in peril of harm,
> And this note I scream out in alarm.

This poem was about the hawk, the king of all birds, who hated and despised the owl that took away his offspring. During the reproductive season, the owl searched for the hawk's nest, pushed out its eggs, and laid her own eggs in the nest. The hawk raised the eggs believing them to be her own, but realized the truth too late when the owl's offspring grew up. The author of this poem, the Duke of Zhou, criticized his three brothers, through this metaphor, for their destruction of the family and for forcing him to go into exile.

Was it a coincidence, In-Mong wondered, that phrase after phrase corresponded to the previous king's life?

> Owl, O owl, hear my request,
> And do not, owl, destroy my nest.
> You have taken my young,
> Though I over them hung,
> With the nursing of love and of care.
> Pity me, pity me! Hear my prayer.

It sounded as if the former king was lamenting that he had put Crown Prince Sado to death, deceived by the Old Doctrine faction members. Now they were trying to destroy the nest as well.

> Ere the clouds the sky had obscured,
> The mulberry roots I secured.
> Door and window around
> Them so firmly I bound.

This phrase seemed to suggest King Yongjo's ascent to the throne after the myriad hardships amid the factional fighting that had continued since his days as crown prince.

King Yongjo had worried constantly, losing sleep, about how to gain the public's confidence after the Revolt of Yi In-jwa. Inside the court, he implemented a policy of grand harmony, employing officials regardless of their affiliation, to mitigate the conflicts among the four factions; and outside the court he implemented the Equal Service Law and the Grain Loan System Reform Act for the benefit of commoners. In addition, relief produce for the drought period was sought after and sweet potatoes were introduced from Japan. "I tugged with my claws and I tore, . . . / And grudged no toil with this intent." Couldn't this phrase refer to the king's efforts?

But all was futile. By the time he dictated the tale of the metal-bound coffer to Chae Che-gong, King Yongjo was seventy-one. He had put his own son to death, the son who would have succeeded him, and he was too old to restrain the ever more tyrannical Old Doctrine faction. Weren't these his sentiments?

> My wings are deplorably torn,
> And my tail is much injured and worn.
> Tossed about by the wind,
> While the rain beats unkind,
> Oh! My house is in peril of harm,
> And this note I scream out in alarm.

Then . . . what did all this mean? What was the message, if the poem were similar to the previous king's life? Was it just a coincidence? Coincidence . . . yes, it could all be In-mong's wild conjectures. Why should the poem be interpreted only in that way? But then why had this particular poem, of all poems, been in Chang's notebook? Wasn't it too much of a coincidence? The threads of Chang's thoughts, which seemed to be almost in his grasp, had never been unraveled.

This is because I have become too high-strung, In-Mong told himself. He had always feared the owl. The owl's cry he had heard during his torture in the State Tribunal had been truly sinister. He smiled bitterly, recalling that time. Suddenly a part of the memorial he had read came back to him: "In general, In-mong's deceptive cunning actions have a thousand faces." A lump formed in his throat.

When those cunning officials spotted someone's vulnerability, they exaggerated it, their imagination in full swing. They had an unusual talent for turning white into black in one sweep. It was also their strength that they had conviction. Equipped with loquacity, they forced their principles on people without paying any attention to other explanations.

> In general, In-mong's deceptive, cunning actions have a thousand faces. In-mong was originally a nameless scholar from an impoverished country home, and none of his ancestors contributed a mote to the improvement of the dynasty. Such a man advanced along the path of government positions, having memorized a mosquito-leg sized body of learning, all thanks to his wife's family in Seoul. In-mong wholeheartedly submitted to the heresies, abandoning what little he had learned. He socialized with the heresy's rabble in Kangnam, and criticized the royal court and tried to harm the Queen Dowager with premeditation, all in the name of

His Majesty. Yet he was not put to death, only banished, all because His Majesty, whose virtue is as vast as the sea, pitied the tender youth. Even during his banishment, In-mong did not discard his wickedness; while discussing the ways of the legendary Three Dynasties in public, he harbored heresies in his heart. The police guessed his designs and attempted to arrest him again, but In-mong divorced his wife to hide his true face, and began to say that he had severed his ties with his wife's family who were tainted with heresy. How can a human being be so abominable?

* * *

The story went back eight years.

King Chongjo had a headache because of the Catholic problem. When incarcerations large and small occurred because of Catholicism, King Chongjo, who had been protective of the Catholics, was driven into a corner. Earlier, the King had issued a proclamation: "Treat the tainted people as human beings, but burn up their books." It was based on the words of Han Yu, and was the mildest way to defend orthodoxy. This was because the Catholics belonged to the Southerners faction, who had supported the king to keep the Old Doctrine in line. In 1792, the King finally came up with a dramatic idea—the so-called restoration of literary style—after mulling over the difficult situation.

The restoration of literary style, in one word, was an attempt to return to the pure style of the Six Ancient Classics, including the *Book of Odes*, the *Book of History*, and the *Book of Changes*, to stamp out the corrupt styles of the Ming and Qing dynasties of China.

King Chongjo asserted that the harms of Catholicism were only superficial, but the more dangerous and flagrant heresy was the novel style of Qing China, as it was used in, for example, *Tale of the Marshes,* by Shi Naian, and *Tale of the Three Kingdoms,* by Luo Guanzhong. This was because writing style was closely related to the customs and morals of the times. According to the king, bad writing style caused the literary scene to deteriorate and disturbed human hearts, preventing people from dedicating themselves to true scholarship. Catholicism would disappear if true scholarship were established, but indulgence in the novel style "corrupts people, turning them into barbarians and animals" without human ethics.

King Chongjo cornered the Old Doctrine faction with such logic and regained his political superiority. He banished a man named Yi Ok to Samnangjin and permanently prohibited him from sitting for the civil examinations because he had written a national examination in fictional style.

In the same year, the king took away government positions and punished those who used the fictional style prevalent among the Old Doctrine faction. Among the accused were Nam Kong-chol, Yi Sang-hwang, Shim Sang-gyu, and Pak Chi-won. The punished officials were forced to lead contrite, quiet lives and to write apologies in the pure, older writing style. There were those who followed the king's orders, like Yi Tok-mu, and those who ignored it, notably Pak Chi-won.

Around this time, Yi In-mong, a reference consultant in the Office of Diplomatic Correspondence, was commanded suddenly by the king to visit Pak Chi-won.

King Chongjo branded Pak Chi-won the father of fictional style after reading his travelogue *Jehol Diary*, and requested In-mong to demand an explanation and bring an apology from him.

Yi Tok-mu, who was gravely sick, managed to write an apology on the twenty-fourth day of the first month of 1793. He died the very next day. Only Pak Chi-won, whom the king had deemed "the cause of the stagnation of literary culture and the deterioration in scholarship," had not submitted his apology. As for In-mong, he had to play the villain. Nevertheless, he had not dreamed that his life would change so much after his encounter with Pak Chi-won.

On the eleventh day of the second month of 1793, In-mong went to see Pak Chi-won at Anui near Chiri Mountain, where Pak was county magistrate. It was a clear winter morning bathed in sunlight, and magpies' cries filled the air. Pak's son Chong-chae was waiting for the guest at the entrance of the village.

As soon as they had exchanged pleasantries, In-mong addressed the main topic. "Teacher Yon-am, why are you being so stubborn? His Majesty is furious. I believe it is right for you to write an apology and submit it to His Majesty."

Pak Chi-won only laughed. "Am I being stubborn? That is not correct. It is not that I will not write it but that I cannot write it. I have a nasty temperament, so I do very well when I make fun and make others laugh, but my hands tremble and will not move when I try elegant compositions intended for His Majesty. Please understand this old man. Things in the world do not unfold as we wish, and it has been hard for me to endure my difficulties. My worthless scribbles became the fictional style, one mistake led to another, and finally they were collected as the *Jehol Diary*. Who would have guessed its popularity? The book is truly vulgar. Why did I scribble trivialities, worthy to cover sauce jars and paper doors, and ruin myself and corrupt the literary style of this world? I am a bad subject who harms this sacred dynasty's teachings, and I am trash on the literary scene. Well, well, please have a drink."

Pak Chi-won was voluble, and told his son to offer drinks to In-mong; but In-mong was not easily deceived. Many people came to extract an apology from Pak in vain, because his tactics confused them.

"Teacher Yon-am!"

"Aha! My ears might fall off because of your shout. What is it?"

"Do you really wish to do this? How many times have you already deceived His Majesty behind his back by saying the restoration of literary style throws Heaven off balance and steals the outdated words of ancient people? Why do you keep doing this? Will you keep ridiculing His Majesty's literary style policy? Please stop talking and write a letter of apology in the pure, correct, older style. You should know that this is your last chance."

Pak Chi-won's face turned white at In-mong's words, although he was not normally easy to intimidate. His son, blinking nervously, was staring up at the ceiling. Neither father nor son had realized that the situation was this serious. Nevertheless, Pak Chi-won was not an ordinary person by any means. He quickly calmed his heart and spoke quietly.

"Do I criticize His Majesty? I do not know who accused me, but the accusation is not true. I once said to my students that each person has different feelings, which is the manifestation of Heaven's balance. Didn't Zhu Xi himself say in the introduction to the *Collected Commentaries on the Book of Odes*, 'Poetry is what remains in a person's heart and is expressed in words, after the human heart has responded to things'? Human nature, endowed by Heaven, is pure and invariant, but the emotions brought by the responses to things are different from person to person. Writings, naturally, have the beauty of uniqueness. What I mean is, one does not need to suppress uniqueness by mimicking the style of the ancients and quoting their phrases."

In-mong retorted, "When Zhu Xi discussed poetry as emotions, he was not speaking of emotional differences, was he? He just emphasized the usefulness of poetry in calming the human heart and evoking lofty emotions as well as cultivating the human mind. The true ideal of poetry is to conceal differences. A poet lends his brush to sing about the governing of the world and the ethics between husband and wife, so as to enhance feelings of resentment or longing. In the end, the real poet is forgotten, and the impression and the sound of the song are carried by the east wind. The poet disappears, but the poem remains. This is the philosophy of the *Book of Odes* and the philosophy of His Majesty, who believes in the reform of the literary style."

"Conceal differences? Returning to the ancient style to conceal differences means writing in quasi-ancient style and plagiarizing old phrases, doesn't it? Then how can a person reveal his vivid natural feelings, so different from the next person's? Consultant Yi, you're so young that you don't know the world. There are many troubles on this earth and one cannot possibly protect oneself from them. His Majesty says that fictional writings express the sad, troubled sounds of discarded civil servants and lowly concubines' children, and thus harm the Way of the world. But do they come from some abstraction? Who likes a tortured cry? Cold and hunger created urgency, various laws of punishment oppressed them, and a sense of fury made them violent. Isn't the dizzy bustle of the world the cause of such style?"

Pak's commentary was the refutation of the usual method of writing. Writing had been based on "Allusions Using Language and Incidents," taken from ancient texts such as the *Book of Odes*. This influenced not only the Four Books and the Three Classics, but also historical writings and Chinese poems of the Han dynasty and the *Anthology of Eight Writers of the Tang and Song Period*, as well as Tang poetry by Li Bo and Du Fu. In *Qunqiu zuozhuan*, one discovers the phrase, "When composing a poem, take its meanings from short literary fragments," as early as the twenty-eighth reign of Duke He. "Taking meanings" signified pulling out phrases from the *Book of Odes* and changing them to fit the context of the current composition, thereby enriching the poetic meaning and enhancing the spirit of the writing.

With the emergence of a new era, starting with Pak Chi-won, this method of writing was disappearing. The Old Doctrine faction, led by the Northern Learning branch, didn't recognize that one could express oneself by depending on ancient writings. They believed that all compositions belonged to the authors, and that was the correct way to keep the balance that Heaven bestowed upon human beings.

King Chongjo's restoration of literary style had been intended to reverse the flow of history. King Chongjo, usually known for his astuteness, was unyielding to the point of irrational inflexibility. The motive for his unreasonable obstinacy would be revealed at the end of *The Encounter of the Stars*. Innocent In-mong had accepted the king's belief at face value.

"But doesn't such a thought negate literature at its roots, the literature we have been familiar with until now?" In-mong argued. "From antiquity, writings have preserved the wisdom of the times. The purpose of the scholar's literature is to learn such traditions in a peaceful rhythm, instilling longing for the moral teachings of Yao and Shun, and enlightening the king for the sake of the country. The real meaning of the Six Ancient Classics lies in this; how can you call it literature if all it does is concern itself with mere trivialities?"

"The Six Ancient Classics," said Pak Chi-won. His wrinkled cheeks twitched and his eyes shone. "I will ask you one thing! Every time you open your mouth, Consultant Yi, you talk about the Six Ancient Classics, but do such elegant, ancient writings exist in this world? Not only were the *Book of Odes*, the *Book of History*, and the *Book of Changes* all secular books of the streets at one point, but also they were recorded using the Han dynasty writing system. The poems in the *Book of Odes* were popular songs sung in the marketplaces of Gaojing, the capital of Zhou; the *Book of History* told the tales about the royal families that had been passed down in the oral tradition; and the *Book of Changes* was a fortunetellers' guide, used by diviners of the court and marketplaces. It would be different if they were the complete writings of Zhou. Confucius expresses a longing for the Zhou dynasty throughout the *Analects*. But . . . any babbling child knows that the current Six Ancient Classics are forgeries, patched up by scholars of the Han dynasty. As for the original of the *Book of History*, when Emperor Wen of Han was searching for old classics all over the country, scholar Fu Sheng dictated what he remembered and the rest was collected from various sources. It amounted to twenty-nine volumes. Afterward, during the reign of Emperor Jing, Kong Anguo, a descendant of Confucius, produced the *Book of History*, written in the authentic ancient system and claimed that he had found it while demolishing a wall in his house, but it turned out to be a forgery. During the reign of Emperor Cheng, Zhang Ba produced the 102-volume *Book of History*, but it was also a fabrication. The one we read now is a compilation by Mei Ze, the scholar of East Chen, who stretched the existing twenty-nine volumes to thirty-three and added twenty-five extra volumes; but Yan Ruozhu and Hui Dong of Qing revealed that this edition was also a fake. All the Six Classics are like that—yet now you talk about returning to the Six Ancient Classics? What absurdity is this?"

In-mong's patience reached its limit. After all, he was only twenty-two at that time and was high spirited.

"What? Now it is clear that you have opposed His Majesty's restoration all along. A short while ago, you pretended to be contrite. How can your views be so sly and your arguments so wrong? His Majesty is angered by today's corrupt literary style and is trying to correct it with a wise order. Would you rather be punished?"

"Punished? Life and death depend on Heaven. People should live quietly, according to their beliefs. This is what my heart and my head tell me, so what is there for me to do now? Is there anything wrong with what I am saying?"

It seemed as if their ages had been switched. Here was an old man, later to be renowned as a peerless liberal philosopher for opening the chapter of modern literature, and a conservative young man who rejected modernity outright.

"What do you mean by that? You are preoccupied with the unsound bibliographical studies of the Qing. It is an effort to attribute every piece of writing to each author. Mei Ze's *Book of History* has been read widely in China, Korea, Japan, and Vietnam for over fifteen hundred years. Were all these people fools, tricked by Mei Ze over a thousand years, as Yan Ruozhu claimed? No, sir. If the twenty-five volumes that Mei Ze added were pieces he had selected carefully after researching old literature, what is wrong with that? If Confucius himself had written the entire text of the *Book of History*, would it have been his own creation word by word? If you try to search for the sources of words, they only retreat further away. What we can gather are the vague thoughts of an author, and the merely imaginary relationship these thoughts have with history. If you ask me, it is a fantasy and reverence for a perfect antiquity."

"Well, well. Now stop it. My head is really confused now, I don't understand a thing you are talking about. Hey, Chong-chae, go and get more wine."

In-mong and Pak Chi-won jousted with words all day. They argued and drank, they debated and drank until the day grew dark. Finally both of them became very drunk. In-mong was impressed by Pak Chi-won. In-mong had never seen such a dear old man. He was frank, open-minded, learned, energetic, and cheerful to the point of impudence even when he was cornered by In-mong's fierce accusations.

Well into the night, Pak Chi-won said, "Look here, Consultant Yi. I will be frank with you. I will continue to resist in this way and I will not write that apology. So forget it."

"Oh? No, no! You can't do that."

"Why can't I do that? We all do it in the name of saving face. But my position is different from His Majesty's. His Majesty is busy with affairs public and private, so he can pretend he has forgotten about it. But what happens if I write an apology? *Jehol Diary*! In His Majesty's eyes, it looks like a mere work of vulgar fiction, but to me it is a tower of obstinacy I erected in exchange for my whole life. I don't have many days left before I die; do you tell me I have to die saying my life was a mistake?"

"Well, you shouldn't think . . ."

"So forget it. Don't you feel any sympathy for this old man? I am the grandson of Pak Pil-gyun, who used to be a second deputy director of the Royal House Administration. His Majesty allowed Hong Kug-yong to torture and kill all the Principle group's men, so my youth was spent fleeing from Hwanghae Province to Pyongan Province. 'I was high once and then fell low, and only then could I see the real friendships of the world.' Is this only the sentiment of Duke Di of the Han dynasty? When my situation changed, no one asked whether I was alive or dead. When I thought I finally survived, my clan was already in decline. Have you been to my house at Poun-dong in Seoul? Do you think the short rafters and coarse roof can withstand wind and rain? They say poverty is a scholar's everyday affair, but it was like that until I was fifty-five. Finally, I have landed this out-of-the-way position and am relieved of the worry of starving to death. I will be sixty soon. Have I made money? Have I seen glories as a government official? My only comfort is I have created a book with what I have written all my life. So will you tell me I should wipe shit all over it with my own hands?"

"Teacher, teacher, please calm down. You don't have to think in this fashion at all."

Pak Chi-won laughed. "Yes, yes. I can really talk to you. Well, well. Have one more wine!"

In-mong felt bewildered, for he knew that he was gradually retreating. He was confused. Pak Chi-won unburdened himself without thinking of saving face or making pretenses.

A new realization began to dawn on In-mong: Not everyone of the Principle group was evil.

In-mong had grown up believing that the Old Doctrine faction members were incarnations of devils, engaged in political intrigues, extortions, deceptions of kings, treacheries, cruelties, avarices, corruptions, and so forth. Pak Chi-won's steadfast belief and guileless innocence engendered a refreshing astonishment.

Of course, In-mong didn't agree with Pak's sentiments. To his dying day, In-mong would not give up his aversion to the lightweight and common style that had begun with Pak; but In-mong knew that no one could choose the epoch in which he lived. One lived as best as one could in one's given time. Like Pak, who had conviction in his heart but tried to survive saying silly things like, "I am a bad subject and trash on the literary scene." Shouldn't In-mong recognize their thoughts to some degree? They were part of the era that was given to In-mong as well.

In-mong wasn't sure whether he was moved or tricked by Pak's wiles. He left empty-handed the next day. Not only did he go without Pak's apology but he made excuses for Pak.

"Your Majesty, Yon-am is in a drunken stupor day in and day out. Consequently his hands shake and his head is muddled."

This was something unthinkable for In-mong. He lied to His Majesty, to none other than His Majesty. His Majesty accepted his words, and his critical inquiries of Pak stopped. The problem was the confusion In-mong felt afterward.

Everything looked empty, every affair trivial. Looking back now, something must have possessed him. He had no energy left, as if the blood had been drained from every part of his body. A sense of futility oppressed him like heavy rain clouds.

"What is the point of living like this?" he asked himself. "Because of that useless old man of the Old Doctrine faction, I lied even to His Majesty. Why did I come up to Seoul in the first place? Why do I pay attention to the fifty thousand meaningless things happening at court? Why do I go around desperately trying to meet people? Why do I torture my heart without respite?"

Such thoughts would occur while he was eating, and his stomach turned. It was the shock he felt after trampling on his own principles. He wanted to live beautifully. That was his principle. He felt his life was a spark that would flame to a high purpose—the high purpose of reviving the king's authority, thereby allowing the people to lead trouble-free lives, and bringing peace to the world.

When the center is disturbed, the parts don't hold together. The peace of the world depends on order. Order can be achieved when the people are equal to one another, under one king. When the king's authority disintegrates, order breaks down, and when order breaks down, the world becomes turbulent.

This was In-mong's understanding of reality, irrational and incomplete though it was. He was a typical Southerner from the southeast. Following the king's intentions was good, and opposing them was a betrayal. With an absolutely pure heart, he was furious at the current situation in which the king's power was only nominal and the Old Doctrine's was potent. He was convinced that he lived to venerate the good king and to punish the evil of Old Doctrine faction, which was responsible for various acts of disloyalty.

The encounter with Pak Chi-won had deflated his confidence. According to his principles, he had compromised with the wicked party and deceived the good king. Such things happen all the time in the course of life. Life is always changing, and principles don't necessarily conform to reality. In-mong was not experienced enough to understand this. He could not accept it that he had strayed from his own convictions. He was angry.

Soon a cool contempt for the remainder of his life surfaced in his heart. Shouldn't he resign and return home?

As he brooded, violent emotions rose up in his heart. Yes. The world regarded him with an ungenerous eye. His talent was meager and his writing was shallow. Yet at a young age he had taken up a post that exceeded his ability. This was because he put more importance on appearances than anyone else did. Without pausing to think whether something suited his ability, he blindly attempted to do everything. Why hadn't there been a disaster? It seemed prudent to extricate himself before he encountered some grand humiliation. Once he became truly miserable, there would be no way out, however much he wanted it.

A thought leaning in one direction tends to become more obsessive. In-Mong developed a habit of sitting in dim candlelight, deep in bitter thought, until he heard the rooster crow.

One day, something happened that lifted him from his depression. In the middle of the night, Yi Kwan-gyu, an assistant section chief in the Board of Rites, and O Sok-jung, a fifth councilor in the Office of Special Advisors, came to In-mong's house. When In-mong asked the purpose of their visit, Yi Kwan-gyu, who had been sitting silently, recited a poem entitled "Yearning with Reverence," from the *Book of Odes*.

> When a man is smart, he establishes the country
> When a woman is smart, she ruins the country.
> That smart woman over there
> Is something like an owl.
> When she has a long tongue and talks too much
> She will become the root of evil for the country.

Suggesting one's own feelings by reciting a poem from the *Book of Odes* is called "poetic allusion." Hearing this poem, In-mong finally realized that Yi Kwan-gyu was hinting at a macabre plan.

"Do you intend to have the Queen Dowager killed?"

"Hush!" O Sok-jung listened carefully for possible movements outside, and Yi Kwan-gyu began to whisper into In-mong's ear. "That is the idea. All the court officials are more afraid of her words than those of His Majesty, and if we don't do anything about it, His Majesty's reforms won't be accomplished even in a hundred years. And it is not normal the way she bustles about goading people inside and outside the court. If we do nothing, we Southerners might be beheaded, accused of being Catholics. This is the way the two of us think. We came to discuss it with you first, and no one else knows about it yet. When the time comes, we will have to discuss it with Chong-hon [Yi Ka-hwan] and Pong-am [Yi Ki-yang]. What do you think?"

In-mong's heart was stirred. With their words, the depression he had felt for previous several months ebbed away.

Queen Dowager Kim, Queen Chongsun, was King Yongjo's second wife, and genealogically King Chongjo's grandmother. She was only two years older than King Chongjo, but nominally she was his grandmother and the head of the royal family. Her character was apparent from the way she phrased her directives to the court officials, written in the Korean script. They all began with the word "you" in the lower form of address, regardless of the recipient among the court officials. Instead of "I hereby ask your lordship to do such and such a thing," she wrote, "You must do such and such a thing." As a daughter of the Principle group, she was by nature arrogant and willful. She had become a fierce protector of that group, all the more because she faced King Chongjo's stubborn resistance.

The significance of this woman's place in the royal family of the Choson dynasty could be compared to the Japanese Invasion of 1592. First of all, she masterminded Crown Prince Sado's death by alienating him from King Yongjo, and later she suppressed the Expediency group, which sympathized with the dead crown prince. She had King Chongjo's brothers, Prince Unshin and Prince Unjon, killed by accusing them of being pretenders to the throne, and after King Chongjo's death she had Prince Unon killed by branding him a Catholic. It was, of course, this woman who had the Catholics, including Yi Ka-hwan, executed, and had Chae Chae-gong stripped of his title.

Alas, the royal family, with a meager number of descendants, was almost brought to extinction by Queen Chongsun.

As we will see later, Yi In-mong would claim that Queen Chongsun had tried to kill the sons of Crown Prince Sado, who harbored strong resentment against her, and had then taken charge of the ascension of Prince Yollyong's great-grandson, a distant relative, to the throne. It was not an unreasonable accusation, considering that Prince Unshin and Prince Unon were banished to Cheju Island toward the end of King Yongjo's reign. She also managed to banish Prince Unon to Kanghwa Island, despite King Chongjo's objections, by personally issuing an order to the court officials. With the birth of Kong (later King Sunjo), her plan ended in failure, but her contribution to the demise of the Choson dynasty was immense. Royal family members, feeling that their lives were threatened, hid in the mountains and islands disguised as lowly farmers. This led to the royal family's plummeting authority and made impossible the education of its descendants. Decades later, King Cholchong would be taken from Kanghwa Island, where he had been living as a woodcutter, and even later, the Taewongun would manage to save his life by acting like a madman.

In-mong concurred without hesitation.

"Of course, I agree. But which method are you thinking of using?"

"We can contact a lady-in-waiting in the Dowager's Palace. We think we can get her to poison the Queen Dowager."

"What? Using deception? No, that is not right," In-mong asserted.

"What do you mean?"

"It is said that with righteousness there is the great righteousness of heroes and the petty righteousness of ordinary men. Don't you remember that Zhang Zifang and Chuang Hai attempted to assassinate the First Emperor of Qin China because they were bitter? But they failed, didn't they? They failed because they resorted to petty righteousness. Although Zi Fang had a talent for turning the world upside down, he didn't take into consideration the tricks of famous ministers, such as Yin Yin and Tai Gongwang. It was sheer luck that he wasn't killed after employing a subterfuge fit for Jing Ge and Nie Zheng. In your plan you are following Zhang Zifang's misjudgment. If you fail, your names will be sullied forever, and if you succeed, there is no guarantee that her cohorts will meekly accept it."

"Then what do you suggest?"

In-mong lowered his flushed face. His heart was thumping. He had been thinking of the same thing as these two men for a long time. He had an idea, but he had to be ready to die.

Death . . . but he was only twenty-two-years-old. He felt a sharp pain in his throat. A true human being should guard his life like a gem and search for something that was worthy of his life. Was this worth dying for?

"I have an idea," In-mong said decisively. "I will accuse Kim Kwan-ju, the Queen Dowager's cousin once removed, as a traitor and ask for his purge."

"What? No, that's too dangerous," Yi Kwang-gyu shook his hand.

"I know that it is dangerous. But writing a memorial to His Majesty to report Kim Kwan-ju's treacherous heart and urging His Majesty to punish this traitor is the most righteous and straightforward way. If Kim Kwan-ju is purged, we can strip the Queen Dowager of her royal privileges and demote her."

Kim Kwan-ju had been noted as a leader, along with Kim Ku-ju, of the Incident of the Clean Name Society in 1772. A confidant of the Queen Dowager, he was constantly kept at a distance with banishments and imprisonments by King Chongjo. If Kim Chong-su, Yun Shi-dong, and Shim Hwan-ji were the visible leaders of the Principle group, Kim Kwan-ju was the veritable power behind the scene.

"But if we write such a memorial, the whole court will turn upside down. The Queen Dowager is at the root of all the disasters most difficult to handle in the world. Indeed, the world harbors unforeseeable disasters, although from the outside it looks entirely peaceful. If we reveal this in a memorial, people won't believe us because they have been lulled into a sense of peace. Don't you know that years ago Yi To-hyon, a scholar from Andong like you, sent the same memorial and was tortured to death?"

"He who writes should be ready to die along with the degenerate foe. I shall compose it," In-mong said, "Perhaps I won't have to die. Compared to the time when Yi To-hyon died, the king's position is no longer weak and isolated." In-mong feigned a smile.

"Then are there grounds for charging him with treachery? In any event, we have to make haste. This is the only way to assert the royal family's control, stabilize the dynasty, and save fellow believers from coming persecutions." Yi Kwan-gyu, a devout Catholic, couldn't hide his anxiety.

"It's been a long time since the rumors began to spread that the Queen Dowager is attempting to replace the throne. Will Kim Kwan-ju remain idle? If we had someone watch over his house, his tail surely would be caught."

The phrase in the memorial accusing In-mong, "He socialized with the heresy's rabble in Kangnam and criticized the royal court and tried to harm the Queen Dowager with premeditation, all in the name of His Majesty," referred to that incident.

After the meeting, Yi Kwan-gyu had someone secretly watch the visitors to Kim Kwan-ju's house. Their hunch proved right. They learned that an unknown scholar coming out of Kim's residence had gone to the house of Yi Cho-min, the great grandson of Prince Yollyong in Hwasong.

In-mong picked up a brush without delay. He had made himself ready by arranging things around him; he had sent his second son down to Andong. If worse came to worst, he wished to avoid the danger of a massacre of his bloodline. It might not be easy to save his oldest son Chun-gi, but perhaps it would be possible for Chun-yong to hide and survive. He began to write.

> This servant reports this in prostration. Your Eminence issued an edict of reproach in order to correct today's corrupt literary style; this is a great attempt that might come only once in a thousand years. Your Majesty's intention is admirable, attempting to rectify the distortions in the righteousness of the world with the enlightening power of literature, but it is an uphill battle. One believes that in the world of this wise king the foundation should be such that good, able people are civil servants, each governing

the masses with his loyalty and wisdom, whereas unrighteous, evil groups retreat fearing their lives.

But what is it like today? In the royal residence, there is a cunning group that suppresses Your Majesty's policies and engages in secret efforts. Your Majesty, please direct your bright eye to the wicked motives nearby. Kwan-ju, a relative of the Queen Dowager, is convening her family members and high government officials who are blinded by personal gain and desires, and colluding with the royal relative Cho-min, thereby committing a crime affecting Heaven . . .

In-mong was arrested before he could send this document to the king.

"Yi In-mong, Reference Consultant in the Office of Diplomatic Correspondence! You should come with us. There is something suspicious about you," the arresting officers said as they pushed him into a palanquin and took him to the interrogation room at the State Tribunal. He was hanged upside down from a beam and thrashed.

They demanded that he reveal who had instigated the vicious words he had written. Only then did In-mong realize that the scheme had been uncovered. The Old Doctrine faction members had made a preemptive move. The content of the memorial was leaked to the Old Doctrine faction and became known as "In-mong's vicious words," according to Kwon Yu, the inspector general. Kwon reported to the king the criticisms against the Queen Dowager circulating around the court, skipping the references to Kim Kwan-ju's treachery, calling them "vicious words spreading in the court."

In-mong had not anticipated the Old Doctrine faction's response. Yi Kwan-gyu and O Sok-jung made efforts to reveal the truth, but this was after the situation had developed and it only added useless sacrifices.

The second day, the torturers had In-mong's feet placed on the beam and nailed six-inch bamboo pegs into them. In-mong screamed and fainted. He thought he was dying futilely when he learned King Chongjo's order. In-mong was to be banished to Yongwol, Kangwon Province; Yi Kwan-gyu to Kwangyang, Cholla Province; and Oh Sok-jung to Chongsong, Hamgyong Province. After the royal order of banishment, Old Doctrine members intended to destroy In-mong's feet so that he might die from the hardships of the journey to his banishment. In-mong shuddered as he left Seoul.

His feet bled extensively. When the bleeding finally stopped, his feet began to fester, for this happened in the hottest days of the summer. It was fortunate, though, that the head of the guards was a kind person. In-mong's wife had borrowed some money and bought a donkey, and she had given some money to the guards. In-mong could ride the donkey after they left the town. He arrived at Yongwol almost a corpse and was confined behind a thorn hedge in the middle of Taehwa Mountain, next to Chongnyongpo, where King Tanjong had been banished many years before.

* * *

In-mong's banishment coincided with the period in which the Southerners took the offensive.

For five years, from 1790 to 1795, the Old Doctrine faction sensed an impending crisis: that they might be wiped out by the Southerners. The government led by State Councilor Chae Che-gong was launched, the construction of Hwasong Fortress was in full swing, and the money that the Old Doctrine faction had collected from the merchants had dried up since the Commercial Equalization Act of 1791. Because of the restoration of literary style, young civil servants of the Old Doctrine faction were stripped of their positions, and the Southerners' offensive began with Chae Che-gong's memorial asserting the suppression of the Old Doctrine. Kim Chong-su, the leader of the Principle group, demanded the punishment of Chae Che-gong, but he himself was banished instead. In-mong was able to return within a year, thanks to the mood of the period.

In September 1794, In-mong came back to Seoul and confined himself to his home. His health was not completely recovered, but his self-confinement was not solely for that reason. "I was high once and then fell low, and only then could I see the real friendships of the world," Yon-am Pak Chi-won had said, and In-mong had the same sentiment. When In-mong was disgraced by the accusations of the Old Doctrine faction, no friend, living near or far, inquired whether he was alive or dead.

It was the following year, in the spring of 1795, that In-mong became acquainted with the Bamboo Orchid Pavilion. This was the name of the pavilion in Chong Yag-yong's residence where rising officials of the Southerners faction, those who were interested in Catholicism, gathered; they were led by Chong Yag-yong and Chae I-suk (Hong-won), and included Yi Yu-su, Hong Shi-je, Yun Chi-nul, Hang Chi-ung, and Han Paek-won. They were all good people. They were discretely considerate of In-mong's feelings. Looking back to that spring, In-mong still felt a pang of sorrow.

That world had been swept away like dust and grass clippings. When would In-Mong and his friends, who used to pour rice wine for each other and appreciate the colors of the evening sky, gather again? He could hear Han Yu's poem "Farewell to Li Yuan Going to Gangu," which Yun Chi-nul recited in a nasal tone whenever he was sprawled out, drunk.

> *Eera*, Pangu is my residence,
> the land of Pangu is my garden,
> the spring of Pangu is good for bathing and for a walk.
> Pangu is rugged, so who would fight over it with me?
> Pangu is roomy because it is deep and wide.
> Ahh, the pleasures of Pangu,
> there is no end to pleasure.

This was the import of the poem: What difference does it make to a virile man like me, who was born into bad times, whether the world is ruled wisely? I don't want to live an ugly life reading the minds of high officials. I will go to Pangu.

Yun's song was like nothing else. He sang it comically, twitching his moustache which resembled rice grains. When everyone finished laughing, Han Chi-ung would take the *komungo* and pluck it, while Yi Yu-su would demand more wine or go out to buy some.

When the sun set and night fell, Madam Hong, Chong's wife, brought out a dinner tray. No special dishes were served in this poor scholar's household. There were bowls of unpolished rice, *kimchi*, and mountain herbs, and there was wine sufficient for only four rounds at best—yet Chong's household was such that if even this meagre spread had to be served to guests every day it would have imposed a burden on its management. Except for In-mong, however, neither the host nor the guests paid any attention to Madam Hong's predicament.

Once Yi Yu-su scolded In-mong when he declined dinner. "What nonsense! This is how one treats guests. Real friendship among scholars is like this: The more often they get together, the more the food shrinks but the more their affections grow. Madam, if there is any cold rice left, bring it out, please!" But as In-mong was slowly gaining confidence in this warm atmosphere, the narrow escape of Father Zhou Wenmo took place.

The Board of Punishments failed to arrest Zhou Wenmo, the Chinese priest, and arrested Korean Catholic leaders instead, including Choe In-gil, Chi Hwang, and Yun Yu-il. The three men died after a long day of cruel torture. The Old Doctrine faction blamed Catholics of the Southerners faction for having a hand in the deaths, in order to shut them up. They claimed that Yi Ka-hwan, Chong Yag-yong, Yi Sung-hun, and Chae Che-gong conspired together and bribed prison officials to poison the criminals. King Chongjo didn't listen to this story, but the persecution by the Old Doctrine faction, led by Pak Chang-sol, the Rank 6B military officer, continued for a long time. In addition, circumstantial evidence, more plausible than fictional accounts, was produced.

This conspiracy was meant to purge the Southerners faction, especially Chong Yag-yong's friends who gathered at the Bamboo Orchid Pavilion.

Chong was subjected to an intensive criminal investigation. Many of the Bamboo Orchid Pavilion guests were implicated, but the most closely threatened was In-mong, the brother-in-law of Yun Yu-il. The very existence of In-mong and his wife was evidence that they could have arranged the collusion between the dead prisoners and the Bamboo Orchid Pavilion group. Furthermore, influenced by her family, Sang-a had been a devout Catholic for many years.

On the day of the arrest, In-mong had to make up his mind about divorcing his wife. It was the custom in literati households that when either of a couple's family committed a grave crime and was punished, the pair divorced by consent, to avoid a chain of punishments.

In-Mong's wife's hand trembled as she held out the brush and an ink stone, and In-mong shed tears as he wrote the divorce paper specifying the division of property. They had spent harmonious years together; they had been married at age fourteen; and they had had two sons together. They knew that their eleven years of harmony would disappear because of a piece of paper. They wept like children, their shoulders shaking.

The children were sent to In-mong's family home in Andong. Although In-mong kept his house in Kwachon, he moved to a rented house in Kahoe-dong, and he gave his house in Itaewon to his wife, for she was being sent to her family.

Of course, the incident didn't end there.

Chong Yag-yong was arrested, followed by Yi Ka-hwan and Yi Sung-hun; and finally In-mong was dragged to the State Tribunal. In-Mong had to undergo the horrifying experience of the interrogation room twice within two years. He fainted many times, and the interrogators would douse him with water to revive him. They would put him in jail for a day and then continue with another session of torture.

They demanded that he confess to poisoning the prisoners—but how could he confess to something that he had not done? They were convinced that Catholicism was heresy and that those who studied the heresy were traitors. In-mong believed that the study of Catholicism was a way to enrich the country and bring peace to the people. Between people holding these two opposed convictions there could be only mutual suspicion.

In-mong's interrogator was Yi Pyong-mo, the third state councilor. He began the interrogation by discussing philosophy.

"Mencius said, 'Sage-kings have ceased to appear. Feudal lords have become reckless, and idle scholars have indulged in unreasonable opinions. The words of Yang Zhu and Mo Di fill the world. If the people do not follow Yang Zhu, they follow Mo Di.' Now is such a time. I have read a Catholic book and discovered that Jesus is no other than Mo Di's follower. He said, 'Love thy neighbors,' thereby putting loyalty to the king and to one's father below universal love. You idiots have studied literature, so how is it possible that you don't see the evil ways of such heresy? You call out for a sage-king, but in your heart you worship the ways of decadent barbarians. How can you be so two-faced?"

By the time he was interrogated, In-mong had undergone severe torture, so holding himself erect was not easy. Yet he showed his mettle, using what little remaining energy he had.

"Two-faced? You don't know the entire story. The teachings of Catholicism appear to be heresy, but if you go to their roots, they correspond with the teachings of the Three Dynasties of Xia, Shang, and Zhou. The sages have taught that originally there were three heavens; the first is the Natural Heaven, the second is the Heaven of the Principle seen in the *Book of Changes*, the third is the Heaven of the God on High. But Zhu Xi asserted that Nature was equivalent to Principle, and therefore, for him and his followers, only the Heaven of the Principle seen in the *Book of Changes* matters. As a result, instead of the Heaven of the God on High that bestows good fortune on the good and misfortune on the evil, an abstract Heaven has been forced onto the people.

"How can a child who cuts weeds, a woman who draws water, and an ordinary misbehaving man with his disheveled hair and dirty face be expected to understand such a difficult and vague Heaven? The ancients worshiped Heaven and the spirits with genuine hearts, because the Heaven they worshiped was easy and simple enough for them to understand. The *Book of Odes* says, 'Fearful command of Heaven, protect us from time to time.' This refers to no other than the Heaven of the God on High. We read Western Learning books not to believe and worship Jesus. We try to return to the real meaning of the Six Classics in order to know about the Heaven of the God on High that bestows good fortune on the good and punishes the wicked."

Yi Pyong-mo was irate. "Shut up. How dare you criticize the Great Zhu Xi? Yes, yes. A dishonest man, steeped in heresy, who disregards Confucian orthodoxy, cannot be expected to know how to respect the sacred and the wise. You are a real enemy, undermining Confucian orthodoxy with fraudulent ideas. Don't you remember the deaths of Yun Hyu and Pak Se-dang? How they were torn to death at the Kwanghwa Gate?"

"Who is the enemy undermining Confucian orthodoxy with fraudulent ideas and who is mocking the sacred and the wise?" In-Mong felt well able to defend his views. "In ancient times sage-kings such as Yao, Shun, Yu, and Tang thought of practical ways to feed the commoners. The sage-kings first promoted industry to provide a broader foundation, opened the way of commerce to allow the people to trade what they have for what they lack, and provided medicine to prevent the people from dying young. Only after that did they establish manners and etiquette, decide the order of the high and low, compose music to relieve depression, and create criminal laws to restrain the rough and the fierce. But what about our country?

"We are a vassal state in the East, but so poor that even His Majesty wears cotton, and we tighten our belts over and over again, but money in this country has dried up. Most of the people don't have barley or sweet potatoes to fill them, let alone rice. We are ignorant about practical matters, and our practical studies give us no answers, any more than what Western Learning offers. Still do you have to reject Western Learning blindly? We look to Western Learning to serve the sage-king in this land. A restoration is not a mere invocation. It is to have the people eat well, sleep well, and warmly clothed. No matter how beautiful a principle is, it can't come before food and clothes for the people."

"Shut up! It seems this crook begs for more beating!"

A board was placed between In-mong's legs, and they twisted it until his shank bones and flesh were crushed. In-mong cried like a starving ghost and lost consciousness.

The concept of restoration mentioned by In-mong needs to be defined.

From today's point of view, In-mong's blind, single-minded royalism, the dream of reinforcing the royal prerogative, appears to be retrogressive in the flow of history. The Old Doctrine faction's position against the royal prerogative might appear more progressive.

In hindsight, however, how did history unfold? From the assassination of King Chongjo, the sage-king, until Korea was colonized by Japan, Korean history was chaotic for a hundred years. There were many troublesome events: the extortion of murderously heavy taxes; the tyranny of low government officials; the endless massacres of Catholics; wandering farmers; bad harvests; starvation; contagious diseases; enormous fires; massive floods; the revolt of Pak Tae-song; the revolt of Hong Kyong-nae; the popular uprising on Cheju; riots prompted by the lack of food; riots by government slaves; disturbances created by concubines' children; the revolt of Chae Hui-je, a large-scale popular revolt in three southern provinces; the riot of the Palace Guards; the Tonghak Uprising; the intervention of foreign powers; and an enormous confusion in the opening of the nation; and, finally, the fall of Korea.

Korea didn't fall because it couldn't incorporate "progressive," parliamentary government, but because it failed to establish the Hongjae Restoration the absolute monarch King Chongjo had envisioned.

All the countries that established independent governments, arising from backward conditions, went through periods of absolute monarchial rule. They needed a transition period to equip themselves domestically with strong governing principles, and to assert their exclusive national interests outwardly and single-mindedly. It is due to the Meiji Restoration that modern Japan exists. Modern Japan was built on an absolute imperial system called *kokutai*, and its parliamentary constitution was imported from England. For the next eighty years, the Japanese fought against the pressures of the Western powers, clinging to absolute imperial sovereignty, rather than to a parliamentary constitution.

With the failure of the Hongjae Restoration, Korean history was retarded by a hundred and sixty years. It was a tragedy for Korea that, instead of King Chongjo's Restoration, Koreans had to experience Park Chung Hee's October Revitalization in 1972. This was like rejecting the wine that was offered as a reward and receiving wine as punishment. Instead of an absolute monarchy governed by wise royal laws, Koreans experienced the coarse, dreadful tyranny of economic development.

Restoration was possible only in In-mong's time, for it meant a renewal of the system by returning the absolute power of the nation to its master. A restoration is not possible in a democracy. The saying that the people are *minju* [masters] is a sort of intellectual syllogism, meaning that no one is the master. The president is a constitutional ruler elected by the people, so he is not the master. But it was different in In-mong's time.

King Chongjo was the master of the nation in both form and substance.

The bureaucrats, called "shepherds" by King Wen of Zhou, were the ones who managed the people, for the master delegated them some authority. Therefore, when a shepherd was corrupt, the master could reclaim the delegated authority any time. In-mong's ideas of Western Learning and dedication to the king should be considered in the context of the period.

In-mong was suddenly released after a week of torture and humiliation at the State Tribunal. The leaders of the Old Doctrine changed their minds and decided to wrap up the incident as soon as possible. There was no proof, and the suspects, including In-mong, stubbornly denied the allegations. In-Mong's release was surely due only to good fortune because he had dared to defend Western Learning. This in itself was a grave crime, but the direction of the interrogation was totally different on this particular occasion.

Yi In-mong was released and Yi Sung-hun was banished to Yesan. Yi Ka-hwan was sent to be the Magistrate of Chungju and Chong Yag-yong to be a seventh-ranking stationmaster in Kumjong. Each was demoted by four ranks.

That was the end of the Bamboo Orchid Pavilion. The comrades, who had been favoring the idea of political meetings in support of King Chongjo's reinforcement of monarchal authority, dispersed to avoid the Old Doctrine's chilling persecution. Some confined themselves in huts outside the walled town, and some left for the countryside where their relatives lived. Those who couldn't do so had to convert, abandoning their principles, and aligned themselves to the Old Doctrine faction. Remembering the end of the Bamboo Orchid Pavilion was still painful for In-mong.

* * *

Quite suddenly, In-Mong's recollections came to an end — the many memories triggered off by His Majesty's abrupt dismissal of In-Mong and by the other events of the momentous day that had begun with the discovery of Chang Chong-o's body in the Royal Library.

He felt a strange sensation at the back of his head, as if someone's eyes were on him. His feet had already carried him past the soup and rice eateries at Off-Horses Vale, Chongno, and now he was near the taverns across from the Supyo Bridge. He stopped short and looked back.

He spotted a few suspicious-looking people. They were on the other side of the Chonggye Stream, across from the Supyo Bridge. Two or three people suddenly dispersed under the eaves. In-mong realized that they were following him — but who were they? He stood on his toes, squinting, to have a better look at them, but now they were hidden by the darkness. This was an in-between time of day — dark, but not yet dark enough for passers-by to come out with shaded candles on holders.

In-mong started walking again, pretending he hadn't noticed anything out of the ordinary, but again he could hear footsteps behind him. He quickened his steps. The bridge was icy and slippery. A freezing wind swept past. In-mong walked hurriedly, bracing the wind. In the distance, the stars were coming out over South Mountain.

When he was near Camp Knoll, he crossed the street along with several men, who were almost running. Two rough-looking guides, clad in jade-green cloaks and hemp hats, were holding shaded candles on sticks. In the middle of their group was an older man in an official's uniform, surrounded by men in military uniform and others wearing gentlemen's coats and holding fans. Wasn't it a rare sight to see a high official's entourage on the southern side of the Chonggye Stream? In-mong cocked his head in wonder and glimpsed the face of the man in the official's uniform.

Surprisingly, it was So Yong-su, the minister of personnel.

Astonished, In-mong pulled himself aside to the edge of the road and bowed deeply. What business had brought him to this poor, foul-smelling district? So was particular about elegance; he didn't wear anything but silk and he always carried musk around his neck.

So Yong-su's eyes met In-mong's. So knew In-mong's face, because he had been the examination supervisor the year In-mong passed the national examinations. When So stopped short and looked at In-mong, his entourage, as one, turned their heads to have a look. In-mong had no choice but to approach the minister and express his respect.

"Your Excellency, how are you?"

"Isn't this Librarian Yi?" So's face, shown in the candlelight, registered embarrassment. His lips were twitching.

"What . . . what has brought you here?"

"Sir, I am on my way home from the palace."

"Ah, yes, yes," the minister laughed. "You are finally going home. You have worked very hard, indeed."

In-mong saw a sweat break out on the minister's forehead.

"Where are you headed at this late hour, sir?"

"Hum? Ah, me?" He laughed again "I heard Kug-ong [Yi Man-su, former Minister of Rites] has a few purple orchids blooming in his men's quarters. I am on my way to smell the flowers. There would be no joy if one neglected friends. Clean smell, clean conversation, and the clean sound of laughter, eh? So we should be diligent about crossing over each other's thresholds for a harmonious life together. And composing poems and cracking jokes in the fragrance of orchids is not an idle pastime. Isn't that so? Well, then . . . "

So's volubility was a surprise. While talking as fast as a bullet, the minister had intermixed his words with laughter, false coughs, and many gestures, and then hurried off without a backward glance. In-mong couldn't help but wonder. So's residence was in Ho-dong. Where in heaven's name had he been if he was on his way to smell the orchids?

In-mong stood still for a moment, looking at So's retreating procession, and then trudged forward again.

By the time he arrived at his house near the Southern Military Encampment, Chonghak-dong, the moon was up.

It was a starry night, but a mist thick as tobacco smoke was crawling up the slopes of South Mountain. Far away, fir trees rocked in the piercing wind, casting shadows into the dusky sky. In the palm-sized patch in front of the house, a few remaining radishes, green and shrunken from the cold wind, were bathed in moonlight.

Between the vegetable patch and the house was a low stone wall, and in the middle of the wall was a narrow gate with a thatched roof, rather than a tiled one. The house was an old one with three rooms, and the veranda in the middle creaked every time someone walked on it. There were no servants' quarters, and the women's quarters and men's quarters were just two separate rooms. Even so, the house was still extravagant for In-mong's situation. Two years before, when he was rehired as the first diarist at the Office of Royal Decrees, he had rented this place for ten thousand *chon*, with the money from the sale of the house in Kwachon and also with some help from his family in Andong.

A dim light emanated from the house, from the women's quarters, where his children slept. On this night, unlike other nights, there was no sound of the children reading aloud. The house was deathly quiet.

"Kia-ya!" As he called out to his son, In-mong's voice cracked. He had to force it out with all his might. This was because of the fever raging throughout his body. He was exhausted and chilled to the bone, but his neck and face were like a ball of fire. Perhaps because of the fever, his eyes were unfocused and hazy.

"Kia-ya!"

In-mong had an auditory hallucination of people murmuring inside the house. As usual, his elder son, who had turned eleven with the New Year, appeared to hurry out to the gate, his straw shoes scuffling. But this was only a brief illusion.

There was no human sound in the house. His heart sank. He pushed the gate. It made a terrible, stomach-churning noise. The gate, which he had thought was locked, yielded easily.

In-mong's face turned ashen as he peered into his home. His head throbbed as if it had been clubbed. All the doorframes were lying about broken, and the ceiling of the outer room, as far as he could see from the gate, showed sword gashes. Books were scattered on the floors and all over the yard. The furniture, including the wardrobe for quilts, was strewn about the veranda and yard.

That was not all. The house was literally devastated. The soil in the yard had been dug up, revealing reddish dirt, as if it had been plowed. He couldn't believe his eyes as he looked at the ravaged scene. He felt as if iron picks were piercing every part of his body.

"Kia-ya! Yong-a-ya! Auntie! Chang-gon-a!" In-mong's shrill voice echoed through the empty house, as he called out to his elder son, his younger son, the relative who was the housekeeper, and the slave. As he rushed into the house like a crazy man, he tripped over a nearby water barrel and fell. A vendor delivered such barrels to the household regularly. The barrel, which was nearlt full of water under a thin layer of ice, tumbled over and soaked In-mong's pants. He couldn't even feel how wet he was. The shock of finding his home deserted and ravaged had temporarily paralyzed his senses.

A day when one misfortune is followed by another is described as "adding frost to a frosty wind." Wasn't this such a day for In-mong?

"Kia-ya! Yong-a-ya!"

As he lay on the ground, his eyes dimmed. He felt himself gradually losing consciousness. His leathery soul had endured a series of drastic misfortunes all day and was almost at a breaking point. A chill traveled up his body to his shoulders and his neck. He was anxious about his family's disappearance. His consciousness was clouded by the nightmarish day. He felt he was left all alone in this world.

Ah, if the day had really been only a nightmare!

He felt something on the ground and grasped it in his hand. It was a shaded candleholder that his family used when they ventured out at night. The paper on one side was torn and the bamboo sticks were exposed. Seeing this familiar object, he quickly regained his full consciousness.

What was he doing? What could he accomplish if he remained stretched out on the ground?

In-mong reached inside his clothes for a flint stone. He ignited the candle and went into the main room holding it. The room was ravaged like a haunted house. Intruders had slashed the ceiling and, as though that were not enough, had torn the floor paper, too. It seemed that they had searched every nook and cranny trying to find something.

In-mong detected the smell of broiling fish wafting through the window from the neighbor's house over the clay wall. It was the house of Clerk Pak, the one who worked at the Southern Military Encampment. They were close neighbors; when guests came to In-mong's house and couldn't be accommodated in the small outer room, In-mong's family would sleep in the Paks home so that the guests could use In-mong's main room. In-Mong took the light, opened the lattice door leading to the backyard, and went to the clay wall separating the neighbors.

"Old Mother! Old Mother!"

After his wife had been expelled, an old relative called Kamchon Auntie had come to live with them. She had been married to a man of the Nakan Oh family in Kamchon, but all her in-laws had died in an epidemic. When she was widowed, she had first returned to her family to live, but for the past four years she had been taking care of In-mong's household in Seoul. She and Pak's old mother were almost the same age and had become good friends. In-mong craned his neck over the clay wall and called Pak's mother.

"Is that the librarian?"

It seemed they had been waiting for his call. Two women, Pak's mother and wife, opened the door of the women's quarters and came out. The older woman, white-haired and bent, slipped her feet into straw shoes and ran to the wall as if on wheels.

"Where have you been and why are you coming this late?" she said, screwing up her face, a face so wrinkled that it looked like a spider web had been thrown over it. Her voice was trembling with fear.

"Old Mother, what happened? Where has my family gone?"

"During the daytime, a woman came with her brother, and she said she was your wife."

"Yes? My wife?" In-mong was startled.

Had Sang-a come here? And her brother? There couldn't be any brother of hers in Seoul. She was an only daughter with two brothers. In 1795, her older brother, Yun Yu-il, had been executed as a traitor. Her younger brother had been banished. The brothers' properties had been confiscated, and the remaining family members had been sent from the capital to their hometown.

"I don't know. Do I know your wife and her family? Your auntie told me."

"What happened to the children and their mother?"

"It was horrible. She looked terrible. Her eyes were sunken and her hair and clothes were dirty and tattered. She looked like a sick beggar. They made a fuss. The children massaged her hands and feet, your auntie boiled thin gruel, and they borrowed medicine to relieve the pain of sword lashes. Dozens of policemen from the Constabulary on the Left came in the evening. Some time later, brawny men in gentlemen's coats came, dozens of them, and searched your house as if they were looking for lice. Your wife had sensed something was happening, so she climbed over this wall and hid in my house. I hid her in the upper closet and helped her flee after the storm died down, but the police and the strong men took away your children and auntie."

"What?"

"Oh Lord. I've never seen such a sight in my sixty years. How could anyone expect that such lightning would hit a palace official's house? They say a palace official is so high and mighty that he fells flying birds. It looks like your wife has done something grave."

The boys!

In-mong's eyebrows arched and his hair stood on end.

He felt a sudden flush despite his exhaustion. Those criminals! He had yearned for his children's bodily warmth whenever he felt defeated by worldly affairs. How could they take away a father's reward, a comfort to him? He believed that in their youth was a new history that might compensate for his defeats. In-mong forgot to express his gratitude, and turned away. He couldn't think of anything else; he only knew that he must find his boys.

"Look, look! Librarian! Wait a moment! Your wife left something. "

"Yes?"

"Look at this." The old woman's hand darted into her neckline and retrieved a half-torn piece of paper. In-mong brought it near the candle. On the paper were ten Chinese characters, written with the stub of a burnt stick, perhaps obtained from the kitchen. The characters were blurry, the soot partially erased, but he was able to make out their meaning: "Officials came to arrest. Leaving home to lean on long bamboo."

Long bamboo?

Ah, yes, Chong-jae Yu Chi-myong. She meant she would go to Yu Chi-myong's house at Saegomjong. In-mong treasured his wife's intelligence afresh. She had used a term only the two of them knew, in case the paper should fall into a pursuer's hand.

One day, the scholars of the Bamboo Orchid Pavilion had invited their wives to an outdoor party where they picked flowers and made flower cakes. When they came home, Sang-a gave nicknames to In-mong's friends who had gathered that day. All the nicknames contained the character for "Bamboo." For example, Yi Yu-su, a dark-complexioned man, was Raven Bamboo; Yun Chi-nul, a heavy smoker, was Long-Pipe Bamboo; Hong Shi-je, a sorrowful-looking man, was Mourning Staff Bamboo; and Yu Chi-myong, a tall fellow, was Long Bamboo.

Chong-jae Yu Chi-myong was the only person among the Bamboo Orchid Pavilion group who still communicated with them. He was five years younger than In-mong, and had yet to sit for the government officials' examinations. He was from the same hometown as In-mong, and the two husbands and the two wives had been very friendly. Chong-jae's house was in a quiet neighborhood at Saegomjong, outside the Hongji Gate. If only Sang-a had arrived there safely! Deep in thought, In-mong heaved a sigh.

"Is the head of the household home?" There was a squeaking sound of the gate opening.

Pak's mother and wife, who had been eyeing In-mong, scurried back to their house. With the light in his hand, In-mong walked around the house to the front yard.

A tall, muscular man was standing at the gate. He was dressed in a gentleman's robe and a large-brimmed horsehair hat. As In-mong appeared in the yard, the stranger slowly entered, bending only his lower body. In his left hand was a three-and-a-half-foot sword, and he held it so naturally that it looked like a part of his arm. He carried himself with inborn dignity.

"I'm the head of the household, but who are you?"

Who was this man? In-mong thought he had seen him before. He raised the candle to illuminate his face. The face, with its straight nose and thin lips, gave an impression of aloofness. It was a face that revealed a clever mind.

"It's been a long time, Consultant Yi. Well, now I should call you Librarian Yi."

"You . . . you are . . . "

As he recognized the man, the blood drained out of In-mong's face. It was Ku Chae-gyom! In-mong's temples throbbed. The two men stood there, each listening to the breath of the other.

"What business do you have this late?"

Ku laughed boisterously. "Why are you so surprised? It looks like your household has been hit by some tremendous misfortune, so I came to help you out."

"I don't need your help! What bravado is this?" In-mong cried, jumping up and down with fury. His arm, holding the light, was shaking. He felt as if a snake had crawled onto his arm. Ku Chae-gyom was none other than the lieutenant in the State Tribunal who had personally tortured him during the furor after Father Zhou escaped in 1795. In-mong stared at him, his face ashen, and his shoulders trembled.

"Help me? How can a former lieutenant in the State Tribunal help me? I heard that you were recently promoted to head cavalier at the Special Cavalry Unit."

Ku laughed. "Well, that's all thanks to everyone's assistance. I am sorry about what happened at the State Tribunal. What could I do when I was under government orders? I am not as nasty a person as you think. Things of the world are accomplished with the help of other people. Perhaps I could be of help to you. There is no family in your house. I know where they are, so I would like to find them for you.

"Where did you take my children? Where are they now?"

"Now, things have become urgent. Let's talk about the details on the way."

"Where?"

He laughed again. "To Myongdok Mountain, to the residence of the former State Councilor Chae Che-gong. You will have to attend the first year anniversary of his death to pay your respects, anyway. If you pay homage and at the same time lend us a hand, we will bring your family back and compensate you financially for the unfortunate things that happened here."

In-mong's face stiffened. "Shut up! So you dragged my children away. You invaded a palace official's house in broad daylight, bound his family in ropes, and took them away. You must be eager to die. You have gone crazy! Stop your bragging and return my children!"

In-mong spat out the words violently, as if he would chew up Ku Chae-gyom on the spot, but Ku didn't even lift his eyebrows. He kept grinning. When Ku's smiling eyes shifted to the veranda of the house, however, In-mong's coarse silk hat suddenly fell and something cold was at his neck.

It was Ku's sword. He hit the hat with the hilt, and with another swing the blade was upon In-mong's neck. In-mong was shocked at the swiftness of it all, and he broke out in a sweat. He had not noticed Ku removing the sword from its sheath.

"Will you reject the wine I offer and drink wine for punishment? Don't speak any more foolishness, and follow me like a nice boy."

"I can't."

"What?" Ku's eyes were furious.

In-mong was frozen. The blue-sharp blade of the sword on In-mong's neck quivered and made a scratch. With Ku's skills, he could chop In-mong's neck with a tilt of his wrist. In-mong restrained himself desperately from the impulse to step back, and faced Ku with calm eyes.

An incredibly long time seemed to pass.

Ku slowly took the sword away from In-mong's neck and grinned again.

"You appear to be under an illusion. In fact, I am not keen on taking you with us. We can accomplish what we intend whether you go with us or not. But a superior said to settle the matter quietly and gently, so I am having this verbal fight with you, against my wishes. If you don't want to go, don't go. In that case I can't guarantee what will happen to your children."

"You insolent, lawless bandits! What do you mean to do to my children? I will go directly to the palace and report your conduct to His Majesty!"

Ku laughed again. "Don't put on airs! You are not in such a comfortable situation. Instead of going to the palace, you are more in a position to be dragged to the State Tribunal. I give you my firm promise. If you help us with this matter, the memorial of this evening will be handled in your favor."

In-mong was aghast. How could this man know that much? Ku looked at In-mong's flabbergasted face and smiled, replacing the sword.

In-mong sweated profusely. "With . . . with this matter? What 'matter' do you mean?"

Ku laughed again. "You should have behaved this way from the beginning. Well, let's go. We'll talk on the way."

Ku clapped his hands. Several martial artists, all of whom were built like Ku, came in, took off In-mong's official uniform, and dressed him in a gentleman's robe and horsehair hat. In-mong bit his lips with a sense of humiliation. He was being treated like a puppet. How could he be this helpless? How could these men with no righteousness and no trust treat him this way? Before he had a chance to think further, two men pulled him out of the gate, each holding one of his arms. The rough way they handled him made the threat about his children seem real.

And . . . in case his wife was indeed hiding at Chong-jae's house, perhaps it was better for her if he went with these men to Myongdok Mountain without resisting. If he had to die, he would die at Myongdok Mountain.

In-mong was astonished by the number of horses and people in the vegetable patch in front of his house. There were more than ten mounted soldiers dressed in blue uniform, three martial artists in plainclothes, and about ten horses. All the horses were of a raw-boned Mongolian breed.

"Hop onto that one." Ku gestured toward the only horse equipped with a leg guard to protect the rider from dirt.

As In-mong approached the horse, a stony-faced soldier with pursed lips held a stirrup for him. In-mong hesitated before mounting the horse. He was astonished to see that the stirrups and the bit were covered with cloth. The man jumped up behind him and held the bridle, his arms around In-mong.

"I know how to ride a horse," protested In-mong in a complaining tone, to let them know that it would be uncomfortable to travel that way.

Ku snickered and mounted his horse. An underling in blue uniform handed Ku his sword, and Ku walked his horse a few steps before he looked back at the group.

"Listen carefully. We will gather at Tonggwan tomb outside of the East Gate. Have you all removed your horseshoes?

"Yes, sir!"

"Start!"

A cavalryman carrying a flag of the Special Cavalry Unit began to trot out first. After him, the rest followed, at intervals of several hundred yards.

In-mong was again surprised at the carefulness of these men. They had covered the stirrups and the bits to muffle the sounds, and had even removed their horseshoes for a night mission. All of them were silent. There was only one road from Seoul to Myongdok Mountain. It passed the Tonggwan tomb outside the East Gate and went on to Anam Brook, Chegi Ridge, Drum Rock, and Over the Water Hill before it arrived at the foot of Myongdok Mountain. In-mong shuddered as he thought of the distance they would have to travel that night. By horse, it would take more than three hours. In-mong's horse shook its mane and started.

In-mong had not ridden a horse since he left his hometown.

He hadn't held reins for ten years. The soldier behind him didn't slow down on the descending slope, but galloped instead. The saddle shook from left to right, and the stirrups and bits clanged and clattered against each other. In-mong's body, still feverish, was exhausted, and his eyes grew blurry. He could have lost consciousness if the reins were not loosened from time to time to reduce the speed on some narrow paths.

In-mong bit his lips until they bled. He was determined to hold onto his flickering consciousness. He wanted to tell the man behind him to slow down, but he didn't want to show his weakness.

"Hey, Librarian Yi! Are you all right? You look like you're about to faint." Ku, who had come up alongside to In-mong, spoke to him. He had switched to the rude form of address, and the expression on his face was the same as five years before.

"I'm . . . I am all right." In-mong barely finished his words. In-mong's face as he muttered this vague, slurred response was no different from five years earlier. With disbelief Ku recalled the witless scholar's behavior at that time. Yi had resisted like a bedeviled demon, his hair down, half of his face covered with blood and the rest with bruises.

"A man should . . . "

Ku slowed down, tightening the reins, and spoke as if to himself. In-mong's horse fell into a trot also.

"A man is better off," Ku went on, "if he remains at the level he used to be when his judgment was simple. That's the smart thing to do. If you think too single-mindedly, does anything improve? What can you accomplish by digging up the crazy dead crown prince's affair? By now his corpse would be completely decayed, a mere skeleton. If he had been normal, would his father have had him put to death? There must have been reasons for killing him."

"You . . . you impertinent rascal! You traitor!" In-mong shouted in despair, but something told him it was strange. Ku had just mentioned "digging up the crazy dead crown prince's affair." Did this imply that the incident at his house today was related to the tale of the metal-bound coffer? Before he could think any further, Ku continued to talk.

"Traitor? What is loyalty and what is treachery? A king is being loyal when he follows what the former kings expected him to do, and he is being treacherous when he goes against the laws and gives his subjects a difficult time. Now the king has distorted the distinction between loyalty and treachery, so the king and his subjects have swerved from the path of duty, and the ethics of the high and the low have become confused. The people are anxious because there may be an upheaval. This is why they have lost the desire to work for their livelihood. If a king is not a person who can be above the people to represent them, naturally he should be punished. Haven't you read Mencius? He said, 'The most important thing in the world is the people, the second is the dynasty, and the king is the least important.'"

"What . . . what impudence!"

"They say a loyal subject doesn't serve two kings or a loyal wife two husbands. But how can a person not serve two kings? During one's lifetime at least two kings, sometimes five kings, take the throne. This only means that the people may change, but the laws of the former kings are passed down, and therefore the former kings and the present king are one and the same. They are different people and their degrees of wisdom or foolishness might differ, but the laws are the same. The former kings' subjects become the present king's subjects. This is how a subject's loyalty is engendered. But what about King Chongjo? Since he took power, how many subjects has he slaughtered, exterminating entire clans, those subjects the previous kings treated with affection? How many loyal soldiers has he thrashed to death? He broached the subject of the crazy previous crown prince, whom his predecessor had forbidden to be mentioned. That was not all. He bestowed a posthumous title on the crown prince and constructed a royal tomb for him. He built a wall around the tomb and visits it almost every month. If this is not to despise the former kings' laws and to threaten the loyal subjects, what is it? The honor between the sovereign and his subjects is the basis for the distinction between loyalty and treachery. His Majesty is a lawless traitor."

"Shut up, you traitor!" In-mong craned his neck and screamed. If he had listened to Ku's words to the end, he might have gathered some hints about this mysterious kidnapping, but he forgot himself in the peak of his fury. "How can a person like you understand His Majesty's sacred intentions of governance based on fundamental laws? The August Ultimate should be established! The August Ultimate! In this world there is no bigger concern than the concern of division, and no bigger difficulty than the difficulties of division. During the peaceful era of the Three Dynasties of Xia, Yin, and

Zhou, the court was at the top, the people under it, and the world shared the same sentiment. People strived for the same goal. In those days, there was the one and only. One king and many subjects. Under the king, numerous subjects were equal! That is the only truth one should know as a subject born into a country. But what about our country? Factions were created, and one was divided into four colors, and the four engaged in extreme partisan squabbles.

"As a result, you rascals, you of the Old Doctrine faction, the privileged class, came into being. You dared to steal the royal prerogative, insolently calling yourselves rulers! You oppressed the people generation after generation, and your main occupation was extortion! You are the ones who are ruining the country! You are preoccupied with your own concerns and schemes! You don't have any respect for the king! You are unscrupulous foes who concentrate on your own interests and profit. You have no feelings for the people. Oh, yes! His Eminence is like the sun and the moon, so how much longer will your mongrel necks be spared? Soon there will be the punishment of evil and the establishment of justice. A revitalization will begin!"

The horse's hoofs accelerated, and In-mong received a blow to the side of his face. Ku had come closer to strike In-mong with the hilt of his sword. In-mong saw a flash in front of his eyes before he lost consciousness.

"Only his mouth is busy. If he talks again, beat him!"

"Yes, sir," the soldier behind In-mong answered, without any expression.

Ku, his face blue with fury, galloped to the front, leaving a cloud of dust behind.

7
The Secret of
The Tale of the Metal-Bound Coffer

*During the Three Dynasties of Xia, Yin, and Zhou,
li (principle) was primary, and after that period, qi
(material force) was ascendant. Emperor Yao and
Emperor Shun lived in the world of principle and
Confucius, Mencius, Chengzi and Zhu Xi lived in
the world of material force.*

*When the sage-kings and benevolent royal subjects
came together and the royal way was followed, that
was the world of order. At the time of the Emperors
Yao and Shun, there were royal subjects such as
Gao Yao and Yu, while at the time of King Tang
and King Wu there were royal subjects such as Yi
Yin and the Duke of Zhou. But the world of vital
force was not like that. While there existed
benevolent subjects such as Confucius, Mencius,
Chengzi, and Zhu Xi, they were not matched by
worthy kings. Consequently the royal way was not
followed in the world.*

*The world of material force has gradually become
corrupted, and our king lives in a private world,
indicating that the end of the world is near. At this
juncture, you should believe in the king as you
believe in the laws of nature. Chong-am Cho
Kwang-jo was a talented man who could assist the
king, and King Chungjong was a sage-king who
recognized his servant's benevolence. When the
benevolent servant and the king met and followed
the royal way once again, customs changed and
enlightenment shook the four corners of the earth.
The thousands of years since the Three Dynasties
during which the royal way was not carried out are
worth no more than one day during the Three*

*Dynasties when the royal way was followed. If the
royal way is again executed, the dark world will
brighten and right order will sprout roots for vital
force.*

*If your mind accepts heavenly principle, have faith
in the king as royal principle. Having faith in the
king is royal principle.*

— O Kwang-un, postscript to *Record of Kimyo*
(1743), Book 15 of *Yaksan Man-go* and the
Veritable Records of King Yongjo, Kabo section of
the fourth month, the ninetheenth year of King
Yongjo.

"My dear!"

Suddenly the sound of the hooves was gone. A silence enveloped In-mong and nothing was visible. The silence was as dangerous as a tottering stone pile.

"My dear!" In-mong felt a breathtaking shock as he opened his eyes.

Where was he? Someone was looking at him. When he recognized who it was, he sat up, startled. Right in front of him were his wife's bright eyes.

"Ahh . . ."

"My dear! You are exhausted. You were talking in your sleep. Now drink this before you go back to sleep."

In-mong stared at the bowl of rice punch on the tray Sang-a was offering him.

This white bowl was unfamiliar, as was the time that was overwhelming him. He was still hovering between the worlds of sleep and reality. His nose was still inhaling the air of his dream.

He cocked his head absentmindedly and looked out of the room. It was a summer night. Rain was falling, although he hadn't realized it at first. The rain that noisily divided the air shook the dim lamplight. The straw bundles and the cornhusks in the corner of the yard were already glistening with dampness. He was in the outer room of his house in Kwachon on a summer night.

What on earth had happened?

He had been screaming at Ku Chae-gyom.

Had he died? Had he died and gone to the underworld? Or had his spirit gone to see the person it had been longing to see one last time, before it left for the underworld? He recollected what the spirit said in the novel by the Chinese writer Li Jingliang, entitled the *Tale of Li Zhangwu*.

> The Milky Way has already gone down
> But the spirit wishes to linger.
> My Love,
> Embrace me one more time.
> Now
> Until the end of the world,
> Is the eternal farewell.

But In-mong was not a spirit. His palms were sweaty. As he pushed aside his hemp covering, he found his neck and chest glistening with sweat.

"It must have been a nightmare," his wife said.

"What? Yes . . . "

"Why were you so agitated? Look! Look at all this sweat!"

His wife, smiling, took out a palm-sized cotton handkerchief from the front flap of her blouse and wiped In-mong's face. He gratefully drank the rice punch his wife had offered, his eyes squinting and his forehead in furrows. Yet his wife's face looked like a strange shadow.

"Your energy is low because it's so hot today. Even with the rain, it is still hot."

"My love!"

"Yes?"

"I had a nightmare. A terrible nightmare. Come to think of it, it was five or six years from now, and I was again employed as an official."

"Yes? Five or six years from now?" Sang-a laughed. "So what position did you hold?"

"Don't laugh. I saw a day and a night, and it was incredibly frightening. It was so real. I was reinstated and I was a librarian in the Royal Library. You had been driven out of our house, because you were a Catholic, and no one knew where you were."

"Really?"

"It was a winter morning. When I woke up, Chang Chong-o was dead in the palace. Chong Yag-yong came and said Chae I-suk had died. I was taken to His Majesty. There was a memorial that falsely accused me of killing Teacher Chae. My whole body ached and I had a fever. And some brutes came and kidnapped me on horseback. Red clouds gathered from the four corners. I couldn't see anything. I was being taken somewhere on a cantering horse when you . . . you woke me up. What happened?"

"Well, you sound like a child. It was just a summer night's dream."

"Just a dream?" In-mong frowned and snapped. "I tell you, it was so real. My dear, a moment's dream is like a day for the dreamer. A day is like his entire life. When you read fortunes, you pick six stalks from the *Book of Changes*, don't you? A dream is the hexagram that governs the dreamer's entire life."

"I don't understand what you . . . "

"What is a human life? Getting up in the morning is the birth, eating and cultivating one's nature is learning, planning in the morning is fixing life's goals in childhood, conducting one's affairs in midday is the career of youth and middle age, achieving less than you hoped for represents the regrets of old age, and going to bed postponing the tasks for tomorrow is like ending life leaving your children behind. A person's lifetime is like a day. The things that happen in a day are like a vivid dream of a moment. Because a lifetime, a day, and a moment's dream are so similar. The only difference between them is the length of time."

"Similar?"

"It means they have the same shape. All circumstances human beings find themselves in during the course of their lives are connected with a web of correlations. If a change is made to one small line in a hexagram, their lives are transformed. This was the basis of the changes Fuxishi talked about. The philosophy of changes means life can't be explained by cause and effect. Our lives are made up of a series of multiple, simultaneous, unrelated occurrences, like fireworks in the night sky. A circumstance changes the things that follow in an unpredictable way, and sometimes dissolves certain things completely. All we can know are the patterns of coincidences that appear again and again within situations, a synchronicity of coincidental correspondences. Of course, the Western Learning, your belief, teaches something different."

"Yes, I think you are right. I think our Father didn't say anything like that. A repetition of coincidences? Then what happens to salvation and the eternal life God has promised?"

Sang-a had already become a devout believer, influenced by her family. Her faith made it difficult for her to accept her husband's lectures about Fuxishi and such. Wasn't it idol worship? She felt anxious about her husband, who had read and studied Catholic books, yet who had no interest in adopting the faith.

"The teachings of Western Learning are based on the belief that history develops in a linear manner" said In-mong. In other words, there was original sin in the beginning of the world, humans were expelled from paradise because of original sin, and therefore Jesus, the son of the God, died to atone for human beings, on their behalf. With the second coming of Jesus, the sinful mankind would be redeemed and the faithful would gain eternal life. Isn't that so?"

Sang-a nodded readily.

"But our philosophy, Chinese in origin, has its feet firmly planted on the ground. So a person who has read the *Analects* finds the teachings of Catholicism nonsensical. A hypothesis that does not fit reality is unacceptable to us Chinese-centered scholars. Between Heaven and Earth there are disasters and good fortunes that number in the tens of thousands, and human fortune, good and ill, makes it impossible for us to comprehend. How can each and every disaster and good fortune be in concert based on one special occasion and one fierce energy?"

"But you always talk about Fuxishi and say that our dynasty should go back to the loftiest ancient times of Yao, Shun, Yu, and Tang. I understand the teachings of the Bible better than those incomprehensible words, and I think the Bible is right, too. What is the difference between the ancient times and the paradise of the beginning of the world?"

"Of course, our Chinese-centered philosophy believes that there is nothing new under the sky and perfect beauty was attained in the ancient era. Confucius said in the *Analects*, 'One interprets, but does not build,' which teaches humility before the historical wisdom handed down from long ago. But the ancient times we talk about are not the root to which all the meanings of history return. It is not the beginning of the world or original sin as the Bible says. When we talk of the "ancient times" when the sages ruled, it has only an ideological meaning, but it is an empty center without definite content. Now His Majesty has proclaimed governance by a sage-king and the worship of ancient things, not to reenact the ancient times as they were, but to reenact the analogical harmony represented by antiquity."

Sang-a remained silent.

"Our period is becoming darker and darker. Treacherous foes and unchecked officials who deny the Six Classics and the August Ultimate are expanding their power very quickly. They haven't achieved their conspiracy yet, but the vicious force will grow bigger and bigger. The August Ultimate has to be established firmly as soon as possible. The August Ultimate . . ."

In-mong stopped talking and glanced at a wall to have a look at the diagram showing the nine points of the Great Plan, found in the *Book of History*, which present nine ways of ruling the world, all centered on the August Ultimate.

But what was wrong? Where there should be a wall there was only blackness. Startled, he looked around.

A pain shot up from his side and a rough man's voice rang in his ears. "Wake up!"

As he opened his eyes, he found himself being kicked by a man. It was Ku Chae-gyom, his eyes shining with a cold gleam.

"Do you think you're in your own room?"

In-mong felt a gust of icy wind blowing in through the door. He shivered with hopeless fear. He couldn't think of anything, and he couldn't move at all. He remembered that they had arrived at an inn in Over the Water Hill and come into the large communal room near the gate. Succumbing to high fever and exhaustion, he had fallen asleep, leaning his head on the wall.

Then had he seen Sang-a in his sleep? He looked around, anxious and doubtful. Indeed. There was the wall and the floor paper, so real, and that hateful face — Ku Chae-gyom.

"What do you want?" In-mong retorted in a husky voice.

Ku offered him a bowl of soup mixed with rice, hot and steamy. A spoon was stuck in the bowl at a slant, and it seemed they expected him to eat it on the spot. His heart was constricted, as if sand had been rubbed against it. His mouth watered immediately. His stomach, starved the entire day, cried out, but he gulped and turned his face. How could he eat food offered by a traitor?

"I do not need it!"

"Huh! They say a *yangban* behaves like a *yangban* even when he's dying from starvation. Your damn face looks like you haven't eaten for three days." Ku slammed down the earthenware bowl and left without looking back. In-mong crawled to the door on his knees and watched Ku's back as he walked away.

They were at an inn in Over the Water Hill, from which Mt. Myongdok could be seen in the distance.

The horsemen, almost fifty of them altogether, were eating bowls of soup mixed with rice. In-mong could see swords, bows, and even guns. The men were armed heavily, heavily enough to catch a tiger. Were all of them going to Mt. Myongdok? What were they going to do? Were they going to kill those who gathered at Chae Che-gong's first-year memorial service? What was the important document that justified this magnitude of military force? The previous king's tale of the metal-bound coffer? It couldn't be. Why would it be at such a place?

In-mong sat hunched, covering his face with his hands, his elbows resting on his lap, and tried to gather his thoughts. The pungent smell of the soup, piercing his nose, wouldn't let him pull his thoughts together. Every part of his body was shaking. He tried unsuccessfully to will it to stop. His forehead was shiny with sweat, but it felt strangely cold. If he ate.... He had changed his mind. He saw now that he should eat. He should eat in order to prevent these traitors' conspiracy. He should eat to be faithful to the king.

In-mong pulled the bowl toward himself cautiously as if he were picking up a sleeping baby.

As he spooned the soup into his mouth, the rice seemed to melt. Hot, soft green onions, vegetables, and morsels of meat tasted like the most delicious food in the world. He devoured the soup, not letting a drop escape his mouth. After he finished the last rice grain, he felt sorry for himself.

Life was really curious. Where did this terrible force of habit come from, demanding that he eat three meals a day? One wasn't born into this world by one's own volition, but once born, one possessed the blind instinct to survive. In the beginning was the instinct to live, that fundamental foundation of life. On account of that instinct one accumulated all kinds of everyday joys and sorrows. The repetition of this strange process formed habits, and then some kind of human order came into being.

As he put the bowl down on the floor, In-mong noticed Ku watching him. He hadn't realized Ku had returned, but he was sitting on the narrow veranda attached to the room, his legs hanging to the ground, and he was wearing a big grin. In-mong's face reddened.

Ku burst out in boisterous laughter. "The famous song says it well: When my stomach is full and I am happy, what does the emperor mean to me? Life begins in the throat and ends at the asshole. Only when rice is stuffed between these two holes does your head begin to work, and only then can such ornaments as loyalty and treachery be gathered. That's life. Get it?

"You Southerners are country bumpkins who don't know anything. You revere moral duty and babble about it, and then think the world will change just like that. The expression, 'dying for ideals' fits you bumpkins."

In-mong felt anxious, looking at Ku, who was talking as if it he had all the time in the world.

Why did this man seem to have such time for leisure? It was past midnight. Yet he was dawdling here, feeding his underlings.

Pessimistic visions unfurled their wings in his head. Didn't these men know that His Majesty had already left for Mt. Myongdok? They must have known it, and yet they had mobilized forces without royal permission. Why were they so sure of themselves?

At that moment a horse neighed and it grew noisy outside. A whiskered man in a gentleman's robe hurriedly approached.

"Director, sir! There are messengers from the State Tribunal and also from groups 3 and 4, who are searching Seoul."

"All right." Ku jumped up, as lithe as a cat, and rushed out the gate.

Seoul? A thorn of anxiety pricked In-mong. As Ku's footsteps retreated, In-mong left the room without bothering to put on his shoes, and approached the bush clover wall. He crouched behind the wall and crept closer and closer until he could hear Ku's voice, albeit faintly.

"You haven't made a discovery yet?"

"No, sir. We have searched not only Yun Yu-il's old house as you ordered, but also the houses of Yi Sung-hun, Oh Sok-chung, Chong Yak-jong, Kwon Chol-shin and Kwon Il-shin, and Hong Nak-min—all from top to bottom. We also have people watching over the high government officials' houses—Yi Ik-un, Chong Yag-yong, and Yi Ka-hwan. And yet . . ."

"Idiots! Eighty people have been bustling all over a palm-sized town all day, but they couldn't lay their hands on one woman!"

"Apologies . . . "

"She couldn't have left the town, could she?"

"Well, that—"

"What is it? I won't hold you responsible, so tell me honestly."

"Guards were placed at the four main gates, but there weren't enough hands for the smaller gates. But they have been all shut since *sulshi*."

"Umm."

In-mong's intuition told him that the woman they were talking about was Sang-a. Every part of his body seemed to have turned into one big ear, directed to the outside.

"Fools! It's almost certain she has left the town. Hey! Civil Officer! Civil Officer!" Ku called out impatiently toward the inn. A middle-aged man, wearing a short-brimmed hat, rushed out, having slipped into his straw shoes hurriedly.

"Did you call me, sir?"

"We have searched all the houses of the Southerners who have been involved in Western Learning, whether in a big way or small. Still, that woman is nowhere to be seen. She must have slipped away in some other direction. Who are the people who have not been involved in Catholicism but have been close to In-mong's household?"

"There are many. That man started in the civil service at an early age, and so he has a rather large circle of acquaintances."

"Idiot! Not including acquaintances, what are the households near the walled town where she could hide herself without difficulty?"

There was the busy sound of a dossier being shuffled, and then the man began talking again. "According to this report, there are four families who are close to Yi In-mong's family, but it is recorded that lately they haven't visited one another. Yi Yu-su, the former third inspector in the Office of the Inspector-General; he lives in front of the Changmok Bridge at Kwanchol-dong. Hong Shi-je, a former fourth inspector in the Office of the Inspector-General; he lives at the Hangangjin quay of Tumopo. Yun Chi-nul, an assistant section chief in the Board of War; he lives in Swaemun-dong in front of the West Gate. Yu Chi-myong, a test-taker who passed the secondary civil service examinations; he lives next to the Northern Military Encampment at Saegomjong."

"Yu Chi-myong? Who is he?"

In-mong's heart sank.

"He is the husband of Tae-san Yi Sang-jong's granddaughter, and a student of Son-jae Nam Han-jo, and it is recorded that he came up to Seoul to sit for the final round of examinations."

"Then is he a bumpkin from Andong, too?"

"Sir? Ah, yes, that is correct."

"That man. He's suspicious. Among those four, Saegomjong is nearest to Mt. Myongdok. And he has regional and academic ties with Yi In-mong. Hey, messengers!"

"Yes, sir."

"Have these four addresses written down for you and go check Yu Chi-myong first. Check every member of his family and search around his neighborhood, too."

"You brutes!" In-mong thought, shuddering. He straightened up and saw the messengers leave with Ku's order. In-mong quickly realized his mistake and bent down again. If he ventured out, it would only confirm Ku's reasoning. Retracing his steps back to the guest room, he heard the civil officer's voice.

"Well, Director, sir. Instead of asking me, how about beating up Yi In-mong and perhaps he . . ."

"No. He just came back from the palace after night duty when we took him, so he doesn't know anything. And he's not the type who would open his mouth if we tortured him. Now that everything we've been waiting for has come, let's leave. We will go on horseback over Taenung. Get ready."

Hurried steps were heard as Ku and the civil officer returned to the inn. In-mong remained in the shadow of the house as he scurried back to the room.

Now what was he supposed to do? This was the moment in which his hopes were crushed, the hopes he had been holding, suppressing his shame for agreeing to come with them. Soon cavalrymen would be sent to Yu Chi-myong's house, but there was nothing he could do about it. Helplessly, he sweated and pictured his wife with longing; his wife was now in danger. Intolerable despair and fright scorched his mouth. He caught sight of a young man brushing by, still sporting braided hair, his symbol of bachelorhood. In-mong's eyes lit up.

"Hey! Look here, young man!" One of his hands waved the boy over, while the other hand was pulling out his purse, string and all.

* * *

It sounded like a murmuring waterfall. Or perhaps more like the chirping of some mysterious insect.

Sang-a woke from a light sleep.

Yu Chi-myong's wife, from the Shin clan of Pyongsan, was sitting at a loom near the door. Her shadow, cast by the lamplight, threw a triangle sail on the paper door. Her hands flitted from left to right as she wove. Each time the shuttle in her hand passed the hemp a faint insect sound emitted. From the hemp thread around the bobbin, the peculiar smell of eyebright wafted out, that unique smell of Andong hemp.

"Younger Sister, you're such a diligent worker," Sang-a commented.

"This is only housekeeping for three people. It's nothing compared to what I used to do at my in-law's house in our hometown." Shin's down-to-earth voice, with a strong trace of regional inflection, was shaking a little. Her attention seemed to be directed to the outside, perhaps because she had some premonition.

"Big Sister, you go back to sleep. You have been so exhausted all day. Don't worry about me. I'll weave until my husband comes home."

"I . . . I might as well keep you company. I see an apparition when I sleep these days."

"An apparition?"

"I keep seeing my husband."

"Ha, ha, ha! Librarian Yi, do you say? Ha, ha, ha! So what does he say?"

"He says that I have died, I have already died . . . in my dream."

"What?" Madam Shin was astonished and turned her head to take a good look at Sang-a.

Sang-a was staring silently at the portable earthen fireplace, her head bowed. Newly added charcoal was burning bright and red. Sang-a's eyes, reflecting the light, shone like red pomegranates. Those eyes and her gaunt face took on a ghostly air that didn't seem to belong to this world. Madam Shin felt a shiver run through her.

"With her heretical beliefs, has she gone crazy?" Madam Shin wondered silently, regretting having welcomed Sang-a into her house.

When Sang-a had appeared, supported by her younger brother, Madam Shin and her husband had just finished their dinner. It was natural that the young couple were taken by surprise and felt nervous and uncomfortable. Even though the two women had been close for a long time, calling each other Big Sister and Younger Sister, Sang-a was not someone they could welcome with an open heart. She was being pursued by the government because she believed in a government-prohibited heresy, and it was said that she had been banished because she had steadfastly refused to renounce her belief, despite her husband's urging. Yet they couldn't refuse to take her in, for she looked as if she would collapse any minute.

After they took her into their main room, however, she told them a horrible story about the tale of the metal-bound coffer His Majesty had entrusted to State Councilor Chae's family.

They learned that the responsibility for guarding the tale of the metal-bound coffer had fallen to Chae I-suk with the death of State Councilor Chae the year before, but then Chae I-suk had been suddenly taken to the Board of Punishments. Before he died, he had revealed the hiding place to Sang-a. She had located it and then had come to their house because the Old Doctrine faction was after her. All these details challenged the imagination of the young couple who had been leading the simplest possible life. They couldn't help but tremble as they listened to her account.

Sang-a pleaded with her host, bowing her head in supplication. "Sir, this is the tale of the metal-bound coffer His Majesty entrusted to State Councilor Chae. Please take it to Mt. Myongdok. If you hand it to the family matriarch, Lady Oh, she will relate to His Majesty the terrible things that have happened."

Madam Shin knew instinctively that this was a favor of frightening dimensions that was being asked of her husband. Her husband belonged to those who had sworn to offer their lives to the Tao of the August Ultimate. How could her husband, still young, say he couldn't do a task of such importance? But the opposition was the Old Doctrine faction, who had killed off Chae I-suk, once a third royal secretary, and her husband was a mere scholar who didn't hold even the lowliest office.

"I understand," was all Yu said after listening silently to Sang-a's tale. He quickly changed into his traveling clothes and left with the bundle Sang-a had given him.

That had happened around *konshi*. Now it was almost midnight, so he should have arrived at the state councilor's house at Mt. Myongdok. If he hadn't arrived . . . Madam Shin felt tears of anxiety gathering in her eyes.

Whether or not Sang-a guessed Madam Shin's thoughts, she seemed to be in her own world, her eyes downcast. Perhaps she felt totally resigned; her eyes were glazed as if she were in a state between reality and dream.

All her energy seemed to have been drained by the wounds inflicted in the jail and the anxieties and fear caused by relentless pursuit. This transitory life . . . why was everything so numbing and painful? She felt that the fate she had been sensing for a long time was catching up with her step by step.

Of course, she knew that one shouldn't despair so easily on the matter of human affairs. As she looked back, sorrows she had thought would never diminish were beginning to fade from her memory. As time passes, bone-aching failures and heartrending torments are transformed into the colors of peaceful, warm evening clouds. If only she could survive, if only she could remain alive! Then the horrible events of today would look the same in retrospect. They would blend into the familiar fabric of life, taking on comical meanings like the masks of the Hahoe *pyolshin* ceremony.

This affair, however, looked as if it would not end well.

Sang-a knew, deep in her heart, that she was too small to shoulder the burden she had been given. It had to do with the survival of the dynasty. As she thought of Chae's last words, her head throbbed. A trifling woman like her had been drawn into this tremendous affair—and today she had to undertake such a breathless flight. Everything seemed hopeless, like fleeting frost on a spring day.

Sang-a had the same dream for several nights. The dream was about her husband, who informed her of her coming death.

As the dream began, she was roaming around a wasteland, not a tree or blade of grass visible. As she looked around, a wind would begin gusting as if it were trying to scratch out her eyeballs. Frightened, Sang-a would run for her life, amid terrifying wails and the howls of wolves from the other side of the dark land.

Had she already died? Had she crossed the Jordan River she had heard so much about? She sometimes recited a passage from the Bible, swept by nameless emotions in her heart. "For thine arrows stick fast in me, and thy hand presseth me sore. . . . I am troubled; I am bowed down greatly; I go mourning all the day long. For my loins are filled with a loathsome disease; and there is no soundness in my flesh. . . . My heart panteth, my strength faileth me: as for the light of mine eyes, it also is gone from me." [Psalms 38: 2-10]

Then her husband, his neck and chest glistening with sweat, would appear in the dream. He was pale, as if he had come from the underworld. He stared at her, his eyes full of doubt.

"I saw you dying in my dream," he said.

"What?"

"You were being chased by something, with your hair down. I ran to you, calling your name. Then horses neighed from all directions and everything became dark. I lost you and wandered around and entered a house. Rain was falling and a lamp was burning and the dim lamplight was shaking in the rain. In one corner were a straw bundle and a sheaf of bound-up corn husks, gleaming with moisture. And you were lying dead next to them. Stabbed by a knife all over your body."

Her husband stopped there. A darkness rose, like sea waves, and covered him up. Then other images would spring up, one after another, but she could not recall them later.

Sang-a shook her head to dispel these oppressive thoughts.

"Madam! Madam! Are you still up?" A voice from the other side of the door interrupted Sang-a's reverie. Recognizing that voice immediately, she bolted up as if scorched by a fire and flung open the door. In front of the veranda she recognized the dark face of Chang-gon, the slave at In-mong's house, who had accompanied her when she fled.

"What is it?"

Chang-gon stood flustered, his scrawny body trembling. Fright rendered him speechless; he rolled his mouse-eyes toward the gate. She followed his gaze and her heart dropped to her feet. From the mouth of the alley, low voices, neighing, and hoofs sounded faintly.

The neighing of the horses rang out in the silent darkness, and came closer and closer. Madam Shin came and stood next to Sang-a; her face showed panic and she seemed to be silently screaming.

"Big Sister? Who could they be? In the middle of the night?"

"Well . . ."

Sang-a's face was blue with fright. She retied her blouse and went back to the room but soon came out holding a bundle containing her clothes and money. Fear and tension coursed through her veins like shooting pain. Her eyes fell on the corner of the yard, lit by dim lamplight. Her heart nearly stopped beating from shock. Her hands, clutching the bundle to the front of her blouse, began to shake.

"Big Sister? What's the matter?" Madam Shin followed Sang-a's gaze.

A lamp was kept burning in the yard for the return of Yu. The dim light was shaking in the wind. Sang-a's gaze was fixed on a straw bundle and the sheaf of corn stalks, wet from the melted snow of the day before.

Could it be possible?

Sang-a was standing on the edge of an abyss.

The torch in the yard, the wet straw bundle and cornhusks, the neighing of horses coming from all directions. . . . This was the very house that her husband said he had seen in her dream.

Faced with this dreadful realization, Sang-a struggled hard not to faint. She felt dizzy and a phantom of light, like the glow of fireflies, wavered in front of her eyes. Oh, Lord . . . but soon a feeling of resignation, a sad, plaintive feeling of resignation, came upon her.

She bit her lip, suppressing her surging emotions. Now the neighing was right outside the wall. Torches came into view. Centered at the gate, the torches beyond the wall illuminated the darkness like red clouds.

"Younger Sister, hide yourself quickly. They have come to take me. Chang-gon-a, help Madam out right away."

"Yes? But you should . . . not me, . . . " stammered Madam Shin.

"No. Take the baby and go right now. If you tarry, you also will be . . ."

Sang-a pushed Madam Shin with a determined face. "Killed right where you're caught!" That was the message Madam Shin read on Sang-a's face.

"Come here!" A rough voice rang out, pounding on the gate, perhaps with a bat.

Everything became obvious. Madam Shin ran as fast as she could, she picked up her only son, who was four years old, and opened the small door of the main room leading to the backyard. She hurried out in her stocking feet. Chang-gon cut through the wall of bushes to make a small hole, but Madam Shin was reluctant to leave Sang-a behind. She looked back. Sang-a gestured to her to hurry up.

"Open up this gate right now!" came the roar, followed by a faint sound, like an unpleasant panting.

The intruders began destroying the wall with an iron pick, and soon there was a crash. Sang-a descended to the shoe ledge and put on her shoes. The gate burst open, and men clad in blue military uniforms swept in.

"You've broken down a civilian's wall and entered lawlessly," Sang-a said bravely. "What is this piracy?"

"Quiet! We are from the State Tribunal. We have information that a Catholic witch is hiding in this house," the man in charge shouted as he approached Sang-a.

He cocked his head in puzzlement and unfurled the scroll in his hand. It was a sketch of a woman on mulberry paper. The man's sharp, cold eyes darted back and forth between the picture and Sang-a. The soldiers around him, all holding swords, glared at Sang-a as if they were going to swallow her up, their eyes darting from her to the picture.

Sang-a shut her eyes and then opened them again. "I am she."

* * *

Around the time the militia from the State Tribunal and the Special Cavalry Unit burst upon Yu Chi-myong's house, In-mong was arriving at the mouth of Myongdok-dong, Mt. Surak.

"Dismount! We will walk from here!" Ku Chae-gyom shouted.

In-mong momentarily felt disoriented, unable to remember how they had arrived here from Over the Water Hill. He had been preoccupied with one thought: Had the boy at the inn reached Sang-a safely? In-mong prayed that he had, even prayed to the God in whom Sang-a believed. Instead, the young man from the inn had already turned around and run away, scared by the guards at the roadside, but In-mong didn't know this. In-mong controlled his trembling legs, leaning on that tiny hope.

The mouth of Myongdok-dong was called Rotting Axes Place, where people enjoyed leisurely games of *go*, forgetting that their axes would fall apart with the passage of time. Chae-gyom left several men behind at Rotting Axes Place to watch over the horses, and the rest began to climb the steep slope, grabbing arrowroot vines for support.

Myongdok-dong was a basin, surrounded by the ring of the peaks of Mt. Surak. There was a little opening in the ring, and that held the path leading to the settlement from Rotting Axes Place.

After they clambered up the slope, they came upon a dense forest. The moon was up, but the tree trunks and branches cast shadows on the path, creating a sinister atmosphere. Before they advanced far, In-mong began to huff and puff. His legs were leaden. The sound of a fierce wind ruffling the trees and vines on either side made his eyelids droop. He thought he was wandering in a nightmare from which he could never wake up.

The wind carried the fierce cry of a lonely animal. In-mong was startled and stopped short. The howl went up high, came down low, and ended with an ear-shattering shriek. In-mong tugged on Ku's sleeve, as they walked together.

"Chief Ku. What do you intend to do, taking me to the Thinking of the Bright King Manor? At least I'd like to know why you're taking me there. How can I go along without knowing?"

Ku merely grunted.

"It is said that a scholar does not endeavor to speak many words, but he should know what he is talking about, and he does not endeavor to do many things, but he should know what he is doing."

"That's in the *School Sayings of Confucius*. Good phrase, eh?" The rough-looking Ku had a surprising clownish quality.

In-mong felt like strangling Ku, who was nodding with his eyes fixed on a distant point. Whether or not he guessed In-mong's feelings, he came closer to In-mong, pulled his arm, and walked on.

"There's nothing you are supposed to do," Ku said.

"What do you mean?"

"Haven't you ever been to a bereaved household to pay your condolences? You just go there to show your respects, meet your friends, and talk with them. We will do the rest."

"What nonsense is this? Are you going to keep doing things this way?"

As they had done before, Ku and In-mong stared at each other with hostility. Again, Ku backed down.

"Hey, hey, it's true. You realize that all these disasters came about because of your wife, don't you? She has a very important document the government is looking for. She disappeared from the Board of Punishments this morning with that thing, so the whole administration is in turmoil now."

"An important document? Are you referring to the previous king's tale of the metal-bound coffer?"

"You certainly are an intuitive fellow; no wonder you're working for the Royal Library. That crazy dog of His Majesty must have spent the whole day looking for it, right?"

"But how can it be possible that someone like my wife has such an invaluable document? You must be mistaken, you've missed the mark by a mile."

"You're too literal, gentleman! Now that it's in the open, I'll tell you. We have been looking for that document for seven years. But we believed that it was hidden somewhere in Changdok Palace. That was because seven years ago His Majesty retrieved the "Song of the Blood-Stained Hemp and the Mourning Staff" from under the spiritual tablet of Queen Chongsong and we were sure that was where it was hidden. So we have searched under each rock, under each patch of grass, with the help of the eunuchs, maidservants, and palace matrons.

"But the sly king foresaw our line of thinking. Seven years ago, right after the fuss made by Chae Che-gong's petition, the tale of the metal-bound coffer was moved to Chae's house from a certain hiding place in the palace. When Chae died a year ago, his son inherited the responsibility for guarding the document. We only learned about it a month ago. And the king is about to relinquish the throne. So what could we do? We had to go and get Chae I-suk, while His Majesty was away from Seoul at the Hwasong Detached Palace."

"You beasts!"

In-mong was disgusted. He felt frightfully confused because he had never suspected such a development, and also because Ku was speaking calmly, as if he were relaying some rumors. "So they are going to decapitate me," he thought. "That is why Ku is divulging everything—because they will kill me off and bury me secretly. Those thugs deserve to be torn limb from limb!"

Ku tossed a glance at In-mong's trembling hands. He perceived everything in In-mong's heart; horror, calculation, fear, and the fleeting desire to murder him.

Nevertheless, he continued nonchalantly. "But things worked out easily.

We were at the end of our tether, so anxious to create an allegation against Chae I-suk, but he himself provided an excuse. The people who had come to stay at his house a few days before were to all appearances Catholics. We descended upon them and arrested Chae I-suk and his guests. We completely cut off Mt. Myongdok here, so his family couldn't do anything about it. And your wife was one of Chae's guests who was arrested.

"But another problem presented itself. The day before His Majesty went on his trip to Hwasong Detached Palace, he had dropped some false information via the director of the eunuchs. The tale of the metal-bound coffer was supposed to be at the Royal Library. We thought we'd go crazy, because this came after Chae I-suk's imprisonment. In fact, we didn't have any evidence that he had the document, and he was denying it obstinately. So what was there for us to do? We were hesitating about what to do, and it was only last night after the king returned that we made the decision to kill Chang Chong-o and take the book that entrusted to him."

"That must have been *Humble Thoughts on the Book of Odes*. Then wasn't that the original of the tale of the metal-bound coffer?"

"I myself wouldn't know. The Eunuch Department took care of the affair. But it can't be the original. If it were, would the ministers be flapping about like fish before a fire?"

"Who are the ministers you're talking about?"

"Hush!" Ku cut short In-mong's question and strode out to the front of the procession.

They had arrived at the upper stream of Waryong Falls, where the Thinking of the Bright King Manor was visible.

"Director, sir!" A man in a gentleman's coat and a large-brimmed horsehair hat rushed up in the dark, but he didn't look like a scholar. "Director, sir! There's trouble." He began to whisper something in Ku's ear in a fast undertone, pointing at various parts of the Thinking of the Bright King Manor.

Ku's face showed that he was shaken. He was nodding, listening to the man. Finally he said, "Group 2! Go back and conceal yourselves at the hidden entry over there. You must not build a fire, however cold it gets. Group One, split into three teams and move to wherever you have been assigned around the manor."

He looked back at his underlings and directed in a firm voice. "Han-su! The second state councilor went to the Thinking of the Bright King Hall. Your unit should follow the state councilor. And Tong-pyo! Take your unit and follow me!"

The forty-odd men dispersed noiselessly in every direction. Ku strode up and pulled In-mong's arm. Walking alongside the water flowing into Waryong Falls, he pushed In-mong to walk.

"Librarian Yi! We brought you as bait, but now things have become urgent, so you cooperate for all your worth. Now let's go where the Southerners are gathered."

Bait? In-mong's face was flushed. He was not a dull man. The implications of the word flashed through his head.

Now that some time had passed, it was possible that Sang-a had delivered the document to someone. No matter who had the document, he couldn't afford to stay away from today's gathering, where all the Southerners were expected. So wouldn't he approach In-mong, Sang-a's husband and an official close to His Majesty? If they had In-mong with them wherever they went. . . . This was how Ku had reckoned — but the report of the underling who had been keeping an eye on the residence had derailed the plan.

It looked as if the Southerners had obtained the document. The important members began to gather one by one in the main hall. Shim Hwan-ji, having been told of this development, rushed there and joined them.

"Then the document has to be intercepted before it is handed over to His Majesty. You should sit with them, and volunteer to deliver it. After all, you are close to His Majesty."

"Damned preposterous trick! His Majesty is a stone's throw away. Do you think this will go as smoothly as you plan?"

"Quiet! If things go astray, your two boys will be killed and they'll be food for crows! You'll have nothing left in the future!" Ku shook a dagger hidden in his sleeve.

In-mong was intimidated and lowered his eyes. At this point, large pavilions — the One Hundred Fragrances Pavilion, the Blue Jewel Pavilion, and the Thinking of the Bright King Hall — came into view within fifty paces.

The Thinking of the Bright King Hall and the Blue Jewel Pavilion were assigned to the Southerners, and the Spring Light Hut, farther away, was reserved for the few members of the Old Doctrine and the Young Doctrine factions. Shim Hwan-ji had just left the Spring Light Hut for the Thinking of the Bright King Hall.

In-mong walked toward the Thinking of the Bright King Hall, propelled by Ku.

The manor consisted of five buildings. At the northern foothill stood the modest living quarters, and a long way off in the middle of the property was the Thinking of the Bright King Hall. Facing it was the Blue Jewel Pavilion, and next to it was the One Hundred Fragrances Pavilion at the Light

Reflecting Pond. The Spring Light Hut was located to the west of the Thinking of the Bright King Hall, off a peach orchard. Although it had five buildings, it was a humble manor, and it looked as if the owners wouldn't be able to buy a decent house in Seoul if they sold it off. It was all Chae Che-gong had left for his family after fifty-six years as a civil servant.

For thirty years, while he had been a high-ranking official, Chae had lived at the Apricot Tree House, a rented home in Poun-dong, with his elderly parents. There was an anecdote about that house.

In the twelfth year of King Chongjo's reign (1788), Chae became a state councilor for the first time. Ten government slaves belonging to the Military Construction Agency were assigned to his residence, as the law dictated, but they returned on the very same day. They had been told to go back because the state councilor's residence didn't have enough food to feed them and had no room to accommodate them. The official in charge was taken by surprise, so he personally visited the state councilor's house in Poun-dong. He found the house teeming with poor relations and others who didn't have anywhere else to go. He saw why they didn't have enough to feed the slaves. The remuneration for the third state councilor was thirty large and six medium sacks of rice and sixteen large sacks of beans per annum. If we calculate that an adult eats from one and a half to two large sacks of rice in a year, this amount of rice would have barely fed twenty people, even if none of the other household expenditures were figured in.

As soon as Chae Che-gong retired at the age of seventy-six in 1795, he sold everything he had and acquired the Thinking of the Bright King Manor, remotely situated in the mountains. People in later generations would be moved when they remembered the name. The name "Thinking of the Bright King Manor" came from a poem: "Thinking of the bright king in times of poverty or glory / one even farms and raises silkworms in a field near the capital." One could sympathize with the aged loyal servant's heart, because, worrying about King Chongjo's precarious situation, he couldn't move farther away to a safer place. Fate had it that, a few years later, Chae's title would be posthumously stripped, his family would go through severe hardships, those who lived under his roof would all be dispersed, and his residence would fall into complete ruin.

Of course, In-mong had no way of knowing the future as he entered the compound.

It was bustling with people, no less than any renowned family's first-year memorial. There seemed to be more than a hundred people who had stayed on into the night. Every room was filled with visitors, and the younger people of In-mong's age sat in the yard where a tent was put up around a bonfire. Despite the number of people, it was deadly quiet, unlike any other first-year memorial. This must have been due to Chae I-suk's tragic death. Where was His Majesty?

"Why, look, isn't it To-won?" People called out as In-mong entered the courtyard between the Thinking of the Bright King Hall and the Blue Jewel Pavilion. They were young Southerners who had come up to Seoul from Andong. There were some friends who had studied with In-mong at Tosan Academy. Unfortunately, In-mong wasn't in the right frame of mind to show his manners. With those glinting eyes behind him, there was a possibility that an innocent man might meet disaster.

One man rushed out, finding his way through the crowd, and tugged In-mong's sleeve.

"Look, To-won! Why are you in such a hurry? It's me! Chong-won!"

"Ah! Big Brother!" In-mong's face registered gladness, even in the confusion of the moment.

It was not simply that he was glad to see Chong-won after a long interval. The person who introduced himself by his personal name, Chong-won, was Kim Yu-jung. He was the youthful current head of the Kim clan from Kwangsan, living in Oenae, Andong. He and Yu Chi-myong had been close neighbors of In-mong.

As he swallowed the words that were about to burst out—"Have you by any chance seen Yu Chi-myong?"—In-mong's Adam's apple moved conspicuously. Ku Chae-gyom and his followers began to watch with suspicion. Hoping for a chance to ask Kim his question, In-mong began to respond.

"You came all this way, Big Brother!"

"People are light and manners are heavy, aren't they? Years ago, Duke Munsuk wrote something for my family even though he was ill in bed. How could I not make this small show of respect?" Duke Munsuk was Chae Che-gong's title, given posthumously by the king.

"Yes, indeed. But the head mourner . . . "

"That's right. What a bolt of lightning to this righteous family! A funeral on the first anniversary of Duke Munsuk's death . . . those bastards deserve death!" Chong-won's face was distorted with sorrow. His eyes were burning. "How can the Royal Way go this far astray! It is only empty words that Heaven helps good people. He was a master who was careful with every-thing, who picked only the right path, and who rarely lost temper if it were not for an issue of justice. And he died accused of being a Catholic, and those cruel sons of bitches, who conspire for every little thing to harm others, enjoy wealth and glory generation after generation. What a despicable world!"

"Indeed . . . indeed you're right. But Big Brother," In-mong cut in. "Who is receiving condolences?"

"It hasn't started yet."

"What do you mean?"

"Teacher Chae I-suk's body has not arrived yet. There was a message from the Board of Punishments this morning to claim his body. His eldest son went up to Seoul, weeping all the way, to have his body moved to the shrine, but they wouldn't release the body, saying people from the Office of the Censor-General and the Office of the Inspector- General should conduct a postmortem. They say there was something suspicious about his death. They were arguing all day, and now night has fallen, so the eldest son and some other family elders are staying in Seoul tonight. At the mourning hall, there's only Duke Munsuk's tablet. The second grandson has become the temporary head mourner, and the preparatory ceremony was held already. A little later, at dawn, the first year memorial ceremony will be held."

"And how is the family matriarch?"

"She has lost consciousness."

"What?"

"It's not hard to see why. A lady over eighty . . . how could she pull herself together to face this unexpected calamity? She fainted a few days ago, and she is still unconscious."

In-mong's face turned ashen.

Chae Che-gong's wife, Oh of Tongbok, was a niece of Yak-san Oh Kwang-un, who was the leader of the Southerners faction during the reign of King Yongjo. He had been the first one to suggest the idea of grand harmony, asserting that strong monarchial authority could control the hard-liners of the factions. His ideas were handed down to Chae Che-gong and became the philosophical basis of the Southerners' strategy to deter the Old Doctrine for the next seventy years. For this reason, Lady Oh was a weighty figure among the Southerners. If she exposed the truth of what had happened to the gathered Southerners, the situation would quickly develop. It was as clear as daylight. His Majesty, who had stubbornly insisted on coming here despite his officials' oppositions, must have wanted to see the old lady. She would know what had happened to the tale of the metal-bound coffer.

She was unconscious on this crucial day . . . In-mong's expectations were crushed again. He looked around, feeling so nervous that his lips were burning. Where was His Majesty? Had he arrived?

Ku Che-gyom, standing behind In-mong, felt his nerves bristle up like the ends of needles. He had just heard a momentous piece of news from his men.

His Majesty was here at the state councilor's residence. He had arrived quietly, concealing his identity, accompanied by Royal Guards, and had gone to the living quarters at the foot of the mountain. This was something they had not counted on. Messages from the palace had stopped since Ku had left for In-mong's house.

Ku was so tense that he felt his tongue was turning into stone. Naturally, he had issued a simple, proper, timely order that every Southerner leaving the Thinking of the Bright King Hall should be followed. If the person looked as if he were going to see the king, he should be deterred by any means.

It was easy to say, but in reality would it unfold as he hoped? A tremendous anxiety gripped him. Until then, Ku had been optimistic, even when he had seen how much the ministers fretted.

First, In-mong's wife would be caught, he thought.

Second, if she weren't, they could find the one who had the document at Chae's first-year memorial service.

Third, if everything else failed, they could control any attempt to approach His Majesty at the palace.

The first and the second calculations had gone awry, and the third seemed not so simple, because His Majesty had come out here. Ku's face flushed as he tried to suppress his agitation and anxiety. His arrogance was crushed and his determination deflated; his face began to reveal a shade of wretchedness. Although he didn't hesitate to spit out blasphemy, he was afraid of the king. Frantically suppressing his fear, he reviewed the situation that had gotten so out of hand.

One thing that was fortunate was the condition of Lady Oh, whom His Majesty was hoping to see. She was eighty-four years-old, and she had fainted of humiliation and shock after her son's arrest. The latest word was that her consciousness had returned but now she was showing symptoms of senility.

If they could get through this night safely . . . Ku wished fervently. The capital was palm-sized. The document could be found in a day or two. When it was found, all they had to do was clean up. He looked at the large, brightly lit room in the Thinking of the Bright King Hall.

Shim Hwan-ji, the second state councilor, who had come here on the pretense of paying his respects to the dead, was sitting in that very room. Apparently he intended to prevent the Southerners from discussing the issue of the tale of the metal-bound coffer.

It was not that there was no hope. Since Father Zhou escaped arrest in 1795, the Southerners' circle had shrunk. Chae Che-gong's death had put the seal on such a trend, and people had defected from the Southerners' camp one by one. In the room were several former Southerners who had joined the Old Doctrine faction, including Mok Man-jung, the censor-general; Yi Ki-kyong, an assistant section chief in the Board of Personnel; and Hong Ui-ho, the chief magistrate of the Seoul Magistracy. Ku Che-gyom hoped they would perform well.

With these thoughts, Ku poked In-mong's side. "Now, let's go in."

In-mong excused himself from Kim Yu-jung and walked to the Thinking of the Bright King Hall, as Ku had instructed. Water drops falling on the dark pond sounded sad. Lit by candles inside, many shadows were reflected on the paper door of the main hall. The eaves held a plaque reading "Thinking of the Bright King Hall."

In-mong and Ku stepped side by side up to the veranda. As the door slid open, they saw about twenty scholars sitting in a large space; a ten-foot door had been removed to make two rooms into one. Opposite In-mong, in the place of honor, sat four old men, the leaders of the four factions of the Old Doctrine and the Southerners. Here were assembled: Shim Hwan-ji of the Principle group of the Old Doctrine faction; Yun Haeng-im of the Expediency group of the Old Doctrine faction; Nam Han-jo of the southeast group of the Southerners faction; and Yi Ka-hwan of the central group of the Southerners faction.

The next place of honor held So Yong-su, the minister of personnel; Mok Man-jung, the censor-general; and Nog-am Kwon Chol-shin. In the lower part of the room sat Southerners in their thirties. The Old Doctrine faction and Southerners sitting in the same room? In-mong doubted his eyes as he squeezed into the lowest row in the lower part of the room.

It was no surprise that tension was enveloping the room like the night before a storm.

Ku Chae-gyom quickly grasped the character of the quiet. It was a silence in which excitement was growing and mounting, hidden yet emanating subtly.

The Old Doctrine faction was directly responsible for Chae's death. When Shim Hwan-ji burst upon them, the Southerners might have hurriedly hidden the document. It was a silent confrontation, each side hiding grave secrets and harboring hatred, contempt, delusion, and fear.

"A picture by Kang Se-hwang." Shim Hwan-ji's voice suddenly broke the silence, but it sounded as if he were talking to himself.

In-mong looked up and saw Shim, sitting crouched like an old spider, gazing at the picture on the right-hand wall.

"His pictures are rather narrow-minded," Shim muttered.

"What do you mean by that?" Someone on his right side asked calmly.

It was Kwon Chol-shin, an elder of Song-ho School.

"This is surely not an educated guess, but the old pine is drawn to fit the characters," Shim said, "The upward strokes for the trunk are old fashioned and the shading is quite archaic, don't you think? Even though it's the same old pine, the one done by Yi In-sang is indeed different."

A light stir went through the scholars.

"I don't understand," Kwon Chol-shin responded, "The eyes of a state councilor and those of a lay scholar must be different. I have seen Yi's old pines several times, but to my eyes his brush technique is unnatural, and he retouches again and again, which looks mediocre to me."

Shim's eyes bulged in displeasure as he looked at Kwon. "He is very creative. That's why."

Kwon didn't hesitate. "Yi's Nine-Dragon Well is strikingly similar to the Qing painter Hong Ren's 'Landscape' and 'Lone Tree on the Cliff.' One could say he copied from them."

Shim was known for his inscrutable expressions, but he wouldn't tolerate this any further, the audience thought. They looked at him, feeling a bit nervous and yet interested. The war of nerves between the Old Doctrine faction and the Southerners had unexpectedly developed into a debate over art criticism.

The philosophical differences between the Old Doctrine faction and the Southerners manifested themselves even in paintings. The Southerners took the traditional viewpoint that supported the concurrence of painting and writing, rejecting realistic paintings and endorsing paintings that depict the inner essence of an object instead. On the other hand, the Old Doctrine strove for more concrete, lifelike depictions, and recognized the independent status of realistic paintings. The Old Doctrine faction praised Chong Son's realistic landscape paintings, in the belief that paintings delineating the unique landscape of Korea had a definite ideology, an ideology of Korean-centeredness, and a dreamy cultural superiority. According to them, the Ming dynasty had been replaced by the barbaric Qing, resulting in the dissolution of Chinese-centered civilization. They believed only Korea maintained the essence of Chinese culture.

This disparity would become meaningless with the appearance of Kim Chong-hui, a maestro who settled such trifling arguments once and for all. However, the mainstream thought of the day was held by the Old Doctrine faction, represented by Chong Son, Cho Yong-sok, and Yi In-sang, while Kang Se-hwang of the Young Doctrine faction held a subtly opposite opinion. Now Kwon Chol-shin defended Kang Se-hwang and dared attack the leading figure of the Old Doctrine art scene. While the rest of the audience stifled their smiles as they gazed at Shim, something flashed through In-mong's head.

Weren't they being taken in by Shim's wiles? Wasn't he deliberately diverting people's attention from Chae's death by starting an irrelevant dispute? Apparently In-mong was not the only one with this thought.

"Teacher Nog-am! You have gone too far!" Someone's chiding voice rang out next to Shim. "What a lack of courtesy for the second state councilor who has come to pay his respects at the memorial service! What's more, today is not only the first-year memorial service for Chae Che-gong, but also the day catastrophe struck his son. It is a good thing that the second state councilor has come, since we can discuss today's disaster."

The room grew silent, as if a pack of noisy mice had suddenly died.

Nam Han-jo opened his mouth in a quiet voice, sitting next to Yi Ka-hwan. "Chong-hon is right. I am only a country bumpkin who has grown old without any accomplishments. My functions are dull and my body is like the setting sun, so it is hard to fully understand many elders' thoughts. But I can't restrain myself from mentioning what happened to Duke Munsuk's family. Was Duke Munsuk an ordinary person? Although he has passed away, this dynasty still relies upon the benefits of his meritorious deeds. Since he entered the path of civil service under the auspices of the previous king, he punished the traitors' schemes in the court and implemented the king's enlightening policies to improve life in the northwest and the three southern provinces. His worthy deeds and loyalty drew the praise of the king, they were the treasure of the nation, and they still shine as a historical record. And no one would disagree about his achievements."

Shim coughed, making a face that indicated he had a hard time accepting Nam Han-jo's statement.

Nam Han-jo didn't acknowledge Shim's discomfort, but continued. "Just because there was temporarily a suspicion of Western Learning in his household, they burst upon him illegally and searched the house. They took his son and his guests and imprisoned them. Then they put them in neck restraints and shackles and thrashed them. Finally, their treatment caused him to die of starvation and cold! It is as though the sky collapsed and the earth caved in. In which country did it happen? Even in beastly barbarian lands, such lawlessness would not occur. The royal law stipulates that officials should make sure that prisoners do not die of severe cold or sweltering heat, of starvation or of sudden illness. If the officials neglect their duties, they are to be investigated and disciplined. I don't have any more to add to this. We should imprison that thug Yi Cho-won, the minister of punishments, and punish him according to the king's law, to confirm the true nature of this incident."

Listening to Nam Han-jo's frosty condemnation, Ku Chae-gyom felt his skin break out in a cold sweat. Allowing them to speak so freely! He questioned what his side was doing now. As though prompted by Ku's silent urging, the censor-general, sitting by Shim Hwan-ji, leaned his body forward.

"Teacher Son-jae! I understand why you are saying that. But Teacher, there cannot be generosity or partiality in the execution of the laws of a country. Nobody is unaware of Duke Munsuk's merits and loyalty, but just because some people are his close family or his close friends, it is not logical to say that they have permission to be patrons of Western Learning, which has been forbidden by the nation."

"Patronage? What do you mean by that? They just read some writing by Matteo Ricci and that was all. Who in the world has not read some Catholic books, if he is young and interested in new studies? If people have to be put in prison for that, arrest this oldster first!" Nam Han-jo growled, repeatedly slapping the floor with a wooden pillow that had been lying near him. The white beard of the seventy year-old man trembled with fury.

He was from the Nam lineage of Uiryong from Sangju, and had been a student of Sang-jong. He was a rare Southerner among the conservative group from the southeast: He had studied Catholicism. The fruits of his research were published in the twelfth volume of the *Son-jae Anthology,* in long treatises entitled "Refuting Objections to An Sun-am's 'Answering Questions about Catholicism'," and "Refuting Objections to Yi Ik's 'A Note on Matteo Ricci's *A True Disputation about the Lord of Heaven'. "* Formally, he took a position as a critic of Catholicism, but he seemed to have considerable understanding of and sympathy with the new religion, judging from the scope of his interest.

Noticing this old man's anger, the censor-general turned white. "One just stated that the law was such. Also, what you said about putting on neck restraints and shackles and thrashing him is not true. Who would dare use such brutal force on I-suk for such a wrongdoing? There were some different circumstances around his death. Astonished by his death, our two offices have investigated the matter, and it was discovered that there was an intervening ruse executed by the Catholics."

"Stop!" A voice rang out from the seat of honor. It did not belong to Nam Han-jo, but to Shim Hwan-ji. "What has the censor-general done so well that he takes it upon himself to argue on and on?"

The room grew silent, as if doused.

"Whatever the reason, it was the fault of the Board of Punishments that Chae I-suk died in prison," Shim continued. "Naturally the officials who are responsible for his arrest should be held accountable. Stop discussing this crystal-clear matter." He scolded the censor-general and turned his head toward Nam Han-jo. He spoke courteously. "Please don't be so angry, Son-jae Elder. It is the habit of us bureaucrats that we cannot overlook the tiniest details." His voice was soft as he bowed his head.

In-mong craned his neck to see this rare performance of Shim. Suddenly someone tugged at his sleeve—a man with thick eyebrows, a darkish complexion, and small, good-natured eyes. In-mong was astonished.

The man was none other than Yu Chi-myong. When had he come in and seated himself among the group? He was sitting next to In-mong. In-mong hurriedly held up his hand to prevent him from talking, and glanced at Ku Chae-gyom on his left side. Ku threw a glance at the two of them, but returned his attention to the upper room. There was no way for Ku to recognize Yu.

Yu understood the situation and nodded. He held In-mong's hand lightly and let it go before he quietly crawled to the door and left the room.

In-mong held in his hand a note that Yu Chi-myong had slipped to him, unseen, in the blink of an eye. In-mong looked around him, wiped the sweat from his forehead, and listened to Nam Han-jo's answer.

"There is nothing to be angry about. But you said a trick of the Catholics, didn't you? Whom do you mean, Censor-General?"

"There is a rumor that the two offices are looking into," Shim said, "It is not certain yet, so it cannot be discussed in a circumstance like this." He burst into laughter before he continued. "Today is the first time that I have met Son-jae Elder, and the lack of manners on my part is inexcusable. In the olden days, there was proper etiquette for the meeting of scholars. When they first met, they found an appropriate poem in the *Book of Odes* to use in conducting a conversation with allusions. This was called the poetry of allusion. Saying what they wanted to say by quoting from a poem rendered the message mild and circumspect. These days scholars do not know this, and what a shame it is that they flush their faces with squabbles at the smallest provocation! Son-jae Elder, please forgive the censor-general for my sake."

Nam Han-jo nodded willingly. He was only a simple, honest man, for he had spent his entire life studying classics. He blushed, having failed to realize Shim's complicated designs.

He said, "That is all right. Now I realize that I vented anger not becoming to my age. Please generously forgive me, Censor-General."

Shim's eyes gleamed. "I overheard briefly as I came in, but you seemed to be talking about the ancient times among yourselves . . ."

It was Yi Ka-hwan who sensed Shim's double entendre. "No, no," he said, "It was just idle talk among ourselves."

"What modesty! It sounded like it had to do with the poetry of allusion. Indeed, it is regretful that the beautiful custom disappeared with the expiration of the ways of Zhou."

"It has not completely disappeared," Yi Ka-hwan said.

"But what is the use of reciting the poetry of allusion in times like this? Reciting a poem from the *Book of Odes* obscures one's true intentions."

"It depends."

The audience had no idea what these two men were talking about. They had been arguing about Chae's death until a moment ago, but now they were deeply involved in an outdated discussion of the *Book of Odes*. Yi Ka-hwan turned his head to the scholars in the other room. "It is getting late. Now please go to the Blue Jewel Pavilion and get some rest."

The floor was so toasty hot, from the full blast of heat fed to the *ondol* from outside, that one could almost smell the roasting of flesh. Most of the scholars, who had been restraining themselves from dozing off, stood up quickly, bowed toward the upper part of the room, and retreated. Only three or four remained who were keeping company with the elders. Ku Chae-gyom signaled to his underlings with the wink of an eye, and followed them out.

Fearing he would lose this opportune moment, In-mong quickly unfolded the note. There were four characters: Wa Ryong Pok Po. Waryong Falls was located to the northwest of the Thinking of the Bright King Hall. Yu would be waiting there.

Yi Ka-hwan was speaking. In-mong quickly tucked the note away and listened attentively.

"Although the poetry of allusion is a formality of ancient times, it can be done by today's king. Because first comes the king and next the songs. The wind blows all over the world, and echoes when it touches people, and that is how a song is born. The source of these echoes is the wind. What is the wind? The king's enlightenment; in other words, the royal enlightening of habits, of teaching, and of customs. Mencius said, 'If the higher class likes something, the lower classes like it more. The virtue of the king is the wind, the virtue of the small people grass. When the wind touches the grass, the grass invariably bows.' Although many poems of the *Book of Odes* were vulgar songs of the marketplaces of Zhou, they have their own beauty and innocence because they were echoes emanating from the king's enlightenment. Therefore it is infinitely possible that even today a king recites the poetry of allusion for the enlightenment of the world."

So Yong-su, who had been sitting next to Shim, adopted a mysterious smile and addressed Yi Ka-hwan. "Teacher Chong-hon is talking very confidently and it appears he has read something like that."

"Ah, no, no. I am simply talking about principles."

"I beg to differ," So said. "You believe that if a king borrows whatever form, in whatever period, it is for enlightenment, do you not? But now we have the teachings of Zhu Xi. Why would a current king bring in worn-out poems from the *Book of Odes* instead of mentioning systematic teachings about the principles of righteousness?"

"It sounds too extreme."

"The ways of Zhou declined, and when Confucius and Mencius died, the tradition of Confucianism was severed. The First Emperor of Qin burned all the classics of Confucianism, and this was soon followed by the revolts of Zhen and Wu Guang. Confucianists took part in the revolts and as a result they were slaughtered. Therefore, during the Han dynasty, the philosophy of the Yellow Emperor Laozi was fashionable, and Buddhism flourished in Jin, Song, Ji, Yang, Wei, Shui, Tang, and Song. If the self-proclaimed Confucianists did not lean on Yang Zhu, they leaned on Mo Di, and if they did not go along with the arguments of Laozi, they went along with Buddhist theories. They have been polluted by heresies all along. Even if the *Book of Odes* is more reliable than the *Book of History*, how can poems that have floated down murky waters retain dead people's intentions? So there is no reason why a king should bring those vulgar poems to his lips, is there?"

It was true that So Young-su was of the Old Doctrine faction, but no one had ever belittled the *Book of Odes* to this extent. His utterly arrogant interpretation had a motive, and that was to infuriate the Southerners in hopes that they would inadvertently reveal some information about the tale of the metal-bound coffer.

Indeed, Kwon Chol-shin did begin to talk, unable to tolerate the attack. "There are many shallow scholars these days who consider the poems in the *Book of Odes* vulgar because they were songs of people in the marketplaces. But do marketplaces and noble places exist separately? Everyone, including you and me, was born in an impoverished household, but has the delusion of an elegant breeding, having no relationship with marketplaces, just because he has read some classics. If you're stained with ink, it should be in the right way! The intellectuals of low echelon come between the king and his people, and pretend they are of a special breed from birth. That is the gravest disease of our nation. They mimic foreign fiction, reciting hard-to-understand phrases, pretending to be high and mighty, but this is only worth a pig's fart."

So Yong-su's eyes bulged with anger, and he groaned.

Kwon eyed Yi Ka-hwan and Nam Han-jo intermittently as if he wanted to know whether he was going too far, but the two men blinked their eyes, wearing stony expressions. Their blinking seemed to indicate that Kwon was on the right track.

"I wouldn't hate them if those good-for-nothings remained quiet. But they frequent powerful people's parties, spend their time composing poems about the clear wind and the bright moon, praise each other for being exemplary and wise, and divide up government positions among themselves. In Heaven's name, how can they be unrecognized men of virtue? Drinking, stroking the *kisaeng*, praising each other enthusiastically, they turn themselves into unsung sages, like the saying that it is thanks to a magistrate a horn can be tooted."

"Stop it, Teacher Nog-am!"

"I won't!" Kwon continued, stroking his moustache. "Our dynasty has declined because of the lords who seized power by colluding with eunuchs and queens' families, not fearing the royal mandate. Why have the powerful become so powerful? Because they planted their own people, saying some were from good families, others were reputed Confucian scholars, and still others were exemplary people or sages. His Majesty, recognizing this wont, tried to abolish the practice of appointment by recommendation. In order to root out the powerful, the national examinations should be implemented strictly and all officials should be selected that way."

"Stop it, Teacher Nog-am!" So Yong-su demanded again. He was usually very calm and unfathomable, but even he lost his head at Kwon's unyielding taunts. Instead of infuriating the Southerners, he became incensed. "Do you think I don't know your hidden motive?"

"Hidden motive? Did you say hidden motive? You bastard! It is said that you can kill a scholar but you cannot humiliate him. How dare you babble about that kind of thing?" The old man stood, rolling up his sleeves. He seemed to want to take advantage of this opportunity to drive away all these interfering Old Doctrine members.

Shim Hwan-ji stood up and restrained Kwon. "Teacher Nog-am, I apologize. I do apologize. Please calm down. It is all because of this old man's weakness. I will apologize on his behalf."

Everyone's eyes widened in surprise. Shim was a true Old Doctrine faction member, known for his inflexibility, crankiness, and arrogance. Now he had put aside his dignity and bowed his head to Kwon. Kwon was so taken aback that he seated himself.

"There are important matters to discuss, so you'd better leave now." Shim addressed those remaining in the other room.

In-mong and the others leapt to their feet and replaced the doors that had been removed between the two rooms. They were all very silent as they opened the door leading to the veranda and left together.

Shim made sure all the footsteps quieted before he opened his mouth. "Truth be told, there is something I would like to discuss with the elders here," he said solemnly

Silence.

Shim Hwan-ji looked at Yun Haeng-im, the leader of the Expediency group of the Old Doctrine faction. Yun was the only one who had remained silent in the confusion, and now he nodded slightly.

Shim continued. "I do not know if you are aware of it, but Chang Chong-o, the book examiner, died at the Royal Library today. He died suddenly in his sleep, of a long-term illness. We found this notebook next to his body." He opened a cloth wrapping to reveal a notebook made of mulberry paper and bound by knotted hemp threads. It looked like the one In-mong had seen that morning.

"What of it?" Yi Ka-hwan asked in a chilly tone. His expression seemed to say he had guessed something.

"On the outside is written 'Notes on *Humble Thoughts on the Book of Odes.*' When you open it, there are phrases copied from three books. I will read."

Shim threw a sharp glace at Yi Ka-hwan and began to read the first part.

"The first phrase is from the fifth section of Zilu chapter of the *Analects*. 'Though a man may be able to recite the three hundred odes, yet if, when entrusted with a government charge, he knows not how to act, or if, when sent to any quarter on a mission, he cannot give his replies unassisted, notwithstanding the extent of his learning, of what practical use is it?'

"The second phrase is from Duke Xiang's nineteeth year in *Qunchiu zuozhuan*. 'Jiwu of No went to Jin to show his gratitude for sending armies at the time of fighting Ji. Jin spread a feast for him. During the party, Fanxuanzi, a minister of Jin, recited a poem entitled "The New Sprout of Millet." Jiwu, in the middle of listening, stood up and kowtowed twice.'

"The third is from the twenty-third year of Duke Luxi, on the country Jin, in *Guoyu*. 'Ziyu went to Qin accompanied by Prince Zhonger. They were granted an audience by Duke Moke, a governor of Qin. Ziyu had made Prince Zhonger recite "The New Sprout of Millet," the Qin governor answered with "The Owl Is Flying." Then the Prince recited "River Water," and the Qin governor answered with "June." Ziyu advised the Prince to step down to the shoe ledge and make a deep bow.' What does Chong-hon think of these quotations?"

"Well, I happen to be a person with shallow learning and no talent and therefore . . ."

"Then I will tell you. It is about the poetry of allusion that was used from

Zhou to the time of Confucius. Should I read the next page? There is a quotation of the entire text of 'The Owl' from the *Book of Odes*. Of course I do not need to read this to the most learned persons of this country. If that had been all, we might have been deceived completely." Shim's voice was high-pitched now, very different from when he had been pleading with Kwon.

The three quotations were indeed about the poetry of allusion.

From Zhou until the period of the Warring States, diplomacy was conducted through the vehicle of poetry of allusion. When envoys came, they were welcomed with a feast. During the party, the guest took a poem from the *Book of Odes* to reveal the purpose of his visit. The host responded by borrowing an appropriate poem from the same book.

As stated in the fifth section of the Zilu chapter of the *Analects*, three hundred poems had to be committed to memory for appropriate quotations for the "job of administration or response on his own as an envoy."

Let us have a look at Jin in *Guoyu*. Prince Zhonger of Jin was a wanderer when he appeared in *Guoyu*, although later he would become Prince Wen of Jin. He left his country due to his stepmother's accusation and wandered the world for eighteen years. Who would have guessed that this wretched man would reclaim Jin in the following year, and that only five years later Jin would emerge as a world power by defeating the strong country of Chu? His old loyal servant Zilu, or Zhao Shuai, followed his master to Qin, with the last kernel of hope.

When he saw the governor of Qin, Zhonger first recited "The New Sprout of Millet" from "Xiaoya" of the *Book of Odes*: "The long-grown sprout of millet / Is wet by rain / The ways of constructing a distant southern country / Are supported by Zhaobo, the illustrious ruler."

The sprout of millet indicated Zhonger's warped life, and the rain referred to the governor of Qin. If the governor helped him, the reclamation of Jin would be achieved. The governor of Qin answered positively by reciting "The Owl Is Flying." When Zhonger expressed his gratitude by reciting "River Water," the governor promised permanent solidarity between Jin and Qin with the poem "June."

There was no doubt that these quotations were records of the poetry of allusion. But where did this recognition lead?

"Second State Councilor, what do you mean by being deceived? I do not understand what you are talking about at all. Who is deceived about what?" Nam Hyon-jo asked, his eyes blinking slowly.

The faces of Yi Ka-hwan and Kwon Chol-shin, who were sitting next to

Nam, had changed. Shim didn't miss their expressions.

"Now look at the next page," Shim said, "Here is the number 38, and the next page has the number 39, and the following page 40."

No one spoke.

"When we first got hold of this notebook, we did not know what the numbers meant, so we overlooked the important secret this notebook held. But we suddenly understood before half the day was over. They are the years of the previous king's reign. The thirty-eighth year was when the crown prince died confined in the rice chest. The thirty-ninth year was when the people connected with the incidents were banished, and then the fortieth year was when State Councilor Chae Che-gong had an exclusive interview with the king and received that tale of the metal-bound coffer."

By this time Shim's face had turned purple. It was surprising that he had suppressed anger of this magnitude up to this point, and a cold-eyed third party might have seen through his theatrical performance.

"Do you know what I mean?" He continued, "There was no such thing as the tale of the metal-bound coffer. His Majesty fabricated that document through Chang Chong-o!"

Everyone seemed to have turned into rock. All directed their surprise at Shim. He appeared happy with the response his bold deduction had elicited, as he looked around. "We looked at this notebook and naturally thought that it was a notebook that had copied the important parts from *Humble Thoughts on the Book of Odes*. But the reality was the other way around. Chang Chong-o created the notebook first, and according to the facts of this notebook, he made a book called *Humble Thoughts on the Book of Odes*, purportedly the previous king's composition. Chang was famous for his talent in copying handwriting so that it would deceive even ghosts. As for *Humble Thoughts on the Book of Odes* – well, do you think we would not know? It is another name for the tale of the metal-bound coffer, which some rat among you brought to your attention a while ago. It must be a forgery. As for the contents, we do not even have to look at the book to know that it contains attacks on the Principle group of the Old Doctrine faction."

His words had his typical vitality and his considerable powers of persuasion.

If Chong Yag-yong and Yi In-mong had been present, they might have accepted Shim's argument with docility. They knew that there was some forgery in the *Chronicle of King Yongjo* in the Royal Shrine. If *Humble Thoughts on the Book of Odes* was a well-crafted forgery, a source for the existence of such a book was required. Shim's explanation went perfectly well with the theory of the forgery in the *Chronicle of King Yongjo*.

Soon, however, someone pointed out a blind spot in Shim's deduction. "Quiet!" shouted Kwon Chol-shin, in a tone as sharp as a knife blade. "Even if you are the second state councilor, your irreverent words and behavior are unpardonable!" He added, "The original documents written or supervised by King Yongjo have royal seals that distinguish the original from mere copies — and the King's seal used ink from Nanjing, which cannot be duplicated by a potato. Do you think we are blind?"

So Yong-su held up his head stiffly. "Now you are talking! You have definitely seen the book, the tale of the metal-bound coffer that had the royal seal. Where is it now?" His face took on the determined look of a savage beast confronting his prey.

Yun Haeng-im, of the Expediency group, deterred So and spoke. His group took a favorable attitude toward the Southerners, and he was a prudent man. Suddenly everyone was attentive to his every word.

"Teacher Son-jae, Teacher Chong-hon, and Teacher Nog-am! We are now faced with suspicion about the patriarch of the nation, which is immensely embarrassing. His Majesty is suspect for having forged the writing of the previous king in a bid to purge a certain group. This suspicion undermines the positions of those who have supported the king up to now. It is a shock of immense magnitude. As you know, traditionally the tale of the metal-bound coffer was something only the king knew and no one else could guess. But if such things were found in a book examiner's notebook, we cannot say the second state Councilor went overboard when he drew such a conclusion."

"It is not the case," Yi Ka-hwan said in a loud voice and bit down on his lip.

His Majesty must have directed Chang Chong-o to make "Notes on *Humble Thoughts on the Book of Odes*" because the Old Doctrine faction's philosophy of style denied the poetry of allusion itself as a form. The poetry of allusion was borrowed to reveal a person's thoughts. His Majesty might have been concerned because the Old Doctrine faction, who believed that writings belonged to the original authors, would not recognize "The Owl" as the previous king's own thoughts. This was Yi Ka-hwan's guess, but he couldn't bring himself to express it. If he did, it would be proof that His Majesty and the Southerners were unsure about the method of expressing themselves through the poetry of allusion. And yet, this immense suspicion . . .

His face full of concern, Yi said with candor, "The tale of the metal-bound coffer is truly original. The royal seal was authentic, as was Duke

Munsuk's handwriting, and we could see it had been sealed with wax for the past thirty-five years. Also the paper, the signature of the previous king, the official royal seal . . . no matter how you looked at it, it was a record of the fortieth year of the previous king's reign, without the slightest doubt!"

"Who has it now? Let's check it right now!" Shim Hwan-ji and others leaned forward as one.

"It is not here."

"Not here?"

"The original belongs to His Majesty. We have sent our people to deliver it to His Majesty!"

"Wha . . . what?"

* * *

As he climbed, the sound of the falls grew louder. In-mong was climbing up the side of the northwest valley toward Waryong Falls. A dense mass of tree branches blocked the moonlight and he couldn't see his own feet. He placed his hands on damp, mossy tree trunks as he made his way, but he kept slipping.

"Elder Brother!" Yu Chi-myong stood in a clearing in front of the falls, sharply outlined in the moonlight.

"It has been a long time," In-mong said.

"I am glad to see you."

"By any chance, did you see my wife today?"

"Yes. She came this evening. She is not well, but she should be sleeping comfortably by now."

"Is that so?" In-mong's face darkened with deep worry. Ku Che-gyom's men must have ravaged Yu's house by now. He was burdened by concerns about Sang-a and felt sorry for Yu. Yu handed him a book made of stiff paper, like the kind used for floor paper. The red title page was blank.

"This is the previous king's tale of the metal-bound coffer. Your wife brought it."

"What? You have this?"

One glance told In-mong that this was not an ordinary book. Each page was sealed with wax. He opened the cover and found that only the first page had no wax seal. In-mong held up the page to see the dense characters written at the top.

On the day of *kapshin*, the ninth month of the fortieth year, His Majesty called me, and in no one else's presence he talked about the matter of the late crown prince and recited "The Owl," shedding tears. This servant, Chae Che-gong, the holder of the positions of the first royal secretary and the second minister of rites, bows with folded hands and humbly writes this down at His Majesty's command.

Ah! Was it possible? In-mong felt as if he had heard a thunderclap.

"His Majesty . . . talked about the matter of the late crown prince and recited "The Owl" shedding tears! Was the tale of the metal-bound coffer a poem alluding to "The Owl"?

"Owl, O owl, hear my request / And do not, owl, destroy my nest. / You have taken my young, / Though I over them hung, / With the nursing of love and of care . . . " Ah, so the previous king had recited "The Owl." That was why Shim Hwan-ji had been talking about the poetry of allusion a while ago at the Thinking of the Bright King Hall. Shim couldn't have seen this book. Ah, yes! "Notes on *Humble Thoughts on the Book of Odes*" had been found next to Chang Chong-o's body.

All the books that In-mong had seen that day began to float in his head.

First there was "Notes on *Humble Thoughts on the Book of Odes*" next to Chang's body. *Humble Thoughts on the Book of Odes* must have been stolen from Chang's room. *Chronicle of King Yongjo* had been found at the Royal Shrine. Chong Yag-yong had told him about "The Song of the Blood Stained Hemp and the Mourning Staff." Now here was the tale of the metal-bound coffer. How were all these books related to one another?

In-mong's head began to hurt.

"Have you shown this to the elders?" he asked.

"Yes, but before we could discuss it, Shim Hwan-ji's entourage burst upon us, so I had to take it out again. Older Brother, please take it."

"Take it?"

"His Majesty is staying in the living quarters at the foot of the northern hill. Many people want to get their hands on this book. Please take it quickly to the king. Imposing royal guards are there, but you are an official close to the king."

"All right. How can I get to the living quarters?"

"Please come with me."

In-mong put the book inside his clothes, near his heart. The two men left the rocks by the waterfall and reentered the forest. The woods were still dark and the deep shadows loomed ominously. Only the sounds of water and the wind could be heard. Soon a narrow path between the dark trees became visible—a rough path buried deep among the tall fir trees. In-mong and Yu followed it.

Yu Chi-myong looked back and said, "They may be looking for us. Let's circumvent them and approach the building by climbing down the back hill."

In-mong only nodded. He didn't have energy left to speak.

After only a few more steps, they froze as a sense of premonition seized them. They heard low voices coming from the path they had just left. As the careless footsteps entered the forest, In-mong heard a faint familiar voice which rang in his ears like a thunderclap.

It was the voice of Ku Chae-gyom.

Soon several tall shadows came into view, still far away in the shadows of the moon-dappled forest.

"Run, now!" In-mong pulled Yu's hand and began to run down the narrow path in the dense forest with all his might.

"Stop right there!" shouted the voices. The footsteps broke into a run and drew closer.

In-mong and Yu were filled with dread as they flew through the forest; their clothes ripped and lashed by the branches. Yu suddenly shrieked and disappeared as if the earth had swallowed him.

"Hey! Chong-jae!" In-mong hoarsely whispered and groped around for his companion.

He quickly realized that Yu had tumbled down a slope in the darkness—but he couldn't stop to save him. Snake-like swords gleamed in the moonlight just ten steps behind him. He bit his lips and began running again but soon tripped over an unseen stone.

"Don't move!" In-mong tried to scramble up but a soldier seized the scruff of his neck.

Then Ku Chae-gyom, all smiles, appeared before In-mong.

"Librarian, sir! You broke your promise. You were supposed to hand us the book when you found it. However hard you run, you will still be in the palm of a Buddha. Can you fly up to the sky or jump into the earth?" He laughed boisterously.

Only then did In-mong realize that his every movement—his meeting with Yu and Yu's transfer of the book to him—had been spied on. In-mong was out of breath and felt paralyzed. He didn't know what to do.

"Search him, boys!"

"Yes, sir."

The man holding In-mong grabbed the front of In-mong's coat and tore it open. The book fell to the ground.

A sudden thought flashed though In-mong's head. "No, you can't do this!" he cried pitifully as he snatched at a corner of the book.

"Let go!" Ku grabbed the hilt of his sword as his other hand gripped the book. In-mong held onto the book with all his might. Ku's sword glittered in the moonlight. In-mong shrieked and blood squirted as the book was torn in half. The pain was as if he had been hit by lightning. He staggered back, flailing his arms, and felt his foot hanging in the air. The slope was steeper than the one on which Yu Chi-myong had fallen.

In-mong shot out into space briefly before he hit and began to roll, bumping down the rocks and pierced by unseen branches. He lost consciousness, feeling as though his body had been pulverized.

"Follow him. Go down right away." Ku shouted.

"There was blood. Wasn't he dead?"

"No. It was a shallow cut," Ku said.

"But he fell off this cliff."

"Shut up! Go and make sure he's dead. What's this small talk? If he's alive, things will be complicated for a long time to come."

One of the men pulled urgently at Ku's sleeve. His hand was trembling. "Chief, sir, Look over there!"

"What is it now?" Ku looked to the right, where his underling pointed.

About ten torches were climbing up from the living quarters.

"The Royal Guards, sir."

A group of Royal Guards approached and began to search the ridge, investigating the strange sounds that had been heard coming from it. If Ku and his men were discovered by the Guards, their every effort would end in futility, as if mucus from their noses had dripped into their cooked rice.

"Damn!" Ku promptly turned back. "We'll come again when it's light. Let's go back."

It was dawn, yet still dark. It was right before *myoshi*, and light had yet to appear in the eastern sky.

8
This World of Dust and Motes

Surprisingly, our King Chongjo passed away in the summer of 1800, and before the period of national mourning had come to an end, Yi Kap-hoe, the magistrate of Andong, threw his father's sixtieth birthday party, with kisaeng *and all, and invited Chang Hyon-kyong and his father. Chang's father said, "When the government offices are closed for national mourning, a feast where people drink and amuse themselves cannot be held." He came out of his room and said to the official who had brought the invitation, "Having a party right after the royal demise means they know how things stand in the world these days."*

In the past Chang Hyon-kyong's father and Yi's father, who were related although they had different surnames, had often discussed rumors circulating in the world when they frequented the government office together. One of the rumors had it that a certain minister had prompted a Royal Infirmary doctor named Shim In to offer the king poison under the pretext of taking care of his health, which resulted in the royal death. Chang Hyon-kyong's father became so furious over the rumor that he shed tears and said, "We have yet to kill that traitor."

—Chong Yag-yong, "A Record of Lady Chang's Family in Kogumdo Island" (1811), vol. 16, *The Complete Collection of Chong Yag-yong.*

The place was Chosan County in Pyong-an Province, at the foot of Yondae Hill. Manchuria was visible in the distance, as well as the point where the Chungman River, flowing from the Tongnim ridge of the Nangnim Mountains, joined the Yalu River.

The sun was sinking slowly, but the sunlight was still hot.

A wagon rolled slowly across the vast, empty plain. Dried stalks were scattered in the fields, for there had not been a drop of rain all summer.

The old man pulling the wagon appeared to be exhausted. He was climbing a slight slope. He braced his shoulders to pull the wagon. He was connected to it by a strap. One hand held the wagon handle, and with the other hand he pulled on the strap. The veins on his neck stood out. He looked ill and his face was yellow with jaundice.

A sudden pain in his ribs caused his legs to buckle. One of the wooden wheels had struck a stone. The frame rattled and a corpse fell from the wagon.

The old man put the handle down, panting. He looked back at the body that had fallen—the body of an old woman in her sixties. Her face was puffy and jaundiced. A cloud of flies had followed the wagon all the way from the village and now buzzed persistently around the sprawled body. The stench was suffocating. The old man frowned, took a dingy bandana from around his neck and covered his mouth and nose with it.

The old man placed stones behind the wheels so that the wagon wouldn't slide down. He put his arms under the body's armpits and dug his heels into the earth. The drooping body was unbelievably heavy. After three groaning efforts, he finally got it back on the wagon, where there were more corpses: two more women, two children around five or six years-old, and a fat young man. Six bodies all together. While the old man was tarrying, another wagon approached.

"Elder Pak, you're working hard."

The old man nodded without speaking and began to pull his wagon.

The other man was middle-aged, around fifty. "It's hard work for an old man. When they hear it's cholera, they flee a thousand miles, so there's never enough hands. Today the magistrate himself brandished his sword and ordered people to work, but these were all he could get."

"That might be so."

The two men followed the mountain path leading up to Aijin Fortress. Half an hour later they came upon four men stripped to the waist, digging graves where the steep slope began. Elder Pak and his companion tilted their wagons and dropped the bodies into one of the empty graves.

Fifteen bodies, large and small, were tumbled into one grave as if they were the carcasses of beasts, but they were the lucky ones. Elder Pak himself and the others who were burying the bodies might well end up being food for the crows, if no one was left to bury them.

The two men staggered across a slash-and-burn patch and collapsed under an old zelkova tree.

This was a desolate place at the foot of the mountain. In the distance, under the pink evening sky, lay a devastated village. They could make out black specks that were burned-down houses and bare patches, like exposed spots on an animal with some skin disease, which had been vegetable gardens. At the beginning of the year, all the people had left the village after burning their houses due to the epidemic. Wherever one went in the land of Korea, there were only these frightful landscapes, the traces of broken lives. Log huts in the mountains and thatched-roof houses in the fields were burned and deserted. Only burnt ruins were left.

"The ninth month is around the corner, so this cholera will ease off a bit, don't you think?" the younger man said.

"That might be so." The exhausted old man moved his arm, as heavy as a thousand weight, to pull out a dog-skin tobacco pouch from his waist fold. He fumbled for a long time, making a rustling sound, until he retrieved a half-palm-sized sheet of mulberry paper, tobacco, and a bamboo box as big as a thumb.

He placed some tobacco leaf in the paper and sprinkled white powder over it from the small box. He carefully rolled the paper and licked the two sides, sticking them together with his saliva before striking his flint stone. Smoke drifted up. He brought the tobacco to his nostrils slowly lest it should spill, and inhaled deeply. Again and again. He kept inhaling until the last whiff of smoke was gone.

Then he leaned against the trunk of the tree. His pains were slowly leaving him, and he felt good.

He was an old man who could live only in the past. The tobacco, sprinkled with opium, transformed his past, the source of his gloomy torment, into a colorful realm of dreams. The person he had been longing for was smiling in that colorful land. Where red dust floated up in the sun, where clouds of smoke danced about. Ah, the elegant music, the majestic palace, the busy marketplace in the walled capital, the lively merchants, the people, the girls who were laughing merrily, the lotus flowers blooming like clouds, the fresh raindrops . . . the rain drops . . . and that person . . .

He beamed. His neck was trembling.

The old man had only one eye. It looked like the trace of a sword had been carved into his left eye, leaving behind tiny thorns. His squinting right eye wavered, almost closed.

The other man shook the old man by the shoulder.

"Elder, sir! Elder!"

"What?" the old man began to regain control of his muscles. As he raised his head and pulled himself up, he heard the long neighing of a horse.

He wiped his eye, and then saw an official with a white beard, dressed in brown military garb and a silk hat. The other man had already prostrated himself toward this official.

"Old man! Are you sick?" asked the official.

"Oh, no, sir." He hurriedly bowed his head.

The official's silk hat indicated that he was the new magistrate of Chosan, who had taken the post a month before. He was an old man himself, almost sixty. The magistrate, to avoid the scorching sun, handed his horse's reins to his slave and sat down in the shade of the tree. The old man had begun to retreat but the official waved his hand.

"Don't mind me. Sit and rest. I was just going to rest my legs for a while. If you were to leave, I'd feel sorry."

"Yes, yes, sir."

Despite the two men's rough appearance, the official spoke to them as if he were talking to neighbors. With his white beard and small bright eyes buried in tiny wrinkles, he had a look of unconventionality not in keeping with his military garb. The furrows on his wide forehead gave him the appearance of a person of generosity who had nevertheless experienced the sourness and bitterness of the world.

"And where do you live, old man?" asked the magistrate, wiping sweat off his forehead.

"This humble person is called Pak Sang-hyo. I live in Songso village. I make a living by doing the job of a teacher."

"Do you still have many students?"

"Ah, no. The times are so terrible that the school is closed for now. I till the slash-and-burn patch in front of my house."

The eyes of the official and the old man met. Suddenly the old man winced and his shoulders shook. An echo of a memory from long ago resounded in his head. Apparently it was not only the old man who was remembering something. The official cocked his head and began to study the old man's face. The old man suppressed his trembling and bowed his head slowly.

"Old man!"

"Yes, sir."

"You don't sound like someone from this region. Didn't you live in Seoul when you were young?"

"Yes? Ah, no ... "

Before the old man could deny it, the middle-aged man hastily interposed. "Yes, sir, that is right. This elder Pak used to live in Seoul and came to Chosan about a dozen years ago."

"Kaedong Father! Why do you babble about something you know nothing about?" The old man sprang up with a determined look. The withered look he had had a while ago disappeared. He quickly bowed toward the official and left the shade. He strode across the patch without looking back.

"Look, old man! old man!" The official ran after him a few steps and then gazed at his back as he walked away.

Kaedong Father was confused. He looked back and forth between the old man and the official, and followed the old man hurriedly. The slave came up to the magistrate, who had been suddenly abandoned.

"Do you know Old Man Kamak?" asked the slave.

"Old Man Kamak?"

"Yes, that is the nickname he is known by around here. When the moon is bright, he always goes to Kamak Stream, drinks, and weeps. He is a truly strange man. Villagers have seen him go up to the mountain to gather wood, but he peels the bark, whitens it, and jots down what looks like poetry with a piece of charcoal. After he finishes his poem, he recites it in a low voice, suddenly weeps, and then scratches out his writing."

"He jots down poems?"

"Yes. And two autumns ago, he got drunk and wielded his scythe over the ripe rice stalks in front of his house. In the blink of an eye, he ruined all the rice in a paddy of five hundred square meters, and he cried his heart out all night. Some book-reading gentlemen praise him as a great scholar, but the villagers look down on him because of his behavior, and almost everyone treats him like a lunatic."

"That old man ... does he have a big family?"

"Not at all, sir. He used to live with his daughter, but she died when she was about fifteen, during the cholera epidemic last year."

The official groaned and his eyes grew smaller. The old man could be seen disappearing with his wagon, far away in the field. The official's eyes followed the lonely, long path in the field, and shifted to the gorge of the mountains over which clouds were floating.

He was not looking at the gorge.

His eyes saw someone hidden in his dim memory. That person was living in such a far-off place in his life that he seemed like a fleeting dream, an enchanting, warm fantasy. This particular memory had a strange comforting power that made him feel that life was not so ephemeral after all.

"Where does he live?"

"He operates a school out of a rented house down from the Somun Pavilion."

While the official and his slave were talking, Old Man Kamak and Kaedong Father were returning to the village. They were walking through the rough field, whose soil hadn't even been turned over this season, and the sun continued to burn hot.

"What mistake did I make? The magistrate looked like he recognized you, so why were you so adamant? Did you do anything wrong in the past?"

The old man was silent.

"That magistrate is really down to earth. He's not like any other official. I heard a few days ago that he used to be a really high official in Seoul."

"Is that so?"

"Yes, he was something called the censor-general and also the third royal secretary. . . . Anyway he was really high up, but he had a hard time because he was not on good terms with the powerful folks. And this time, too, he wrote a memorial, and that was why he was demoted to this out-of-the way post in the countryside."

"Is that so?" the old man asked absentmindedly, his face expressionless.

The work was finished before long. The bodies, which had been left in the streets for over a month, had all been buried by the end of the day. That day in their district thirteen hundred bodies had been buried and three hundred and fifty houses had been burned.

The numbers of the previous month were similar. The old man passed the village where death dwelt and dragged his exhausted body to his house under the Somun Pavilion.

Cholera, which suddenly appeared in the twenty-first year of King Sunjo, in 1821, was different from any of the other epidemics Koreans had known. Ways had been developed to avoid epidemics such as typhoid fever and smallpox, which first appeared in the Koryo dynasty (918-1392), and syphilis, which first appeared right after the Imjin Japanese Invasion in 1592. The symptoms of cholera, however, were bizarre, and the disease was more infectious and more fatal than any other. A high fever hit, diarrhea and convulsions from a raging fever lasted a day, and death quickly came from dehydration.

This contagious disease first appeared in Pakistan in 1817 and took only four years to travel to the south, ravaging all of India; to the north, laying waste the entire nation of China; to Korea through Shanhaiguan, devastating Korea before crossing over to Japan. Considering how contagious it was, it was no wonder everyone was talking about Heaven's Mandate.

The old man lived in a log house, teeming with bedbugs.

He collapsed on the straw-covered dirt floor and made himself get up only after the subtle pink sky of the sunset had turned to a dim gray. He started a fire by using a flint stone to light thin resinous pine twigs cut to uniform length. In this remote village, it was unthinkable to use oil for a lamp when there was not enough oil for cooking.

The old man put the twigs on a flat stone that he had brought into the room, and pulled a box from a corner. The box functioned as both a clothes bin and a desk. He took out a thick, tattered notebook, a brush, and an ink stone.

As he was rubbing the ink bar on the stone, he realized that something was wrong with him. Heat surged from deep in his nose to his earlobes. Startled, he breathed deeply. The top of his head began to throb and suddenly he couldn't breathe.

The symptoms had developed only recently. The pain brought tears to the corners of his eyes yet he persisted in making ink. Finally, when the ink was ready, he moistened his brush and began to write.

> *Ulmi* day of the eighth month. Drafted in for corvee labor service and moved fifty-six corpses. The corpses buried in the district today amounted to thirteen hundred. It has already been thirty-five years since the Loved One left. The king has changed twice, but again this year there was a drought during which cholera rampaged nationwide. Ah, this misery! The people's lives are so miserable. The civilian houses lining the villages have turned into ashes. With the disappearance of the sage-king, the earth dried up, the sky turned murky, and all kinds of contagious diseases and disasters kept assaulting us. Because everything is on the wrong path, everywhere there is only desolate silence and the shadows of death.

He managed to write thus far, but an agonizing pain squeezed his neck and chest.

He dropped his brush. Trembling, he took out his dog-skin pouch to roll some tobacco. As he spread the tobacco evenly across the paper with trembling hands, he thought of his daughter, who had died the year before. Then he sprinkled all the white powder he had on top of the tobacco. He had started smoking opium to relieve the heartbreak of losing his daughter.

He smoked. The fever and pain all over his body disappeared as if by magic. He even felt he had regained some energy. He drew in the last whiff. His eyes were bright now.

He took up his notebook and riffled through the first few pages, looking at some entries he had made the year before. When he wrote these, he had thought he would leave this village forever, after he had buried his daughter on the hill. Slowly he began to read one passage.

> Heaven and Earth created human beings to differentiate them from the beasts. Heaven has a special affection for humans, so they were given propriety and institutions, which are no other than the laws and ordinances revealed clear and bright in the immortal world. Propriety and institutions originate from the sole entity of the king, and because there is a king, Heaven's Heart is revealed, laws are established on earth, and human beings are differentiated from beasts. On whom do human beings rely when they follow the three fundamental principles and five moral disciplines in human relationships to reveal Heaven's Heart? It is the king, the essential being in the world and the one that can never be replaced.

> My life, like a floating cloud between the sky and the earth, is about to disperse, and my hair has turned white. Looking back, this life, which was short on joy and long on sorrows, is so far away that it looks like a dream. The only thing that floats up in my dim eyes is the king himself, whom I saw as a young man. I was indebted to His Grace for enlightening me and cultivating me, but how immense is my guilt for repaying his Sacred Virtues with disloyalty! When I die, how can I dare see King Chongjo, and how can I face the scholars of later years?

> The words I record on this paper concern an astonishing incident that I witnessed and experienced as a young man. Everything in that incident is mixed with the guilt of my stupidity and churlishness, and my brush point trembles already. I record these perilous words, suppressing the pain and regret in my heart, because I cannot be assured of the conveyance of evidence, because there is no one to whom I can relay the terrible things that happened in the twenty-fourth year of King Chongjo. If the scholars of the coming decades can judge the right and the wrong

of the historical records based on my incoherent writing, this old man's guilt will be somewhat alleviated. But who will keep this notebook in which I write in a hut in a remote village, using a dull brush? When this book is finished, I will depart for an unknown place.

Why do I write this and for whom?

Again today, the wind of the western province blows lonely, sweeping hazy, sandy dust to the sky. Winter is not far away from this northwest region. When I leave here, my life will end wherever the remainder of my strength will have been spent. I will lay my body in a silent, dusty road in some mountains in whirling snow, and the path before me will be forever closed.

But those of you who read this writing should not pity me. I have wished for death in an unknown place for the past thirty-four years. I have wandered over half of this country during that period. I have lived as a traveler in an isolated hamlet, a teacher at a tiny school, a slash-and-burn farmer, and sometimes a sick beggar. At one point I was a prisoner of a dank, dark local office, and another time I lived in a dirt-floored room as the man of a young woman who eked out a living by making ox fodder.

A daughter was born between myself and that young woman. This was twenty years after the two sons I had with my former wife died. With the deaths of my sons, my home had disappeared. I had to walk endlessly toward some unknown place, driven by the fiery wind of pursuers on my heels.

The nineteenth day of the first month of the twenty-fourth year of the previous king. It was on that dreadful day that I lost my eye. A twig pierced it as I fell off a cliff. By the time I pulled myself together and regained my wits, His Majesty had already taken to his bed and the court had fallen into the hands of the Old Doctrine faction, led by Queen Chongsun. I hid myself in an acquaintance's house in Kwachon for a few months, and then I left. When I reached Haeju, Hwanghae Province, by boat via Kanghwa Island, I heard that His Majesty had passed away.

What a shame and heartbreak! How persistent life can be!

I have meant to die since that day, but I have lived on until now.

In the first few years, I moved between several places in Pyoksong near Haeju. Finally I was arrested and imprisoned, but I managed to break away and I have been on the run ever since. I was on the move for seven years from Sariwon, to Pyongang, to Kangso. At Kangso, I had to burn my house and leave, pursued by prison guards. I passed through Sunchon, Maengchon, and Tokchon. I hid myself in Mt. Myohyang and subsisted among slash-and-burn farmers. After that, I was a beggar in Yongbyon for a year.

My wandering life has lasted more than thirty years, and now my body and my heart are old.

I have admired the Way, but I have never seen it or heard it. When I saw my wife and my daughter, whom I acquired accidentally, cold and hungry, I could not wander in the land of Taoism. There is no fixed address for a wanderer, and I do not know where I will end up. The red sun is setting and the path to the Underworld is beginning to brighten. I will become a wanderer of a thousand miles. When I leave here, will I head for somewhere near water or the foothills of a mountain?

The old man managed to read this far before he collapsed on his side.

When he had first bound the notebook and held the brush, he hadn't imagined it would take this long. Everything had happened on one day, the nineteenth day of the first month of the former king's twenty-fourth year. Yet after a year he was still writing about what had happened in such a short span of time.

How many stories can a day hold? The things that had seemed so obvious had become utterly complicated, and the faces that he had thought were so clear in his memory that he could almost touch had retreated far, far away.

Ah, how fundamentally foolish he was, and how narrow and dim in learning! He couldn't even articulate what happened in the course of a day. He had searched the *Book of Changes* to find the seven numbers of that day to divide up the events accordingly. After he finished the events of the seventh part of the day, something was still lacking. He tried to figure out what it was while he recorded his diary every day, starting each entry in the style of "*Ulmi* day of the eighth month."

The harder he tried, the farther the events of that day retreated into the past.

He felt as if he had lived in Chosan all his life, without venturing out once. Of course "Pak Sang-hyo," the name of the school teacher, was a pseudonym; but his real name, "Yi In-mong," also seemed like a fictional name. He envisioned infinite living moments on the smooth, firm chain of eternity, without a beginning and without an end. "Yi In-mong" was not a name of reality, only a momentary name like a drop of water, like the day about which the old man failed to write well.

There was only one country in this chain of eternity that human beings had made—Zhou. The countries before it were but dreams trying to achieve it, and the countries after it were but dreams trying to return to it. Who was he? What did he live for? His life was but one drop of water in the eternal dream. It was a dream within a dream.

The old man's body was burning like fire.

A voice called his name. It reached his ears, but it didn't register in his consciousness. Only the things that happened thirty-four years ago, upon which he had reflected endlessly, still undulated in his mind.

Finally the door creaked open.

The magistrate who had met In-mong earlier that day was at the door with several clerks. Overwhelmed by the dark, dank, stench-filled room they simply stood. The magistrate had changed into an ordinary gentleman's coat and hat. After a time, he took off his shoes and stepped up into the dirt-floored room. He gazed at the old man with sad eyes for a long time. Then he shook him.

"Older Brother! . . . Older Brother!"

"Sir, isn't it the epidemic?" a clerk with a lush moustache asked in a trembling voice.

The others jumped back, startled.

"No. This old man has smoked tobacco sprinkled with opium, a little too much. You may wait outside."

When they were gone, the magistrate sat down cross-legged, next to the old man. This official, Yu Chi-myong, who had fled with In-mong in that dawn years ago, was suddenly overcome by a feeling of helplessness. Starlight came in between the logs of the roof.

To the old man all exterior sounds were mere buzzes. His consciousness was drifting toward a deeper world of dreams. His blood, stimulated by the opium, made the sound of gurgling water, generating fantasies of all shapes and colors. The last energy of his life summoned the memories he had failed to write down.

Was he old now?

Was death coming to him?

The old man's eyeballs moved rapidly under his eyelids. A sense of permanence covered all the torments. Suddenly a poem by Yi Sang-un came to him, one that he had read as a young man: "Ringing the bell of the lonely day in which the darkness descends, / I lean on a staff leisurely. / This world is made of dust and motes, / so how can there be love and hatred left for me? . . . Memories fell like snow. He saw a bright face, overlapping the snowflakes of memories. A bell rang.

"To-won!"

Silence.

"To-won!"

"Yes.
"Yes.
"Yes, Your Majesty.
"Your Majesty . . ."

Chronology

1790: Kim Chong-su retires to mourn his mother. His retirement marks the inauguration of a government led by a single state councilor, Chae Che-gong, a Southerners faction member. Kim Mun-sun, minister of taxation, of the Principle group, manipulates merchants to bring about a large-scale scarcity of goods in the capital.

1791: Chae Che-gong announces the Commercial Equalization Act of 1791, which abolishes the privileges of market merchants and allows unrestricted buying and selling. A Catholic burns an ancestral tablet in Chinsan, and consequently, the ownership of Western books is prohibited.

1793: King Louis XVI of France is executed. The Chinese Qianlong Emperor intensifies prosecutions against Catholics. Chae Che-gong pleads for royal punishment against the Principle group of the Old Doctrine faction. "The previous king's tale of the metal-bound coffer" comes to light.

1794: Chae Che-gong again insists on royal punishments. Kim Chong-su, the leader of the Principle group, demands the punishment of Chae, but Kim is banished instead. Hwasong Detached Palace is completed. Zhou Wenmo, a Catholic priest from Qing China, enters Korea secretly.

1795: The attempt to arrest Father Zhou Wenmo ends in failure. Kwon Yu, inspector general, impeaches Yi Sung-hun, Yi Ka-hwan, and Chong Yag-yong, claiming that they killed the arrested Catholics to silence them, and that the mastermind is Chae Che-gong. King Chongjo banishes Yi Sung-hun to Yesan, while demoting Yi Ka-hwan to magistrate of Chungju and Chong Yag-yong to stationmaster of Kumjong.

1796: Hwasong Fortress is completed.

1797: After continuous impeachments, Chong Yag-yong resigns from his post in the Royal Secretariat, admitting that he has been corrupted by heresy. King Chongjo appoints Chong Yag-yong as magistrate of Koksan. Yun Shi-dong, the leader of the Principle group, dies.

1798: From the fifth month, the Principle group starts clamoring for the persecution of Catholics. King Chongjo gives permission to mine gold, despite the opposition of the Principle group. The organization of the Royal Defense Garrison is fully established.

1799: Chae Che-gong, the leader of the Southerners, dies. Kim Chong-su, the leader of the Principle group, dies. A new government is started, with Yi Pyong-mo as chief state councilor, Shim Hwan-ji as second state councilor, and Yi Shi-su as third state councilor.

1800: Prince Kong is designated the crown prince. The daughter of Kim Cho-sun is selected to be the wife of the crown prince. King Chongjo strongly promotes abolishing the distinction between the proper lineage and the concubines' lineage. King Chongjo dies on the twenty-eighth day of the sixth month. Chae Che-gong is stripped of his title.

1801: Yi Ka-hwan and Kwon Chol-shin are thrashed to death in prison. Chong Yak-jong, Hong Nak-min, and Hwang Sa-yong are executed. Yi Sung-hun and Kwon Il-shin are executed where they had been banished. Chong Yak-jon, Yi Ki-yang, and Oh Sok-chung die of disease in exile.

Glossary

Ai: An interjection expressing dismay or disappointment.

Aigo: An interjection used to express mild surprise, dismay, apology and sympathy.

Chon: An old money unit.

Chongshimhwan (*qing xin wan* in Chinese): An emergency tablet that relieves the blockage of the heart meridian in Chinese medicine.

Choraeng-i: A comic character of the Hahoe *pyolshin* ceremony.

Chusok (Full Moon Festival): A major Korean holiday held during the full moon of the eighth lunar month, usually in September or October. On this day, an ancestral ceremony is held using newly harvested crops, and people visit the graves of their ancestors.

Eit (*ei*): An interjection expressing anger.

Egugu: An interjection used to express dismay and pain.

Eera: An ejaculation expressing disappointment or urging oneself to stop thinking about something.

Feng shui: A theory that first became popular toward the end of the later Han period in China (A.D. 25–220). It is based on the theory of the Five Elements and Yin-Yang. The direction and the seat of a grave or a house are believed to determine the fortunes of descendants or inhabitants. Koreans have been greatly influenced by this theory since the end of the Shilla Kingdom (57 B.C.–A.D. 935).

Flower cards (*hwatu*): A game with forty-eight picture cards representing the twelve lunar months, such as pine needles for the first month and maple leaves for the tenth month.

Go: Japanese word for the game called *paduk* in Korean. The game for two is played with black and white stones. The goal is to enclose a larger area on the board than your opponent does. This game, which originated in ancient China, is sometimes called Chinese chess.

Kapshin: The twenty-first unit of the sixty-number cycle, used for counting days and years.

Kimchi: A fermented cabbage dish eaten by Koreans with nearly every meal.

Kisaeng: A woman who has been formally trained to entertain upper-class men by singing, dancing, playing musical instruments, and sometimes composing poems.

Konshi: Between three and four o'clock in the afternoon.

Komungo: A six-string zither.

Kyongshi: Between five and six o'clock in the afternoon.

Li: Translated as "principle," "form," or "order." Zhu Xi's dualistic philosophy asserted that the great immutable *li* principles of form give shape to *qi* material force.

Mah-jongg: A Chinese parlor game using 136 ivory blocks.

Meiji: The period 1868–1912 in Japan.

Mishi: Between one and three o'clock in the afternoon.

Myoshi: Between 6:30 and 7:30 in the morning.

Ondol: A unique subfloor heating system invented long ago in Korea and still used today. Flues beneath the floor heat its surface; people sit and sleep on the floor to be close to the warmth.

Pyolshin ceremony: A shamanistic ceremony performed by fishermen or shamans. The Hahoe ceremony is best known. Its ritual masks date back to the fourteenth century.

Qi: Translated as "material force" or "vital force." Zhu Xi asserted that *qi* creates existent reality, which is shaped by *li*.

Sashi: Between ten and eleven o'clock in the morning.

Shinshi: Between 6:30 and 7:30 in the evening.

Showa: A Japanese word used to refer to the period of reign from 1926 to 1989.

Sulshi: Between 7:30 and 8:30 in the evening.

Ulmi: The thirty-second unit of the sixty-number cycle. It is used for counting days and years.

Yangban: Literally, the officials of two orders (civil and military) that first emerged in the thirteenth century during the Koryo dynasty (918–1392). Later, during the Choson dynasty (1392–1910), the *yangban* emerged as the dominant social class, directing the government, economy, and culture. The Choson dynasty is often described as a *yangban* society.

Yutnori: A board game played by two teams using four sticks with four stone markers on each side. The team that finishes the course first becomes the winner.

Everlasting Empire

Yi In-hwa is the pen name of You Chul-gun, a professor of Korean Language and Literature at Ewha Womans University in Seoul. He received the first Writers' World Literature Award for his novel *Who Can Say What I Am?* in 1992. He is also the recipient of the Korean government's 1995 Today's Young Artist Award and the Chinese government's first Korea-China Youth scholarship award. In 2000, Yi received the prestigious Yi Sang Ward for his short story "A Poet's Star."

Yu Young-nan is a freelance translator based in Seoul. She has translated several Korean short stories and novels into English, including *The Naked Tree*, by Pak Wan-so. Her translations of Yi Mu-yong's "Lesson One, Chapter One" and *Farmers* received the Korean Modern Literature Translation Award in 1991 and 1992.

EastBridge
Signature Books
Doug Merwin, Imprint Editor

Signature Books is dedicated to presenting a wide range of exceptional books in the field of Asian and related studies. The principal concentrations include: texts and supplementary materials for academic courses; literature-in-translation; and the writings of Westerners who experienced Asia as journalists, scholars, diplomats, and travelers.

Doug Merwin, Publisher and Editor-in-Chief of EastBridge and Imprint Editor of its Signature Books imprint, has more than thirty years' experience as an editor of books and journals on Asia. He was the founding editor of the East Gate Books imprint at M.E. Sharpe. He received a BS in Public Law and Government and an MA and A.B.D. in East Asian Languages and Cultures from Columbia University.